The Summer Queen

MARGARET PEMBERTON

PAN BOOKS

First published 2019 by Pan Books
an imprint of Pan Macmillan
20 New Wharf Road, London N1 9RR
Associated companies throughout the world
www.panmacmillan.com

ISBN 978-1-5098-4178-3

1 3 5 7 9 8 6 4 2

A CIP catalogue record for this book is available from the British Library.

Typeset in Ehrhardt MT Std by Palimpsest Book Production Ltd, Falkirk, Stirlingshire
Printed and bound by CPI Group (UK) Ltd, Croydon, CR0 4YY

For my much-loved husband,
Mike, in the year of our Golden Wedding

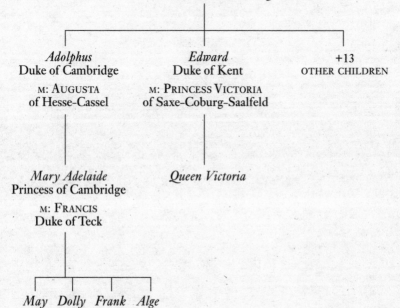

King George III
M: CHARLOTTE of Mecklenburg-Strelitz

Adolphus
Duke of Cambridge

M: AUGUSTA
of Hesse-Cassel

Edward
Duke of Kent

M: PRINCESS VICTORIA
of Saxe-Coburg-Saalfeld

+13
OTHER CHILDREN

Mary Adelaide
Princess of Cambridge

M: FRANCIS
Duke of Teck

Queen Victoria

May   Dolly   Frank   Alge

Queen Victoria
M: PRINCE ALBERT of Saxe-Coburg-Gotha

Vicky	Bertie	Alice	Affie	Lenchen	+4
M: FREDERICK III (Fritz)	M: ALEXANDRA of Denmark	M: LOUIS of Hesse	M: MARIE of Russia	M: CHRISTIAN of Schleswig-Holstein	OTHER CHILDREN

Willy	Eddy	Vicky	Missy	Christle
Charlotte	Georgie	Ella	Ducky	Thora
Heinrich	Looloo	Irene	+3	Marie-Louise
Moretta	Toria	Ernie		+1
Sophie	Maudie	Alicky		
Mossy	+1	+2		
+2				

PART ONE

VOWS

Chapter One

Queen Victoria's favourite summer residence stood on a high knoll overlooking the narrow sea channel separating the Isle of Wight from mainland England. Designed by her late beloved Albert, it had been built in the style of an Italian Renaissance palace and, with its cool spaciousness, cream-stone colonnades and balustraded terraces looking out over rolling lawns and light woodland to the glittering expanse of the sea, it was the perfect setting for family gatherings.

The gathering now taking place was one that Victoria held annually in the last week of August, for 26 August had been her beloved Albert's birthday. Much to the relief of the vast number of children and grandchildren that the Dear Beloved had left behind him, and whose presence at Osborne was compulsory, the 26th had now come and gone. The mood had lightened and the English, Danish, German – and, in one instance, Russian – sides of the family were all enjoying catching up with each other's news.

The day was blissfully hot and a light breeze from the sea was gently stirring the needles of a giant cedar. At the centre-piece of an immaculately manicured lawn on which a score of elegantly dressed couples were strolling, and where children were playing, the wide-spreading branches were giving shade to the Queen, who, small and squat and dressed entirely in black, was seated in a bath chair.

As always at the August get-together, the Queen was taking the opportunity of conducting a series of one-to-one in-depth chats with those members of her family who were approaching the age when a dynastic marriage for them needed arranging.

May Teck, who was twelve and too young for such a tête-à-tête, watched from a safe distance as sixteen-year-old Princess Victoria of Hesse and by Rhine was seated next to the bath chair while the Queen embarked on what, in her eyes, was a very necessary grandmotherly interrogation.

Hoping it would also be a gentle one, for Vicky's mother had died only eight months earlier, May scanned the lawn in the hope of catching sight of Vicky's slightly younger sister, Ella, and her much younger sister, seven-year-old Alicky.

Their bereaved father was standing nearby in conversation with the Prince of Wales. All children in the family referred to the adults as either Aunt or Uncle, no matter what their actual relationship to them was. So although the Prince of Wales was her second cousin, to May he was 'Uncle Wales' because of the age difference between them, just as the Queen was 'Aunt Queen'.

Uncle Wales was one of her least favourite people, because he chaffed – teased in a way that was unkind. Not wanting to draw his attention, May moved away, walking across to where, at a white-clothed table, her mother, Princess Mary Adelaide – known by her royal title as the Duchess of Teck – was indulging her passion for cream cakes in the company of the Princess of Wales. Although May always went out of her way to avoid her Uncle Wales, she adored his graceful, stylish Danish wife, Alix.

'Why are you on your own, May?' Alix asked, with the gentle smile that had won not only the hearts of the family she had married into, but those of her new country as well. 'My little chicks would love to be spending time with you.'

The little chicks in question – twelve-year-old Louise (always known as Looloo), eleven-year-old Victoria (known as Toria, to differentiate her from all the other Victorias in the family) and nine-year-old Maud – were a little distance away, sitting on a blanket and arguing over a game of Jacks.

May didn't find the thought of joining them enticing. Not when, only minutes ago, Toria had pointed out to her that she lacked the pedigree that she, Louise and Maud possessed.

'A Serene Highness is far less royal than a Royal Highness,' she had said, annoyed that May had beaten her at Halma. 'You'll never be a country's queen, but I will, and so will Looloo and Maudie.'

'No, I won't,' Maudie had said, resetting the Halma board. 'I'm going to marry May's brother, Frank.'

'But Frank's also a Serene Highness, you silly girl,' Toria had said, exasperated. 'Don't you know anything, Maudie?'

'I don't know very much,' Maudie had admitted, 'but I do know that Frank is the nicest and best person in the whole wide world.'

May, the only girl in a family of four, was well practised at peace-making and, aware that Toria's annoyance with Maudie was now close to the hair-pulling stage, she'd said hurriedly, 'I don't care that I'm not likely to marry the heir to a throne, Toria. I just want to marry someone who loves me.'

'And who you are in love with,' Maudie had said. Out of the three Wales girls, she was the only one May regarded as a genuine friend. 'That's very important, May. And now is this next game of Halma going to be you and me against Toria and Looloo? And if it is, which pawns do you want to play with? I'm taking the blue, because blue is my lucky colour.'

Remembering the incident, May said now, 'I'll come back a

little later and play Jacks, Aunt Alix. For the moment, I'm looking for Ella and Alicky. You don't know where they are, do you?'

Although only in her mid-thirties, the Princess of Wales was deaf and, when she looked blank, May's mother, guessing the question hadn't been heard clearly, helpfully answered for her, saying, 'As they're nowhere in sight, May, they will probably be on the beach.'

'Oh yes, of course, Mama. Thank you.' The suggestion was so obvious that May couldn't think why she hadn't thought of it for herself.

Blowing a kiss to her mother and Alix, and giving the Wales girls and their blanket a wide berth, she began heading across the lawn in the direction of the wooded walk that led down to a private stretch of seashore. It took her a little while to reach the trees, for she had to weave her way between little knots of relatives, the men formally dressed despite the heat, the women a sea of colour in trailing silk gowns worn over bustles to give them a fashionable, swan-like S-shape.

She was so busy skirting around the Crown Prince and Crown Princess of Prussia that she accidentally bumped into one of her aunts.

'Do look where you are going, May,' her Russian-born Aunt Marie said, with an air of long-suffering patience. 'You're too gawky to wander around with your eyes closed. One of these days you'll injure someone.'

Aunt Marie had a carrying voice, and fourteen-year-old Georgie Wales, who was standing nearby with his older brother Eddy, cracked with laughter.

May, conscious of how tall she was for her age, felt her cheeks flush scarlet.

'I'm sorry, Aunt Marie,' she said, wishing Georgie and Eddy – particularly Eddy – a million miles away. 'I'll take more care in future.'

Her aunt gave a nod of her head to indicate she had accepted the apology, then moved her lace-edged parasol from one shoulder to the other and returned her attention to the sister-in-law she had been speaking to.

'Nice work, May,' Georgie said, highly amused. 'You nearly knocked down an Imperial Highness.'

May, who had forgotten that Aunt Marie was the only daughter of the Tsar of Russia, said crossly, 'Yes, I did, didn't I? And me only a Serene Highness – something your sister Toria has just left me in no doubt about, and which I don't need to have pointed out a second time, thank you very much.'

'No need to be touchy. It's not your fault. You can't help not being *ebenbürtig* and of equal birth. Do you fancy a game of croquet?'

'No.' The blood had drained from May's face. No one, absolutely no one, ever mentioned the word *ebenbürtig* to her. Even Toria, when pointing out that May stood no chance of ever marrying an heir to a royal throne, hadn't done so. To have referred so bluntly to the stain in her father's lineage would – even for someone as insensitive as Toria – have been a step too far. In a shaky voice she added, 'I don't want to play croquet with you, Georgie Wales. I don't think I shall want to play croquet or anything else with you, ever again.'

She pushed past him, painfully aware of Eddy having been a witness to her humiliation. When she was safely a good half-dozen yards away she slowed down and looked behind her.

Both Wales boys were standing perfectly still, staring after her, Georgie in comical mystification, Eddy inscrutably – the fashionable way he was dressed making the near two-year difference between him and Georgie seem years greater than it actually was. As his dark eyes met hers, May's heart began to thud and she whipped her head back round so that he wouldn't see the effect he had on her.

Even though she was the Wales children's third cousin, she had always spent more time with them than she had with any of her other cousins. Marlborough House, the Wales family's London home, was as familiar as her own home, which made Toria and Georgie's remarks about her semi-royal status doubly distressing.

She began to give herself a good talking-to and, although still hurt and angry, her emotions came once again under tight control. If Georgie was going to grow up as insensitive of people's feelings as his father, then there was nothing she could do about it. Eddy, thank goodness, was nothing like his father, although he was an enigma to everyone but his adoring mother. May knew one thing, where Eddy was concerned, and that was that he wasn't insensitive. His sensitivity was one of the reasons she had such a crush on him – that and his mesmerizing gold-flecked eyes.

Just as she reached the thickest part of the woodland she was waylaid by a forlorn-looking Hélène of Orleans, the eight-year-old daughter of the Count of Paris. 'The Parises', as Queen Victoria always referred to Hélène's family, lived in exile from France in Buckinghamshire and were accepted as being almost family.

'I'm looking for Eddy,' Hélène said, appearing to be on the verge of tears. 'He said he would teach me how to whistle, but I can't find him anywhere.'

'He's on the top lawn, with Georgie.'

'Is he?' Hélène's face brightened. 'Thank you ever so much, May.' And she set off at a run in the direction of the house.

When May reached the bay, she was a little surprised to see that it was nearly empty. As there had been no sign of Ella and Alicky on any of Osborne's lawns, she had supposed she would find them here with her brothers, but there were only two people in sight. One of them was Alicky, who was sitting in a huddle, crying; the other was their twenty-year-old German cousin Willy, who was squatting on his haunches, facing her.

Willy had a reputation for being a bully and, assuming him to be the cause of Alicky's distress, May burst into an urgent sprint. It wasn't until she was almost on top of them that she realized that, far from being unkind to Alicky, Willy was trying to comfort her.

'Your mama is in heaven with the angels,' he was saying as May floundered to a halt beside them. 'She's looking down on you and wants you to be happy, not sad.'

'But it was my fault she died.' Tears flooded Alicky's cheeks. 'Mine and Vicky's and Irène's and even Ernie's.'

'Of course it wasn't!' Appalled that Alicky should think such a thing, and wondering why Alicky hadn't also thought Ella responsible for their mother's death, May dropped to her knees on the sand and put an arm around her. 'Darling Alicky, how on earth could your brother and sisters have been responsible for your dear mama's death?'

Alicky's face was ashen. 'Because if she hadn't nursed us when we had the diphtheria, she wouldn't have caught it and wouldn't have died.'

She hiccupped, the tears still falling.

Willy, whose mother was Alicky's aunt and who knew all the details of his aunt's death – and was aware that May clearly didn't – said to May, 'Just before Christmas, Vicky fell ill with diphtheria, and then Alicky, Marie, Irène and Ernest soon followed. Ella was spared, because she was staying with relatives. Despite the doctors' and Aunt Alice's nursing care, Marie couldn't be saved, and then Aunt Alice caught it and died – and the way she died . . .'

He left the rest of his sentence unsaid, and May understood

why. When someone died from diphtheria, they choked to death. Did Alicky know that was how her mother had died? If she did – even worse, if she had been nearby at the time – it was no wonder she was still so grief-stricken at the horror of it.

She tried in vain to think of some way of comforting or distracting Alicky, but couldn't. May rarely felt out of her depth, but grief combined with guilt – no matter how irrational that guilt – was something totally outside her experience. To her great surprise, it was Willy – generally accepted as being the oddest of the many oddballs in the vast tribe of their family – who came to the rescue by bringing Alicky's attention to the deformity that he usually went to huge lengths to hide.

'Everyone has something terrible happen to them, Alicky.' He indicated his foreshortened and withered left arm, with its abnormally small hand. 'Look at this. This is because, when I was born, I came out all wrong.'

Alicky hiccupped again and stopped sobbing, her attention caught now. She didn't quite know what he meant by 'having come out all wrong', because storks brought babies and she thought they would be careful about doing so. Like May, she had never previously known Willy to voluntarily remove his hand from one of his specially tailored jacket pockets and, as he did so now, she was riveted.

So was May.

Willy's deformity would have been dreadful for anyone. For someone who was already a prince, and who would one day be Crown Prince and eventually Emperor, it was dreadful on a scale that was truly calamitous. Kings and emperors were not supposed to be disabled. They were supposed to be fine figures of men who rode on magnificent white horses at the head of glorious ceremonial parades, and Willy had horrendous difficulties with anything that needed balance and physical coordination.

Just as the rest of the male members of the family were in formal dress at an informal party, so was Willy, although in his case, because he was a lieutenant in the 1st Foot Guards, he was wearing military uniform. As Alicky seemed about to begin crying again, he quickly removed the glove on his left hand. His little paw was as white and flaccid as a small, beached sea creature.

Alicky wiped her tears away. 'Is it always like that? Does it ever move?'

'Only if I move it with my good hand.' To prove his point, he lifted it with his right hand and then let it fall, so that it once again lay inert on his thigh, the fingers clawed.

A seagull was circling around them, hopeful of food. May shooed it away. Alicky said with a perplexed frown, 'Were you born like that, Cousin Willy? Or did it just happen to you, like catching diphtheria happened to me and Mama?'

Willy hesitated and May, whose mother chatted to her with no holds barred, wasn't surprised. The story of Willy's gory birth was not suitable for a sensitive seven-year-old. It had been what her mother had described as a 'breech birth', which apparently meant that he'd been born bottom-first. In the struggle to bring Willy into the world, the court physician used forceps and, in doing so, the ligaments and nerves in Willy's left shoulder were hideously damaged, resulting in an arm that had never grown or functioned properly and which, for Willy, was a complete and utter catastrophe.

Alicky asked again, 'Were you born like that, Cousin Willy, or did it just happen?'

Willy said, mercifully not elaborating, 'I was born like this.'

A braid of red-gold hair had fallen forward over Alicky's shoulder and she flicked it back. 'Does it make you feel different from everyone else?'

Willy gave a mirthless laugh. 'I'm as different as the Man

9

in the Moon is from everyone else. How could I not be? Do you know how my grandfather refers to me? He calls me the "defective" prince. Even worse, my mother is of the same opinion. You have no idea of the tortures I had to endure as a child. All carried out not for my sake, but because having been brought up to believe herself perfect, my mother couldn't bear to be seen as having given birth to a child so glaringly imperfect. She insisted that the arm had to be made good, no matter how much I suffered in the attempt.'

'But how could it be made good?' May knew it was indelicate to ask, but she couldn't help herself. In all the family gatherings she had been to at Osborne, she had never previously had such an interesting time. 'What could the doctors do?'

'When I was approaching toddlerhood, my right arm was strapped to my side, in the hope it would miraculously result in my using the left arm. I didn't, of course. How could I? All it did was hinder my learning to walk, because it affected my balance and meant I did nothing for years but fall over. And when strapping my good arm to my side didn't work, I was given animal baths.'

'Animal baths?' May stared at him wide-eyed. 'What are animal baths?'

'It's when an injured limb is placed inside a freshly killed animal. In my case, the animal was a hare. I was only four at the time, and I can't begin to tell you how terrifying the experience was.'

May felt ill. 'But why on earth . . . ?'

'God only knows. Presumably the doctors thought doing so would energize my arm, but the only result was that I had nightmares about dead furry things for years.' Willy shielded his eyes, looking out to sea, to where the Danish royal yacht lay at anchor. 'After dead hares, I had electric-shock treatments, which were supposed to jolt my arm into life; and when they failed, I was strapped into an iron arm-stretching machine for an hour every day. The only outcome, for the years and years of medieval torture, was that it emphasized my difference from everybody else in the family. I'm so much of an outsider that sometimes I don't feel part of the family at all.'

May drew in an unsteady breath. That anyone else in the family should feel as she did – even if for a very different reason – was such a revelation that it made her feel dizzy. Even though Willy was eight years her senior and an adult, she suddenly identified with him in a way she had never done with any of her other cousins.

Willy began one-handedly taking off his footwear. 'I fancy a paddle to cool down. Are you coming, Alicky? May?'

Alicky looked doubtful, but May, who didn't want the unity that had so unexpectedly been forged between the three of them to come to an end, said encouragingly, 'Come on, Alicky. I'm going in. Do you know Granny Queen has a bathing machine so that she can go into the sea and sea-bathe?'

Alicky hadn't known and, as May began undoing the buttons on her white boots, she said, 'Is Granny Queen your granny as well, May?'

'No.' May took off her boots and began undoing Alicky's. 'The Queen is my mother's first cousin, and though she isn't my aunt, she allows me to address her as if she is, and it is how I always think of her.'

With their boots off, they peeled off their long white stockings and then, hand-in-hand, began running towards the sea.

'I wish I'd brought my bathing costume,' Willy shouted, his trouser legs rolled up to his knees.

May also wished she had her bathing costume with her. She could have changed into it in the privacy of the bathing machine. Scooping her skirt and petticoats as high and as far away from the water as she could, she splashed towards him, amazed at how much fun Cousin Willy – whom she had always regarded as being no fun at all – could be.

Suddenly he frowned. Shielding his eyes from the sun, he looked towards the far end of the beach where two figures could be seen. 'Do you think that's Ella?' He was rigid with tension. 'And is that Louis of Battenberg with her?'

'Yes, it's Louis.' May had exceptionally good eyesight. 'But it's not Ella he's with. It's Vicky.' Willy's shoulders sagged in relief and she said, 'Why would it have mattered if it had been Ella?'

'Because I'm in love with Ella, and I'm going to marry her. I made up my mind about it a year ago. The last thing I need is Grandmama matchmaking Ella with anyone.'

May's eyebrows rose. Ella was just fifteen and she thought even Aunt Queen would think that a little on the young side for serious courtship.

Alicky pulled on May's hand, whispering anxiously to her behind Willy's back, 'Ella won't want to marry him. She doesn't like him. Do you think we should tell him? It doesn't seem fair for him to be hopeful, when he's going to be so disappointed.'

'I don't think any good would come of telling him,' May whispered back. 'It would only upset him.'

She didn't add that, as his grandmother would already have a bride lined up for Willy, there was no point. She wondered who the bride would be and rather thought that in four years' time, when she would be sixteen, it would be Looloo. For what could be more dynastically perfect than another marriage between the House of Coburg and the House of Hohenzollern? That they were first cousins wouldn't be seen as a drawback. Aunt Queen had never made a secret of her belief that marriages between first cousins strengthened the royal blood-line.

Suddenly Willy said, 'Time for us to leave.'

May saw why. Uncle Wales was strolling from the woodland onto the beach, and with him were Alicky's father and the Duke of Connaught.

Willy was already striding rapidly out of the water, but not rapidly enough.

'Whoa there, Willy!' Uncle Wales shouted, cigar in hand. 'What's this love of the sea? Are you thinking of leaving the Foot Guards for the Navy? And which navy?' He bellowed with laughter. 'The Royal Navy, the oldest and biggest in the world, or the Kaiserliche Marine, the newest and the smallest?'

May couldn't see Willy's face for he was bending over, rolling his trouser bottoms down, but she see could that he was tense with rage at the slur on the size of his country's navy.

Certain that his uncle would make more of what he always referred to as his 'teases', if he were to put his boots on one-handedly in front of him, Willy scooped them up and, without turning his head to say goodbye to May and Alicky, marched off in the direction of the footpath, his shoulders ramrod-straight, the back of his neck still crimson.

May and Alicky were left facing a wall of disapproval, sensing that one of the reasons for it was that Alicky's nanny wasn't with them. Before Alicky's father could say so, May pre-empted his scolding by saying, 'Cousin Willy has been awfully good at looking after us, Uncle Ludwig. Because he's an army officer, we felt very safe.'

Picking up their stockings and boots, she took firm hold of Alicky's hand. 'And now, if it's all right, we're going to join Looloo, Toria and Maudie on the lawn for a game of Jacks.'

Without waiting for a reply, and still holding Alicky's hand, she set off towards the trees, walking as speedily as Willy had. Only when they had reached them did she come to a halt.

'I wasn't fibbing when I said we were going back to the lawn to play Jacks with the Wales girls,' she said, helping Alicky on with her boots. 'It's something I promised Aunt Alix I would do. You don't mind, do you?'

'No. I like playing Jacks, and I like Looloo and Maudie.'

'What about Toria?'

Alicky frowned. 'I don't like Toria so much.'

'Why?' May was intrigued.

'Because she's a cat,' Alicky said and, in complete agreement about Cousin Toria, they set off at a run up the woodland path.

Chapter Two

Osborne was May's favourite of all her Aunt Queen's royal residences. Whenever she stayed there, and if Ella was there at the same time, they always shared a bedroom and stayed up talking long after they should have been asleep.

'What did Aunt Queen want to talk to Vicky about this afternoon?' May asked, sitting up in bed in the darkness, her arms hugging her knees. 'Was it a prospective husband discussion?'

Ella made herself comfortable against the feather-filled pillows. 'It was, and it didn't end well. Granny Queen has two suitors in mind for Vicky, and Vicky says she'll die before accepting either of them. One candidate was in his thirties and the other had a wooden leg. Can you imagine?'

May couldn't.

'And what makes it worse for Vicky is that she has a desperate crush on Louis of Battenberg, and for her to marry a Battenberg is out of the question.'

May was about to ask why, when she remembered that Louis's parents' marriage had been a *mésalliance*, just as her paternal grandparents' marriage had been. Like her, Louis was a Serene Highness and, when it came to being eligible in the family's marriage market, being a Serene and not a Royal

15

simply wasn't good enough. Quickly she changed the subject. 'Do you know Cousin Willy is in love with you, and that when you're old enough to be married, he plans on marrying you?'

'Yes. He's a pest. I didn't know his hope was public knowledge, though. Who told you?'

'He did.'

At the stunned expression on Ella's face, May giggled. 'Alicky and I spent some of the afternoon with him down on the beach, where, incidentally, I saw Vicky walking with Louis of Battenberg.'

The fact that, after her conversation with their grandmother, her sister had immediately sought out Louis interested Ella, but something else interested her even more.

'Why on earth were you with Cousin Willy? He's such a bore – people go to great lengths to avoid him, they don't seek him out. Once, at Balmoral, when Papa saw Willy approaching him down a corridor, he opened the first door he saw and darted into what he thought was a room. Only it wasn't a room, it was a cupboard. Even though no one saw him hide, Papa says he felt an awful fool.'

Amused at the thought of the Grand Duke of Hesse's embarrassment, May said, 'I think the family have got Cousin Willy quite wrong. He was niceness itself to Alicky and me.'

'That's because you're twelve and Alicky is seven, and he obviously didn't feel he had to impress you. Papa says Willy's bad manners and bullying are a way of covering up a secret lack of self-confidence.'

'Because of his deformed arm and hand?'

'I expect so. It's a ghastly handicap. Do you know he needs someone to cut his food up for him? How did his desire to marry me one day come up in conversation? What was he saying about me?'

'He hadn't been saying anything. He'd been telling us about

the nightmarish time when he was little and all sorts of hideous things were done to him, in the hope of making his arm grow properly. And suddenly he saw Vicky at the far end of the beach, walking with Louis – only at first he thought it was *you* with Louis. His mood changed so immediately when I told him it wasn't you; and when I asked him why, he told me.'

Ella swung her legs from the bed. 'Even if I fancied Willy – which I don't – Papa would never in a million years give his permission. It was Prussian warmongering that forced our family's grand duchy into the newly formed German empire, and it's something Papa will never forgive. He would rather see me married to a Turk than married to a prince of Prussia. I fancy a biscuit. Do you want one? Granny always has some Garibaldis tucked away in a dresser drawer.'

With the Garibaldis retrieved, Ella sat on the side of May's bed. 'I hate this having to make a suitable dynastic-marriage business,' she said. 'Luckily, Granny Queen doesn't have Willy in mind for me; she's far more keen on a marriage that will strengthen the ties between the new Germany and England.'

'But how?' May was bewildered. The only eligible young men high-ranking enough to achieve such a purpose were Eddy and Georgie. Although it was obvious they would one day have to enter into politically advantageous marriages, it had never occurred to her that one of the brides might be Ella. Dry-mouthed and praying the groom wouldn't be Eddy, she added, 'And who with?'

Ella brushed Garibaldi crumbs from the front of her night-dress. 'Eddy. I can't say I'm enthused. He's too much of a mystery. You never know what he's thinking. But after Granny Queen's death and after Uncle Wales becomes King and he dies, Eddy will be King – although he won't be titled King Edward or King Eddy, as his Christian name is actually Albert

Victor – and as Granny Queen is now Empress of India, he'll be an emperor as well. All of which means I will then be both a queen *and* an empress.' She stood up and crossed over to her own bed. 'Which isn't bad for a princess of a little duchy like Hesse, is it?' she asked, sliding down beneath the covers. 'Goodnight, best friend May. Sweet dreams.'

May's dreams were anything but sweet, and the next morning her mood was glum and would have remained glum if it hadn't been for Alicky seeking her out. 'I've given Nanny Orchie the slip again, so that we can have another nice time on the beach with Cousin Willy,' she said, taking hold of her hand. 'He's gone down to Granny Queen's sketching alcove to write a letter to Ella and, when he's finished writing it, I'm to give it to her. He says if he tried to give it her, she wouldn't take it from him.'

The semicircular sketching alcove had been built on the far end of the beach so that Queen Victoria could sit in the shade and, enjoying the view, indulge her passion for sketching in watercolours. There was a wooden bench built into the curve of the blue-tiled inside wall, and the ceiling tiles were prettily decorated with exotic yellow stars.

As May didn't fancy the idea of anyone else's company, and as the Queen wouldn't be sketching when she had so many family members visiting, she thought a visit to the alcove as good an idea as any. Walking across the terrace and skirting the island beds of geraniums, zinnias and marigolds, she wondered if it would be a kindness or a cruelty to tell Willy that his grandmother's plans were for Ella to marry Eddy.

By the time they were walking down the steps to the lower terrace she had decided it would be an unnecessary cruelty – especially as most royal bridegrooms didn't marry until their early twenties, and Eddy was still only fifteen She wondered if Eddy knew of the plans his grandmother had for him and, if he did marry Ella, if he would be happy.

Because her mother gossiped with her on subjects that girls her age were usually in ignorance of, May knew that some arranged royal marriages – although not many – were happy. Willy's parents' marriage was a love match and a happy marriage. Her Aunt Alix's sister's marriage to the Tsar of Russia was also, according to her mother, happy. 'Which is a miracle,' her mother had said, 'for Minny was first engaged to Tsar Uncle Sasha's older brother, and it was only when his older brother suddenly died that she was handed on, so to speak, to Tsar Uncle Sasha.' In those kinds of circumstances, May thought her Aunt Minnie's happy marriage was nothing short of a miracle.

As she walked over an immaculately clipped lawn towards the belt of woodland, it occurred to her that there was another side of the coin to not being *ebenbürtig*. She would never be in Vicky's position of having, for dynastic reasons, to marry a man who was not of her choice, when she was in love elsewhere – as May was sure Vicky was with Louis. But would anyone not royal, but aristocratic, marry her, when she would come to marriage without a dowry? And was marriage to someone not aristocratic out of the question, because it would simply never be allowed?

May knew that at her age she shouldn't be worrying about her future marriage prospects in this way, but she couldn't help it and, up to now, there had never been anyone she felt she could share her worries with. Now, however, there was. There was Cousin Willy.

He was already seated in the sketching alcove as they walked up to it, and the first thing he did, on rising to his feet, was to hand Alicky a sealed envelope with the House of Hohenzollern crest on it.

'There's something I want to talk to you about,' May said to him, as Alicky put the letter safely in her peggy-purse. 'The Queen has been talking to cousins not much older than I am about their future marriage prospects, but she's never going to have a chat like that with me, because I'm not *ebenbürtig*.'

'That's a funny word.' Alicky looked up, interested. 'What does it mean?'

'It means "of equal birth".'

Seeing that Alicky was still puzzled, May added, 'It means I'm semi-royal and that I don't have the title Royal Highness, only Serene Highness.'

'And what is it about being a Serene Highness, and not a Royal Highness, that you want to talk to me about?' Willy asked.

'Because I'm not of equal birth and no royal marriage will be arranged for me, what will happen to me? Will anyone aristocratic want to marry me, when I'm not an heiress? Papa has no fortune, for he was only an officer in the Austrian Army when he and Mama married, and he and Mama are always in financial difficulties.'

Willy frowned and twirled an end of his narrow, upturned moustache. 'Then perhaps the Queen will settle a dowry on you.' He didn't sound hopeful. 'Or perhaps a rich member of the peerage – so rich it won't matter to him that you are not an heiress – will fall in love with you?'

'But is that likely to happen, when I'm so very gawky and plain? And as I'm gawky and plain now, I suppose I will still be gawky and plain in another four or five years' time.'

Unable to deny that what she'd said was a very likely possibility, Willy said nothing.

Not having expected him to, May said dejectedly, 'And so what is to become of me, Willy? Will I have to marry a commoner?'

'*Lieber Gott*, May! You will never be allowed to do that.' When he was at Osborne, Willy's English seldom lapsed into German unless other relatives were speaking it, or unless the Queen – in memory of her late beloved husband – interjected a German expression into the conversation. That Willy had done so showed May more clearly than anything else that marrying a commoner was never going to be an option.

Alicky's pretty face was deeply concerned. 'Does that mean you are too royal to marry anyone who isn't, May? And that you are not royal enough to marry anyone who is?'

May squeezed her hand. 'Yes, Alicky, I think it does. And it makes me feel an outsider and as if I'm not quite part of the family – just as Cousin Willy's arm makes him feel an outsider and as if he's not part of the family.'

Willy put his good arm around her shoulders. 'Then, May, we are kindred spirits. And now we should walk back, so that Alicky can deliver my letter to Ella.'

As they rose to their feet, Alicky said, 'What is a "kindred spirit", Cousin Willy?'

'A kindred spirit is someone with whom you share an experience that no one else shares with you, or truly understands and feels about as you do.'

'Then I'm a kindred spirit, too.'

'And why is that?'

'Because even though Ella, Irène, Vicky and Ernie miss Mama dreadfully, they don't feel about her dying the way I do. That's because I sometimes see her, and even though I was a baby when my little brother Frittie died, I sometimes used to see him, too. When I said so, everyone apart from Mama said I was weird.'

From the expression on Willy's face, May could see that Willie also thought seeing dead people was weird.

'And that is why I'm not like anyone else in the family,'

Alicky continued, 'and if I'm not, then I'm a kindred spirit with you and Cousin May.'

Afraid that Willy was about to disillusion Alicky, May said swiftly, 'Of course you are.'

'Then if the three of us are kindred spirits, we should make a pact so that we never ever forget it.'

Willy, who loved anything theatrical, said, 'And how would we do that, little Alicky?'

'I'll show you, if you let me hold the medal you are wearing.'

Intrigued, Willy obligingly unpinned a beribboned gilt eagle from his jacket and handed it to her.

With her pale face set in concentration, Alicky drew the medal's brooch-pin so hard against the side of her wrist that drops of blood appeared.

Then she handed the medal to a horrified May.

'Now you have to do the same, May, and so does Cousin Willy. Then we rub our wrists together to make the blood mix, and that makes a solemn pact of kindred-spiritness that can never be broken, not ever.'

'No, Alicky. Absolutely not.' Filled with revulsion, May tried to hand the medal back to her and, when Alicky refused to take it, she turned to Willy for help.

Instead of backing her up and telling Alicky she was behaving very badly, he was staring at the blood in riveted fascination.

'I think,' he said slowly, 'I think a blood-pact is a very good idea, but as I am one-handed I will need help.' Taking the medal from Alicky, he handed it to May. 'If you please, May.'

He was eight years older than her and an adult. Wanting to refuse and yet not seeing how she could, without destroying the closeness that had been forged between the three of them, May unhappily – and feeling a little sick – drew the medal's pin across the side of his wrist.

'And now you, May,' Alicky said. 'You have to do it as well.'

Wishing herself a million miles away, and with extreme reluctance, May scratched her wrist deep enough to draw a line of gleaming blood. Then she joined with Alicky and Willy in rubbing their wrists together.

It was a shockingly primeval, intimate sensation.

'What happens,' she said unsteadily when the deed was done, 'if the pact is broken?'

'It can't be broken. To break it would be to bring about something more terrible than you can ever imagine; something so terrible it would be like the end of the world.'

It was such childish superstition that, as they walked back across the beach to the woods, May was already pushing the unpleasant little ceremony as far to the back of her mind as it could possibly go.

Not for decades would it resurface and, when it did, she was to know with bitter grief that Alicky hadn't been exaggerating. For their pact had broken and, for all three of them, their worlds had ended – and in ways far more terrible than could have been dreamed, on that long-ago, innocent summer day.

Chapter Three

JANUARY 1883, WHITE LODGE

It was 5 January, and May was helping her father dismantle the drawing room's Christmas tree and was wondering, as she did so, how her family was going to get out of the dire financial pickle it had got itself into over the last four years. That they had a roof over their heads was due only to the Queen's kindness, for when May's parents had married, she had allowed them the use of a large apartment in Kensington Palace. A few years later and at her mother's request, the Queen had granted permission for them to occupy, as a second home, White Lodge, a Crown property in Richmond Park.

May knew that White Lodge had only come about as their country *pied-à-terre* after her mother had pestered the Queen for it, in a manner no one else but a close first cousin would have had the temerity to do. The problem was that they still retained their Kensington Palace apartment and, as the running cost and staffing of one home had been beyond their means, the cost of running and staffing two had plunged them into a level of debt there was no obvious way of getting out of.

'Mama simply doesn't understand money,' her father said gravely as, from a stepladder, he handed May a delicate papier-mâché angel with gauze wings. 'God knows, I have tried hard enough to make her understand that we must live within our means – as have the Queen, the Prime Minister, Baroness Burdett-Coutts of Coutts Bank and the friends who so repeatedly and generously lend her money, but it falls on deaf ears. She simply will not rein in her expenditure, and soon bailiffs will be knocking on our door.'

May knew it wasn't an idle threat. She had grown up with the knowledge that her loving, carefree, generous mother was also heedlessly extravagant. Her favourite charities always received huge and regular donations. No one coming to her in need ever went away empty-handed. As Mama was a great party-lover, no one – not even the Waleses – could equal her in the lavishness of her hospitality, and there was nothing she liked better than entertaining and throwing grand dinner parties for her royal relations, especially relations visiting from Germany.

When it came to clothes, too, only the best would do and, as she had tried to explain when her husband chastised her for the enormous expenditure on 'only the best', because of her size – at a cautious estimate, her weight was close to eighteen stone – all her gowns needed double material, and so she had to pay double the price.

Having wrapped the angel in cotton wadding, May said with a troubled frown, 'Perhaps if Mama spoke to Aunt Queen . . . ?'

The Duke of Teck removed a silver star from the top of the tree. 'The Queen is as exasperated as I am at Mama's inability to live within any kind of a budget and, fond as she is of Mama, she has refused to loan her any more money.'

May hadn't known that the Queen had loaned her mother money – money that had obviously not been repaid – and her cheeks burned with mortification. She took the star from him and placed it carefully with the other decorations in a large box that was thick with more wadding. 'What will happen when tradesmen refuse us any more credit, Papa?'

'I don't know.' Her father climbed down from the ladder, his face haggard with worry. 'A solution has been suggested, but it is not one Mama will be happy with.'

'But if it gets us out of this hideous debt, surely it will be worth trying?'

There was such hope in her voice that her father, knowing what May's reaction was going to be when he told her what the suggestion was, could hardly bear it. He fumbled in his trouser pocket for the pipe that he was seldom without and at last said reluctantly, 'It has been suggested that we remove ourselves to the continent, where it is possible to live much more cheaply than we do here.'

May's jaw dropped. 'But if we were to do that, Papa, everyone will know why!' The horror of such humiliation made her feel faint. 'It would be too shaming. It would be mortifying beyond belief.'

She thought of the Waleses knowing it; of Vicky, Ella and Alicky knowing it; of everyone at the Prussian court – especially Willy – knowing it. Hard though she was trying not to show the depth of her distress, tears stung the back of her eyes. 'It is a nonsensical suggestion, Papa. You must tell whoever made it how stupid they have been.'

'I'm afraid that is not possible, Pussy-cat.'

'Dear Papa, of course it is!' Panic rose in May's throat. 'How can we possibly leave England? How can we leave White Lodge and Kensington Palace? The person who suggested that we do so deserves to have their ears boxed!'

Looking old beyond his years, the Duke of Teck sat down heavily at the room's vast dining table.

May's heart caught in her throat. She loved her temperamental father dearly. Although he frequently erupted with exasperation at the annoyances of daily life, and when dealing with her brothers, Dolly, Alge and Frank, he never did so with her. Something else she liked about him was that, unlike other men in the family, he far preferred artistic pursuits to the eternal round of long weekends hunting, shooting and fishing. No one could create a garden as spectacularly as her father, or tend one as lovingly. No one could choose and arrange furniture with such an unerring eye, or know which of his wife's hats went best with which of her dresses. She had long sensed that these admirable qualities were sniggered at by some male members of the family, and particularly by her Uncle Wales.

As soon as Uncle Wales came into her mind, May was certain she knew where the offensive suggestion of exile had come from.

'Exile is Uncle Wales's idea, isn't it? And it's one of his cruel teases, Papa. It isn't something to be taken seriously.' She was so relieved it was a tease that she could have cried.

Instead of sharing her relief, her father winced. Fiddling with his still-unlit pipe, he hesitated and then, knowing the moment could be put off no longer, said, 'The suggestion wasn't made by Uncle Wales, May. It came from the palace.'

She stared at him, still not understanding.

'The suggestion was made by the Queen, so now you understand how impossible it is to for me to take no notice of it or,' he added, in a bleak attempt at humour, 'for me to box her ears.'

May didn't respond with even a glimmer of a smile. She felt as if she'd been hit by a sledgehammer. Coming from Aunt Queen, the suggestion had all the force of a royal command. Slowly she sat down at the table next to him.

He put his pipe down and took her hands in his. 'I have still to tell Mama, and intend doing so this evening. I am telling you now because I want you with me when I break the news to her. Perhaps a couple of years abroad will not be so bad. We could stay with Mama's relatives at Neu Strelitz, or with my relatives in Stuttgart.'

May shuddered. Fond as she was of her mother's Mecklenburg-Strelitz relatives and her father's Württemberg relatives, she had always been glad that visits to their very stiff and formal courts had never lasted too long. The thought of spending the next couple of years, or perhaps even more, as guests in one of them was a prospect that chilled her to the bone.

'And so,' her father continued, 'this evening I must break the news to your mama and I would like you and Adolphus with me when I do so.'

'And Frank as well?'

'I think not. At fourteen, Adolphus is old enough – and, like yourself, sensible enough – to be a support to me.'

'Frank is only a year younger, Papa.'

'There is a big difference between being nearly thirteen and being fourteen – and besides, like you, Dolly has a sensible head on his shoulders. Francis hasn't. Francis would see exile as an adventure, not a disaster.'

Ten hours later, bolstered by the presence of May and Dolly and fortified by brandy, the Duke of Teck told his wife of Queen Victoria's remedy for their financial difficulties.

Her reaction was neither shock nor horror. Instead, seated on two chairs, for one chair was never wide enough for her to sit comfortably, she laughed it merrily away as if it was all the greatest joke.

May's father, always ineffectual when dealing with his wife, looked towards May for help.

May said in deep concern, 'It isn't a joke, Mama. Papa says bailiffs will soon be at the door and, unless we come up with another solution as to how to live more cheaply, there is going to be no alternative but to do as Aunt Queen suggests.'

Her mother patted her daughter reassuringly on the hand. 'Nonsense, sweetheart. You forget how close my relationship to Victoria is. I am her closest cousin and I have known her far longer, and far better, than anyone else – be they in or out of the family. The suggestion would have been made when she was temporarily out of sorts, and by now she will have forgotten all about it – as I shall do.' She beamed sunnily. 'And I have news that will cheer us all up, for I have come from arranging a lavish redecoration of White Lodge. Just think of it, my darlings. When it is complete we will be as grand as the Waleses are at Marlborough House!'

Facing such blatant disregard of all that had just been said, her husband dropped his head into his hands. Dolly looked disbelieving. May was horrified.

Unperturbed by their reactions, the Duchess said happily, 'And now, pet lambs, I think it's time for a late-night snack. Hot chocolate with cream, cheese on toast and Abernethy biscuits, I think. May sweetheart, will you ring the bell?'

For six months it seemed to May as if her mother was right that the word 'exile' would not be mentioned again. Then, in mid-July, as the anxiety was beginning to fade, her mother received a note from the Queen saying that she would like to receive a visit from her at Windsor.

'How delightful,' May's mother said blithely, not fearing the worst. 'And you must come with me, May. I know the Hessians are there on a summer visit, and I believe the Edinburghs are at the castle as well. It will be so nice for you, May, meeting up with your little Edinburgh cousins, and with Ella. At eighteen, it's high time Ella was married. I wonder if that is why she and her family are now at Windsor? I wonder if an announcement is about to be made?'

* * *

'An announcement?' Ella asked, after she and May had found an unoccupied room in one of Windsor Castle's turrets and were sitting opposite each other on a cushioned window-seat, their knees pulled up to their chests, their feet toe-to-toe. 'Absolutely not – although Granny Queen living in the hope of one is why I'm here.'

'And is her bridegroom of choice still Eddy?' May asked tentatively, trying to disguise in her voice the hope that it wasn't.

'Yes. He was here when I arrived. Granny Queen's idea was that the two of us could spend time acclimatizing ourselves to the prospect of spending the rest of our lives together and that, when we had, an announcement would be made. Only it isn't going to be made because – unlike so many of our aunts and cousins – I am not going to be bullied by Granny Queen into a marriage I don't want. I'm not going to marry Eddy. He's far too unreadable and we just don't suit each other. I'm going to marry Sergei.'

Hard on the heels of relief that she wouldn't have to attend Ella and Eddy's wedding came complete bewilderment. Sergei? May's mind raced. Who on earth was Sergei?

As if May had put her thoughts into words, Ella said, 'Sergei is a younger brother of Tsar Uncle Sasha. His mother is a princess of Hesse, and so he's been visiting my family all his life.' She giggled. 'He tells me he once bathed me when I was a baby, but I don't think I believe him. He's twenty-six, so he would only have been seven or eight at the time.'

May tried to get her head around the idea of a little boy of seven or eight bathing a baby and couldn't. To her, it all sounded most odd.

Something else seemed even odder, for if Sergei was a brother of Uncle Sasha, who had inherited the Russian throne two years ago after his father's assassination, then he was the brother of her Aunt Marie. And that Ella was contemplating marriage to someone she had grown up referring to as 'uncle' was, to say the very least, bizarre. Not letting her thoughts show, she asked, 'And has Sergei asked you to marry him?'

Ella shot her a happy smile. 'No, but I know he's going to soon.'

May had never before been so aware of the age difference between them. At sixteen, she hadn't as yet officially 'come out', but Ella, only two years older, had twice been offered the opportunity to one day be both a queen and an empress, for if she hadn't rejected Willy, she would one day have been the German Empress and Queen Consort of Prussia; and if she hadn't rejected Eddy, she would one day have been the Queen Consort of England and Empress Consort of India. And now, almost unbelievably, she was looking forward to receiving a third proposal of marriage – one that this time she intended accepting.

Aware that her own chances of receiving even one proposal were so slight as to be not worth thinking about, May returned her thoughts to Eddy. With Ella unshakeable about not marrying him, had Aunt Queen already got another prospective bride in mind? And if so, who? And where *was* Eddy? Was he still at Windsor, or had he already left? The last time she had seen him had been four years ago, for immediately after the family party at Osborne he and Georgie had left the country aboard a Royal Navy ship.

'And as naval cadets, they are going to be away for three years,' her mother had said at the time. 'Aunt Alix is distraught about such a long separation from her darling boys, but Bertie is adamant. He believes that living under strict naval discipline will be to Eddy and Georgie's advantage, although never having lived under it himself, I fail to see how he can possibly know.'

Bertie was Uncle Wales and, as Eddy and Georgie's father,

his word had been law. Almost immediately after the boys' return – and without it becoming known whether the hopes of the voyage had been achieved – they had been sent to Lausanne for six months in order to improve their French.

When they had returned a month ago, only Eddy had remained in England, for it had been decided that the Navy was to be Georgie's career. 'And he's now aboard a ship called a corvette, heading for the West Indies,' her mother had said, on returning from afternoon tea at Marlborough House. 'Poor dear Alix is prostrate.'

Not wanting to betray her interest in Eddy to her mother, May hadn't asked where Eddy was, or what it was that he was doing.

Just as she was about to casually ask Ella if he was still at Windsor, Ella said, 'Eddy left for Sandringham yesterday. He wasn't happy about it, as he is to spend the next couple of months holed up there, cramming in preparation for Trinity College in October.'

That he wasn't still at Windsor was a body-blow of disappointment. Hiding it, as she did so many of her feelings, May said, 'Is Trinity an Oxford college?'

'No, Cambridge. It's hard to believe, isn't it? One of the Waleses at university? I've never seen any of them with a book in their hands. And that goes for Uncle Wales and Aunt Alix as well.'

That the stylish Prince and Princess of Wales were philistines when it came to the arts, and that their lack of interest in the quality of their children's education had resulted in their children being seriously under-educated, was something everyone in the family was well aware of. May knew that none of her other cousins would have had to be sent to Lausanne for six months to improve their French, for by the time they were six or seven they had all spoken both French and German fluently, and in many cases – though not hers – Russian as well.

'Eddy may well begin to enjoy reading, once he's somewhere that reading isn't an activity to be scoffed at,' she said, not seeing why he should be blamed for something that wasn't his fault. 'Mama says Eddy and Georgie's tutor was hopeless and bored them to tears, by only ever giving them things to learn by rote. And although I think Georgie quite enjoyed his years at sea as a naval cadet, I don't think Eddy did. I think Eddy hated it.'

'Why? Has he said so?'

'No. It's just a feeling I have. I think he's . . .' She hesitated, not wanting Ella to laugh. 'I think he's a little like my papa. I think he's artistic.'

'Then I don't envy him.' There was dark humour in Ella's voice. 'If he is artistic, he won't be allowed to give any expression to it at Marlborough House.' She swung her feet to the floor and changed the subject to one that was troubling her. 'What did you think of Willy having married plain and pious Dona of Schleswig-Holstein?'

'It came as a surprise.' May stood up and slid a hand through the crook of Ella's arm. 'Did he do it on the rebound?'

'Yes. I'd told him, after the letter he sent to me via Alicky when we were last at Osborne, that I was never going to marry him; that I was going to marry Sergei. He said I was the love of his life and that if he couldn't marry me, it didn't matter whom he married. And three weeks later his engagement to Dona was announced. I'm just so desperately hoping they will be happy together, because if they aren't . . . if they aren't, I shall feel so responsible.'

May's common sense seldom let her down. 'There's no reason why you should feel responsible for anything to do with Willy and Dona's relationship,' she said robustly. 'You never gave him any encouragement, and he should have accepted years ago that you were never going to marry him. If he had, he would most likely have been over you by now. As it is, he isn't and he's chosen to marry Dona – who Mama says adores him and will never give Willy the slightest trouble – and his happiness is now in his own hands. It isn't something you should feel responsible for.'

'Thank you, May.' Ella's relief at May's response was profound. 'You are so clear-sighted about things, and there are times when I'm not. Have we to go and find the Edinburghs? As I'm set on Aunt Marie becoming my sister-in-law, I've been spending as much time with her as I can. Do you know she smokes Black Russian cigarettes? And that she always makes a conscious effort to wear more jewellery than anyone else? She says that, being both the daughter of the late Tsar and the sister of the present one, it's her duty to do so.'

They left the room and began clattering down the spiral stone steps.

'Our little cousins are just as bad,' Ella continued. 'When she plays at dressing-up, Missy does so with a Romanov tiara on her head and a rope of Catherine the Great's black pearls reaching down to her feet.'

At the bottom of the steps, May said, 'I can understand Cousin Marie having been nicknamed "Missy". It's a nice nickname. But how on earth did Victoria Melita get the nickname "Ducky"?'

'I've no idea. Perhaps it's to do with ducks and water, Uncle Affie being the only one of Granny Queen's children to be a naval man? I believe it caused quite a stir in the family when he married the then-Tsar's only surviving daughter. It's strange, isn't it, that when Missy and Ducky are only half-Russian, they always seem wholly Russian? The nice thing about it is that their temperaments, like Sergei's, are too fiery for them ever to be dull.'

May was wary of fiery temperaments and certainly wouldn't have found one an advantage in a prospective husband, but it didn't seem the right time to say so.

As they walked towards the Crimson Drawing Room she struggled over whether or not to tell Ella about the suggestion of exile that the Queen had made, and which she might now be making for a second time – only this time to her mother, and with far more force.

She thought of how horrified and sympathetic Ella would be, and decided against it. If it did come to living in exile, she didn't want sympathy. Sympathy would be more than she could bear. And if she was wrong about the purpose of her mother's invitation to Windsor, then there was no need for her to let anyone, even Ella, know how shamefully close a call it had been.

In the long Grand Corridor they were nearly knocked over, as Missy and Ducky careened towards them on roller-skates, with one of the Queen's small terriers barking excitedly at their heels.

'Oh, goody!' Six-year-old Ducky swerved to a tottering halt. 'Alicky's gone off and left us, and we don't have anyone to time how fast we are going from one end of the corridor to the other. The footmen are being mean and won't do it, so will you?'

'Yes,' Ella said.

May asked, 'Where has Alicky gone, Ducky? Do you know?'

'No. She's nice for a little while, and then she always falls quiet and goes off on her own.'

May had no intention of leaving Windsor without having spent time with Alicky, and she was just about to tell Ella that she was going off to find her, when her mother entered the far end of the Grand Corridor, looking visibly distressed.

There could only be one reason for her always happy-go-lucky mother to have lost such self-control. Certain of what it was, it felt for a moment to May as if the world had stopped spinning. Sucking air into her lungs, she began running as fast as she could towards her distraught mama.

Chapter Four

An hour later, on the short carriage ride from Windsor to White Lodge, her mother was still complaining bitterly at what she termed the 'barbaric' treatment they were receiving.

'Although not from Victoria,' she had said emphatically as, with a handkerchief, she had dried her eyes. 'Poor, dear Victoria was almost as distressed as I at having to insist we live more cheaply abroad, and she only did so because – and you will hardly believe this, May – because all of my *closest* family – your maternal grandmama, my sister and my brother – have *all* insisted that we abandon White Lodge and that we do not even keep our apartment at Kensington Palace. It is they who *begged* Victoria to intervene in this matter. It is outrageous that family who should be helping us financially have said they will do so *no longer*, when they know that, of all people, I am the person *least* prone to extravagance and that I am not *at all* responsible for our situation. If it hadn't been for your Teck grandmama having been non-royal, Papa would be heir to the throne of Württemberg now and we would be living in Stuttgart, with no financial difficulties whatsoever.'

She drew in a deep, shuddering breath, but to May's relief was no longer crying.

'And to think of all the little economies I have been driven

37

to practise,' her mother continued indignantly as the carriage rattled through the gates of White Lodge 'Hoarding pieces of string! Keeping used paper from parcels! And it has been suggested that when we remove ourselves to the continent – which we are to do almost immediately – we occupy a small apartment in Frankfurt. Over my dead body will I live in a small apartment in Frankfurt!'

A few hours later, as a family discussion was being held around the dining table, she said emphatically, 'Wherever we remove to, it will never be Frankfurt.'

'Or Neu Strelitz,' her husband said, not having the slightest desire to be surrounded by his wife's close relatives for what could well be a permanent stay.

'Or Stuttgart,' said Dolly, who hated the rigid formality they had to endure there.

A box of chocolates was conveniently to hand and, helping herself to a strawberry cream, Princess Mary Adelaide said firmly, 'Wherever we go, it *must* be somewhere suitably fashionable. I understand from Aunt Marie that Florence is a great favourite with Russian royals.'

The Duke of Teck said encouragingly, 'And not only with Russians, my pet. Queen Natalie of Serbia spends several months each year in Florence, and Mecklenburg-Strelitz and Württemberg cousins visit the city regularly. We shall not be without society, and there will be museums and galleries to interest May.'

'Then Florence it is!' From being in the depths of despair, their mother's natural optimism was beginning to resurface. 'And now I must order new gowns and furs. I cannot risk being thought a dowd by Russian royals.'

Later that night May wrote three letters. The first was to Ella:

Dearest Ella,

I have no idea for how much longer you are to be at Windsor, but I doubt Mama and I will be there again before you return to Hesse and there is news I want to tell, before you are told it by others. Mama's distress this afternoon was because something we have long feared has now become a certainty. White Lodge and our apartment at Kensington Palace are to be given up and we are soon to leave for a new life in Italy. The move is not one of choice, but of a very essential need to live more economically (although my mama, out on another shopping trip, hasn't grasped this yet). I didn't say anything this afternoon, as I was hoping another way would be found to resolve Mama and Papa's unhappy financial situation. When we are settled I will forward you an address so that you can write to me. I do so want to be kept in touch with everyone and with extended family gossip – especially anything to do with your love life and with Vicky's love life!

Best love, May x

Not wanting Alicky, who was so much younger, to be distressed on her behalf, she wrote:

Dearest Alicky,

Just a little note to tell you some very exciting news. I am shortly going to be leaving dear old England and moving to Italy with my mama and papa and three brothers. (Although only my youngest brother, Alge, will be staying permanently with us in Italy, as my older brothers, Dolly and Frank, attend an English boarding school and will continue doing so.) Italy is going to be a wonderful adventure and, when I have an address, I will make sure I send it to you. I'm so sorry Mama and I had to leave Windsor yesterday before I'd

*had the chance to meet up with you, but Mama was taken
a little unwell and so we had to leave for home in rather a
hurry. (And please don't worry about my mama. She is
much better now.)*

Much love, your Kindred Spirit, May x

And to Willy she wrote:

Dear Cousin Willy,

*You will no doubt soon hear on the grapevine that, in
their best interests, my mama and papa have been asked to
withdraw to the continent for a period of some years. I, of
course, will be going with them and so, as well as being of
unequal birth, I will be an exile as well – all of which will
make me a double outsider. Not something that anyone else
in the family (apart from Alicky) has the faintest perception
of. To everyone else I shall, of course, be putting an
extremely brave face on things, but it is a welcome relief, in
this short letter to you, not to have to do so. Please give my
best regards to Dona and to your parents.*

With much affection, your Kindred Spirit, Cousin May

The next few weeks were a frenzy of activity, none of which
helped May come to terms with the thought of leaving the
only two homes she had ever known. Even worse was when
the bailiffs came to White Lodge. Her mother avoided the
humiliation by fainting upon their arrival. May and her father
had no option but to endure it. Just as bad, if not worse, was
when it was decided (although not by her mother) that, in
order to pay off their creditors, many personally owned
contents from Kensington Palace would have to be sold at
public auction.

Torturing herself to the utmost, May attended the auction,

not showing a flicker of her inner agony as people pawed over and speculated on her family's much-loved paintings and pieces of furniture. The stuffy smell of the saleroom, the sound of the gavel coming down time and time again, as one item and then another disappeared into the ownership of strangers, was a nightmare she would never, to the end of her very long life, forget. By September, with the agreement that their future living expenses would be funded with money to be paid back when May's maternal grandmother died and her mother came into her inheritance, they were ready to leave. It was also money that would be under the care of an administrator, and which neither her mother nor her father would have direct access to.

'Which I think a very *great* indignity,' her mother said, hardly able to believe that life could be so unfair. 'That a granddaughter of King George should have to *ask* for money that is rightfully hers is a monstrosity. If the dear general public knew of it, there would be an uprising!'

Her mother's popularity with the British public was such that May thought her mother might not, for once, be exaggerating. In contrast to the Queen, who spent the best part of the year at the remote Balmoral Castle and never dressed in anything but black, Princess Mary Adelaide's carriage was constantly spotted on London's streets. Even in the middle of winter she travelled with the window down, so that when she was recognized and people called out a greeting – often referring to her affectionately as 'Fat Mary' – she could lean out and, with her hat bedecked with stylish feathers and swathed in furs, respond with one of her life-enhancing smiles and a cheery wave.

There was one last thunderbolt before they were to leave England ignominiously behind them.

'It has been requested that we travel incognito.' The Duke

of Teck tried to sound as if this was expected and came as no surprise. He failed miserably.

'Not travel under our own names, Papa?' May was incredulous. 'But why? Are we suddenly to be ashamed of them?' Angry colour spotted her cheeks. 'If we are not to travel under our own names, what names *are* we to travel under?'

'Your Hungarian grandmother was granted the title "Countess of Hohenstein" on her marriage, and that is the name we shall all be travelling under.'

'So I shall be travelling – and living in Italy – as May Hohenstein?'

'Not quite, Pussy-cat. When we travel, you won't be doing so under your family pet name, but under your baptismal name.'

'And so I will answer to Victoria Mary Hohenstein?'

'Yes.' With his eyes not meeting hers, he turned away from her; May knew why. Her dear papa was just as mortified at the subterfuge they would be living under as she was.

It was impossible to keep the news of their enforced exile from the inmates of Marlborough House, and May had to suffer Toria distancing herself from her as if she had a catchable disease, Looloo's horrified disbelief and Maudie's tender sympathy. For once, she was grateful that Eddy was still at Sandringham and, for several days, she wondered if she dared to write to him. Not a long letter of course, just a line to say that for the foreseeable future she and her family would be living in Florence.

The fear that if she did write to him, Eddy wouldn't trouble himself to respond – or that if he did, it wouldn't be in the manner she was hoping for, but would be in a way that would entirely crush her – ensured that she never got further than writing *Dear Cousin Eddy* several times, before screwing the sheets of notepaper into a tight ball and, sick at heart, throwing them into a waste-paper basket.

By the time the morning of their departure arrived, May had already said goodbye to their spacious apartment at Kensington Palace. She had done so knowing there was very little likelihood she would ever live in it again. As she had closed the door of the bedroom she had been born in – a bedroom that had once, before she had ascended the throne, been her Aunt Queen's bedroom – she had known that she was not only closing a door on a host of happy memories, but on a part of her life that was irrevocably over; and that she had no real idea of what was to come next. Saying goodbye to White Lodge was not quite as traumatic, for it had been decided that her mother was to retain the Lodge in the hope that sometime in the future they would be able to live in it again.

The plan was for them to cross on the night-boat from Dover to Calais, from where they would not travel directly to Florence, but to Rorschach on Lake Constance for a stay with their Württemberg relations.

'For as Rorschach is en route to Florence, it would be *criminal* not to accept their kind invitation that we break our journey and stay with them for a few weeks, to "catch our breath", as your Papa's great-aunt so kindly puts it,' her mother had said.

Frank, who never enjoyed staying with his father's Württemberg relations, had raised his eyes to heaven and sloped off in the company of Maudie, who, at every opportunity, was sticking to him like glue.

May watched bleakly as, in the deepening dusk, their trunks and travelling bags were loaded into the waiting carriages. Maudie, she knew, was heartsick at the prospect of Frank spending holidays from his public school in Florence, and not at White Lodge or Kensington Palace. It meant that whenever he was home she could no longer look forward to seeing him, and for the last few weeks her face had been permanently wan and frequently tear-stained.

May felt great sympathy for her, but she also knew that the sooner Maudie got over her fixation of one day marrying Frank, the better it would be, for it was a daydream that was never likely to happen. For one thing, although Frank liked Maudie and tolerated the way she sought him out and trailed in his wake, he didn't have a crush on her as she had on him – and even if he'd had a crush on her, marriage would never be on the cards. As a daughter of the Prince of Wales, a suitably prestigious, dynastic marriage would already have been arranged for Maudie and she would have no option but to do her royal duty – duty that had been instilled in her, and in Toria, Looloo, Georgie and Eddy, from birth.

Royal duty was the reason a homesick Georgie was now firmly embarked on a career in the Royal Navy and was on the other side of the world. Royal duty was the reason Eddy had suffered years as a naval cadet, when May was certain that, given the choice, he would never have left dry land for even an hour. Royal duty was why, if Ella had been willing, Eddy would have been obliged to marry her, no matter what his private feelings might have been. Royal duty was why he would eventually marry someone else who had been selected for him – someone whose father was heir to the throne of a country that Britain wanted to forge closer, unbreakable ties with. To be royal (even to be semi-royal, as she was) was to not have a life of one's own. If she had been able to have a life of her own, May would not now be about to leave the country of her birth, a country she identified with utterly and loved passionately.

'Hurry along, Pussy-cat,' her father said impatiently. 'The last thing we want is to miss the train.'

As the carriages carrying their trunks and bags rattled off

down the drive, followed by the carriage carrying five members of their household staff who were to travel with them, May stepped reluctantly into the carriage. As the horses moved off, she looked over her shoulder only once and then, with tears burning the backs of her eyes, she dug her nails deep into her palms, refusing to let any fall. Whatever lay ahead, she would make the best of it – for making the best of things was what she always did – but that she would be doing so in a land far from her beloved England was a knife-wound to her heart so deep that she could hardly bear it.

Chapter Five

The little medieval town of Darmstadt in the Grand Duchy of Hesse and by Rhine was in a fever of excitement over the imminent wedding of the Grand Duke's eldest daughter, Princess Victoria, to her father's first cousin, the handsome Prince Louis of Battenberg.

Royal wedding guests were arriving in an endless stream at the town's toy-like railway station and the town's brass band welcomed them ceaselessly with whatever English, Danish, Prussian or Russian anthem was appropriate. Crowds of spectators thronged the streets, waving flags and cheering lustily as horse-drawn landaus carried the guests away from the station and through streets of steeply roofed houses, in the direction of the ancient market square that fronted the palace. Sometimes landaus converged with each other and there would be squeals of recognition from the occupants. Horses would be hastily reined to a halt while, in the middle of a cobbled street, a Danish party of royals fell into the arms of Russian relations, or a Prussian party of royals fell into the arms of the latest batch of arriving English cousins. What Queen Victoria referred to as the 'Royal Mob' was out in full force, and the citizens of Darmstadt were loving every minute of it.

The only person not doing so was Alicky, who still felt the

same dislike of crowded family get-togethers that she had felt five years ago at Osborne; and this particular get-together didn't have the compensating factor of having either May or Willy as part of it.

'The Tecks are still acclimatizing themselves to being exiles and are probably not yet ready to face the family en masse,' Sergei, one of Nicky's uncles, said when Alicky told him how disappointed she was that May wouldn't be at the wedding. 'And that Willy's parents are here is reason enough for Willy and Dona not to be.'

Sergei was tall and, although narrow-shouldered, imposing, dark-eyed, dark-haired and with a well-trimmed pointed beard. Few people were comfortable with him, for his manner, other than when he was with children, was too cold and austere for casual friendship. Only on his visits to his mother's relatives in Hesse-Darmstadt did he relax, turning into a man that few of his fellow countrymen would have recognized.

'I know that Cousin Willy's relationship with his mother isn't all it should be,' Alicky said, stroking the pet rabbit that was asleep on her lap, 'but that's to do with his poor arm and all he was put through because of it, when he was a child. I didn't know he didn't get on with his father, either.'

'He doesn't get on with his father because they have very different opinions as to how a country should be ruled. When his father becomes Germany's emperor, he intends to rule as a constitutional monarch.'

That Ella's husband-to-be treated her as if she was an adult – as she felt May did, in her regular letters to her, and as Willy did in his sporadic letters to her – was one of the reasons Alicky liked her brother-in-law-to-be, but there were times when his conversation went above her head.

She stopped stroking the rabbit. 'What,' she asked, 'does "constitutional" mean?'

They were sitting on one of the broad stone steps that led from the palace to the tree-studded park in which it was set. Making himself more comfortable, Sergei pulled a knee up to his chest, hooked an arm around it and stretched his other leg straight out.

'A constitutional monarch is King or Queen of a country that has an elected parliament, and the parliament makes and passes laws, not the King or Queen. Your granny, Queen Victoria, is a constitutional monarch – and although that may be all right for Britain and its empire, Willy doesn't think the newly united Germany should be governed in the same way; and as that is the way his father intends ruling, it is the reason the two of them do not see eye-to-eye.'

Alicky thought this over for a few moments and then said, 'I like Cousin Willy. I'm a Kindred Spirit with him and Cousin May, but I don't think he can be right on this. My governess says that Granny Queen is the most powerful monarch in the whole wide world – and so her way of being a queen and an empress must be the right one.'

Eleven-year-old Alicky was soon to be Sergei's sister-in-law, for immediately after Vicky and Louis's wedding, his own and Ella's engagement was to be announced. It was important to him that Alicky, as well as Ella, understood the gigantic differences between the way Queen Victoria ruled, the way the newly united Germany was presently ruled and the way Russia had always been ruled.

He said, 'Different countries have different histories, Alicky, and both Germany and Russia have very different histories from Great Britain, and so they need ruling differently. They need an autocratic ruler; a ruler who rules without the interference of a parliament; a ruler who is answerable only to God.'

'And is that how Uncle Sasha rules Russia?'

'It is, and he does so for a very good reason. When our father was Tsar, he was known as "the Liberator" because he made so many reforms. He freed the serfs. He reformed the justice system. He encouraged local self-government. He did all the kind of things your Granny Queen approved of – and if those reforms had been carried out elsewhere, he would have been thanked for them. But they weren't carried out elsewhere. They were carried out in Russia, and what your Granny Queen and Willy's father don't understand is that Russia is so vast and medieval that it can't be governed in the same way a country with a long history of parliamentary rule is governed. It can only be governed by force and with a whip.'

He came to a sudden halt, a pulse throbbing at the corner of his jaw. Sensing that he was thinking twice about saying anything any further, Alicky asked, 'And what happened? What is it you aren't telling me?'

Sergei breathed in hard. 'My father's reforms merely inflamed the revolutionaries even more. They made three attempts to assassinate him. On the fourth attempt they succeeded. A bomb was thrown at his carriage as he was approaching the Winter Palace. I was there when he was carried into the palace, his face streaming with blood, his stomach ripped open, his right leg torn off, his left leg shattered. I was there when he died in agony. And so that is why my brother doesn't rule as a liberator, but as an autocrat, because a strong autocrat – answerable to no one but himself – is the only kind of ruler Russia respects.'

'Stop hobnobbing, you two!' Ernie, Alicky's brother, called out to them from the terrace. 'We've just heard that the Queen's train has drawn in at the station. Her carriage will be here any minute.'

Alicky gently shooed the rabbit from her lap and sprang to her feet. She knew that she was Granny Queen's favourite granddaughter, and she wanted to be first of all her grand-children to run up to her for a hug.

Sergei remained where he was. Despite his sister Marie being the Queen's daughter-in-law, he knew Queen Victoria had no time for Russia and that she certainly wouldn't be happy when she learned that Ella would shortly be leaving Darmstadt for a life as a grand duchess in St Petersburg. That she wouldn't be happy didn't bother him at all. Ella's widowed father had consented to their marriage, and so what a stout old lady dressed in black silk thought was, where he was concerned, of no account whatsoever.

Musingly he turned his thoughts back to Alicky. She was a funny little thing; very fine-featured and pretty, and yet very withdrawn. He wondered what on earth she meant by saying that she was kindred spirits with her cousin Willy and with May Teck. Not in a million years could he imagine what she could possibly have in common with either of them. Willy was a self-opinionated know-all who, in reality, knew next to nothing; and although he had never met the Teck girl, Sergei knew she wasn't even full-blown royalty and that her parents lived a hair's breadth away from being inmates of a debtors' prison.

He took a cigarette from a diamond-studded cigarette case and lit it. Queen Victoria was a notorious matchmaker and would no doubt be putting her skills to good use during her stay in Darmstadt. Her motherless Hesse granddaughters held a special place in her heart and he was fairly sure that, having failed to make a match between Ella and Eddy, Victoria already had another prospective bridegroom in mind for Ella. If she had, the surprise she was about to get when his and Ella's engagement was announced was going to be doubly unpleasant.

But what about Alicky? In four years' time she would be of marriageable age and Queen Victoria no doubt had a bridegroom in mind for her. Would it once again – where a Hesse granddaughter was concerned – be Eddy? He rather thought it would. When Alicky was sixteen, Eddy would be twenty-four and, if she accepted his proposal, she would, as his wife, one day be Queen and Empress of over a quarter of the world's population.

Except that Sergei was determined she wouldn't be.

He ground his cigarette out beneath his booted heel and lit another one. He had long ago decided that his future sister-in-law would be Russia's next empress. Russian royalty had a long history of marrying princesses from the little duchies and kingdoms of Germany, and his beloved late mother had been a princess of Hesse. Once, when he had visited Darmstadt with her and Alicky was no more than three or four years old, his mother had turned to her lady-in-waiting and said, 'Kiss this child's hand. She is your Empress-to-be.'

It was something he had never forgotten, and something he was determined to bring to fruition.

His nephew Nicky, the Tsesarevich, was almost sixteen. Once he and Ella were married and living in St Petersburg, Sergei was going to ensure Alicky visited them frequently and that she and Nicky spent as much time together as possible. His plan was that in four years' time, and with the right encouragement, Nicky would propose to Alicky, be accepted and that when Nicky inherited the throne, his mother's prophecy would be fulfilled and Alicky would be Her Imperial Majesty The Empress of all the Russias. Best of all, when she was, she would be bound to him by the closest of family ties, and his influence over both her and Nicky would be total.

Despite the press of family thronging around her in the main drawing room, the Queen gave Alicky her undivided attention for far longer than she gave it to anyone else. Yet there was a tension in the air and, when it was suggested that the children should leave the room, Alicky had no choice but to go with them.

'What's the matter?' she asked Ella, as Ella shepherded her from the room. 'Why is everyone so on edge?'

'People are always edgy before a wedding, Alicky. Wedding nerves are nothing to get worried about.'

Alicky wasn't convinced. A familiar knot of anxiety began growing in her tummy. Her father was nowhere to be seen – which was most odd, under the circumstances. Adult cousins, aunts and uncles were also now leaving the drawing room in an undignified hurry. As far as Alicky could tell, only Vicky, Irène and Ernie now remained with the Queen.

As Ella headed straight back to the drawing room, closing the door firmly behind her, Alicky frowned. If her three sisters and her brother were now closeted in privacy with Granny Queen, why wasn't she? Had Granny Queen decided she didn't want Vicky to marry nice Louis of Battenberg? Or had nice Louis of Battenberg decided he didn't want to marry Vicky? What was going on?

Judging by the buzz of conversation and the expressions on people's faces, her relations were all as much in the dark as she was. She thought possibly Sergei might know, but he was nowhere to be seen. The only other person she could think of who might know was Madame de Kolémine. Pretty, kind-hearted Alexandrine de Kolémine was her father's special friend and for the past few years had become part of their household. No one had minded, for everyone liked her, and their father was far better-tempered when Alexandrine was around than when she wasn't.

She went in search of Madgie, her governess. Away from the palace, Madgie was Miss Margaret Jackson, but within it she was the much friendlier-sounding 'Madgie'. Madgie sent monthly reports on Alicky's schoolwork to the Queen, who responded by taking a deep interest in Alicky's impressive scholastic progress.

'Madgie,' Alicky said when she found her, 'do you know where Alexandrine is? Something odd is going on, now that Granny Queen has arrived. The only people with her in the drawing room are Vicky, Irène, Ella and Ernie. Everyone else has been ushered out, and a footman is now standing outside the door so that no one can enter. If it's because Vicky is telling Granny Queen that there's not going to be a wedding after all, Alexandrine will know, but I can't find her.'

Margaret Jackson pushed her wire-rimmed spectacles up into her hair. She knew very well why the Grand Duke's adult children were closeted with the Queen. It was because their father intended to marry Alexandrine and was too cowardly to break the news to his mother-in-law himself.

She quite understood his cowardice. His late wife had been one of Queen Victoria's much-loved daughters and although it was five years since Princess Alice had died, five years was nothing to a woman who was still in black-garbed mourning for a husband who had died twenty-two and a half years ago.

That the Queen would not have expected the Grand Duke to even consider marrying again was not the only reason he would be nervous of breaking his news to her. There were several other reasons – the main four being that Alexandrine was a commoner, a divorcée, Polish and Russian Orthodox.

'I don't think you will find her in the palace, Alicky,' she said equably. 'Madame de Kolémine is not family, and she thinks it best that at such a family-orientated event she keeps a low profile. There is no need for you to worry about Vicky and Louis's wedding being called off. Whatever Vicky, Irène, Ella and Ernie are discussing with the Queen, I know for a certainty it has nothing to do with tomorrow's wedding.'

53

Alicky breathed a sigh of relief. She thought it a shame, though, that Alexandrine was not going to be at the wedding. She was certain it was something Alexandrine would have enjoyed.

Queen Victoria was white-lipped with rage. She had travelled to Darmstadt in the happy expectation of a gala reunion with her children, grandchildren, nieces, nephews and her many German cousins. Vicky and Louis's wedding was one that had her full blessing. He and his two brothers were handsome and charming young men, and Louis had, in her eyes, the added lustre of being a serving officer in the United Kingdom's Royal Navy. At an event so happy, what could possibly go wrong? The answer, within minutes of her arrival, was plenty.

'Your papa wishes to do *what*?' The shock she'd been dealt was so great that if she hadn't already been seated, Queen Victoria would have had to be lifted from the floor. Without waiting for an answer from Vicky, she continued without pausing for breath, 'Your papa cannot possibly marry such a person! For what possible reason can he wish to do so?' Beneath acres of black silk, her massive bosom heaved. 'Never – *never* – could I defend such a choice! If your papa was to carry out his intention, he would lose the respect of *everyone*, both in Germany and in England. To choose a lady who is *divorced*, who is of another *religion*, is beyond all reason. You must go and tell him so, and tell him that it is never to be mentioned again. Not ever, is that understood? Not ever!'

Sergei's mouth twitched when Ella told him of the scene that had taken place.

'Poor dear Granny Queen was beside herself at the prospect of Papa marrying Alexandrine,' she said as they snatched a few minutes' privacy together in the palace's palm-filled conservatory. 'It is a great shame she is so firmly set against them marrying, as we all like Alexandrine enormously and all of us would be very happy to have her as our stepmama. Vicky says Papa was quite ashen when she told him what Granny Queen had said.' She bit her lip. 'You don't think she might have a similar reaction when our engagement is announced, do you? I couldn't bear it if she was just as opposed to our getting married.'

Sergei tucked her hand into the crook of his arm. 'She isn't going to be pleased about it, but it is something she will accept – even if only grudgingly – especially as, unlike Madame de Kolémine, you are not divorced, a commoner, Polish or, as yet, Russian Orthodox.'

'No, indeed.' Ella's response was grave, because although it had been agreed between them that for the moment she would keep to her own Lutheran Protestantism, it was under-stood that once she was in Russia she would take instruction in the Orthodox Church and would convert, as German prin-cesses in the past who had married Romanovs had done.

It was a prospect that didn't disturb her. There was nothing about marrying Sergei that disturbed her. She was aware that when people knew of her decision they would be mystified by it, for Sergei was not a popular member of their vast extended family. His attitude to everyone but her was stern and arrogant. He was seven years older than she was and, until now, had been so oddly reluctant to marry that there were rumours about his sexuality. She, on the other hand, was considered the most beautiful and nice-natured princess in Europe.

Five years ago, at Osborne, she had indicated to May that the prospect of one day becoming a queen and an empress had filled her with a certain satisfaction – but that had been five years ago, and she knew a great deal more about life now than she had then. She knew that the vast majority of royal marriages were, where the brides were concerned, desperately unhappy. The men, married to a wife who was suitably royal and fulfilled dynastic requirements, found love and passion outside marriage. But the same option wasn't open to their long-suffering wives.

It was public knowledge, for instance, that Uncle Bertie was serially unfaithful to Aunt Alix with actresses and other ladies of the demi-monde, and that nearly all married men in the family behaved in a similar manner – and did so blatantly.

It was not the kind of marriage Ella wanted; nor did she want the other kind of marriage: the faithful kind that was built around close physical intimacy. For a long time her secret desire had been to become a nun, but knowing how such a desire would be received by Granny Queen at Windsor had been enough to make her see the impossibility of it. Sergei, too, had no wish for any kind of physical relationship in marriage. His true interests lay elsewhere, although his fierce Russian Orthodoxy and innate Puritanism ensured he didn't pursue them. The two of them understood exactly the kind of marriage they were about to embark on and, having been close companions since childhood, it was one they were certain was going to suit them – and if it didn't, it was absolutely no one's business but their own.

The next few days were a misery for Alicky. The palace, the palace gardens, even Darmstadt itself were thronged with relatives, and finding somewhere she could sit in the seclusion that was so necessary to her was impossible. Not even her schoolroom was sacrosanct, for when she opened its door, it was to find her one-eyed Uncle Christian displaying his collection of coloured glass eyes to Toria, Looloo, Maudie, Missy, Ducky and his daughter, Marie-Louise. She and Marie-Louise were to be two of tomorrow's twelve bridesmaids and, as they were the same age and the same height, they had been paired together to walk hand-in-hand behind the bridal couple.

But that was tomorrow. For now, Alicky wanted somewhere quiet where she could anticipate seeing Vicky in the bridal gown that had been their mother's. As her uncle replaced one glass eye in his eye socket with another and his audience shrieked in enjoyable horror, Alicky closed the door on them. She had thought of one room in the palace where no one was likely to be, and that was Frittie's bedroom.

She didn't remember Frittie, for she had been a baby when, after falling through an open bedroom window, he had bled to death, a victim of the family bleeding disease, haemophilia. Her mother had, however, often spoken to her about Frittie and of how they would all one day meet in heaven – something she devoutly believed her mother and Frittie had now done. Frittie's bedroom had been kept exactly as it had been on the day he had died, and Alicky knew it would be nice and quiet in there and that she would be able to think of tomorrow and of how one day she, too, would be a beautiful bride.

A fierce glow spread through her from head to toe. When that day came, she would have someone of her very own – someone even more special than a Kindred Spirit; someone who would be her soulmate forever and ever; someone who would be her soulmate for eternity.

The day preceding the wedding was a hive of frenzied activity. Last-minute alterations to bridesmaid dresses were made, ancient family silver was given a last hard polishing and, under Irène's careful eyes, the gardeners brought in armful after armful of white roses from the palace gardens.

'And now for the best bit of the wedding preparations,' Irène said, taking Alicky by the hand, 'the decorating of the chapel with the roses. I had intended doing it on my own, but on reflection, I think I'm going to need a little help.'

Alicky's cheeks flushed with pleasure. 'Will there be white roses in my bridesmaid's bouquet?' she asked as they made their way to the family's private chapel in the east wing of the palace.

'No, sweetheart. You and Marie-Louise will be carrying posies of lily-of-the-valley.'

Alicky was disappointed, but was too polite to let her disappointment show. 'And what will be in Vicky's bouquet?' she asked, as the general hubbub taking place in the main rooms of the palace receded.

Irène, who was much enjoying this interlude of private time with her little sister, said, 'Vicky's bouquet will be white roses mixed with white gardenias and stephanotis. Stephanotis,' she added as they entered the chapel, 'signifies "marital happiness" and I'm quite sure that is what Vicky will enjoy with Louis.'

Alicky was to remember the afternoon she spent carefully wrapping rose stems in white satin ribbon, pinning fan-shaped bouquets of them on the ends of the pews, filling vase after vase to mass the many stained-glass windows – paying particular attention to Frittie's commemoration window – as the last time that, for days, her stomach wasn't a knot of churning nerves.

The nerves started with the dress rehearsal for the wedding. The white kid slippers she was to wear with her bridesmaid dress were too tight, and she was terrified she wouldn't be able to walk down the aisle without limping and that, if she did limp, it would look as if she was making fun of Vicky, who had jumped over a coal scuttle for good luck and had injured her leg so badly that she thought she would have to use a stick to get her down the aisle.

It didn't help that her father had completely abandoned playing host to his scores of guests and had shut himself away in his study, in order, he said, to memorize his Father-of-the-Bride speech; that Granny Queen was still furiously angry at his even contemplating marrying a non-royal divorcee; and that Russian Aunt Marie was causing pandemonium by declaring that the pearl-and-diamond tiara she had been going to wear to the service had been stolen – only for it to be found where she had left it, underneath a shower cap in her bathroom.

'Let's hope everything runs like clockwork tomorrow,' Marie-Louise's mother said fervently to anyone who would listen. 'I don't think I could survive another day like today. Truly I don't.'

Much to everyone's relief, she didn't have to. The next morning Alicky swapped slippers with Marie-Louise, who had been given a pair of slippers a size too big, and which fitted Alicky as perfectly as Alicky's slippers fitted Marie-Louise. Vicky announced that her leg was no longer painful and she would be walking down the aisle without the aid of a stick. And Alicky's father emerged from his study full of nervous *bonhomie*.

Alicky was nervous, too, but in a way that was full of sickly dread – dread that grew as her pretty, satin-sashed bridesmaid dress was slipped over her head and her red-gold hair was crowned with a coronet of lilies-of-the-valley.

'Hold hands prettily with Marie-Louise,' she heard her Aunt Lenchen say, as the time came for them to walk in procession towards the east wing and the chapel. 'As the youngest two bridesmaids, you are going to receive far more attention than the older ones.'

That was the very last thing Alicky wanted to hear. Her fingers tightened on the posy of flowers she was carrying.

Somehow she had to get through the agony of being stared at by more than a hundred pairs of eyes, but how?

As they approached the chapel, and in a moment she was never to forget, the solution occurred to her. She would simply pretend that the vast clan of extended family was not there; that there wasn't a member of the House of Saxe-Coburg-Gotha, of Hohenzollern, of Mecklenburg-Strelitz, of Romanov (apart from Sergei) in sight. That there was no aged German Emperor, no German Crown Prince and Princess; no Uncle Wales and Aunt Alix; no Uncle Affie – a brother of whom her mother had not been fond – and Aunt Marie; no Uncle Christian and Aunt Lenchen, who had been her mother's favourite sister; no spinster Aunt Beatrice; none of the groom's Battenberg relations; none of the army of cousins who were not part of the bridal party. The only two guests she would mentally acknowledge as being there were Granny Queen and Sergei and, in that way, glacially composed and not allowing a flicker of expression to cross her face, she would survive the experience of being on public show. It was a trick she learned that – with disastrous consequences – she would depend on for the rest of her life.

Chapter Six

Once the wedding breakfast was under way, some of Alicky's tension began to ebb. Conversation and laughter – bellows of it, where Uncle Wales was concerned – filled the vast room, and Alicky was able to do what she liked doing best: sitting as unobtrusively out of sight as possible and watching what was going on around her, without the torment of being an active part of it.

The palace where the wedding breakfast was taking place had been built only a few years before her birth and was known as the New Palace. Her mother had had a very large say in its design and, like Osborne, it was elegantly Italianate. The rooms were large and airy, with high ceilings and French doors opening onto delicately arched loggias. In every room were reminders that her mother had been very much an English princess: a daughter of Queen Victoria. A portrait of Granny Queen with Grandpa Albert dominated the main drawing room, while on other walls there were individual portraits of all her mother's eight siblings, from Vicky, now Crown Princess of Prussia and Willy's mother, all the way down to Princess Beatrice, the only one of Granny Queen's children still unmarried.

In the ballroom where the wedding breakfast was taking place was a full-size portrait of her great-great-grandfather,

61

King George III, resplendent in his coronation robes and painted at a time when he was still young and rosy-cheeked.

On the walls of the bedroom Alicky had slept in, ever since she could remember, were watercolour sketches of Osborne, Windsor and Balmoral. All of them had been painted by Granny Queen; and hanging on the wall of one of the palace's many corridors was an oil painting of Dash, the Cavalier King Charles spaniel that had been the first in a long line of dogs that Granny Queen had owned and doted on. All through her life Alicky had been surrounded by reminders that she was just as much English as she was German and, with an English nanny and then an English governess, she had grown up not only speaking English fluently – although with a German accent – but often thinking in English as well.

Looking to where her father was seated next to Granny Queen, she could tell that he was tense with barely suppressed excitement, and she was certain it was because he was about to stun all Vicky and Louis's wedding guests by announcing Ella and Sergei's engagement.

Not far away from her, her Aunt Beatrice was paying no attention to anyone but the groom's very handsome brother, Henry. Alicky wondered if Beatrice had been purposely seated directly in Henry's sightline. At twenty-seven, Beatrice, plain but kind, was very much a royal old maid. Was Granny Queen up to her matchmaking tricks again? Because of a blip on the Battenberg family tree, all the Battenberg brothers were Serene Highnesses, not Royal Highnesses, something that played very much against them in the royal marriage market. It hadn't affected Louis, for Vicky had been too head-over-heels in love with him to care that he was not of equal birth; and Alicky doubted very much if Aunt Beatrice, facing a lifetime of spinsterhood, would care very much about Henry not being of equal birth, either – especially not as Henry was tall and broad-shouldered, and just as strikingly handsome and charming as his three brothers. For Henry, marriage to one of Queen Victoria's daughters would be quite a step up in royal ranking and consequently, even though Beatrice was plain, quite a temptation.

On the other side of the room her sister Irène also looked as if she had been smitten by a Henry, although this time by a fully royal one, Prince Heinrich of Prussia – Kindred Spirit Willy's younger brother. Alicky wondered if it was always like this at weddings; as if simply being at a wedding induced romantic thoughts in guests who had not yet taken the plunge. Certainly it was the best occasion to see, in the flesh, possible future marriage partners, for there was no question of marrying outside the exclusive caste of which they were all members. This meant there was a very narrow selection field, and it became even narrower when dynastic and political alliances were taken into account. Vicky was very fortunate in marrying a man she was in love with, and of whom Granny Queen approved; and Alicky hoped that when Ella and Sergei's engagement was announced, Granny Queen was going to be similarly pleased at the prospect of Sergei as a grandson-in-law.

All the main speeches had long since been made and there was a ripple of surprise as her father again rose to his feet and footmen flooded the room, recharging the champagne flutes. Not since their mother died had Alicky ever seen her father looking so pleased with life.

'Your Majesty,' he beamed towards Granny Queen, 'on this wonderfully happy occasion allow me to announce another joyful event, the engagement of my daughter, Ella, to Grand Duke Sergei Alexandrovich Romanov.'

There was a second of stunned silence and then – with the exception of the Hohenzollern contingent, who were well aware that Willy had asked Ella several times to marry him and had been spurned every time, which was, to them, the equivalent of their country being spurned; and of Granny Queen, who had a face like thunder – the room erupted in a storm of congratulations. A Romanov wedding meant a St Petersburg wedding; and a St Petersburg wedding meant another Royal Mob get-together – this time on a scale of almost impossible-to-imagine splendour and lavishness.

Alicky watched in pleasure as Aunt Marie rushed to Ella's side, hugging her and telling her how pleased she was that Ella was about to become a Romanov. Missy and Ducky were jumping up and down and squealing that she would now be their aunt as well as their cousin. Every red-blooded male in the family was lining up to tell Sergei that he was a damned lucky fellow and, as Ella was far and away the most beautiful girl in the room, meaning it. And then Alicky saw Lady Ely, Queen Victoria's lady-in-waiting, cross the room towards Ella and speak to her. Almost instantly Ella excused herself from her well-wishers and, as Granny Queen swept from the room, Ella – accompanied by their now apprehensive-looking father – followed swiftly in her wake.

In normal circumstances Queen Victoria was an indulgent grandmother – something her government ministers, accustomed only to her stubbornness and her refusal to compromise, would have found hard to believe. Ella, well aware that there was another side to Granny Queen and that she was about to be faced with it, steeled herself for the coming storm as the doors of a nearby drawing room closed behind the three of them.

Seating herself in an armchair and looking as imperious as if the chair were her coronation throne, the Queen fixed the son-in-law she had previously always regarded with deep affection with gimlet-hard eyes.

'Never,' she said emphatically, '*never*, Ludwig, have my wishes been so disregarded! For you not to have informed me *beforehand* about the announcement is *such* a breach of bad manners and protocol it takes my breath away. You know my feelings, where Russia and the Romanovs are concerned. You *know* that I had a far different match in mind for Ella. And yet, without taking into account my wishes, you have sanctioned an engagement between Ella and a Romanov – a Romanov who, I have on good authority, is so *autocratic* as to be regarded in St Petersburg and Moscow as a *tyrant*! And now I wish to speak with Ella – and I will speak to her on her own.'

Summarily dismissed and looking unnaturally pale, the Grand Duke of Hesse shot a helpless look towards his daughter and beat a hasty retreat.

'And now, Ella,' the Queen said, striving for patience, 'an explanation, if you please, as to why you have refused to consider either Willy or Eddy as a future husband and have instead settled on a Russian grand duke of dubious reputation.'

Ella regarded her grandmother gravely. 'Because I know it is the right thing for me to do, Granny, and because I know that marrying Willy, or Eddy, would have been the wrong thing for me to do.'

It was said with such quiet certainty that Queen Victoria sensed she stood no chance of getting Ella to change her mind. Nevertheless there were things she wanted to say, and she *was* going to say them. She patted the footstool next to her chair and, when Ella had sat down upon it, took hold of her hand.

'Many German princesses before you have married into the House of Romanov,' she said, deep concern now replacing her anger, 'and none of their marriages were happy. With the exception of the present Tsar, Romanov men do not make good husbands. Do you know why Sergei was such a regular visitor with his mother to Darmstadt when you were a child? It was because his father, the late Tsar, had moved his mistress into the Winter Palace in a suite of rooms immediately above her; a mistress whom, the moment his wife died of a broken heart, he married. Even your Aunt Marie's marriage to Uncle Affie is not a happy one. English and Russian temperaments are just as incompatible as German and Russian temperaments. I fear very much for your future happiness, dear Ella, if you persist in this ill-advised engagement, most especially because of the unpleasant rumours as to Grand Duke Sergei's tyrannical nature.'

Ella squeezed the pudgy, aged-spotted hand. 'Dearest Granny, I suspect that all the marriages you are speaking of were arranged marriages, where the bride and groom were given very little time to get to know each other. That doesn't apply to Sergei and me. I've known him since before I could walk – and I am well aware of the unpleasant gossip that surrounds him, but gossipmongers rarely ever speak the truth, and I don't believe they do so where Sergei is concerned. It is true he has a brusque manner and that in his role as Command-er of the 1st Battalion Preobrazhensky Regiment he can be a little harsh, but marriage to me will be good for him. My love will soften his nature and will ease his grief and rage over the hideous manner of his father's assassination. Sergei needs me, Granny.' Her eyes held the Queen's, shining with love and conviction. 'And I need to be needed, Granny. Over the last year I've discovered that being needed is what fulfils me.'

When she emerged from their tête-à-tête, Ella did so composed and dry-eyed. Deeply satisfied with the way she had obviously handled a tricky situation, Sergei strode to her side and put his arm around her waist. The congratulations for them continued. It was Willy's hoydenish sister Charlotte, never seen without a cigarette in her hand, who asked the question Alicky thought the most important.

'So how long before the wedding, Ella?' she asked bluntly. 'Willy won't want to be a guest at it. You do know that, don't you?'

'That's up to Willy,' Sergei said before Ella could make a diplomatic reply. 'And to answer your question, Charlotte, the wedding will be in six weeks' time.'

It was an answer that pleased everyone, apart from Alicky. Happy as she was that Ella was going to marry Sergei, she most certainly wasn't happy at the prospect of being a brides-maid again – and especially a bridesmaid at a wedding that would, she knew, be far grander and more opulent than Vicky and Louis's wedding had been.

'Why so glum?' Irène asked her.

Alicky told her.

'I think you can stop worrying, poppet.' Irène's eyes were still on Willy's brother, Heinrich, who was deep in conversa-tion with Uncle Wales. 'It's going to be a huge Russian Orthodox affair, and I'm fairly sure there will be no Protestant bridesmaids in attendance. In fact there may not be any brides-maids at all. Russian Orthodox weddings are very different from Protestant weddings. All I know is that there will be lots of incense and that the ceremony will go on for hours, prob-ably days.' She changed the subject. 'It's a shame Uncle Wales put the kibosh on Eddy and Georgie being here today. According to Toria, he simply refused to allow them to take time off from their studies.'

'Studies?'

As Alicky looked blank, Irène said helpfully, 'Eddy is at Trinity College, Cambridge, and Georgie is training to be an officer at the Royal Naval College, Greenwich.'

Apart from Maudie, Alicky wasn't much interested in her Wales cousins. Nor was she much interested in having a horde of her relatives telling her how much she had grown, and how she had to stop blushing with shyness whenever she was the focus of attention.

She was just about to slide away and feed her rabbit when Vicky marched up to them, not looking at all like the radiant bride of a little while ago. 'Papa is nowhere to be found,' she said tautly to Irène. 'I've got the most dreadful feeling that he's gone to ask Alexandrine to join us and that, when she has, he's going to announce their engagement.'

'In front of Granny Queen – and after the way she reacted to news of Ella's engagement to Sergei?' Irène was disbelieving. 'I don't think so, Vicky. Not even Papa could be so rash.'

'Let's hope he isn't, but he isn't circulating among the family and I think we need to go in search of him. You check out the east wing of the palace, and take Ella with you. I'll round up Ernie and do a search of the west wing.'

Still without a word to Alicky, they set off in different directions.

Alicky hesitated, but only for a moment. And then, not wanting to be left out of anything interesting, she set off at a brisk trot in the same direction Vicky had taken.

By now, with the wedding breakfast over, relatives were gathered in little clusters all over the palace, catching up on gossip, exchanging titbits of scandal, discussing how odd it was that Ella should have accepted a proposal from the stern and uncompromising Sergei, when it was well known that she had turned down proposals from both Eddy and Willy. They were also speculating on what had gone on behind closed doors between the Queen and Ludwig, and between the Queen and Ella. Nowhere, though, was there a sign of their father and Alexandrine.

Forty minutes later, Irène, Ella and Alicky met up with Vicky and Ernie in the New Palace's grand entrance hall.

'Not a sign of either of them,' Ernie said, tired of the

exercise and impatient to get back to catching up with his Battenberg cousins. 'And if Pa wishes to marry Madame de Kolémine, surely that's his affair and no one else's.'

'Alexandrine is a divorcee,' Irène said, annoyed by how dense her brother could be. 'That one fact alone is enough to make Papa intending to marry her very much Granny Queen's affair.'

'Well, neither of them are in the palace, so I suggest we put it to the back of our minds. By now everyone will be wondering where Vicky is, so let's continue enjoying her wedding day and forget all about Papa. He'll put in an appearance when he's good and ready. After all, there's nowhere else for us to look.'

'Yes, there is.'

As usual, everyone had been ignoring Alicky. Vicky, Ella and Irène now turned to look at her.

'Where?' Vicky demanded.

'The family chapel.'

'It's a possibility,' Ella said to Vicky, 'but why would they be there?'

Even before she'd finished asking the question, the answer was obvious.

The colour left Irène's cheeks. 'Papa wouldn't . . . . He couldn't . . .'

'He's wanted to for long enough,' Ernie said bluntly. 'But I can't see a Lutheran pastor marrying him to a divorced woman, can you? If – and when – they marry, it will be a civil ceremony.'

'A civil ceremony could still be conducted in the chapel.' Irène looked towards Vicky.

Vicky didn't speak. She simply hitched her floor-length wedding gown up to her knees and, with everyone following her, set off at a run towards the east wing of the palace and the chapel. They never reached it, for strolling away from it, arm-in-arm, were their father and Alexandrine. Their glow of happiness, and the bouquet Alexandrine was carrying, told them everything they needed to know.

'Be happy for us,' Ludwig said swiftly as they all skidded to a shocked, disbelieving halt. 'When I knew that on Vicky and Louis's wedding day I would be announcing Ella and Sergei's engagement, I thought how wonderful it would be to make a hat-trick of it, by marrying Alexandrine – and because of Alexandrine being a divorcee—'

'And of her being totally non-royal,' Ernie interjected.

'And because of other inconvenient difficulties,' his father continued, 'I thought it best that we marry as quietly and unobtrusively as possible.'

'Quietly and unobtrusively?' There were times when Vicky feared for her father's sanity. 'Papa, nearly every crowned head in Europe is at present in the palace. I'm truly happy to have Alexandrine as a stepmama, and I know Ella, Irène, Alicky and Ernie are as well, but to do so now? And when Granny Queen is here?' Words failed her.

'I quite appreciate what your grandmother's reaction is likely to be, which is why I shall not be making our marriage public today. Only when the time is right – perhaps in another few weeks – will I be making an announcement. Until then, my marriage to Alexandrine is to remain a secret.'

Alicky, who had slid her hand into Alexandrine's, said, 'I don't think it's a secret you will be able to keep, Papa.'

'And why is that, sweetheart?' Her father smiled at her indulgently.

'Because Ernie isn't with us any more, and the only possible reason that he isn't is because he has already gone to spread the news.'

Chapter Seven

MAY 1884, FLORENCE

The Villa I Cedri stood within sight of the River Arno, only a short walk from Florence's medieval Porta San Niccolò gate. It was an ancient house, its flat roof prettily tiled, its pale-yellow walls covered in a riot of sweet-smelling bougainvillea. May was seated in its garden – a garden planted in the English manner with cedars and magnolias – with the letter that had arrived for her that morning lying still unopened on her lap.

Having now been in Italy for a little over eight months any letter keeping her in touch with family events was eagerly received. From the postmark, she knew the letter was from Alicky and had purposely delayed opening it until she could do so in privacy. With the garden to herself, that moment had now arrived and, in considerable anticipation, she opened it:

Dearest Kindred Spirit,
    I do wish you had been a guest at Vicky's wedding to Louis, for then I wouldn't have to be writing such a long letter telling you all about Papa's wedding to Madame de Kolémine and of the uproar that followed it, although there would have been no uproar at all, if Ernie hadn't spilt the beans. However, he did, and it was as if the world had ended. Kindred Spirit Willy's grandfather refused to stay

71

*another night in Darmstadt. He said he'd never heard
anything more disgraceful in his life than a widower
marrying on the same day, and in the same chapel, that his
eldest daughter had married; and of course, being the Kaiser,
when he left, all our other Hohenzollern relations left with
him. Willy wasn't there – did I mention that? His not being
there was perhaps a good thing, as Papa announced Ella's
engagement to Sergei Romanov at the wedding breakfast and
everyone would have been looking at Willy to see his
reaction, and he would have been terribly upset and would
have hated people seeing how upset he was.*

*Anyway, no one in Darmstadt was upset at Papa
marrying Alexandrine ('Alexandrine' is Madame de
Kolémine's Christian name), because she's been Papa's
special friend for a long time and we all love her – even
Ernie, who spoilt things by giving away their secret
(although I don't think he realized how much of a secret it
was meant to be). Once he had told one person, the news
spread like wildfire and, when Granny Queen heard of what
Papa had done (I think it was her lady-in-waiting, Lady
Ely, who told her), Aunt Beatrice said Granny Queen was
so angry that she feared for her life. What happened next
was that Granny Queen instructed Uncle Wales to speak
with Alexandrine and, when he did, he told her that her
marriage to Papa was to be annoulled (I think that's how
it's spelt).*

*An annoulled marriage means that it's as if it's never
happened. I'm sure Papa didn't want his marriage annoulled,
but Madgie (my governess) says that Granny Queen isn't
Queen Empress for nothing and that Papa should have
realized what the outcome was going to be. I've stopped
crying now, but I cried for ages and ages after Alexandrine
said goodbye to Vicky, Ella, Irène and me – and she had to*

*say goodbye. Uncle Wales was implacable about that. She
didn't say goodbye to Ernie, but I expect that was because if
it hadn't been for him, she and Papa would have been able to
keep their secret for a little longer.*

*It's all so sad that I can hardly bear it. The entire
wedding party broke up with everyone scurrying off home
(once Granny Queen's ultimatum had been given, she left for
England and Windsor, with all the Waleses in her wake).
Ella's wedding to Sergei is only a few weeks away and, as
Granny Queen doesn't approve of it and isn't going to attend
it, Papa's relief is vast.*

*I think that's all for now. I've written so much my wrist is
hurting. Please write back and tell me what living in
Florence is like. I miss you and I hope that although you
and your mama and papa weren't at Vicky's wedding, that
you will be at Ella and Sergei's.*

Much, much love, your Kindred Spirit Alicky xxxxxxxx

May laid the letter down on her lap. She felt deeply sorry
for Alicky's father, but thought he should have had more sense
than to believe the Queen would have approved of his marrying
a divorced woman, especially when his late wife had been one
of her much-loved daughters. She wondered where Madame
de Kolémine was now and, wherever she was, if anyone would
ever hear from her again.

Her writing case was on her knee and she took a pen from
it and began writing a reply:

Dearest Alicky,

*It was so nice to receive your letter, although it made me
very sad to learn of the very unhappy outcome of your
papa's marriage to Madame de Kolémine. I am afraid that
not all my news is good news, either, for a few weeks ago my*

*dear papa suffered a stroke and although we hope that he is
slowly beginning to recover, his left arm is still paralysed and
his left leg is no good at all for walking, which is a great
shame since walking in the flower-filled countryside around
here had become one of his greatest pleasures.*

*You ask what living in Florence is like and so, starting
with the Villa I Cedri, I will tell you. In English the name
'I Cedri' means 'The Cedars'. It is a very old house. Miss
Bianca Light, the English lady who has kindly loaned it to
us, claims it was built as long ago as the fifteenth century
and I like to imagine Renaissance Florentines such as
Lorenzo de Medici or Donatello riding past it on their way
to Lucca and Padua.*

*Mama entertains a great deal, and we give and are
invited to lots of tennis parties and, as the weather is so
blissful and we do not have to worry about rain spoiling
garden tea-parties, we give and go to a lot of tea-parties.
We had a lovely such tea-party when it was my seventeenth
birthday.*

She stopped writing and thought about her seventeenth
birthday. The tea-party to celebrate it had been a great success.
It had been attended by lots of the new friends that she and
her parents had made since moving to Florence, and she had
received some very nice presents. Her mother had raided her
jewellery box and given her a pair of her diamond earrings
and two of her bracelets with pearl clasps. Other presents had
included a gold bangle, a beautifully hand-embroidered
cushion, an exquisite hand-painted fan, a white leather book
for photographs, a prettily beribboned box of chocolate-
covered bonbons and a Chinese silk shawl.

Conspicuous by their absence had been presents or cards
from anyone in England. In previous years Aunt Queen had

always remembered her birthday, as had Aunt Alix and her Wales cousins. This year none of them had sent so much as a birthday card. Nothing could have shown her more clearly that, as an exile, she was out of sight and out of mind.

It didn't trouble her too much that Aunt Alix had forgotten about her, or that Georgie, Toria, Looloo and Maudie had forgotten about her, but she had been hurt that Aunt Queen had forgotten her. And then there was Eddy. It wasn't surprising, of course, that she hadn't received a card from him. Even in past years, when Eddy had always dutifully sent her one, she had suspected it had only been because he'd been chivvied into doing so by his mother. This knowledge didn't alter the fact that if he had sent a card – or, better still, a short letter – it would have meant an awful lot to her.

She bit her lip. It was no use thinking of what might have happened. The reality was that it hadn't happened, and dwelling on things that hadn't happened was pointless. She picked up her pen again:

When not playing tennis, or attending tea-parties, I visit museums and galleries – there are lots and lots of wonderful art galleries in Florence – and I accompany my mother when she takes her daily carriage ride through the city's central park, the Cascine. I have also been busy sitting for my portrait (if you can call sitting perfectly still while someone paints a portrait of you being busy). The artist is one of the new friends that, as a family, we have made. His name is Thaddeus Jones and I am sure that if you were to meet him, you would like him. He is known to everyone as Mr Thaddy, and he is Irish.

May paused, the pen still in her hand. There was a lot more that she could write about Mr Thaddy, but a sixth sense told her it might be best if she didn't write that he was only six years older than her, that he was terrific fun and possessed the dramatic good looks of a certain type of Irishman, having blue-black hair and ravishing blue eyes. Such a true description could, if Alicky were to share the letter with her father, be misconstrued. She didn't want lurid rumours about the nature of her feelings for Mr Thaddy spreading from Darmstadt to Windsor and Marlborough House, and Aunt Queen telegramming her that their friendship was most unsuitable and one that had to be terminated immediately.

She chewed the corner of her lip and then, to emphasize Mr Thaddy's respectability, wrote:

Shortly after we arrived in Florence, Mr Thaddy was introduced to Papa by the President of the English Club, and he and Papa have become great friends. Since Papa's stroke, Mr Thaddy has been kindness itself to Papa, sitting with him and keeping him amused in a way that, under the circumstances, isn't easy.

She then added, to make it clear that Mr Thaddy wasn't an amateur artist:

He has trained both in London and in Paris. In Florence, a city famed for its art, his work is very highly regarded.

Which was true, for although the portrait he was painting of her had not been commissioned, portraits that he had been commissioned to paint included one of Russian Princess Woronzoff, wearing twelve ropes of priceless pearls, and one of Queen Natalie of Serbia, her little Pomeranian dog in her arms.

Thinking it best, May now changed the subject:

My life is now far busier than it was when I lived in England. I go to singing lessons, painting lessons, and Italian and French lessons. Thanks to my many visits to the Uffizi and Pitti galleries, I am also becoming quite knowledgeable about Italian Renaissance art and can tell a Bellini from a Botticelli at a glance. (Something that wouldn't, I think, ever have happened if I had remained living in England.) As for the family wedding in St Petersburg, we shall sadly not be attending it, as to do so would be very costly for us and our being there would be too obviously an instance of Mama still being heedless of her expenditure – something none of us want to bring to Aunt Queen's attention.

Her writing came to yet another halt. Certainly her parents knew of the St Petersburg wedding, for her mother had brought up the subject of how extraordinary it was that the Romanovs were uncaring of the possibility that Ella might bring her branch of the family's bleeding disease into their bloodline. No one, of course, knew when, or if, the bleeding disease might strike, and in lots and lots of cases it never struck at all, which was presumably why Louis of Battenberg, with so much to gain from his marriage to Vicky, had thought marriage to her well worth the risk. Another reason was that neither he nor Vicky was in direct line of succession to Aunt Queen's throne, and so if a child of theirs did inherit the disease, the tragedy would be a personal one, not a major dynastic one.

It was different, however, for Sergei, who was the Tsar's next brother in age and who, although not in immediate line of succession to the Romanov throne, was certainly high up in line.

May raised her face to the blissful heat of the Umbrian sun and continued thinking about the hereditary sickness that ran like an ancient curse through the lives of Aunt Queen's children and grandchildren, and which – as she wasn't a direct descendant of Aunt Queen – mercifully hadn't affected her and her brothers. Its medical name was haemophilia, but 'the bleeding disease' was how it was always referred to within the family. The first person to suffer from it had been her Uncle Leopold, Aunt Queen's eighth child, whose blood ever since babyhood had refused to clot in the normal manner.

'When your poor dear Aunt Queen was told Leopold was a haemophiliac, she was utterly bewildered,' her mother had said when explaining it to her. 'Why would a disease, which Aunt Queen's doctors have told her is only passed down in the female line and only affects male offspring, have suddenly showed itself in her lineage? There is absolutely no explanation for it. Even worse for Aunt Queen is the knowledge that although her daughters and granddaughters will never suffer from the disease, they are carriers of it, and any sons they have are at risk of being born with it.'

After a life of pain when every bump and knock caused excruciating bleeding into his joints, her nice, kind Uncle Leopold had died of a brain haemorrhage. It was the same way that, after a fall, Alicky's haemophiliac little brother Frittie had died. In the extended family descended directly from Aunt Queen, 'haemophilia' was a word that was never spoken, but was never far from their thoughts.

Wishing her own thoughts hadn't veered onto a subject so dark, May turned them to something lighter: the St Petersburg wedding list. Uncle Wales and Aunt Alix would be among the wedding guests; Uncle Wales because he would be there representing Aunt Queen, and Aunt Alix because her sister was both the Tsarina and Sergei's sister-in-law.

Although Uncle Wales hadn't allowed Eddy and Georgie to attend Vicky and Louis's wedding, she was fairly sure he would want them to attend Ella and Sergei's. He wouldn't want to waste an opportunity for them to get to know their Romanov cousins better, especially as Cousin Nicky, who was only four years older than Eddy, would, on his father's death, be Tsar of all the Russias at probably the same kind of time as Eddy would be King of the United Kingdom and Emperor of India.

She wondered who else would be there and realized that, at such a big wedding, everyone she could possibly think of would be there. As their mother was the groom's sister, Missy and Ducky would be there. Toria, Looloo and Maudie would be there. Aunt Lenchen, Uncle Christian and all four of their children, Christle, Albert, Thora and Marie-Louise, would be there, as would her Hohenzollern cousins – with the likely exception of Willy, who certainly wouldn't want to see another man marrying Ella. Relatives from nearly every country in Europe would be in St Petersburg. The only family members not there would be her parents and herself.

With the letter she was in the middle of writing now almost forgotten, May wondered how she felt about being so excluded. The answer was immediate, for she didn't feel bad about it at all, and that was because she was enjoying her life in Italy so much. It was a way of life she had never previously experienced; a way of life 100 per cent preferable to the rigid formality the wedding guests would soon be enduring at the Winter Palace in St Petersburg.

She stared thoughtfully into the middle distance at the broad, glittering surface of the Arno, realizing for the first time that it was even preferable to her former life in England. In England, her social life had revolved around the occasional visit with her mother to Aunt Queen at Windsor; to the Edinburgh family at Clarence House; and, with far greater frequency, to the Waleses at Marlborough House. At no time had she socialized with anyone other than family and extended family. Everyone had been royal or, as she herself was, semi-royal.

In Florence, life was far different. Some of their new friends were royal, but many others were not. What had been an eye-opener to her was how, in Florence, her parents happily socialized with fellow exiles who were not even aristocratic and possessed no other title than Mr, Mrs or Miss. Even more extraordinary was that they had been happy for May to make similar friendships, and at the art-history class that she attended at the Uffizi she had made friends with Rowena Daly, who was an American, and with Belinda Light, who was a niece of Miss Bianca Light who had loaned her parents I Cedri.

In England she would never have been allowed to make such friendships, and she most certainly wouldn't have been allowed to saunter down Bond Street – or anywhere else – unaccompanied by anyone except a couple of girlfriends. Now, in Florence, her parents turned a blind eye when, after art class was over and in the company of Rowena and Belinda, she explored the little shops that lined the nearby Ponte Vecchio. Even better was when she strolled in the countryside around I Cedri, picking wild flowers to press, in the company of her mother, Miss Bianca Light and Mr Thaddy; and some-times, even better, with Belinda, Belinda's aunt and Mr Thaddy.

It was a taste of life that was unremarkable to her two friends, but which May had never experienced before, and the dizzying novelty was compensation aplenty for not attending Ella and Sergei's wedding.

She picked up her pen again, wrote *Never before have I been so happy*, and came to a halt, overwhelmed by the realization of why she was so happy. Quite simply, it was because she no longer felt herself to be an outsider. Among her new-found friends, and in her new-found way of life, it didn't matter that she was *ebenbürtig. Ebenbürtig* was an ugly word that her Florentine friends didn't know and, if they had known, wouldn't have cared about. The reserved, withdrawn young woman May had once been was – now that no such shield was needed as protection from hurtful remarks – no longer reserved and withdrawn. Instead she was outgoing, carefree and not only laughed easily and often, but did so out loud in a way that at Windsor, or at Marlborough House, would have been considered extremely vulgar. It was a transformation so wonderful that she never wanted it to end.

For the first time, it occurred to her that being born royal was to be born in a kind of prison. Rowena and Belinda could fall in love with whomsoever they pleased and marry whomsoever they pleased – an option that when her family's exile finally came to an end, and she and her parents returned to England, would not be open to her.

All that would be open to her was either marriage to someone semi-royal who, for very good reasons, no one else in the family was willing to marry, or spinsterhood. Neither option was remotely enticing.

But what if, when her family's exile came to an end and they returned to England, she didn't remain there? What if she returned to Florence and met and fell in love with someone who, like Mr Thaddy, was handsome and fun and non-royal? And what if this unknown person in her future loved her passionately in return and wanted to marry her? It was a scenario so revolutionary the blood pounded in her ears.

She thought of how out of sight and out of mind she had already become. Who, within the vast family that she was such a fringe member of, was likely to care if plain May Teck kicked over the traces and, living far enough away not to be an embarrassment, married someone non-royal? The answer was that she couldn't imagine anyone caring very much.

In a nearby cedar tree, two chaffinches wrangled noisily. She rose to her feet and the birds immediately ended their quarrel, flying away in the direction of the river. May watched them until she could see them no longer, knowing she had come to a realization that, if she allowed it to, would alter the course of her life

Writing *All my love, your Kindred Spirit May*, she finished her letter and then, picking up her writing case, began walking back to I Cedri. There, full of his devastating Irish charm, Mr Thaddy would shortly be arriving in order to continue work on her portrait.

Chapter Eight

It was barely dawn; still dark, and they were coming for Willy again. They were coming to force him into the iron monstrosity, to strap him into it for hours and hours, his head at an impossibly awkward angle, his body convulsed in pain. They were dragging him from his bed. He was kicking and screaming, shrieking for his mama, begging her to tell the men to let him go; but his mama was saying it was for his own good. His mama was saying he had to be put into the iron machine so that one day he would look as other boys looked; so that he would be able to run and ride, and eat with a knife and fork just like other boys; so that he would no longer be an embarrassment to her and a shame to Prussia, the country that he would one day rule. The hard leather of the straps bit into his four-year-old body. The icy cold of an iron restraint pressed hard against his forehead. '*No!*' he was shouting. '*No! No! No!*'

As always, Willy's own terrified shouts woke him. He was bathed in sweat, his heart pounding, his pulse racing. He fought free of the tangled sheets; screamed, '*Get out!*' at the almost equally terrified valet who, as ever on such occasions, had nervously entered the room; swung his legs over the edge of the bed and, like the small petrified child he had once been, covered his face with his hands and wept.

Later, when he had recovered a semblance of control, Willy wiped the tears away, heaved himself to his feet and shrugged himself into a tartan dressing gown. Then he walked wearily to the window and pulled one of the two heavy curtains to one side.

His bedroom overlooked a lake that stretched the entire east side of the palace and, in the ethereal light of breaking dawn, two swans glided serenely upon it. Having mated for life, the pair were always together. Mercifully, always being together was not something that applied to Willy and Dona. Her bedroom was a conventional distance away from his on the other side of their separate bathrooms, dressing rooms and sitting rooms and, even if she had heard his terrified shouts, he doubted if Dona would have had the nerve to walk in on him and try to wake him.

And he most certainly wouldn't have wanted her to. Dear God, he didn't want anyone ever to see him screaming with fear and sobbing like a child: not his valets, not his wife, not anyone. It was too far removed from the image he projected of himself, an image that was far different from the real Willy – the timid, not-very-clever Willy whom he had long learned to keep hidden under a cloak of constant pretence; a pretence that had become a way of life.

He had been six when he discovered what a difference and a comfort pretending to be someone he wasn't could be. It had been a cold autumn day and he was to accompany his grandfather, the Kaiser, to the parade ground at Potsdam. Dressed appropriately in a Foot Guards uniform made especially for him, he was marching up and down, practising, in the hope that his grandfather would allow him to march with the soldiers.

Watching from a distance, his mother had called Willy across to her and he had run to her, eager for her praise, for praise from his mother was seldom, if ever, given. With his face shining in happy expectation, he had floundered to a halt in front of her and waited for her to tell him what a wonderful little soldier he was, and how proud his grandfather would be of him when he saw him in his uniform. Instead she'd said tartly, 'Do stop making such an exhibition of yourself, Willy. In uniform you look like an organ-grinder's monkey.'

His happiness had been destroyed at a stroke and he had hated her for destroying it; hated her for – as she always did – making him feel ridiculous and insignificant. He had sought refuge in his playroom and had stood in front of a mirror, tears scalding his face. 'I do not look like a monkey! I do not! I do not! I do not!' he had shouted at his reflection time and again.

When he had shouted himself hoarse, he dragged a scarlet cloak from his dressing-up box and flung it around his shoulders. Then, still wearing the helmet that was part of his uniform, he snatched up a toy sword and, in front of the mirror and uttering war whoops, began swirling it round and round above his head. Suddenly he was a crusader knight storming the walls of Jerusalem to free the city from the infidels; he was Alexander the Great, conquering the known world; he was his grandfather leading the Prussian Army to glorious victory in the Austro-Prussian War of twenty years ago.

And even when, without the cloak, it was time to leave for the parade ground, the sensation that he had aroused in himself remained, for Willy had discovered a precious secret. If he imagined himself to be invincible, then he *became* invincible.

He hadn't known at six years old what an inferiority complex was, or why he had one, but he had discovered a way of living with one. He simply pretended to be all the things he wanted to be and wasn't; and, because he never let the pretence down, the world didn't know the real Willy – the not-very-brave, not-very-clever Willy. They only saw his steely gaze and his aggressive bearing; his arrogance and swagger and know-it-all superiority. It was a pretence lived so utterly and completely that even his mother no longer knew the true Willy – and Dona had never known him.

It was growing lighter now. The first fingers of dawn stabbed the sky, no longer so pale as to be barely visible, but a pure and piercing deep gold and rose-pink.

With his hands plunged deep in the pockets of his dressing gown – one that had been a gift to him from his grandmother on his last visit to Windsor – he thought about his mother. Even now that he was a grown man, she was still as brutally critical towards him as she had been when he'd been six. The difference now, though, was that he no longer cared.

A couple of years after the organ-grinder monkey incident, his grandfather had begun to take an interest in him, as had Bismarck, his grandfather's formidable Chancellor. They were the two people he idolized most in the world. His grandfather because he had led the Prussian Army into battle against Napoleon, and Bismarck because, with blood and iron, he had welded together a hotchpotch of kingdoms, principalities and grand duchies into a strong, unified empire. And both men disliked his mother just as much as Willy did.

When he had asked his grandfather why he disliked his mother so much, his grandfather had replied bluntly, 'Because she is an *Engländarin*. Because she has infected your father with English liberal ideas and because she rules her husband in a way no German wife would ever dare to do.'

He had then gripped Willy hard around his shoulders. 'Promise me,' he'd said, his white handlebar moustache quivering with the force of his emotion, 'promise me you will only ever marry a German princess. A German princess will know her place. She will never try to rule you, as your mother rules your father. All you will need from her is that she bears you sons, for to father sons is the duty of a hereditary monarch. Do you understand, Wilhelm? Do you promise?'

He had promised. And he had kept his promise. He had married Dona, who, before their marriage, had been Her Serene Highness Princess Augusta Viktoria of Schleswig-Holstein and who was now Her Royal Highness Princess Wilhelm of Prussia.

He hadn't been in love with her. He'd been in love with Ella, and he was still in love with Ella. He would always, until the day he died, be in love with Ella. But Ella had rejected him for Sergei Romanov, a man so unappealing that in a crowded room he was always to be found standing alone. Blind with bewilderment and hurt, desperate to save his pride, Willy had left immediately for Schleswig-Holstein and had proposed to Dona, the daughter of one of his father's friends.

It had been an act of impulse, but then he was always impulsive. Being impulsive was something he simply couldn't help. It was part of his psyche. And he'd known there wasn't a one-in-a-million chance of suffering another rejection. As a Serene Highness, the homely and dim-witted Dona was insignificant in the royal marriage stakes. So much so that it would never have occurred to her, or to her family, that she stood the slightest chance of a distinguished marriage – far less of marriage to a man who would one day be Germany's emperor.

Her homeliness hadn't mattered to Willy. Although far from beautiful, when she smiled she was pleasant-looking and he'd never been stirred by any woman's beauty other than by Ella's, and neither did he expect he ever would be. Dona's dim-wittedness hadn't mattered, either. Instead he'd counted it one of her advantages, for the last thing he'd wanted was a fiercely intelligent woman who would meddle in political affairs, as his mother constantly did. All he'd wanted from his marriage was a wife who would be dutifully submissive, would bear him strong sons and, as a future empress, would look the part – and although she was plain, Dona did carry herself with impressive dignity.

He sighed heavily. In that she was submissive beyond reproach and, in three years of marriage, had given birth to three strong boys – the last only days ago – she had certainly fulfilled all he'd thought he wanted. What he hadn't taken into account was that she would love him so cloyingly; that she would expect so much of his time and attention and that, God help him, she would bore him to such an extent there were times when he thought his nerves would give way under the strain of enduring it.

His way of coping had been to spend as little time with Dona as possible. They breakfasted together and then, making courteous insincere apologies about not being able to spend more of the day with her, he speedily departed for regimental headquarters, where he ensured that his duties as colonel and commander of the Hussar Guards kept him away from the palace not only for the whole day, but every evening as well.

Spending time with his regiment was no hardship. It was what he lived for. He had always felt far more comfortable with men than he had with women. Riding with his fellow officers, parading with them and, in the evenings in the officers' mess, drinking and enjoying practical jokes with them gave him a sense of completeness that he never experienced at any other time. The regiment was his safe harbour and refuge.

That safe harbour and refuge belonged, though, to the pretend Willy, not the real Willy. The real Willy was buried so deep that even he only recognized the person he really was when – as now, in the aftermath of a nightmare – all pretence was stripped away.

The sun was rising. The swans were completing a second

lap of the lake. The palace was stirring. Knowing he would not be disturbed until he chose to be, he remained at the window, pondering whether, as an adult, he had ever interacted as the real Willy with anyone.

From out of nowhere, memory smote him with vivid, physical force. There *had* been such a time. It had been at Osborne when, five years ago and on an otherwise deserted beach, he had come across Ella's little sister sobbing her heart out because she thought it was her own, and her siblings', fault that their mother had died of diphtheria.

If Alicky hadn't been Ella's little sister, would he have stopped to comfort her? Willy didn't know. The thing was, he *had* stopped and he *had* tried to comfort her, and whilst he'd been doing so, May of Teck had run up to them and from then on, whenever he'd been with her and Alicky, he'd forgotten all about being the pretend Willy. 'Kindred spirits,' Alicky had called the three of them, and beneath the childish tosh there had been an element of truth. Never before had he revealed so much of his inner self to anyone as he had to May and Alicky when their mutual confidences had begun. Being himself, instead of his pretend self, had been a unique, extraordinary experience – as had the scoring of their wrists with his 1st Foot Guards medal brooch-pin and the mixing of their blood. Even now he still mentally prefaced May's name with the words 'Kindred Spirit', just as he did Alicky's name.

He breathed in deeply, aware that his pulse was no longer pounding, his heart was no longer racing and he was no longer sweating. It was over, thank God. Day had fully dawned, the miasma of nightmare had fled and his pretend personality was rushing headlong through his veins and along his nerve endings. He could feel himself becoming once again the Willy the world knew; the Willy who was braver and cleverer than anyone else; the Willy who was invincible.

He swung away from the window, slammed his fist on the bell that would summon his valet and was in such good humour that it occurred to him that he could, just for once, return to the palace after his morning at headquarters and take Dona for an after-luncheon carriage ride. She would like that and would be deeply grateful – and when it suited him, he liked people to be grateful to him. It increased his sense of superiority.

As his valet stumbled hurriedly into the room, Willy roared at him for not having entered the room sooner and then, full of satisfaction at his magnanimity where Dona was concerned, His Royal Highness Prince Wilhelm of Prussia embarked on his day.

Chapter Nine

The New Palace was in uproar with wedding and travel preparations. Ladies-in-waiting and chambermaids were scurrying here, there and everywhere with armfuls of day gowns, afternoon gowns and lavish evening gowns, which all, folded in layer upon layer of tissue paper, were then packed into enormous travelling trunks. Even though it was high summer, furs aplenty were also being carefully packed, for to travel without furs – especially to St Petersburg – was unthinkable.

'I don't see why Ella has to take furs with her,' Alicky said to Vicky, who was supervising the packing of their jewellery into locked travelling cases. 'Not when Sergei will be drowning her in Russian sable when she arrives in St Petersburg – and with jewels,' she added. 'Madgie says the Romanovs' jewellery collection is the largest in the world.'

'And I dare say your governess is right, although I'm surprised she was vulgar enough to say so to you. And although having enough jewellery will never be a problem now for Ella – who doesn't, incidentally, give two hoots about jewellery and furs – it would be very shameful to arrive as if we didn't have a diamond to our name.'

'I'm not sure I do have a diamond to my name.' Being only twelve, Alicky's jewellery was still restricted to pearls. 'It seems to me that everyone is much more excited about this wedding than they were about yours. Don't you mind?'

'Silly goose, of course I don't mind. All Romanov weddings are hugely magnificent events, and Sergei isn't just any Romanov. He's the Tsar's brother. And although the wedding will be impossibly splendid, I will always think my own wedding was even more wonderful, for how could it not be when I was marrying Louis, and when I love Louis so very, very much?'

'And Ella loves Sergei very, very much, doesn't she?'

She'd meant it as a statement, not a question, but Vicky pursed her lips, handed the jewellery case to her maid, saying, 'Would you put this box with the rest of the jewellery cases, Jenny?' and then, as the maid left the room, said, 'I'm sure she does, Alicky. But not, I think, in the same way.'

Alicky frowned, sensing a secret she wasn't supposed to know. 'Then in what way?'

'She feels that Sergei needs her. Papa says he is a different kind of person when he is at home in Russia, and that he isn't much liked. Ella believes she can change that.'

'It doesn't sound a very exciting reason to marry someone.'

'No, it doesn't.' Vicky thought of the other reason why Ella was marrying Sergei, but it wasn't one she could share with Alicky.

'Sergei being twenty-seven and not yet married is causing open speculation,' Ella had said to Vicky in confidence on the day before her engagement to Sergei was announced, 'and he wants to put an end to it.'

Vicky's eyebrows had risen. 'You mean the same kind of speculation that our little brother Ernie is beginning to arouse?'

Ella had nodded. At sixteen, Ernie's lack of interest in girls and his interest in the family's male members of staff were obvious. Their father was forever sacking footmen who had encouraged Ernie's attention, or finding replacements for those who had left because of it.

Vicky hadn't asked Ella if marriage to a man who was rumoured to prefer his own sex was the kind of marriage she wanted, because it was quite obvious to her that Ella was embarking on her marriage with her eyes wide open, and for reasons that suited her own, not very run-of-the-mill emotional needs.

She said now, 'People marry each other for all kinds of reasons, Alicky, and when people are royal, the reasons can be complex. Thankfully, my reason for wanting to marry Louis wasn't complex at all. I married him because I couldn't even begin to envisage marrying anyone else. I married him because I'm heedlessly, hopelessly in love with him.' Her cheeks warmed as she remembered their lovemaking of the previous night. 'We share a grand, all-engulfing passion, Alicky. It's as simple as that.'

Alicky sighed rapturously. She knew all about grand, all-engulfing passions because she was often taken to the opera, and what Vicky was describing was the kind of operatic grand passion that thrilled her to the depths of her being. It was a passion that, when she was older, she fervently hoped to experience for herself. All that had to happen was for her to meet her one true love. An ecstatic shiver ran down her spine. When she did, she knew she would recognize him before he even spoke to her. Without a shadow of a doubt, she knew she would recognize him the instant their eyes met.

The journey to Russia was the longest Alicky had ever taken. Even though they were travelling by train, it took three days. For most of the way the track hugged the Baltic coastline and the land was flat and bleak, interspersed only occasionally by mist-shrouded, medieval-looking villages. Whenever the track turned a little way inland there was nothing but endless reed-beds and chains of eerily desolate lakes; and then, as they progressed deeper into Russia, the lonely lakes gave way to mile after mile of dark, mysterious forests of spruce and fir.

Vicky, Irène and Ernie found the journey tedious and spent it playing cards and solitaire. Alicky didn't find it tedious at all. She thought the colossal scale of the landscape and the strange northern summer light it was bathed in were mesmer-izing. Russia! How could anyone think forests that were home to bears and wolves, and goodness knew how many other wild creatures, tedious? Russia wasn't just another country; it was another world, so strange and exotic that it seemed barely possible her sister was soon to be a part of it.

'Even my Christian name of Elizabeth will change to Russian spelling and pronunciation,' Ella said to her as their private train steamed ever further north-east. Outside the train window they watched as a flock of geese flew over the surface of a perfectly still silver-grey lake. 'After my marriage, I will be known as Yelizaveta – Grand Duchess Yelizaveta Feodorovna Romanova.'

It sounded wonderfully grand and the only thing spoiling it was that May would not be at the wedding, and Alicky's disappointment that she wouldn't be having a reunion with her was vast. As May would be missing out on what was going to be a very special family occasion, Alicky decided that she would write her long descriptive letters so that, even at a distance, her Kindred Spirit might not feel too left out of everything.

As the flock of geese disappeared from view she said, 'Where will we be staying when we reach St Petersburg, Ella? Will we be staying at the Winter Palace, or at another of the Romanov palaces?'

'I don't know, pet lamb. I do know that the wedding is to

take place at the Winter Palace, but that a favourite family residence is at Peterhof, which is fifteen miles from St Petersburg on the Gulf of Finland. Papa thinks it quite possible that for some of the time we will be staying there.'

Alicky was just about to ask if that meant the Winter Palace was the equivalent of Buckingham Palace, and Peterhof the equivalent of Windsor Castle, when Ernie strolled into their otherwise-deserted carriage and plopped himself down into one of its many comfy armchairs. Throwing a leg over one of the chair's plush arms, he said to Ella, 'Lord, is this journey ever going to end? Why couldn't we have come by sea, like the Waleses are doing? At least it would have been more interesting.'

'We don't possess a yacht, that's why,' Ella said drily. 'The Waleses have the use of Granny Queen's *Victoria and Albert*.'

'Lucky dogs.' Ernie, thinking of muscular sailors in bell-bottomed trousers, withdrew a cigarette case and a lighter from his jacket pocket. 'At least if Irène's pash on Prussian Henry comes to fruition, the wedding will be on home ground and, if not on home ground, it will only be a hop and a skip to Berlin.'

At the thought of a third wedding in the family, Alicky's eyes widened.

'Don't spread rumours,' Ella chided. 'Irène may well have a crush on Henry, but I don't think it's being reciprocated. At least not yet.'

'Ah, but there will be further opportunities for Irène to wow him with her charms at St Petersburg. The Hohenzollerns are going to be there in full force, aren't they?'

Ella, who wasn't at all sure that Willy would be there, said, 'I imagine so. Everyone in the entire family has been invited. The Waleses, the Edinburghs, the Connaughts, the Albanys, the Battenbergs, the Hohenzollerns, the Schleswig-Holsteins, the Saxe-Meiningens and then there will be all the Romanovs – and goodness only knows how many of them there will be. The Winter Palace and Peterhof will be knee-deep in Russian royalty even before we arrive.'

She said it without any sign of concern. Alicky envied her. How could Ella be so relaxed when, during the wedding service, she would be the focus of hundreds of pairs of eyes? When, on her carriage ride through St Petersburg's streets, she would be the focus of *thousands* of pairs of eyes? The mere thought of being the object of such public exposure made Alicky feel faint, and she was grateful to the bottom of her heart that at this family wedding she wasn't expected to be a bridesmaid.

'Only girls who are Russian Orthodox can be bridesmaids at a Russian Orthodox wedding,' Vicky had explained to her when arrangements for the wedding were being made, 'and so all the bridesmaids will be members of Sergei's family. I hope it isn't too much of a disappointment?'

Hugely relieved, Alicky had shaken her head to show that it wasn't. Later, though, she had said, puzzled, 'How is it that the bridesmaids have to be Russian Orthodox when the bride is a Lutheran Protestant?'

Vicky had looked uncomfortable and Alicky had known it was a question her sister had rather she hadn't asked. 'Ella is taking instruction,' she had said, her eyes not meeting hers. 'Sergei expects her to convert to Russian Orthodoxy in the not-too-distant future.'

If it hadn't been for Ernie joining them, Alicky would have asked Ella how she felt about taking instruction in a way of worship that was vastly different from the one they had all been brought up in, but she doubted Ella would want to talk about such a subject in front of Ernie. Ernie was carelessly flippant about everything, and one thing Alicky was certain of was that changing from Lutheran Protestantism to Russian

Orthodoxy was not a subject to be flippant about. She would talk about it later with Ella when they were next on their own.

Ernie was now gossiping about the Waleses and of how, although Maudie was fun, Toria and Looloo were tedious beyond belief.

'They're so pathetically infantile. Do you know that for Cousin Toria's sixteenth birthday next month, Aunt Alix is going to give a children's party for her? A *children's* party! Can you believe it?' His snort of disgust was the last thing Alicky heard before the rhythmic rocking of the train sent her to sleep.

She had expected their arrival at the train station in St Petersburg to be similar to their royal welcomes whenever they stayed with Granny Queen at Windsor Castle, or Osborne House, or Balmoral. A red carpet and immaculate formality, but nothing so excessive that it would plunge her into agonies of shyness.

The noise and the crush when they stepped from their train onto the station platform, to be met by Sergei and his uniformed and bemedalled entourage, were totally unlike anything she had ever experienced, or even imagined. Flags – the red and white of Hesse-Darmstadt, the gold and black of the House of Romanov and even, here and there, the red, white and blue of Granny Queen's Union Jack – waved in what appeared to be an endless sea. Brass bands played deafeningly. Church bells rang out. The coaches waiting for them were as ornately gilded as Britain's coronation coach.

'The Romanovs don't believe in doing things by halves, do they?' Ernie said admiringly as the coach he was sharing with Alicky and Irène moved off, drawn by eight white horses postilion-ridden and accompanied by footmen in powdered wigs and scarlet livery.

All the way to the Winter Palace, Alicky kept her eyes not

on the cheering people lining the streets, but on her lap and her lace-gloved hands. It was nice that the people of St Petersburg were welcoming Ella so eagerly, and she was very glad they were doing so, but crowds of any kind unnerved her, no matter how hard she tried not to let them do so.

'Oh, look, Alicky!' Irène grabbed hold of her arm. 'The Neva! I'd no idea it would be far, far wider than the Thames. Do look, Alicky. Please.'

Reluctantly she raised her head. They were crossing a bridge and although it was lined by flag-waving Russians, over their heads was a mesmerizing view of the broadest, most awe-inspiring river she had ever seen. And it wasn't only the river that took her breath away. Pale-stone mansions as big as palaces lined both banks and beyond the mansions, and as far as the eye could see, delicate spires rose ethereally; pumpkin-shaped domes glittered; towers and steeples pierced the sky; turrets and pinnacles gleamed with gold. It was a scene of such awe-inspiring beauty that the breath caught in Alicky's throat. Why had no one told her that St Petersburg was a city straight from a fairy-tale? Why had no one warned her that once she had seen it, she would want to remain in it forever?

Nothing over the next couple of days made Alicky change her opinion. Sergei had told her that the Winter Palace was magnificent beyond description, but as he was a Romanov speaking of the most famous of all Romanov palaces, she had thought his description nothing but natural pride and exaggeration. It wasn't. Buckingham Palace was splendid, its grandeur impressive, but elegantly restrained. There was nothing restrained about the interior of the Winter Palace.

They had stepped from their coach into the palace's central courtyard and, with Cossacks lining every foot of the way, and walking just behind Ella and Sergei, they had been escorted through a grandiose entrance into a room colonnaded with gilded columns. At the far end of the room, bathed in light from a cathedral-high bank of windows and walls of glittering mirrors, rose a staircase of breathtaking splendour. A vision of white marble and gold, it rose in two separate curving wings to meet on a balconied landing. There, framed by gold-topped jasper pillars, the Tsar and Tsarina of all the Russias were waiting to greet them.

Alicky sucked in her breath and slid her hand into Irène's. Irène gave it a reassuring squeeze. 'I know you haven't met Uncle Sasha since you were too young to remember, and that you haven't met Aunt Minny for ages,' she whispered, 'but they are your godparents. There is absolutely no reason at all to be shy.'

Her Uncle Sasha was a bear of a man, six-and-a-half feet tall, his shoulders massive, his face heavily bearded. With flushed cheeks, Alicky sank into a curtsey. Jovially he put out a hand and raised her to her feet. 'The last time I saw you, little squirrel, you were small enough for me to throw into the air and catch!' His voice was deep and booming, not at all like Sergei's, but he was looking at her with the same kind of family interest that Sergei always looked at her with, and remembering that he was Sergei's brother enabled her to fight down her shyness.

There was no need for shyness in the presence of her thirty-six-year-old aunt, for she was Aunt Alix Wales's sister and she was so like Aunt Alix, and her manner so reassuringly similar, that Alicky's nervous tension soon evaporated.

When they had gathered in a formal reception room that linked the state rooms to the private rooms, her aunt said, 'Nicky and the children are on their way from Peterhof and are very much looking forward to meeting you.'

For a second, Alicky had no idea to whom her aunt was

referring, and then she remembered that Nicky was Uncle Sasha's son and heir, the sixteen-year-old Tsesarevich, and that the children she had spoken of must be his younger siblings.

Later, when she was with Irène in the bedroom they were to share, and after she had endured hours of being introduced to a seemingly endless parade of Romanov royalty, Alicky said unhappily, 'I can't face this evening's reception, Irène. Truly I can't.'

'Of course you can. It's going to be wonderful. It isn't only Romanovs we're meeting for the first time. There are distant cousins of Mama's here that we've never met before. Meeting them is going to be absolutely thrilling.'

Alicky didn't think it would be thrilling at all. To her it sounded unbelievably daunting. She said hopefully, 'Can't you tell Papa I have a headache?'

'Absolutely not.' Irène regarded her in exasperation. 'A great exception is being made in allowing someone of your age to attend an evening reception and consequently people will think your shyness quite natural, and perhaps even appealing, but it is a shyness you have to get over, Alicky. You are a royal princess, and royal princesses have to be perfectly composed in the public eye. You can't continue to turn beetroot-red whenever anyone who isn't intimate family speaks to you.'

Alicky bit her lip, knowing it was a battle she couldn't win and would just have to endure.

What made the enduring more difficult than normal that evening was that because Vicky, Ella, Irène and Ernie were so enjoying the Romanov experience, they weren't, as they often did, shielding her from unwanted attention.

As the hours passed, Alicky's heart pounded more and more painfully and she knew red blotches were staining her cheeks. Making her shyness worse than usual was the fact that only

Aunt Minny and Uncle Sasha spoke to her in English. Although they were Russian, everyone else spoke French to her, and her French wasn't good enough for her to say even a few words in it without it being an embarrassing struggle. It all added to her nerves and sense of awkwardness. And then, just when she thought she wasn't going to be able to survive another minute, she found herself facing a handsome young man with the bluest, gentlest eyes she had ever seen.

Time stood still.

She drew in a deep, unsteady breath. Unbelievably, wonderfully, it was the moment she had dreamed of. The moment when she knew herself to be facing the one person in the whole wide world who was destined to be her everlasting true love.

In flawless English and with an engaging smile, he said, 'Hello, Alicky. I've been so looking forward to meeting you. I'm Nicky. Would you like me to show you the Knights' Hall? There are wonderful life-size bronzes of knights on horseback in it.'

'Yes,' she said gratefully, knowing that he was instinctively removing her from the oppressive crush of his intimidating relations; and certain she would never feel nervous with him, never feel shy. 'Yes, Nicky. I'd like that very, very much.'

And with her cheeks no longer stained red, and her heart singing like a bird, she left the room with him, happy to go wherever it was he wished to take her; happier than she could ever remember being.

Chapter Ten

It was mid-July and, for May, the heat in Florence was over-powering, far too hot to be out in the countryside gathering wild flowers, sketching or sitting companionably nearby with Rowena and Belinda, or with her mother and Miss Light as Mr Thaddy painted views of the Arno. Instead she was enjoying the shade of I Cedri's rooftop loggia. Its outer wall, supported by delicate stone arches, was open to the elements and, as well as affording a wonderful view of the river, captured the occasional welcoming light breeze.

The loggia was furnished with cushioned wicker chairs and May was sitting in one of them, with two unopened letters on her lap. Both of them had arrived at I Cedri that morning. One, with a Sandringham postmark, was in Maudie's unmistakeable near-indecipherable scrawl. The other, in Alicky's far neater handwriting, had been posted from Darmstadt.

May bit the corner of her lip. Which should she open first? Alicky's letter would be full of gossip about Ella and Sergei's St Petersburg wedding, but Maudie's would have Wales family news in it – and that meant there was a good chance of there being news of Eddy in it.

With hope in her heart, she opened the envelope bearing the Sandringham postmark:

Dearest lovely May,

I'm missing you. For how much longer are you going to be in Italy? Toria says that if you stay out there much longer you are going to return to England with skin as dark as a little native boy's. You won't believe this but we (Toria, Looloo et moi) now have both a German governess and a French governess. The German governess is also teaching us – and Mama – how to spin. Can you imagine it? My mama spinning? I think it the greatest hoot ever. Toria and Looloo are embarrassingly duff at both French and German, but I'm not. I've discovered I like languages and I am also (although this is something of a secret) beginning to learn a little Russian. I can't wait until Sergei makes a visit to England with Ella and I can astound him by greeting him in his own language!

I have another secret, too. When Eddy and Georgie were at sea together and went on shore in Tokyo, they got themselves tattooed. Georgie's tattoos are quite modest, but Eddy's aren't. He has blue-and-red dragons writhing all the way down his arms! Although he is now twenty and Granny Queen thinks it high time a suitable marriage was arranged for him, Mama insists otherwise, and for once Papa is in agreement with her. As you can imagine, Granny Queen is not best pleased.

I can't help wondering who it is that Granny Queen has in mind for Eddy. Both Toria and Looloo think that, until Ella's engagement to Sergei, it was Ella. I did as well. When it comes to her many grandchildren, Ella has always been Granny Queen's number-one favourite and I think she would very much have liked Ella to be crowned Queen Consort when Eddy becomes King. We Wales girls have never been high on her list of favourites: Toria and Looloo because they always have coughs and colds (Granny Queen once offended

*Mama greatly by referring to them as puny), and me
because she thinks I'm too much of a tomboy and not
ladylike enough.*

*Perhaps, as Mama is reluctant for Eddy to marry until
he is well into his twenties, Granny Queen will now have
another of the Hesse-Darmstadt girls in mind as a future
Queen of England. How old is Irène now? Seventeen?
Eighteen? And if not Irène, there is always Alicky. By the
time Eddy is twenty-four or twenty-five, Alicky will be of
marriageable age. When it comes to who I would prefer as a
future sister-in-law, I would much prefer it to be Irène.
Alicky is a strange little thing. You never know what is going
on inside her head.*

*What other news? Eddy is still at Cambridge and not, I
think, enjoying it very much. In September he is to go to
Heidelberg for a few months to improve his German.
(Knowing Eddy, he won't enjoy this, either, but will endure
it silently and then have his tutor accuse him of being
indolent and inattentive.) Georgie is still at the Royal Naval
College and, as Papa has instructed that he shouldn't leave
the college except to go places that he (Papa) has first
approved of, and not unless he is accompanied by a senior
member of the college staff, I don't imagine he is having
much of a fun time, either.*

*I envy you in Florence – and a mama who allows you the
freedom to make friends outside the family. How I would
love to be with you when you picnic with Rowena and
Belinda and Miss Light on the banks of the Arno. All I
have to look forward to is an end-of-summer stay at
Abergeldie and, instead of the blissful-sounding Arno, the
all-too-chill River Dee.*

Love always, Maudie x

PS: If you have any news of Frank, will you please write me with it? I haven't seen him in ages and he doesn't write. At least, not to me.

PPS: Rumour is that my Aunt Beatrice wants to marry Henry of Battenberg and that Granny Queen is not as happy as might have been expected. Mama says this is because Aunt Bea is Granny Queen's last unmarried daughter and she relies on her for companionship and doesn't want to lose her. I feel sorry for Aunt Bea. To have been a spinster for so long and then to have one of the to-die-for-handsome Battenberg brothers asking for her hand in marriage – and for Granny Queen to object – must be very hard. Love again, Maudie x

May put the letter down on her lap. Was Maudie right in thinking that, with Ella married to Sergei, Irène might now be next in line as a future prospective bride for Eddy? The Queen had always taken a particular interest in all four of her mother-less Hesse-Darmstadt grandchildren, and the best future possible for Irène would be as Eddy's bride – or would be, unless Irène made a surprising, unexpected marriage elsewhere first.

She looked into the distance where the Arno, flanked by wide green meadows, shimmered in the sun. Would Irène ever come to understand Eddy as she did? Would she come to realize that the only reason he appeared indifferent to everything was because he was never given the opportunity to do anything that interested him? Certainly his years as a naval cadet had held no interest for him. She couldn't even begin to imagine how awful it must have been, enduring three years at sea when he had no love of it and when, unlike Georgie, who was to follow the traditional path of a royal second brother by becoming a naval officer, for Eddy it had all been for no good purpose.

She knew, without being told, that no one had ever asked Eddy if he wanted to study at Cambridge; that no one had ever asked either him or Georgie what it was they wanted to do – what it was they liked doing best. Because Georgie had a natural aptitude for seamanship, the years at sea would have been no particular hardship for him, and he would probably be enjoying his officer training at Greenwich. But what about Eddy? Was Maudie right in thinking that he wasn't enjoying Cambridge? May had no way of knowing. Although her mother received the occasional letter from Aunt Queen, and the even more occasional letter from Aunt Alix, no one – apart from Maudie and, of course, Alicky – ever troubled to write to her, and news of Eddy in the letters her mother received was not the kind of personal news she craved.

Telling herself that things could be much worse, and that at least Maudie hadn't been writing with news that Eddy had become engaged, she opened the letter from Alicky:

Dearest Kindred Spirit,

I have so much to tell you, I don't know where to start. I want to begin by telling you of the most wonderful, amazing thing that has happened to me – of how I have met the one person I am destined to go through life and eternity with. But if I do that, I will never get round to telling you about St Petersburg and about Ella's wedding, which was spectacular beyond belief and which, because there had to be a Lutheran service as well as an Orthodox one, went on for what seemed like forever. The wedding took place in the chapel of the Winter Palace, which is not at all like a Lutheran chapel and is all white and gold, and all through the service it was full of the smoky scent of incense (which I liked, but which made my papa cough dreadfully). Ella wore a Russian-style dress of white and silver that fell into an

ermine-edged train, yards and yards long. Her veil was held
in place by a jewelled coronet that had once belonged to
Catherine the Great, and she looked so untouchably beautiful
that I found it hard to believe she was my sister.

What you will not believe is that I was one of the
bridesmaids and my gown was white muslin and I wore a
coronet of roses. I didn't know I was to be one of the
bridesmaids until the very last moment, for Papa had been
told that Ella was to have only Romanov bridesmaids. If I
had known beforehand, I would have pretended to be sick and
would never have left Darmstadt, but I was given very little
time to be terrified beforehand and then, throughout the long
candlelit ceremony, the person I know is always going to be
my other half was standing by the side of the altar and his
eyes held mine all the time, and so I wasn't sick with nerves.

Have you guessed yet who this very special person is? He
is Sergei's nephew, Nicholas (and also one of my second or
third cousins). He is sixteen and the kindest, gentlest person
in the world. He is also the most tremendous fun. The royal
family do not live in the Winter Palace. They live nearly all
the time at Peterhof, which is a summer palace set amidst
vast gardens and lakes and fountains a few miles from St
Petersburg. It's within sight of the sea, and that is where we
all stayed in the days after the wedding.

We had such good times, May. I do wish you had been with
us. Nicky has two brothers and two sisters. Georgy is thirteen.
Xenia is nine. Misha is five and Olga is two. They are all
terrifically nice and I played with them every day I was there.
Nicky doesn't call me Alicky; he calls me by my second
baptismal name, Alix. My first name is Victoria, after Granny
Queen, and I expect your first name is, too. Because of Aunt
Alix, my being called Alix makes me feel very grown-up, but I
don't want everyone calling me Alix. Only Nicky.

Before we left Peterhof we scratched our names into a pane of glass in a little summerhouse so that our names will be there forever and ever. Don't you think that is romantic? And please, please, please don't say that we are too young to be romantic. Kindred Spirit Willy's mama was only fourteen when his papa offered for her, and in Shakespeare's Romeo and Juliet, *Juliet is only thirteen. And when everything in your head and your heart tells you that someone is the right person for you, then it doesn't matter how old you are when it happens. I'm back home in Darmstadt now, but Ella says she will invite me to stay with her and Sergei, and I can't wait to be in St Petersburg again. It's the most magical place you can imagine.*

Filled with an unpleasant feeling of unease, May stopped reading. Of all the people for Alicky to have developed a crush on, Nicholas Romanov, who, on his father's death, would be Tsar Nicholas, Emperor and Autocrat of all the Russias, was about the most unsuitable – and the most unlikely. Unsuitable because there was no way Aunt Queen's deep Russophobia would tolerate a second Hesse-Darmstadt granddaughter marrying a Romanov, especially when she would one day be Russia's Tsarina, and when Russia's tsars – although not the present one – had a long history of treating their wives extremely badly. And unlikely because she knew Alicky's shyness was so intense that she became physically ill when she was the centre of attention. A future life with Nicky – which was surely what Alicky was now dreaming of – would mean a life spent constantly in the public eye.

A butterfly flew into the loggia and, as May watched it, she reflected that Alicky was only twelve and that in another few months she would most likely have a crush on someone else. The butterfly landed on the loggia's balustrade, its wings a brilliant azure in the strong sunlight. Still watching it, she reminded herself that she had only been twelve when she had developed a crush on Eddy, a crush she had still not entirely recovered from, although common sense had long since ensured that she no longer allowed herself romantic daydreams that couldn't possibly come true.

Other daydreams had replaced those of Eddy being in love with her – daydreams of being able to stay in Florence long after it had been deemed that her family could return to England; daydreams of a life free of the restrictions that, being a Serene Princess, she had always, until coming to Florence, had to live by. A faint touch of colour heightened her cheeks as she imagined marrying someone neither royal nor aristo-cratic, but someone who loved her, and whom she loved in return.

One of the maids hurried out onto the loggia, saying breath-lessly, for the stairs to the loggia were steep, *'Mi scusi per il disturbo. La signorina Light aspetta fuori per andare al Duomo con il signor Thaddy.'*

'Grazie mille.' May tucked both letters into the pocket of her skirt. A few days ago, when he had accompanied Miss Light to tea at I Cedri, Mr Thaddy had been surprised that Miss Light, on her many visits to the Duomo, had never given any attention to the tomb sculpture of Bishop Antonio degli Orsi.

'Are you,' Miss Light had said uncertainly, flustered at being thought not quite *au fait* with the Duomo's many treasures, 'referring to the tomb of one of the popes, sculpted by Donatello and Michelozzo?'

'Not at all,' Mr Thaddy had said kindly in his slight but very attractive brogue, 'for as you have discovered, that is a tomb monument too big to be ignored. The sculpture of Bishop Orsi is far smaller and is by a Siennese sculptor, Tino di

Camaino. It is placed very high and unobtrusively on the inner facade wall of the Duomo and is a particular favourite of mine, and of May's, Rowena's and Belinda's.'

Miss Light had looked towards her in bewilderment. 'But why on earth, May? I can never imagine a tomb monument as a favourite sculpture.'

'Because of the way he is sitting, and his expression. He has his hands crossed at the wrists and drooping downwards in front of him, and he looks so glum and bored with being dead, it is impossible not to be amused by him.'

'Then I must see him and be amused by him, too,' Miss Light had said decisively. 'Perhaps on Friday, if Friday is convenient to both you and Mr Thaddy?'

It had indeed been convenient, and now Miss Light, in her very comfortable horse-drawn barouche, was at I Cedri and waiting for May.

'I have arranged with Mr Thaddy that we will meet him at five o'clock in the Piazza di San Giovanni,' she said, when May stepped into the barouche beside her. She repositioned her lace-edged parasol so that it wouldn't collide with May's. 'The nice thing about a late-afternoon visit to the cathedral is that the Duomo is always so blessedly cool.'

May agreed with her and then, as she enjoyed the breeze from the Arno and the sight of Florence's distinctive skyline drawing ever nearer, allowed Miss Light's chatter to flow over her.

Only as their carriage rolled into the bustling piazza did she realize that Miss Light's subject of conversation had turned to Mr Thaddy. 'Can you see him, May?' she asked as their carriage rocked to a halt on the piazza's cobbles. 'I can't, and it would be so unlike Mr Thaddy to be late.'

For a moment or two May couldn't see him, either, and then a group of tourists moved away from where they had been watching workmen redoing the cathedral's facade in white-and-green marble and she had a clear view of him. Dressed in a cream cutaway jacket, white flannels, a flamboyantly patterned floppy silk bow-tie and a straw boater, he was in conversation with a well-dressed Italian.

For a few seconds, enjoying being able to look at Mr Thaddy when he was unaware of her doing so, May didn't draw Miss Light's attention to him. Below his boater, his dark hair curled low into his neck and, against sun-bronzed skin, his blue-black immaculately trimmed pencil moustache gave him an even more Italian look than that of the man he was speaking to.

She drew in a quick little breath, aware, for the first time, of the similarities between Mr Thaddy and Eddy. At twenty-three, Mr Thaddy was only three years older than Eddy and both of them were tall, dark-haired and, although Eddy wasn't sun-bronzed, he had such a naturally olive-tone to his complexion that it was a Wales family joke that dear Eddy didn't look at all English. Just as she was wondering if she was destined to go through life being attracted only to men who looked Mediterranean, Miss Light closed her parasol with a snap, saying triumphantly, 'There he is! Mr Thaddy! Mr Thaddy!'

He waved in acknowledgement, ended his conversation and, with loose-limbed ease, strode across to them.

'I am so looking forward to this, Mr Thaddy,' Miss Light said as they entered the cathedral's vast, impressive interior. 'I can't tell you how foolish I feel for not already being familiar with this particular sculpture.'

'Then I hope it will not disappoint.'

When they were ten yards into the cathedral he came to a halt and gently turned her around.

'Now, Miss Light. Look upwards and to your left.'

Miss Light did so, drew in her breath and said, 'Oh, I *am* glad you have pointed him out to me. You are quite right in that he looks very bored and also, I think, rather lonely, positioned as he is away from all the cathedral's other tomb memorials.'

'That, I think, is because he is not one of Florence's better-known bishops.'

'Indeed he is not,' a plummy elderly male voice said from behind them. 'How nice to run into you so unexpectedly, Bianca. Would your young friends mind if I stole your company for a half-hour or so, in order to catch up on family gossip?'

Miss Light was kissed on either cheek, introductions were made and it was agreed that Miss Light and her cousin, a gentleman who was relying heavily on a walking stick, would spend some time sitting companionably together in the coolness of the Duomo.

May and Thaddeus watched them make their way towards the nave and a pew, and then Thaddeus quirked an eyebrow. 'As we are both so familiar with the Duomo, would you like to spend the next half an hour having an iced lemonade at one of the cafes in the piazza?'

It was a loaded question. Even though he had become so close a friend of the family that her parents regarded him almost as if he *were* family, convention ensured that she had never been alone with him. When he came to I Cedri to paint her portrait, her mother always joined them. On countryside excursions, when Rowena and Belinda were also with them, so was Miss Light – a chaperone, even though she was never openly referred to as such. In the many months they had known each other, this was the first time they been alone together.

May knew what her response should be. She should decline

the invitation and instead remain with Mr Thaddy in the Duomo, admiring artworks long familiar to both of them and keeping well within sight of Miss Light and her cousin.

Instead she said, 'Thank you, Mr Thaddy. Iced lemonade would be most welcome.'

He proffered his arm. She slid her net-gloved hand into its crook and, before Miss Light could remember her duties as a chaperone and hastily re-join them, they walked briskly together out of the Duomo and into the still-strong sunlight.

'The heat doesn't seem to trouble you as much as it does your mother,' he commented as they began crossing the crowded piazza.

'No, it doesn't. At I Cedri I can nearly always find a cool place to sit, and I enjoy Florence's heat. It's far preferable to an often-chill English summer.'

He shot her a quick smile. 'Or a distinctly wet Irish one, which is why I like living here.'

'I like living here as well.' She was relieved that he was as easy to talk to when they were on their own as he was when they were with other people. 'I like it so much I never want to live anywhere else.'

'Where Florence is concerned, I feel like that, too, although I suppose I will eventually return to Dublin.' They sidestepped a man selling toy monkeys-on-a-stick from a tray. 'Your father tells me you have another year – perhaps even another two years – before you all return to London.'

'What I would like,' she said, putting her daydream into words for the first time, 'is not to return to London at all. I would like to continue living in Florence. I would like Florence to be my home, not just for a year or two while my parents are here, but for always.'

His eyebrows rose. 'But surely such a thing is not possible? It would never be allowed for any young unmarried woman

– and certainly not one who addresses Queen Victoria as "Aunt Queen"!'

'It might be allowed, if I have a suitable lady companion living with me. Someone similar to Miss Light, for instance.'

They had reached the far side of the piazza, and a cafe with outdoor tables set beneath an awning. Waiters hurried over. Chairs were pulled out for them. Careful to make enough room for her bustle, May sat down.

Shocked at the realization of how serious she was, Thaddeus suppressed the desire for a large whiskey and said to the young man waiting for their order, '*Due limonate con ghiaccio, per favore.*'

The waiter nodded and hurried away and Thaddeus said, concerned, 'I'm sorry, May. I'm afraid not even Miss Light's presence would make the situation you are envisaging possible.'

She bit her lip and looked away from him, but not before he had seen that he had dashed something she had been seriously hoping for. After a few moments she said bleakly, 'I'm sorry. At heart, I always knew it was impossible. It would have been so nice, though, if it hadn't been.'

'But why?' He was mystified. Although he had always been sensible enough not to show it and to embarrass either May or himself, he was deeply attracted to her. He liked her quiet manner, her natural dignity, her sense of fun and quick intelligence. He liked the way her hair was neither blonde nor brown, but a tantalizing mixture of both shades, and the way it was shot through with strands of dark gold. He liked the way she had become so passionate about Renaissance art, and how her eyes shone with enthusiasm whenever it was under discussion.

The waiter served them their lemonades and May replied, 'In London, being royal means I live a very different kind of life from that which I live here. Friendships can only be made within the family – and no one within the family is interested in the kind of things that I'm interested in.'

'Which are?'

'Art and history, and making visits to galleries and museums.'

He frowned. 'But some of them must be, surely? In their palaces and castles the British royal family is surrounded by some of the greatest paintings in the world.'

'True, but the walls could be bare and, other than Papa and me, no one would notice. Although I think Eddy would,' she added. 'I think if someone took the time to introduce Eddy to art, he would be very interested in it.'

'Eddy?' Thaddeus was regretting his decision not to have ordered a whiskey. 'Eddy, as in His Royal Highness Prince Albert Victor?'

May nodded, and he was interested to see a faint rise of colour in her cheeks. He took a long sip of his lemonade. Their conversation had crossed boundaries that had never been discussed before. In revealing her desire to remain in Florence permanently, May had been treating him not just as a family friend, but as an intimate personal friend who could be trusted with a confidence. As such, there was something he wanted to ask her.

'I would like it,' he said, as they rose to their feet to leave, 'if you dropped the name your mama has christened me with, and which everyone uses now, and began calling me Thaddeus.'

'Thank you, Thaddeus.' The faint colour in her cheeks deepened. 'I would like that very much.'

She slipped her hand into the crook of his arm and together, looking like a very handsome couple, they stepped out of the shade of the awning and into the brilliant sunshine of the piazza.

Chapter Eleven

'Come on, Maudie. Don't be a spoilsport,' Frank Teck pleaded.

In the privacy of a neglected summerhouse, he had succeeded in fighting his way beyond the innumerable pearl buttons on the bodice of her dress, had defeated a silk chemise, an underbodice, a corset protector and was now at the last bastion: her corset.

The milky-pale half-moons of her breasts rose tantalizingly above stiff whaleboning and he urgently wanted to free them. He wanted to cup them in his hands. He wanted to see if her nipples were a rosy-red or a pale pink and, whatever colour they were, he wanted to kiss them. He wanted to kiss them so much he could hardly breathe.

Maudie had no intention of letting him do any such thing. Over the last few months she had discovered that the only way she could be sure of Frank's company was if she allowed him certain liberties – liberties that, if anyone else knew about them, would result in disastrous consequences for both of them. It wasn't as if she had even embarked on her debutante year yet, and Frank was several months younger than she was.

'Please.' He was breathing heavily, feeling as if he was going to burst. 'If you won't let me lift them out, lift them out yourself, Maudie. It would mean such a lot to me. Really it would.'

Because all through her childhood she had trailed after Frank, longing for him to take notice of her, and because he had only rarely done so, the new-found power that her body had over him was intoxicating.

'I will,' she said, 'if you promise, on your mother's life, that you will only look and won't try and touch them.'

Frank groaned. Looking wasn't what he'd had in mind, but he was desperate enough to know that it was better than nothing – and that, after doing it once, a barrier would be broken and she would be happy to do it again, whenever he asked it of her.

'All right, Maudie. You win. I promise.'

Fascinated that it took so little to bring a sixteen-year-old to his knees, Maudie obliged.

Frank seriously began to wonder if he should ask his parents if he could marry Maudie. When not pushed up by her corset, her breasts were smaller than he had imagined, but they were pert and as firm as apples, and her nipples were a wonderful deep silky red. The Maudie who was able to offer such delights was a far cry from the Maudie who, until a few weeks ago, he had regarded as a tiresome nuisance.

'That's it. You've looked long enough.'

Maudie stuffed her nipples back below the hard rim of her corset and began rearranging her corset protector, underbodice and chemise.

'Help me with these buttons, will you?' she said, when it came to buttoning up the bodice of her dress. 'There must be at least twenty of them.'

He did as she asked and then said, 'Another kiss before we go back to the house, Maudie.'

'No.' It wasn't that she didn't want to kiss him again, but

an instinct as old as time told her that the more she rationed the liberties she was giving him, the more eager for them Frank would be.

Having enough sense to realize she meant what she said, Frank followed her out of the summerhouse and across the vast rear lawn of Marlborough House. Until his new-found relationship with Maudie, he had never been as regular a visitor there as May and his older brother, Dolly, had always been. Toria and Looloo had never been of any interest to him and there was a five- and six-year age difference between him and Georgie and Eddy. When they had been children, it had been an age difference that had mattered. Now, when it might not have mattered quite so much, Georgie was a lieutenant aboard Uncle Affie Edinburgh's flagship in the Mediterranean and was seldom home on leave and, after he had left Cambridge, Eddy had begun officer training at the Hussars' riding school at Aldershot.

He didn't envy Georgie his life at sea, but he did envy Eddy the glamour of his Hussars uniform and what he suspected was now, unknown to his parents and his grandmother, the raciness of his private life. His own future was also to be the Army, and Frank couldn't wait until the day he began officer training at Sandhurst and, as he was sure Eddy was doing, started a secret life of gambling and womanizing.

'Do get a move on, Frank.' Maudie was striding out as much as her narrow ankle-length day-gown allowed her to. 'It's beginning to rain.'

Frank hurried unenthusiastically to catch up. Now the weather had changed, there would be no alternative but to join May, Looloo and Toria in one of the drawing rooms, and that would mean passing the time playing cards – although not for money and so, to Frank, pointless – or in a game of Halma, or helping with a jigsaw.

He cheered himself up by thinking of how, when Maudie joined in with one of her family's boring pastimes, he could beat the boredom by mentally summoning up the image of her standing before him in the summerhouse, her gown unbuttoned to the waist, her underclothes in disarray and her wonderful tip-tilted, creamy-white breasts fully exposed to his appreciative gaze.

'Where on earth have you two been?' Toria asked as they walked into the drawing room. 'We wanted to play Halma, but as there were only three of us, we couldn't.'

'Two of you could have.' Frank did his best to sound reasonable and not exasperated, 'and as there are now five of us, if you do have a game, one of us will have to sit it out. And before you start puzzling who that should be, Toria, I'll be the one to volunteer.'

Toria, who would have preferred it to be Maudie who volunteered, began setting the board with more force than was necessary.

'Did you play much Halma to while away the tedium when you lived in Florence, May?' Looloo asked, her curiosity sincere.

'No, I don't believe we did.' May seated herself at the table, ready to play. 'I don't remember there being any tedium when we were in Florence.'

'But what did you do? I thought there was nothing to do in Florence but visit boring galleries and museums?'

'There are certainly plenty of both of those, but they are far from being boring, and I loved visiting them.' She was so overcome with the longing to be back in Florence that she had difficulty keeping her voice steady. 'There is also lovely countryside within easy walking distance of the town, and the most stunning wild flowers – flowers that we never see in England. There were always lots of parties being given: afternoon parties, tennis parties, even musical mandolin parties. There were Saturday dinner parties, and my mama would sing and we would play charades. Sometimes there was a small dance. And on top of all that, there were painting classes and singing lessons to go to, and lots of new people to make friends with.'

She thought of Rowena, Belinda, Miss Light and Thaddeus, and a lump formed in her throat. In the two years since she had left Florence, all four of them had written to her, and she had received a letter from Thaddeus only that morning. His letter had been posted not from Florence, but from Algiers, where he had gone to study Oriental art. His interest in Orientalism had sparked her own interest in it, and whenever she could persuade her mother to accompany her, May had visited London galleries to see first-hand examples of Orientalist paintings.

Frank had called her a bluestocking, which meant he thought her passion for self-education was distinctly unfeminine.

'I don't see why it should be thought so,' she had said crossly. 'I'd far rather read a book, or visit a gallery, than sit gossiping about which member of the family is destined to marry another member of the family – especially when it's often someone they barely know and, if they do know, have no particular liking for.'

As if she had been reading May's mind, Toria said, as she made the opening move on the Halma board, 'Aunt Beatrice says Granny Queen has a list of German princesses, any one of which would make Eddy a suitable bride – or will make him a suitable bride, when they become of marriageable age.'

Maudie's eyebrows lifted. 'Poor Eddy. He's not going to want to be pushed into marriage in the same way he was pushed into spending years at sea with Georgie. He's only twenty-two.'

From the depths of an armchair where he had been

pretending to be interested in a *Horse & Hound* magazine, while all the while imagining Maudie with her gown unbuttoned to the waist, Frank said, 'Your Grandpa Albert was only twenty when he married Granny Queen, and your papa was only twenty-one when he and your mama married. Going by family example, Eddy is being very lax in his reluctance to marry at twenty-two.'

With Maudie's attention being taken up by Frank, and with May staring at the Halma board without giving any indication of actually seeing it, Toria took the opportunity to hop-jump her checker four squares across the board.

'Mossy would make a nice sister-in-law,' Looloo said. 'I wonder if she is on Granny Queen's list? I like Mossy.'

Mossy was fourteen-year-old Margaret of Prussia, Willy's youngest sister and, unlike Toria, Looloo and Maudie, not a member of the family with whom May had ever spent time.

'Not Mossy, when her sister Moretta is at least five years older and still not spoken for.' Maudie was trying to keep her attention on the Halma board and the conversation, but it was difficult when she was so aware of Frank looking at her with a very lustful expression in his eyes.

General speculation followed, concerning who else might be on their grandmother's list of prospective brides for Eddy. Aware that Doomsday could come and go before her name appeared on the list, and that it had certainly never entered Toria, Looloo or Maudie's head to mention her as a possible bridal candidate, May gritted her teeth and soldiered on with the game.

The rain that had been moderate a little while ago was now heavy and was making so much noise against the windows that, even though the drawing room was at the front of the house, none of them heard the clatter of a carriage drawing up to the front portico.

When, a few minutes later, the drawing-room door opened and Eddy walked in, his sisters sprang to their feet and rushed to greet him.

'Darling Eddy! Why didn't you let us know you were going to be home today?' Toria rarely showed delight at anything, but her face shone with happiness at his unexpected arrival.

Looloo hugged him as if he was Georgie, returning home after a year at sea.

Maudie tucked her hand eagerly through his arm. 'Have you got unexpected leave, Eddy dear, or have you gone absent without leave?'

'The latter, I hope,' Frank said teasingly, nearly as pleased to see Eddy as his sisters were, but disappointed that Eddy was not in his distinctive gold-braided Hussar's uniform. He tossed his copy of *Horse & Hound* to one side. At least now Eddy was here, he would be able to talk horseracing with him, which would be a welcome change from listening to the girls' inane chatter about which German princess was destined to be their future sister-in-law.

'Did you strike it lucky with Willie Hamilton's horse at Newmarket last week?' he asked, knowing that if they talked about horseracing, the six-year age difference between the two of them would disappear.

Eddy disentangled himself from Looloo's exuberant embrace. 'No, I backed Sun Dawn, not Miss Jummy.'

He acknowledged May's presence with an inclination of his head and a brief 'Cousin May', and then did a double-take. The Cousin May he remembered had been nothing spectacular to look at – and she still wasn't, in comparison with a lot of the young women he spent time with – but she had certainly blossomed. Tall and slender and with china-blue eyes, she had a poise about her that none of his sisters, all of whom were around her age, possessed.

Seating himself in a companion armchair to Frank's, Eddy said chummily, 'I take it you backed Miss Jummy and came out of things handsomely, Frank?' He took a cigarette case from his inner jacket pocket, proffering one to Frank, before lighting up himself.

Frank had been smoking since he was twelve, and the surge of pleasure he felt wasn't because Eddy thought him old enough to smoke, but because he and Eddy were having a one-to-one chat without the interfering presence of anyone else. The girls didn't count, even though, with the exception of May, they were all clustering around the armchairs. Maudie perched on the arm of Eddy's chair, while Toria and Looloo drew up fat leather pouffes so that they could sit at the foot of it.

'I did rather,' he replied. He shot May a quick glance, but as she was toying with the Halma-board chequers and seemed lost in thought, he risked saying, 'And I scooped the jackpot at Epsom Downs with Firefly at sixty-six to one.'

He kept his voice low, for his growing passion for gambling was not something he wanted either May or his parents to become aware of.

Eddy was impressed, as Frank had hoped he would be. 'You're obviously a lucky cub when it comes to the turf.' He shot Frank his slow, sweet smile. 'Perhaps you can give me some tips.'

Frank was more than willing, and was also more than a little relieved when May rose from the games table and walked to the bank of long windows at the far end of the drawing room.

She did so looking perfectly composed, but that was only thanks to steely self-discipline. Eddy's sudden arrival had filled her first with elation, then with crippling shyness and lastly, after his brief acknowledgement of her, with bleak acceptance that she was not of the slightest interest to him.

Making matters worse had been Toria, Looloo and Maudie leaving her marooned on her own, for there was no way she could have joined them in drawing up a pouffe to Eddy's armchair or perched on a chair arm. It was all right for his sisters to behave in such a way, but for her to have done so would have looked very odd indeed.

Something else that had looked odd was the way she had been left so conspicuously alone at the games table, which was why she had walked to the windows. At least there she could have her back to everyone and, with feigned interest, look out at the rain-lashed garden.

If she could have summoned the carriage that had brought them from White Lodge, she would have done so, but she and Frank couldn't leave without their mother, and their mother was with Aunt Alix, discussing Needlework Guild matters. The Guild provided clothing for the poor and was a charity that her mother gave a great deal of time to.

May was just thinking how odd it was that her mother should be so efficient when it came to the charitable work she undertook, given that she was so inefficient in every other area of her life, when she became aware of someone walking up and standing beside her.

She knew, without turning her head, that it was Eddy.

'I haven't had a chance to talk with you since you returned from Rome,' he said in the lazy drawl she found so attractive.

'Florence.' Her heart was beating in thick, slamming strokes. 'A little less than a year ago we returned from Florence, not Rome.'

'Ah, yes.' He gave a lopsided smile. Florence accounted for why May had changed so much from how he remembered her. 'You lived there for ages, didn't you? I know Maudie missed you terribly.'

'We were there two years.' Her hands were clasped so tightly that her nails were digging into her flesh. Please, she prayed silently. Please God, let him say that he missed me too!

He didn't. Standing so close to her that his shoulder was brushing hers, Eddy said in a friendly manner, 'It must have been very strange for you, living so long in a country that doesn't speak English.'

Surprise jolted her out of her almost paralysing shyness. 'Oh, but lots of the people we mixed with were English expatriates, and from the first day we were there I took Italian lessons. It meant I was soon able to make myself understood and, as well as having English friends, and an American friend, I soon had lots of Italian friends as well.'

'Good Lord!' His surprise was genuine. 'I must say I find that extremely enterprising of you, May. I've always been a duffer at languages. Because my mother is Danish, I speak Danish, but I've never been able to get the hang of either French or German.'

Although Eddy standing so close to her was still making her heart race, May's nervous tension had ebbed. 'That's because you were only taught French and German by an English teacher, in an English classroom. For me, because I was living in Italy, learning Italian was relatively easy.'

'You're probably right.' He hesitated and then said, 'One of the reasons I wanted to speak to you without anyone else hearing is because the girls are discussing whom I might choose as a bride, from my grandmother's list of possibles, and when I realized I was on the point of telling them – and filling them with disappointment – I thought it best to walk away.'

The blood drummed in May's ears. From out of nowhere had come a subject so unexpected, she wondered if she had misheard him.

He said wryly, 'They all expect me to plump for Mossy.'

She hadn't misheard him. Scarcely able to believe Eddy was

trusting her with such information, she turned to face him, her hand at her throat. 'And . . . you haven't done so?'

'No. I know from Maudie that you never gossip, Cousin May, and that I can trust you not to let this go any further, but when I was at Balmoral a few months ago, so were the two younger Hesse-Darmstadt girls, and it was then that I knew who I was going to marry.'

The drumming in May's ears became deafening.

Irène. He was going to marry Irène. And unlike the princesses on the list who were not of marriageable age, Irène was nearly twenty now, which meant the official announcement would not be very long in coming.

She had always known that when Eddy married, it would be to someone in her Aunt Queen's vast extended family network, but she had been hoping it would be to someone like Mossy; someone she barely knew and therefore wasn't on friendly terms with.

'Granny Queen will be pleased.' He gave her another of the slow, sweet smiles that she found so sexy, and which sent tingles down her spine. 'Alicky will be sixteen in two years' time,' he added, 'and her name has always been the one at the top of her list.'

May's hand was still at her throat. The high collar of her gown was pinned with a brooch and beneath the tips of her fingers the jewels were cold and hard and sharp. She thought of Alicky's letters to her. Letters full of her certainty that Nicky Romanov was her one true love, and that she knew with all her heart they would be together until the end of time.

It was a dream that would now end in ashes, for there was another side to the small, squat figure who always dressed in black. Their Aunt Queen and Granny Queen was also Queen Victoria, and as such, when it came to what she perceived as her royal duty – or anyone else's royal duty – she was as implacable and immovable as the Rock of Gibraltar. She would tell Alicky that her destiny lay in England; that it was her duty to marry Eddy and be a future Queen Consort of England, not a future Tsarina of Russia. And just as a long line of the Queen's Prime Ministers had done before her, Alicky would be pressured into obeying, and royal duty would win out over love.

Alicky would marry Eddy, even though her heart lay elsewhere. Eddy would discover that he had married someone incapable of loving him. And she, May, would most likely never be loved at all.

A flash of lightning forked across the sky, followed by a crack of thunder so deafening that the chandeliers shook. Toria and Looloo jumped to their feet with little hysterical squeals.

Eddy said, 'It was good talking to you, May, but I'd best get back to the girls. Thunderstorms scare the life out of them.' And, turning away from her, he strode back over to them.

May, too, was afraid; not of the thunder and lightning, but of the future and what it might hold for Alicky, Eddy and, having been a debutante for nearly a year without attracting even one suitor, herself. Yet again she felt an outsider. She was a Serene Princess who was not royal enough to feature on a list of possible brides for Eddy; not royal enough to attract any other royal suitor; and not pretty enough to encourage an aristocratic suitor to overlook her lack of a dowry. All of which meant she was very unlikely ever to have a home of her own, or children.

She straightened her already very straight posture. Self-pity had never been one of her weaknesses and she had no intention of indulging in it now. She would deal in a positive way with the hand that fate had dealt her. She was already acting as her mother's lady-in-waiting and she would begin acting as her secretary, in order that her mother could take on even more charitable work. When her brothers married and had children, she would be the best possible aunt to them, and she would continue with what she found so fulfilling – her interest in art and literature. In the future, whenever moments of bleakness took her unawares, she would remind herself that it was better not to be married at all than to be trapped in a loveless marriage.

Full of strong resolutions, and with her emotions again under control, May continued watching the storm grow in intensity, fiercely hoping that when Alicky married Eddy, she wouldn't – at her Kindred Spirit's request – be one of the bridesmaids walking down the aisle behind them.

Chapter Twelve

MARCH 1888, MARLBOROUGH HOUSE

Well muffled up against a cold breeze, May, who was now twenty, and Alicky, who was only three months away from being sixteen, were swinging gently backwards and forwards on swings that had been erected at Marlborough House as an eighth-birthday present for Toria.

May had grown into an intelligent, quietly confident young woman who, although serious by nature, also possessed a sense of the ridiculous and was fun to be with. Her naturally dark gold hair held intriguing copper highlights and she wore it, as she had always worn it, pulled back high and tight at the sides and with a frizzled low fringe. It suited her and was distinctive – and May liked to be distinctive.

'It's good to be together again,' she said to Alicky, whose riotous red-gold hair was scooped up beneath a fur hat that came down over her ears.

'Yes. Family life is crazy, isn't it? We didn't meet up for ages and ages after becoming Kindred Spirits at Osborne, and now here we are, together again less than a year after Granny Queen's Golden Jubilee.'

'But this time without having a smoulderingly angry Willy to contend with.'

'No, thank goodness.' Alicky's swing had come to rest and,

with the toe of a high-buttoned boot, she pushed it into motion again. 'Our secret Kindred Spirit has never been one of Uncle Bertie and Aunt Alix's favourite nephews, so it's no surprise they didn't want him at their Silver Wedding celebrations.'

May's arms were hooked around the chains of her swing, leaving her gloved hands free. She'd always thought there was an aura of glamour about twenty-nine-year-old Willy, but was well aware it wasn't how his close relatives viewed him. She tucked her hands into the large fur muff that was resting on her knees and said, 'Although he behaved badly at the Jubilee celebrations, I felt a lot of sympathy for him. After all, he is the Queen's firstborn grandchild and if she had invited him to be her aide-de-camp for the day – as she did Eddy and Georgie – he could, like them, have ridden beside her carriage all along the processional route and would have been seen to be that little bit more special than any of the other world royalties taking part in it.'

'And that would have made him happy?'

'Yes, of course it would.' May sometimes thought she was the only person in the family who understood Cousin Willy even a little. 'Willy likes to shine and be the centre of attention. If he had been allowed to shine at the Jubilee, he would have oozed charm all week. I've no idea why the Queen is so out of sorts with him, but you must have noticed that when it came to the formal celebration dinner at Buckingham Palace, he and Dona were seated so far away from her they were practically in another room.'

'Yes, I did notice, and I know why.' Alicky put her foot to the ground to bring her swing to a halt. A year ago her sister Irène had become engaged to Willy's brother, Heinrich, and as a result she knew far more about what was going on in the Hohenzollern family than May did. 'It was because Willy and Aunt Vicky were at loggerheads about his father's medical treatment, and Granny Queen was angry with him for causing his mother additional distress at such a difficult time. You do know Uncle Fritz has throat cancer, don't you?'

'Yes, of course I know. What I didn't know was that Willy's always-unhappy relationship with his mother had been made even worse because of it.' May brought the swing to a halt. 'Do you remember what Willy told us about the way he suffered when, because she was so ashamed of his deformed arm, she allowed the doctors to use barbaric practices in an attempt to lengthen it? Whatever is going on with Uncle Fritz's treatment, Willy could be quite right to object to it.'

'It's a different situation this time. The bad feeling is because Aunt Vicky refuses to believe Uncle Fritz has cancer and doesn't want him to have surgery, whereas Willy believes that only drastic surgery will save his father's life. Whatever the truth of it, May, the battle lines have been drawn and I think it's a relief to everyone that Willy and Dona aren't among the guests this week.'

It was such an unhappy thing to be talking about that they fell silent for several minutes and then, bringing up a subject she definitely wanted to talk to May about while they were on their own, Alicky said, 'Granny Queen has become very heated in her insistence that it's time I fell in with her marriage plans. She wants me to become engaged to Eddy and I had to endure a week at Balmoral with him – the idea being that by the end of the week our engagement would be announced. Naturally, it wasn't. Eddy declared himself to be heartbroken with disappointment, but whether he really was I'm not quite sure. The problem for both him and Granny Queen is that although Germany and Denmark are littered with cousins and second cousins who tick all the right boxes, when it comes to their eligibility as a future Princess of Wales and then, further down the line, a future Queen of England, none of them are, at the moment, the right age.'

'Moretta, Willy's sister is.' May was finding the subject almost as painful as the previous one. 'She's twenty-one.'

'Maybe, but she isn't Granny Queen's favourite grandchild. I am, and she's set her heart on me marrying Eddy, but even though I can see there is something very sexy about him – those slumberous, dark eyes and the way you can never quite tell what he's thinking – I'm not going to marry him, because he isn't my soulmate. Nicky Romanov is my soulmate and it's something Granny Queen is just going to have to come to terms with.' She pushed her swing into movement again, adding, 'And although Granny Queen doesn't yet know it, I shall be seeing lots and lots of Nicky before the year is out, for Ella and Sergei have invited me to spend the autumn and winter with them in St Petersburg, and Papa, God bless him, is in full agreement that I should go.'

May was enjoying all the fun and family hilarity that formed the keynote of any party held at Marlborough House. For her, Uncle Bertie and Aunt Alix were master party hosts, and over the last two days she had been able to spend time with family she rarely saw – family such as Ducky and Missy, who were now eleven and twelve and were both exhilaratingly high-spirited. Together with Alicky, Irène and their brother Ernie, the six of them, at Ducky's suggestion, had spent a riotous hour sliding down a Marlborough House staircase on tea-trays.

That evening, as her mother chatted to her and her dresser helped her into a sumptuous gown of shimmering turquoise silk, May told her mother what fun the tea-tray sliding had been.

Her mother clapped her podgy hands, which were covered with rings, in delight. 'That is exactly the kind of fun dear Mr Thaddy would have joined in with, and I would have done so as well, had there been a tea-tray big enough!'

They were still laughing at the thought when there came

the sound of several bedroom doors being opened and, almost immediately, being slammed shut, and the noise of footsteps hurrying down the corridor towards their room.

'What on earth—?' her mother exclaimed as, after only the briefest of knocks, the door to their room was flung open. Standing in the doorway, Frank said, 'Better change into something a bit more sombre than turquoise, May. A telegram has just arrived announcing that the Kaiser has passed away. He was ninety so no great surprise there, but terrible news for Uncle Fritz. How is he going to cope with being the new Kaiser, when he has throat cancer?'

It wasn't a question he expected an answer to and, saying, 'Tonight's family dinner is still on, but the Grand Ball tomorrow night isn't,' he slammed the door behind him and hurried off to break the bad news elsewhere.

May's mother sat down heavily on the nearest chair. 'Poor, dear Fritz. How will he cope?' Always kind-hearted, she had tears in her eyes. 'To have waited for the throne for so long, and then to inherit when he is so ill. It doesn't bear thinking about.'

May had never met Willy's grandfather and so, with the best will in the world, she didn't feel any personal grief at the news of his death. Like her mother, though, she did feel great sympathy for Uncle Fritz, who, already bearing the colossal burden of his ill health, now had another gigantic burden to shoulder; and she also felt a crushing disappointment that the Grand Ball she had been so looking forward to was not now going to take place. The hope that Eddy would dance with her at least once had always been slight, but now it wasn't even that. Royal kinship would necessitate full court mourning. Dancing of any kind was out of the question, possibly for weeks.

* * *

The next morning, with all organized jollities considerably scaled down, Irène and May braved the March wind and walked together through Marlborough House's formal gardens.

'I wonder how Willy is reacting to the news?' Irène said, a frown creasing her forehead. 'Uncle Fritz is only in his fifties. Under normal circumstances, Willy would have had another twenty years or more of waiting before succeeding him as Kaiser, but with Uncle Fritz's health the way it is, it's something that could happen at any moment.' Her eyes widened in alarm. 'Goodness, I hope it doesn't happen before my wedding!' She shuddered at the thought of Uncle Fritz dying before he became her father-in-law. 'The truth is, May, I'm finding the thought of marrying into the Hohenzollerns tricky enough, as it is. The only person who is even-tempered and on good terms with everyone is my darling Heinrich, and he's an angel, but as for the rest of them . . .'

She spread gloved hands out in a gesture of despair. 'Aunt Vicky is just as argumentative as Willy. Everything is either black or white. There is never a middle way. She simply doesn't know the meaning of the word "compromise". And as if the situation over Uncle Fritz's illness isn't bad enough, Willy has been neglecting Dona. She adores him, but he spends all his time, both days and evenings, with his regiment – he is a colonel and commander of the Hussar Guards – and so when they are together, which is only at breakfast, all that can be heard are voices raised in argument, and then Willy slamming out of the palace with his six-foot-tall blond aide-de-camp, and Dona crying. It's hardly happy families.'

There were times when May found her own home life difficult. Four years ago, when they had been living in Florence, her father had suffered a stroke and although he had recovered from it remarkably well, he had since grown increasingly short-tempered and she was constantly being called upon to act as a buffer between him and her mother. It was a trying situation, but one that was not nearly as stressful as the one apparently taking place on a daily basis in Potsdam's Neues Palais.

They rounded a corner of the gravelled path. Both edges of it were lined by long swathes of sharply yellow daffodils, leading towards a bleakly dry fountain. Seated on its bronze rim, glumly smoking a cigarette, was Georgie.

May's heart skipped a beat. At family get-togethers such as the present one, Georgie and Eddy were usually inseparable. This time, however, there was no sign of Eddy and she fought her disappointment, her heart steadying.

'If you've come out here to avoid company, we won't stop and talk,' Irène said as they approached him.

'As it's you two, I don't mind you stopping to talk, and I could do with a bit of bucking up.' He rose politely to his feet. 'It's bad timing, the old Kaiser pegging it when Uncle Fritz is in such a bad way, isn't it? You'd think, as he'd made it to ninety, he could have hung on a little bit longer. Two more years in which to recover his health would have made all the difference to Uncle Fritz.'

As May followed Irène's example and seated herself on the fountain's broad bronze rim, she wondered how two brothers so close together in age could be so dissimilar in looks and personality. Georgie had grown a beard, but it still didn't make him look his age, which, in three months' time, would be twenty-three. It didn't help that he wasn't very tall – certainly not as tall as she was, without heeled shoes and boots – and that, with his rosy cheeks and slightly protuberant blue eyes, there was a fresh-faced boyish openness about him.

There was nothing boyish about Eddy. Tall and lean and always dashingly dressed, Eddy was all handsome sophistication. There was something about him that was far more continental than it was English. In Florence and amongst Italians, Georgie would have stuck out like a sore thumb. Eddy wouldn't have done so. With his glossy dark hair, gold-flecked eyes and a fashionable moustache waxed and turned upwards at the ends, he would have fitted in perfectly.

They were just as different in other ways. Georgie was addicted to stamp-collecting. Eddy, often accused of being 'dreamy' and 'not interested in anything', played hockey and polo – games that needed perfectly controlled aggression in order to be played well; and, giving the lie to what was said about him, Eddy played them very well. Like his father, Georgie teased people and, also like his father, he often teased unkindly. Eddy didn't tease. Within the huge royal clan that was their family, he kept himself very much to himself.

'Unnervingly secretive' was how she had heard her father describe Eddy. 'It's rumoured he makes friends outside the royal circle.' 'Enigmatic' was the description her mother used.

May simply thought him an ideal specimen of masculine beauty.

Her train of thought was interrupted as she became aware of Irène saying to Georgie, 'Do you need bucking up because your parents' Silver Wedding Grand Ball has had to be cancelled, or is it because you feel so sorry for Uncle Fritz becoming Kaiser at a time when he's so ill?'

'No,' Georgie said bluntly as he remained standing, facing the two of them. 'Although naturally I'm disappointed about the ball being cancelled, and I do feel sorry for Uncle Fritz.' His shoulders were slumped, his hands were shoved deep into his coat pockets and his face was a picture of misery.

'Then what is it? You look as if you've lost a pound and found a penny.'

Unable to keep his unhappiness to himself any longer, he said explosively, 'I've lost more than a pound, Irène. Thanks to damnable royal protocol, I've just been told I can't marry Julie.'

May nearly fell off the fountain. Julie? Who on earth was Julie? It wasn't a name much used within the family. She couldn't think of a single first or second cousin called Julie.

'Who,' Irène asked, as taken aback as May, 'is Julie? And why can't you marry her?'

Georgie ran a hand over his hair. 'Julie is Julie Stoner. Her grandfather was one of Granny Queen's Prime Ministers, and her late mother was once a lady-in-waiting to my mother. Her family live very close to Sandringham and I've known Julie all my life. She's so pretty and sweet-natured . . .'

His voice broke and, for a hideous moment, May thought he was going to burst into tears.

'. . . and damn it all, when Julie was orphaned, Motherdear *encouraged* me to spend time with her and to be kind to her.' It was the second time Georgie had been so het up that he'd used a swear word in front of them without even noticing, let alone apologizing for it. 'When I'm away at sea we write to each other all the time, and we've known that we love each other for ages and ages. It never occurred to me that I wouldn't be allowed to marry her. It's Eddy who is going to be King one day; not me, thank God. He's the one who has to have a wife of flawless royal pedigree.'

May felt sick at heart for him. To love someone so much you wanted to marry them, and for them to love you in the same way and then to be unable to marry because of a difference in status, was a situation so hideous it didn't bear thinking about.

It was, however, a situation that Georgie should have been aware of, long before his relationship with Julie had reached the point it had. After his father and then Eddy, he was third in line to the throne. It was generally accepted within the family that Georgie wasn't much of a thinker, but even he must have realized that marrying a commoner wasn't something someone in his position would ever be allowed to do.

She was just trying to think of something encouraging to say to him, when he blew his nose and said, 'Motherdear says she wishes things could be different, because she adores Julie. How could she not, when Julie is so special in every way? But she says the Roman Catholic thing is simply too much of an obstacle.'

'The Roman Catholic thing?' May wasn't sure she'd heard correctly. 'Is Julie a Roman Catholic as well as a commoner?'

'Yes, but I don't see why it matters. Julie wouldn't expect me to become a Roman Catholic, and I don't mind her being one, so where is the problem?'

May drew in a deep, unsteady breath. 'The problem, Georgie,' she said slowly, hardly able to believe he didn't know about the Act of Settlement, 'is that you are third in the line of succession, and ever since 1702 no one who becomes a Roman Catholic – or who marries a Roman Catholic – can succeed to the British throne.'

He stared at her in stunned disbelief. 'So, even if a miracle happened and I was given permission to marry a commoner, I still couldn't marry my darling Julie?'

'No, Georgie. I'm afraid not.'

She stepped towards him, sliding her hand through his arm and giving it a comforting hug. 'Being royal can be beastly, can't it?'

'It's more than beastly; it's a bugger.' With eyes full of tears, he turned away from her and Irène and stomped off down the path, his hunched shoulders shaking with sobs that he could no longer hold at bay.

Chapter Thirteen

In the Neues Palais, Willy was cock-a-hoop. As Kaiser Wilhelm II, he was Germany's Emperor, the 'All-Highest', master of all he surveyed. And how he loved being so! Seven months ago, the very second his cancer-ridden papa had passed away, he had started out as he meant to go on – and that was as a powerful, autocratic ruler, answerable to no one but God. Like the Tsar of Russia, he was his own man. He appointed his own ministers and, if they proved tiresome, he replaced them with the same spur-of-the-moment speed.

Wearing a white, gold-braided and bemedalled uniform – he never wore anything other than one of his score of military uniforms, unless he was visiting his grandmother at Balmoral, when he wore full Highland rig in Royal Stewart tartan – he was awaiting the arrival of Mr Henry Thaddeus Jones. It was May Teck who had brought Mr Jones to his attention. In one of her letters she had written:

When living in Florence some years ago, my parents had a family portrait painted by a young Irish artist, Mr Henry Thaddeus Jones. The painting has been shown at the Royal Academy and has been very highly praised. In Florence he was commissioned by several Russian royals, and in Rome he

*received two papal commissions, one of them being to paint
Pope Leo XIII's portrait. I was invited, together with my
mama, to afternoon tea at Windsor earlier this month and,
while there, Aunt Queen told us of a portrait that a German
artist had painted of you, standing on the terrace at Osborne
House wearing the uniform of a British Admiral of the
Fleet. It sounds magnificent, but it occurred to me that you
might also like to have your portrait painted by Thaddeus
Jones (Mr Jones never refers to himself by his first Christian
name), only this time with a Marble Palace background and
wearing one of your magnificent Prussian uniforms?*

May had then gone on with family news:

*Looloo is in love with Lord Fife, and wishes to marry him.
He is nearly twenty years older than her and a friend of
Uncle Bertie's. Toria says she can't believe Granny Queen
will give permission for Looloo to marry a non-royal, but
knowing Granny Queen's love of Scotland, and as Fife is a
Scot and so wealthy he owns half the Highlands, I think
Looloo may well be in with a chance. (Georgie has wickedly
suggested that Granny Queen ask one of her Highland
ghillies to act as Fife's best man!)*

And there was more: mention of how, since their marriage
and a visit to Osborne House, Irène and Heinrich had become
so popular with the English branch of their family that they
had been nicknamed 'The Amiables'. Of how Eddy had been
made a Knight Justice of the Order of St John of Jerusalem,
and how Georgie was serving in the Mediterranean fleet. That
he was seeing a lot of Aunt Marie, Ducky and Missy for, as
Uncle Affie was commander-in-chief of the Mediterranean
fleet, his family had taken up temporary residence in Malta,

so Georgie had begun staying with them whenever he had shore leave.

Alicky, she had added as a postscript, had recently left for a long stay with Ella and Sergei in St Petersburg; she had no up-to-date news with regard to Ella, although she was sure Alicky would soon be sending her some.

Willy had very much liked the idea of having his portrait painted by Mr Jones, and the arrangement that he should do so had swiftly been put into place, which was why, in a few minutes' time and suitably escorted by a clutch of his favourite aides-de-camp, he was about to make his way to the Audience Room, where he would meet the painter.

For the moment, though, he wished to remain alone in his study to think about Ella. Her photograph stood on the desk in front of him. Having it there was no insult to Dona, for no one entered his study except at his invitation, and in eight years of marriage he had never extended that invitation to his wife.

Ella – a stab of pain knifed through him. How could he have so wanted to marry her, and for her not to have wanted to marry him? Even worse, how could she then have married Sergei Romanov? Although not much was known about Sergei outside Russia, other than that he was arrogant and not much liked, the rumours about him within Russia were sinister enough to make Willy's flesh crawl. 'I have it on good authority that he is a sadist,' Willy's Ambassador to St Petersburg had told him.

Even thinking about Ella being married to such a man made bile rise in Willy's throat. How could his darling Ella, the most loving, caring and compassionate of girls, have married such a man? And not only have married him, but continually have insisted that her marriage was a happy one?

Desperately he tried to think of something else and forced himself to focus on Looloo and her desire to marry the non-royal and middle-aged Lord Fife. His Aunt Alix was a claustrophobically possessive mother and he knew, from time spent in her company, that she had no desire for any of 'her chicks', as she persisted in calling her daughters, to marry. 'Why should they?' he had once heard her say gaily, 'when they have lovely Sandringham and Marlborough House to live in, and horses to ride; and when their Motherdear loves them so much and would be so distraught if they were to marry and leave her?'

Although it had always been easiest to think of Toria as the eldest of the sisters, it was the self-effacing Looloo who was actually the eldest and he knew that she was May's age, which was twenty-one. Being twenty-one in a family with a history of arranging marriages when a girl was as young as fourteen, and where it was commonplace for them to marry at sixteen, was to be on the shelf, especially as it meant that even as a debutante, no proposal had been received. It was no wonder then that, if Looloo had received a proposal from Fife, she was eager to accept it.

Willy's thoughts reverted to Ella. How could they not, now that he knew Alicky was staying with her in St Petersburg? His jaw tightened and he clenched his good hand into a fist. Ever since Ella had so adamantly refused to marry him, he had vowed never to see her again; not because his love had turned to hate, but because the pain of seeing her would have been more than he could bear.

Although it had attracted comment, he hadn't attended her wedding. At any family get-together where Ella and Sergei were expected to put in an appearance, he had not done so. She had captured his heart when she had been little more than a child, and when he had been a student in a city so near to Darmstadt that it had been only natural he should visit relations who were living there. No other girl had ever affected him as Ella had then and, in the years since, neither had any other woman.

Not that there had been many women. He had always found sex a laborious and unsatisfactory business. There had been a handful of brief love affairs before his marriage to Dona, because it was what was expected of him. For him not to have had love affairs would have aroused comment. There had even been a couple of love affairs since his marriage, and mainly for the same reason. It was what was expected of a man at the peak of his virility – and he'd be damned before he'd be seen as being anything else.

'And nor will you be,' his closest and much-loved friend, Phili, had said reassuringly. 'With five sons already in the palace nursery, you have more than done your duty where securing the succession to the throne is concerned. Women are not as important in a man's life as they like to think. How can they be, when they are incapable of focusing on the loftier things in life, things such as music and literature and, dare I say it, the mysteries of the occult?'

Remembering that conversation, Willy underwent one of his fast-as-light mood changes and bellowed with laughter. Phili had known he could say such a thing, because ever since Phili had been introduced to him, nothing had ever arisen between the two of them that wasn't permissible. Phili was Count Philipp zu Eulenburg. At the time of their introduction he had been a lowly diplomat in the Prussian legation. Now, thanks to Willy's intervention, Phili was an envoy, next in status to an ambassador.

'Male camaraderie, Your Majesty,' Phili had said to him in the early days of their friendship, 'and with friends of a like individuality – that is where the true pleasures of life are to be found.'

It was a sentiment Willy fully agreed with and, faced with

the delicious decision as to whether to wear an ornate military uniform, Clan Stewart Highland dress or the costume of a war-like Norse god in his portrait sittings with Thaddeus Jones, he strode off in the direction of the Audience Room, surrounded by a posse of long-limbed, blond-haired Hussars.

On a train steaming towards the Russian border, Alicky was almost faint with excited anticipation. She would soon be in St Petersburg. Would Nicky be as pleased to see her as he had been four and a half years ago, the last time she had been there? Four and a half years was a long time. She had been twelve then, little more than a child. Now, nearly seventeen, she was a child no longer. Would he still like her now as much as he had then? And when she saw him again, would he still be her soulmate or would he have become a stranger? She remembered how the two of them had scratched their names within a heart on the windowpane of a little summerhouse. Would Nicky still remember doing so? Would he recall how they had felt about each other?

As the train ate up the miles, its engine blowing clouds of smoke past the carriage windows, she stared into the white billows, her gloved hands clasped so hard that her knuckles hurt.

'Please God, let Nicky like me as much now as he once did,' she whispered beneath her breath, when her father and Ernie left the carriage in order to enjoy cigars in the corridor. And then, with the fevered intensity that was so much a part of her nature: 'Please God, let him more than like me. Let him love, love, love me!'

As they stepped off the train at St Petersburg station, not only were Tsar Uncle Sasha and Ella and Sergei on the platform waiting to greet them, but so were Sergei's brothers, a brass band and, best of all, Nicky. The last time she had seen him he had been sixteen and, being slightly built and nowhere near as tall as his father and his uncles, had been a young-looking sixteen. Now he was twenty and, wearing a splendid white and gold-braided military uniform and sporting a neat Van Dyke beard, he suddenly seemed to be someone she was meeting for the first time.

As she made her curtsey to Uncle Sasha, Alicky felt her head spin and her stomach churn. Had she been living in a fantasy world for the last four and a half years? Was Nicky only at the station to meet her, and her father and Ernie, because Romanov etiquette dictated he should do so? And then, as her father exchanged pleasantries with Uncle Sasha, Nicky stepped towards her.

With her heart hammering and the blood beating in her ears, knowing that every atom of her future happiness depended on the next few moments, Alicky raised her eyes to his.

In their blue depths was everything that she had hoped to see. The kindness and gentleness that marked him out as a rare and very special kind of man, and as well as the kindness and gentleness – qualities that were of vital importance to her – there was blatant, undisguised pleasure at seeing her again.

Her relief was so vast that she gasped and then, aware of how many eyes were on her, disguised the gasp by turning it into a hiccup.

'Welcome to St Petersburg,' Nicky said, as he would have said to anyone he was meeting formally at the station, but the smile he gave her and the expression in his eyes told Alicky she wasn't just anyone, but someone who was very, very special to him.

Her father was afforded the honour of travelling with Uncle Sasha and Nicky to the Anitchkov Palace, where Aunt Minny was waiting to greet them, while Alicky and Ernie travelled in another carriage, accompanied by Ella and Sergei.

'Why is Aunt Minny at the Anitchkov and not the Winter Palace, Ella?' Ernie asked. 'If the Winter Palace was my palace, I'd never move out of it.'

'Uncle Sasha finds the Winter Palace too vast and chilly at this time of year, which incidentally is my favourite time of year. Have you ever seen anywhere as beautiful as St Petersburg under snow?'

Alicky hadn't. Snow, so blinding-white it hurt the eyes, lay in drifts several feet high at the sides of all the wide boulevards. It glittered like crystal on the city's hundreds of onion-shaped domes and elegant spires. It coated the leafless branches of the trees and rose in flurries from beneath the hooves of the royal horses. As their carriage turned into Nevsky Prospekt, Alicky saw that the nearby Fontanka River was frozen to a sheet of shining silver and was crowded not with boats, but with skaters.

'Even the Neva freezes in the winter,' Ella said as their carriage turned in through the Anitchkov Palace's great triple-arched entrance. 'We'll be going to lots of skating parties while you are with us, Alicky.'

'And toboggan parties,' Sergei added. 'Nicky loves toboggan parties, and you will be seeing a lot of Nicky.'

Over the top of Alicky's head, Sergei's eyes met Ella's, and although Alicky didn't see the look they exchanged, Ernie did.

He sucked in his breath. Were Ella and Sergei hoping to snare Nicky – a man who would one day rule over one-sixth of the world's surface – as a husband for his little sister? If so, it was one heck of an ambitious project. Sergei might have married a princess of Hesse, but he wasn't heir to the Romanov throne. Nicky was. When it came to his marriage, Uncle Sasha and Aunt Minny would be looking for a marriage alliance that would bring dynastic and political advantages to Russia – and that wouldn't be achieved by Nicky marrying Alicky.

In the palace, Aunt Minny, petite, dark-eyed and, even though it was only late afternoon, laden with jewels, greeted them with a warmth that Alicky found reassuring.

They were too small a family group for her and Nicky to exchange eager, urgent glances, but as they moved from where Aunt Minny had greeted them and along an ornately gilded gallery to where, in a jasper-columned drawing room a steaming-hot samovar and refreshments were waiting for them, Nicky managed to whisper from close behind her, 'Dearest Alicky, I thought you were pretty the last time you visited St Petersburg, but you are even prettier now.'

Alicky flushed scarlet, but because she blushed so often when uncomfortable at the social situations she found herself in, no one – not even Ella or Ernie – suspected that this time the scarlet banners in her cheeks had been caused by dazzling, heart-stopping happiness.

Later, as he readied himself for the ball that was to take place that evening, Ernie pondered what was, to him, the odd character of both his cousin, Nicky, and his brother-in-law, Sergei.

Because they were both the same age, and because his oddness was baffling and not, as in Sergei's case, unsettling, Nicky was the easiest conundrum. At twenty, there was still something immature about him, and in a young man who would one day be Emperor-Tsar-Autocrat over a country so vast that as the night was falling on its western borders, day was breaking on its eastern shore, his gentleness and the air of submissiveness that Ernie detected in him seemed bizarre. One thing he was quite sure of, though, was that Nicky wasn't – as he was – homosexual.

That wasn't a certainty he felt, where Sergei was concerned. Ernie had grown up feeling comfortable around Sergei, who had always been such a regular visitor to Darmstadt. Sergei and Ella's marriage had been a surprise, but only because Ella was so beautiful and had such a magical quality about her that Ernie had assumed she would be snapped up by someone able to offer her a throne; someone like Eddy, or Willy. Her choosing to marry Sergei, who was so much older than her and had an off-puttingly austere manner, had been decidedly unexpected.

And then, over time, had come the rumours that the reason Sergei and Ella had no children was because he was a homosexual; or, if not a homosexual, a sadist. The accusation of sadism didn't ring true to Ernie, for if Sergei was a sadist, surely he would have sensed it? Ella's marital happiness was obvious, and he couldn't see how that was possible if Sergei gained sexual pleasure from inflicting pain.

So that left only the rumour of homosexuality, something that was always a possibility. Even he, a happy and untroubled homosexual, had to be fiercely secretive about being one, and Sergei was a highly decorated military officer and Major-General of the elite 1st Battalion Preobrazhensky Life Guards Regiment. If the rumours about him were ever substantiated, it would mean Sergei being stripped of his rank, his military decorations and, most probably – and most devastating of all for a Russian – exile.

Was that why, in the royal world of early marriages, Sergei had waited until he was nearly thirty before he had married Ella? For anyone who was sexually deviant, marriage was the greatest of all cover-ups, and something nearly all men of his own persuasion resorted to eventually. It was something Ernie knew that he, too, would resort to one day, but with luck, that day still lay some way in the future.

The ball that evening was to take place in the Winter Palace, and Ella and Alicky, assisted by half a dozen ladies' maids each, dressed for it in the palace together. Ella wore a dazzling

Parisian gown of the same ruby-red as the rubies at her ears, throat, wrists and at the centre of her diamond tiara. Alicky, because of her age, was all in white. Her décolleté, off-the-shoulder gown was of silver-beaded chiffon, sashed in silk, and in her hair were white roses that had been sent by train from the Crimea. Her jewellery was demure: a single string of pearls and matching drop-earrings that had once belonged to her mother.

Looking in the mirror, wearing her white elbow-length gloves and carrying a swan-feather fan, Alicky realized for the first time that although she wasn't beautiful in the way Ella was, she was beautiful in her own, very different way.

As if reading Alicky's thoughts, Ella said, 'You look as beautiful as a snow princess from a Russian fairy-tale, but try and remember not to give the impression of being as icily cold and frigid as a snow princess. I know how you hate being amongst vast numbers of people who aren't familiar to you, but as my sister and as a visitor, you will attract a lot of attention. If you keep a smile on your face, there will be nothing for you to worry about. Everyone will love you.'

Alicky steeled herself for the aspect of the evening that she knew was going to be an ordeal. Struggling to keep the nervousness she now felt from showing in her voice, she asked, 'How many people are likely to be at the ball, Ella? Three hundred? Four hundred?'

'Goodness, no.' There was loving laughter in Ella's voice. 'This isn't Darmstadt. The standard number at a Winter Palace ball is three thousand, and the ballroom and the galleries surrounding it are so vast they can accommodate that number of people easily.'

Alicky was seized by panic. Until now, all her thoughts about the ball had centred solely on Nicky: on how he would hold her in his arms and, beneath glittering chandeliers, waltz her round and round to the heavenly music of Glinka and Tchaikovsky. Now reality was sinking in. In order to enjoy the bliss she had dreamed about for so long, she was going to have to endure being the focus of many more pairs of eyes than she had expected. She steadied her breathing, forcing herself to remain calm. If she had to suffer an evening of such torture so that she could be held in Nicky's arms, then it was a price she was willingly going to pay.

Nothing she had ever experienced before – not at home in Darmstadt, or at Buckingham Palace or Windsor – had prepared her for the sheer size and splendour of what lay ahead.

Velvet-carpeted corridors were lined every step of the way by scarlet-uniformed Cossacks; the galleries opening onto the Nicholas Hall, where the ball was to be held, were each as high and vast as a cathedral, a vista of soaring gold-framed mirrors, glistening marble columns and priceless statues. Beneath the shimmering light of crystal and gold chandeliers, Russia's royalty, aristocracy, court officials and senior members of the country's navy and army greeted each other and, as they waited for the entrance of the Tsar and Tsarina, exchanged the latest gossip, looking towards Alicky with blatant curiosity as they did so.

She was already well aware of how popular Ella was in St Petersburg. What she hadn't taken into account was how much interest there would be in her, simply because she was Ella's sister.

'Smile, Alicky,' Ella instructed, not letting the smile on her own lips slip for an instant. 'Let people know how happy you are to be in St Petersburg.'

Alicky *was* happy to be in St Petersburg, but she wasn't happy at being the centre of attention. Instead she was petrified and far too frozen with panic to emulate Ella's easy, gracious smile.

And then salvation came. The Master of Ceremonies brought the Nicholas Hall to an instant hush by striking the floor with a golden-topped staff and then, having called for silence, announcing thunderously, 'Their Imperial Majesties!'

Every woman in the room, Ella and Alicky included, sank into a curtsey as the Tsar and Tsarina entered the ballroom and then, as Alicky stood straight again, she saw with stupefying relief that Nicky was only a few steps behind his parents.

His eyes sought and found hers, and she read the message in them clearly: *Etiquette decrees that you dance first with your father and then with Sergei, whose personal guest you are, and then with your brother. Then, and only then, will it be proper for us to dance together.*

Across a kaleidoscope of dazzlingly coloured evening gowns, jewelled tiaras and a forest of blue and scarlet uniforms, she sent back her own joyous message: *I know. I understand.*

The opening dance was a stately polonaise. To her surprise, her father danced it very well, but it was also a dance that, being processional, made it easy for other dancers to get a clear, close-up view of her. Determined not to let Ella down, Alicky kept a fixed, frozen smile on her face, knowing that every minute she endured was a minute closer to being with Nicky again.

After the polonaise it was a waltz, and Sergei, handsome and unbelievably tall and erect, waltzed her with military precision around the crowded ballroom floor. Occasionally she caught sight of Nicky waltzing with a beautiful dark-haired girl. Diamonds were threaded through the girl's hair, and she and Nicky were talking animatedly to each other. Nicky wasn't looking at the girl in the way he looked at her, though. One more dance. That was all that had to be lived through. Just one more dance.

'Trust me to have drawn a mazurka,' Ernie said in mock

despair, when Sergei had returned her to Ella. 'Am I allowed to improvise?'

'If you draw a shred more attention to me than I am already receiving,' she said through gritted teeth, 'I swear I will never speak to you again as long as I live.'

Ernie laughed and then, as she had known he would, danced the intricate heel-clicking, foot-stamping steps perfectly. Because of its exhilaratingly fast tempo, the mazurka was one of Alicky's favourite dances, but, for the first time ever, she couldn't wait for it to end.

As she stood once again at Ella's side, her heart beating fast and light, she saw Nicky begin walking towards her; saw people making way for him; saw how closely they were watching to see who it was he was about to dance with.

He came to a halt in front of her and bowed. 'My dance, I believe, Cousin Alix.'

The dance was another waltz and as the orchestra began playing Strauss's 'By the Beautiful Blue Danube', she slid rapturously into his arms.

He said with a shy smile in his voice, 'You don't mind me calling you "Cousin Alix", do you?'

'No.' Incredibly she, who suffered from such crippling shyness that she could barely function socially, was not at all shy. In Nicky's arms she had never felt safer, more secure or more confident, and that he – the Tsesarevich and an army officer – was shy won her heart in a way no amount of self-important arrogance could ever have done. 'I have forgotten,' she said, 'in what way we are cousins, for I know that we are not first cousins.'

'Your great-grandmama, Wilhelmina of Baden, was also my great-grandmama.' As they waltzed in graceful circles to the music, his voice thickened. 'I wonder if you remember your final day, on your last visit to St Petersburg, sweetest Alix? Do you remember the way we scratched our initials and a heart in a windowpane of the little summerhouse at Peterhof?'

'Oh yes!' There was scarcely any difference in their height and, as her eyes met his, she said, 'And no matter how old I may grow, I will never forget doing so, Nicky. Not ever.'

Absorbed in each other, they were oblivious of the attention they were attracting, for whispers concerning the interest that the Tsesarevich was showing in Grand Duke Sergei's young sister-in-law were spreading around the Nicholas Hall like wildfire.

Aware of the whispers, and the reason for them, Ella and Sergei sucked in deep, satisfied breaths. Ella was doing so because a marriage between Alicky and Nicky would be the most prestigious marriage possible for her sister; Sergei because he, like Ernie, sensed Nicky's innate submissiveness and was certain that if Alicky and Nicky married, Nicky would always follow Alicky's advice, just as he was certain that Alicky would always follow his, Sergei's, advice.

All of which meant that when the day came that Nicky became Emperor and Autocrat of all the Russias, the person wielding power over one-sixth of the world's surface wouldn't be kind, diffident Tsar Nicholas II. Via Alicky he, Sergei, would be the one wielding the power. His eyes blazed and his mouth hardened as he thought of how, if his plans came to fruition, he would one day – in everything but name – rule the largest country on earth.

PART TWO

HOPES

Chapter Fourteen

Standing on the private deck of a cross-Channel ferry, Eddy looked towards Dover's white cliffs with mixed feelings. He had been away for seven months on a royal tour of India and part of him couldn't wait to be reunited with his mother and sisters, while an equally large part of him dreaded the thought of the obligations and the lack of choices he was so soon to be faced with.

When his grandmother welcomed him home – something he knew she would do very swiftly – the first subject she would bring up would be that of his future marriage. Her heart had been set on him marrying Alicky, as, for a short space of time, had his own. Now, with Alicky having refused him – and having done so with such determination that his confidence still hadn't fully recovered – there were not many prospective brides left for him to propose to, royal and Protestant princesses of the right age being thin on the ground.

In his grandmother's eyes, the only contenders of flawless pedigree were two of Cousin Willy's sisters, Moretta and Mossy. Neither of them aroused enthusiasm in him. It had been common knowledge for years that Moretta was infatuated with one of the Battenberg brothers and, when permission for them to marry had been refused, she had publicly announced that as she couldn't marry him, she was going to kill herself. She hadn't, of course. Even so, he had no desire to marry someone who had once felt such strong passion for someone else, and quite possibly still did.

That left Mossy. He liked Mossy. She was nice and uncomplicated. Unfortunately she was also extremely plain and, with the best will in the world, he knew he would never, in a million years, feel the remotest spark of desire for her. As this was a situation that underpinned the vast majority of royal marriages, no one was going to think his lack of physical desire a justified reason for not proposing to her. One did one's duty by marrying in a suitably dynastic and politically acceptable way and, when it came to love, one found it with a mistress. It was what kings and their direct heirs had always done.

It wasn't, however, what Eddy wanted to do. He wanted to love the girl he married, and he wanted to be loved in return. And that was the crux of his dilemma, because someone who married him because it had been arranged by others that they should do so was as unlikely to be in love with him as he was to be in love with her.

With luck, of course, the person in question would like him, and he knew cousin Mossy liked him, just as he liked her. But liking wasn't love, and it was love that he craved. His family loved him, of course, but ever since he could remember, Eddy had known it was a love laced heavily with disappointment in him and, where his father was concerned, often with barely disguised dislike.

Folkestone harbour came into view and he stared unseeingly at it through a late-afternoon mist, recalling the way that both he and Georgie had always suffered from their father's 'chaffing' – the cruelly barbed taunts and the humiliating, confidence-destroying name-calling that their father thought great sport. Georgie, blessed with little sensitivity, had always been more resilient to their father's verbal attacks than Eddy had been and, more than capable of a little bullying himself, had grown up as their father's favourite.

If Eddy had been their mother's favourite there would have been balance, but much as he loved his mother – and he absolutely adored her – he hadn't been her favourite. Noisy, boisterous and ill-behaved Georgie had been her favourite because, as he had once overheard her say to his Russian Aunt Marie, 'Georgie is so typically a boy and is what one expects of a boy, whereas dear Eddy is too daydreamy for words.'

That he knew himself to be daydreamy didn't lessen the pain her words had caused him. Being daydreamy was the only way Eddy knew of surviving the treadmill of a life where his sensitivity and vulnerability were never taken into account and where what he did, and where he went, was mapped out without a thought for what he might actually like to do, and what would be best for him.

The worst example had been when he was thirteen. As the second son, Georgie had always been destined for a career in the Royal Navy, something he was eagerly enthusiastic about; and when Georgie was twelve, it was decided that for the next two years his education should continue aboard the Royal Naval training ship *Britannia*, where, along with forty-eight other cadets – all from aristocratic backgrounds – he would 'have the edges knocked off him' as a prelude and preparation for his future life at sea.

As an afterthought it was arranged that he, Eddy, who had no edges to be knocked off, should accompany him. For Georgie, who although small for his age could stick up for himself and relished a fight, it had been challenging, but also exhilarating. For him, Eddy, it had been hell. Nothing in his life had prepared him for the rowdyism and bullying of communal living.

Worst of all had been the knowledge that all his time spent learning about seamanship was pointless when, even if he had wanted to – which he didn't – he was never going to make a career of the sea. His future career was to be second in line to the throne until his grandmother died and his father became King, when he would then inherit his father's present title and, on his father's death, be crowned King of the United Kingdom and the British Dominions and Emperor of India – something else he wasn't at all looking forward to.

No one ever spoke to him about his future role of king. Even after his own and Georgie's time on the *Britannia* had come to a merciful end, it was all sea, sea, sea. This time it had been three years of acute homesickness, keeping Georgie company aboard the *Bacchante*, where, once again, his waking hours had been planned from six in the morning until late at night. Only after he had joined the Hussars had he gained a sliver of freedom and choice; and, after a lifetime of not being able to make his own decisions, some of the choices he had then made had been ones that he had come to regret.

His equerry came up to him and, breaking in on his thoughts, said, 'We're about to dock, sir', and then, 'There looks to be quite a crowd waiting to greet you home, sir.'

There was. The British public could always be relied upon to turn out with welcoming cheers whenever he or Georgie, or indeed any member of the royal family, returned home after a trip overseas. There was also a red carpet waiting for him, and a mayoral address to be endured.

His arrival at Charing Cross was far different. His parents were on the platform waiting to greet him, and so were Toria, Maudie and Looloo, and Looloo's new husband, Fife. At the sight of them, Eddy's throat tightened. No matter what the outcome of his tête-à-tête with his grandmother, it was good to be home. All that was needed to make it perfect was to be told that Cousin Mossy had become engaged elsewhere.

Next morning and after enjoying breakfast out of doors, Queen Victoria fixed Eddy with a beady eye. 'It has already been announced in the *New York Times* – and with the usual American vulgarity – that you are to marry Princess Margaret of Prussia before the summer is over.' She drummed the tips of her short, stubby fingers on the top of the small ivory-inlaid table that was placed conveniently by the side of her chair. 'Precipitate and unfortunate as the announcement has been, now that her name has been published in the American press, it means there must be no further delay in you proposing to Mossy and an official announcement being made.'

Eddy opened his mouth, but before he could speak, she raised a silencing hand. 'Your absence for the last seven months has been reason enough for the delay, but now the delay must end. You are now twenty-six. Your papa was twenty-one when he married. Your beloved grandpapa was even younger when he made me the happiest and most fortunate woman in Christendom.' She paused for a moment, her eyes overly bright, overcome with emotion, as she always was, whenever she spoke of her late beloved Albert.

The despair Eddy had felt on entering the room was deepening with every passing second. He looked around in the vain hope of finding help, but saw only his Aunt Beatrice who, despite her marriage to Henry of Battenberg, was still her mother's constant companion – something Toria had told him had been one of the Queen's conditions when she had given Beatrice and Henry permission to marry; and the other person in the room was the Munshi, the Queen's Indian servant, who was kept even more permanently in the royal presence than poor, put-upon Beatrice. Resplendent in a turban and Indian robes, he was standing in front of the room's closed double doors, his arms folded, as if daring Eddy to make a bolt for it.

With all hope at rock-bottom, Eddy returned his attention to his implacable grandmother. 'Willy,' she said, resolutely pursuing her agenda, 'is growing very irate at this long, drawn-out wait for matters to be settled. He feels your procrastination in not yet having formally proposed to Mossy is not only an insult to his sister, but an insult to him.'

For a terrifying moment Eddy thought she was about to add that it was an insult to her, as well. Mercifully she didn't do so, but his stomach still heaved. Even as a child, when Cousin Willy was irate, he had been like a bull in a china shop. Now that he was the Kaiser, there was no telling how he might give rein to his temper; he might even go so far as to break off diplomatic relations with England.

'I'm sorry Willy should feel like that,' he said, the reminder that marriage to Mossy would make Willy his brother-in-law only making him more determined than ever that he wasn't going to be brow-beaten into proposing to her. Summoning up all his courage, he said, 'But I think Willy would be even more irate if I was to marry Mossy and, when I do not love her, make her unhappy.'

'Between two healthy young people it is very easy for love to grow.'

'Or for it not to, Grandmama.' He wondered if he should cite as examples his Uncle Affie's marriage to Russian Aunt Marie, for everyone knew that although they put up a good front, Aunt Marie bitterly regretted marrying Uncle Affie; or his Aunt Louise's marriage to Lord Lorne, which was so unsatisfactory they rarely lived together.

There was silence and Eddy wondered if his last response was about to bring the world tumbling down upon his head.

His Aunt Beatrice, who was wondering the same thing, shot him an agonized glance.

The Munshi smirked.

Queen Victoria, who beneath all her sternness had a soft heart and who was also, although she tried to hide it, a great romantic, said in a different, far gentler voice, 'I would not willingly see you in an unhappy marriage, Eddy dear, but all through your life you are going to be called upon to do your duty, where the good of the country is concerned, and your decision now is, I think, a case in point. Mossy would not, as you well know, have been my first choice as a future Queen of England and Empress of India, for in my opinion she does not have the necessary bearing or gravitas. However, as Alicky has so foolishly refused the highest position there is, in my estimation Mossy is the second-best choice possible, for she is very amiable, half-English and has a great love for England.'

Seeing a window of hope in his grandmother's altered tone of voice, and before she abandoned her new mellow attitude, Eddy said swiftly, 'Will you allow me a few more months of bachelorhood, Grandmama? Perhaps until my birthday in January?'

Queen Victoria regarded him fondly. Eddy was a good-looking, nice-mannered young man and, unlike his much smaller, homely, far more robust younger brother, reminded her very much of her late beloved Albert. This last fact was reason enough for her to cut him a little slack.

'Until January,' she said, seeing relief flood through him. 'And then, Eddy, there will be an official engagement announcement.'

All three of his sisters rushed up to Eddy, the minute he entered the main drawing room at Marlborough House.

'What did Granny Queen say?' Toria demanded even before he'd sat down. 'Has she made you fix a wedding date with Mossy?'

'Because we do hope she hasn't,' Maudie said. 'We've changed our minds about wanting you to marry Mossy.'

Eddy ejected one of their mother's small dogs from a comfortably cushioned chair. Sitting down, he said, 'Yes and no. I'm going to have to marry Mossy, but Granny has agreed I can delay proposing and making it official until my birthday, which – as it is only eight months away – is a reprieve, but not much of one.'

'And so if, in the next eight months, you fall in love with someone you *do* want to marry – and who is suitably royal, of course – then you can marry her?' Looloo looked ecstatic.

Eddy couldn't for the life of him think why.

He said patiently, 'The whole point of the jam I'm in, Looloo, is that there is no one else suitable. Although Granny didn't mention them, there are apparently two Strelitz princesses of the right age, but Louis of Battenberg tells me they are not being considered, as neither of them is quite right in the head.'

Toria pulled a well-worn pouffe to the foot of his chair and sat down on it. 'Darling, darling Eddy. You are going to be so happy in a few minutes, because there *is* someone I'm sure you could very easily fall in love with, and who is the right age and is royal. It's someone so obvious I can't think why Granny Queen, and Papa and Motherdear, haven't suggested her already.'

Eddy frowned. 'Are you thinking of Cousin May? Because if you are, I'm sure she has already been thought of. She's a Serene and her name has never been suggested, because of her bloodline not being up to snuff.'

'And she's plain and, at twenty-three, already something of an Old Maid,' Toria said, conveniently forgetting that both labels could equally apply to her.

Maudie opened her mouth to spring to May's defence, but Eddy got there before her.

'Cousin May is actually quite pretty,' he said, feeling that it was rather an exaggeration, but that as he quite liked her, he should show some gallantry. 'Anyhow, I take it this person you are thinking of isn't May Teck.' He took a cigarette from his cigarette case and lit it. 'Who is it, whose name hasn't yet occurred to Granny Queen?'

With triumph in her voice, Toria said, 'Princess Hélène of Orleans!'

Eddy blinked, opened his mouth and shut it again.

Maudie said, 'Hélène is *perfect* for you, Eddy. She's eighteen, beautiful and, being a daughter of the Count of Paris, is suitably royal.'

'And we all know dear Hélène so well,' Looloo said, as if this settled the matter.

Eddy was transfixed, his cigarette held in mid-air. Hélène: why hadn't he, or anyone else, previously thought of her? She was certainly royal enough, for her father, the Count of Paris, was the legitimate claimant to the French throne. As such, the family had, for as long as he could remember, lived in exile in England and had always been on the very best of terms with English royalty. Why, then, hadn't his grandmother ever mentioned Hélène as a suitable candidate, when it came to the question of his marriage?

He put his puzzlement into words and Looloo said gently, 'Hélène and her family are at Windsor and Osborne so often, and someone who is under your nose can easily be the last person to be thought of.'

For once, Eddy thought, Looloo might be speaking sense.

Exhilarating hope surged along every nerve and vein in his body. Ever since he had been thirteen, he had spent very little time at home and so had not had the opportunity to form the kind of friendship with Hélène that he knew his sisters had. He tried to remember when he had last seen her to talk to, and rather thought it had been at Ascot, three years ago.

But, given the opportunity, would someone as beautiful as Hélène have him? He remembered how confident he had been of Alicky accepting his proposal, and how devastating to his confidence her refusal had been. What if the same thing happened again? If it did, he doubted he would survive it.

'Even if I proposed, she might not have me. She's such an acclaimed beauty and so delightfully French and . . .'

'And here comes the best bit!' As Eddy seemed intent on letting his cigarette burn away unsmoked, Maudie took it from him, inhaled, blew smoke into the air and said, 'She *will* have you, Eddy dear, because she has told us that ever since she was sixteen she has been in love with you.'

For a hideous second, Eddy wondered if his sisters were having a huge tease at his expense.

'It's true, Eddy.' Looloo slipped her hand into his and gave it a reassuring squeeze, 'and since my married home in London is East Sheen Lodge, and since the Parises live less than a mile away at Sheen House, nothing could be easier than for you and Hélène to get to know each other better, by meeting at the Lodge as my guests. And Hélène would have no need of a chaperone, because as I am an old married lady now, I can chaperone her.'

His gratitude was so deep he barely trusted himself to speak. That someone as beautiful as Hélène should love him – and had done so for more than three years – was so wonderful he hardly dared believe it was true. When he had entered the room ten minutes ago he had been certain that his future held only a dutiful marriage to someone he liked, but knew he could never love. Now, in a matter of minutes, all that had changed.

If Hélène loved him, then she would accept his proposal of marriage.

And if she accepted his proposal of marriage, all his troubles would be over and he would be the happiest man on the planet.

Chapter Fifteen

May and Maudie were walking out of the Royal Academy after viewing the Summer Exhibition.

'I'm so glad you weren't otherwise engaged this morning,' Maudie said, linking arms with May. 'I know you nearly always have an engagement to attend with your mama, but I did so want to have a chat with you, away from the rest of the family.'

'If you hadn't telephoned, I would have been with her at a Needlework Guild meeting, but when I told her of your suggestion she said she could quite happily attend the meeting on her own.'

As that was not quite what her mother had said, May avoided Maudie's eyes by opening up her parasol.

What her mother had actually said was: 'Maudie wants to speak to you, without there being any other listening ears? Then it can only be about Frank, and as I suspect he is playing with dear Maudie's affections in a most regrettable manner, you should certainly meet her and find out exactly what is going on between the two of them. I don't want an unpleasant run-in with your Uncle Bertie, and if Frank really is overstepping the mark with Maudie, that is something that will most certainly happen.'

The family carriage they had arrived in was waiting in the

Academy's courtyard and, before they reached it, Maudie came to a halt.

'I wanted to see you so that I could talk to you about Frank. I thought I could perhaps do so as we walked around the exhibition, but the minute we arrived I realized it wasn't the right place.' She looked towards the waiting carriage. 'Would you mind if we walked down Piccadilly, towards the Circus? It will be crowded, but we should have more privacy than in the Academy. And Jim will keep us in sight and will be only yards away, when we are ready to return to Marlborough House.'

'Jim?'

'The coachman. He's quite a chum and regularly covers up for me.'

This knowledge did nothing to ease May's peace of mind.

Moments later they walked out in the street, their parasols shading their faces to lessen the likelihood of anyone recognizing them.

'It's Frank,' Maudie said. 'He wants to marry me, but he says that because he is only semi-royal, neither Granny Queen nor Papa would give their permission.'

Whatever May had been expecting, it certainly wasn't that Frank wanted to marry Maudie, and that he had told Maudie so without first speaking to her father, or Aunt Queen. She was so taken aback she couldn't think of a suitable response, for how could she congratulate Maudie, when she knew Frank was quite right in supposing that he and Maudie were unlikely to be given permission to marry?

'And because Frank is so certain that permission wouldn't be given,' Maudie continued, 'he hasn't asked for it, which I think is too silly for words. After all, until he asks, how can he know? And if Looloo has been allowed to marry a non-royal aristocrat, surely I – the unimportant baby of the family – will be given permission to marry a Serene Highness?'

Logically, May didn't see why she shouldn't, but she was old enough to know that logic didn't have a lot do with royal marriages. Maudie being allowed to marry Frank would be just as unthinkable as she, May, being allowed to marry Eddy, or Georgie.

Aware that such an idea would never enter Eddy or Georgie's head and that, even if it did, it would never get off the ground, she said carefully, 'I think Looloo was lucky in that, as the eldest daughter of the heir to the throne, permission was given for her to marry into the aristocracy instead of to a fellow royal; and I'm sure Fife being a Scot, and his owning half of Scotland, had a lot to do with it, where Granny Queen was concerned. It's such a great pity that your childhood closeness to Frank has been allowed to grow into a serious romance, Maudie. And for that, Frank is to blame.'

'No, it isn't. Not really. Frank took a lot of chasing, before he began feeling the same way about me as I do about him. And it's all so *unfair*, May. Looloo is unbelievably happy with Fife. Georgie has now recovered from his heartache over Julia Stoner and fancies himself in love with Missy – a result of all the leaves that he has spent with the Edinburghs on Malta – and if she'll have him, there will be no objections at all to his marrying her. And dear, darling Eddy is at last in love with someone he will be allowed to marry.'

May missed her step and stumbled.

'And so why,' Maudie continued as May regained her balance, 'can't I marry Frank? I don't give tuppence about him being semi-royal. It isn't as if I'm ever going to succeed to the throne. Eddy, Georgie, Looloo and Toria are all in front of me, when it comes to that – and so it doesn't matter a fig that Frank isn't of equal birth.'

'Who,' May said, as a crowded horse-drawn bus rattled nosily past them, 'is Eddy in love with?'

'Aunt Louise says all this fuss about whose grandfather or grandmother married beneath them, resulting in their children and grandchildren being ineligible to reign, is a lot of bosh and should be struck from off the Royal Statute Books. That is, if it is written in them, which I assume it is.'

'Who,' May said again, 'is Eddy in love with?'

'Princess Hélène of Orléans. And so I want you to speak to your parents, May. I don't think Frank has spoken to them about wanting to marry me, but it would be so helpful if I knew they knew, and it would be so encouraging if they were happy for us to marry, for they might be able to bring pressure to bear on Granny Queen; and if Granny Queen was happy for us to marry, then Papa would have to be as well.'

There was a certain logic in what Maudie was saying, but May couldn't focus on it. She was still coming to terms with the thought of Eddy being in love with Hélène. 'How long,' she asked, stepping out of the way of an elderly woman selling lavender, 'has it been going on?'

The brim of Maudie's hat was laden with artificial flowers, and beneath them her eyebrows shot up in surprise. 'But you know how long, May. I've always been in love with Frank. I can't remember ever not being.'

'Sorry, Maudie. I was referring to Eddy and Hélène.'

'About a month – and I don't think you're concentrating on what I'm saying, May. I don't think you appreciate how important it is that permission is given for Frank and me to marry.'

May thought of all the reasons why no such permission would be given. There was the fact that Frank wasn't of equal birth; but there were lots of other reasons as well. For one thing, Frank's surname was Teck and, much as she hated admitting it, their family name came with a lot of damaging baggage.

Her mother's carelessness with money – a carelessness Frank had inherited – had led to bailiffs pawing over their possessions; the shame of having the contents of their home sold at public auction; and a very public two-year exile in Florence. Uncle Bertie couldn't help his cousinship to her mother, but he certainly wouldn't want their family ties to become even closer. She wondered, if it had been Dolly and not Frank that Maudie was in love with, if things might have been different, for at least with Dolly there had never been a hint of regrettable behaviour.

The same couldn't be said for Frank, who had gained a reputation for outrageousness when, as a schoolboy, he had been expelled from his prestigious public school for tossing the headmaster over a hedge. Dark-haired and swarthily handsome, he was a free spirit who didn't care what people thought, or said, about him. A compulsive gambler, he was always at a racecourse, dog track or casino, and was either gleeful at his winnings or carelessly indifferent to his losses, and it was impossible to imagine the Prince and Princess of Wales giving him permission to marry their daughter.

'And so will you speak to your parents, May?' Maudie asked as they reached Piccadilly Circus and came to a halt. 'I'm quite sure if you did, it would turn things around in a flash.'

May could never remember being in such a quandary. Not only was Frank a reckless gambler, but according to Dolly he had also acquired the reputation of being a womanizer, something Maudie was presumably unaware of. Just as worrying was that Frank hadn't given the slightest indication that his feelings for Maudie were such that he would marry her, if he could; and, knowing her brother as she did, May doubted if what he had said had been sincerely meant.

Not wanting to encourage Maudie in her hope that her relationship with Frank was going to have a happy ending, and wanting to protect her from hurt, she replied, 'If you really want me to, I'll speak to my parents in the way that you've asked, but I truly think the best thing you can do for your future happiness is to end your romance with Frank, because I honestly don't believe it can have a happy ending.'

People were bustling past them in a never-ending throng. Bicycles, horse-drawn buses, carts and carriages rattled and clattered as they rounded the fountain in the centre of the Circus and streamed off into Piccadilly, Regent Street and Shaftesbury Avenue. Over the general din, Maudie said cheerfully, 'Oh, but it will have a happy ending, May. My romance with Frank has gone too far down the road for it not to.'

Out of the corner of her eye, May saw with relief that Jim had brought the carriage-horses to a halt and was waiting for them only yards away.

'I'm sure it must seem like that, when you've known each for as long as both of you can remember—'

'That isn't what I meant by Frank and me having gone too far down the road for us not to be allowed to marry.' The expression in Maudie's cornflower-blue eyes was both defiant and triumphant. 'Frank and I are lovers, May. We are lovers in the most full and wonderful way possible. So you see, if the worst comes to the worst and the answer is no, when Frank finally asks Papa and Granny Queen if he can marry me, then I shall tell them that unless I'm allowed to marry Frank, gossip will get out about my having lost my virginity and the result will be no one else ever asking for my hand in marriage. Poor, dear Toria will be tainted by association, and Granny Queen will die of heart failure.'

May thought that she, too, might die of heart failure. How could she be in a public place – and not just any public place, but Piccadilly Circus – listening to dearest, lovely Maudie telling her that she was no longer a virgin, and that the person responsible was her brother Frank? She tried to imagine the repercussions if the Queen was to get to know of it, but her imagination simply wouldn't stretch that far.

'And so you will tell your mama that Frank wants to marry me, and you will ask your mama to speak with Granny Queen about her giving permission for him to do so, won't you? Everything will be so much nicer if no notice is taken of the silly old unequal-birth thing, and Frank and I can have a lovely wedding at Buckingham Palace.'

'Yes.' May fought off a wave of dizziness by focusing on the bronze statue on top of the fountain. 'Yes, I will speak with Mama, Maudie.'

'But not about how far down the road Frank and I have gone? I want to save that as a last resort.'

It was a last resort that May fervently hoped would never be used.

'Frank wants to marry Maudie?' Princess Mary Adelaide's reaction was one of amazement, swiftly followed by delight. Out of Bertie and Alix's five children, Maudie had always been her favourite and she could think of nothing nicer than to have Maudie as a daughter-in-law. 'But why hasn't Frank spoken to Papa about wishing to do so? And he hasn't. Papa wouldn't keep that kind of news to himself.'

'Maudie says Frank is certain that if he were to ask her father and Aunt Queen for permission to marry her, permission would be refused on the grounds of his being a Serene, and Frank wouldn't have wanted to remind Papa of the unequal-birth thing in his lineage. You know how mention of that always upsets him.'

Her mother knew it only too well.

'And so if you and Papa are happy at the thought of her marrying Frank, Maudie wanted me to ask if you will approach

Aunt Queen about the two of them marrying. As Aunt Queen broke an old-established rule by allowing Looloo to marry a non-royal, I don't see why she wouldn't do the same thing for Maudie.'

'And neither do I.' To May's vast relief, there was firm conviction in her mother's voice. 'Being her first cousin, I understand dear Victoria far better than anyone else, and I know, from my own experience, that she takes a surprisingly relaxed view where the subject of equal birth is concerned; far more relaxed than those of continental royalties. When I was about to marry your Papa, she wrote me a very kind letter in which she said she had always thought it wrong and absurd that because dear Papa's mother was not a princess, he was unable to succeed to the Württemberg throne.'

'And so do you think Frank and Maudie can be hopeful about getting permission to marry?'

'I think they can be *exceedingly* hopeful, and I shall ask Papa to telegram dear Frank at his Royal Dragoons barracks, telling him so. For now I am going to send word by messenger to Aunt Queen asking her if I may visit her at her earliest convenience. Fetch me pen and paper, May. Oh dear, my poor old heart. It's racing fit to burst!'

The next morning, and accompanied by May, Princess Mary Adelaide was happily en route to Windsor.

'Papa is beside himself at the thought of having even closer family ties to the Waleses.' She leaned out of the carriage to wave to a small group of children standing by the roadside, all of whom waved back enthusiastically. 'With Frank married to Maudie, perhaps dear Victoria will finally agree to giving Papa the title of Royal Highness, which he so longs for.'

May made a polite sound to show sympathy with her mother's hopes, but her thoughts weren't on what advantages might come to her father if Frank and Maudie were allowed to marry; they were on Eddy.

She hadn't seen him since he had returned from India a month ago, and because there had been no house parties recently that might have included the Parises, or any family weddings or christenings they may have been invited to, she couldn't imagine when and where Eddy and Hélène had so recently fallen in love.

What was understandable, though, was Eddy having fallen in love with Hélène. She was beautiful, sweet-natured and possessed enviable French *chic*, wearing clothes with head-turning elegance and style. If they really were in love and married, Hélène, with her dark hair and dark eyes, would one day be the most ravishing queen England had ever had.

The prospect filled May with a turbulent mix of emotions: happiness that Eddy would be marrying someone he loved and who loved him in return, and painful regret that her most secret daydream would have to end.

Once they had arrived at Windsor, her mother hurried off to speak to the Queen in privacy, and May was kept company in the White Drawing Room by her Aunt Beatrice. She had barely taken a sip of the Indian tea that the two of them had been served when a footman announced Frank's arrival. He strode into the room, looking as tense as a tightly wound spring.

Overjoyed at seeing him, May sprang to her feet, saying swiftly in order to ease his tension, 'Mama is already speaking with Aunt Queen.'

He didn't look towards her. Instead he said urgently to Beatrice, 'Please interrupt my mother's conversation with the Queen. It's vitally important she doesn't ask on my behalf what she has come here to ask.'

May's jaw dropped.

The teaspoon Beatrice had been holding clattered into its saucer.

'Please, Beatrice!' There was panic in his voice as well as urgency. 'It's vital you do as I ask.'

'But my dear Frank, I can't possibly do such a thing.' Beatrice couldn't have looked more horrified if Frank had asked her to stand on a table and dance the cancan.

May said, struggling to understand Frank's request, 'Are you frightened of Aunt Queen saying permission for you to marry Maudie is out of the question?'

'No! The opposite! Beatrice, if you don't interrupt my mother's conversation with the Queen, I will.'

The thought of Frank Teck bursting in on her mother, when she had asked not to be disturbed, was so horrifying Beatrice stumbled to her feet and almost ran from the room.

May said bewilderedly, 'What on earth is the matter, Frank? In all probability, Aunt Queen is telling Mama that if you and Maudie wish to marry, then you can.'

'Hell's bells, May! Didn't you understand what I said a second ago?' He ran a hand through his hair. 'I don't *want* to marry Maudie. I don't want to marry anyone! I'm not the marrying kind, and it's because I don't want to marry Maudie – and because I care for her too much to want to hurt her feelings, by admitting to it – that I told her I would never be given permission to do so. I said it, God help me, because it was the only reasonable excuse I could think of for my not proposing to her!'

May put a hand on the nearest small table to steady herself, overcome by the horror of Frank having led Maudie on in the way he had, when he never had the slightest intention of marrying her. That he had behaved so dishonourably was almost more than she could grasp.

She said hoarsely, 'Then you shouldn't have compromised her!'

He sucked in his breath, stunned by how much she knew about his own and Maudie's relationship.

'And because you have compromised her, if Aunt Queen tells Mama she will give permission for you and Maudie to marry, then that is what you are honour-bound to do.'

'I know.' There were beads of sweat on his forehead. 'But if I do have to propose to her, there will be little chance of her accepting me, when I tell her how unfaithful I have been to her. Of how incapable I am of fidelity and of how, for the last six months, I have been in love with a married woman several years older than myself. If, when I admit all this, she still wants to marry me, then I will do the right thing and marry her, but somehow I don't think Maudie will still want to marry me, do you? In fact, I don't think she'll ever want to see me again.'

They were interrupted by Beatrice hurrying back into the room and saying, with a smile on her face, certain that the news she was bringing was good news, 'Your mama will be with you both in a couple of minutes, and she has asked me to tell you that her premonition was correct and that all is well.'

Frank drew in a deep, steadying breath and then said, 'Thank you for the message, Aunt Beatrice. When my mother joins you, will you please give her my apologies and tell her I've left for Marlborough House?'

And then, ashen-faced and without another word, he strode from the room.

Chapter Sixteen

The next few weeks were deeply distressful for May. Frank had proposed to Maudie and, after admitting to her that he had never been faithful to her and was presently having an affair with a married woman – and that it was an affair he had no desire to end – it was a proposal she had broken-heartedly turned down.

Not knowing the circumstances, both his mother and his father were almost hysterical with disappointment – Princess Mary Adelaide because the wedding would have been such a prestigious one for Frank, and the Duke of Teck because he had imagined that, on becoming father-in-law to one of the Prince of Wales's daughters, the Queen would fulfil his heart's desire and bestow on him the title of Royal Highness. It was a distress that doubled when Frank abruptly left the country, doing so for an unspecified destination and for an unspecified length of time.

Her parents and the Queen believed he had done so because he'd been jilted by Maudie and therefore couldn't bear the pain of constantly seeing her at family events. Everyone else believed that things had simply got too hot for Frank, where his gambling debts were concerned, and that he had fled abroad until things had cooled down.

Most painful of all, to May, had been Maudie's heartbroken despair. In Marlborough House's secluded summerhouse she had said, between hiccupping sobs, 'I thought Frank loved me, May. And he didn't. Knowing that he didn't – that he never had – was far worse than knowing he had been unfaithful to me.' Tears had streamed down her face and dripped onto her dress. 'I could have forgiven all that – did forgive all that – but I couldn't accept a proposal he was only making under duress. I couldn't marry him, knowing how unhappy I would make him. I couldn't bear the thought of making Frank unhappy. I love him far too much to do that to him.' And she had leaned her head on May's shoulder and, with May's arm sympathetically around her, had cried and cried until she was too exhausted to cry any more.

At the end of June the Queen made Eddy a duke, which puzzled May. 'I don't understand,' she had said as she accompanied her mother to yet another Needlework Guild event. 'Duke of what? And why? I've never heard of a prince being demoted to a duke before. Surely the only possible change of title is when the Prince becomes King?'

Princess Mary Adelaide fussed with the arrangement of her gossamer-light shawl. 'It's all to do with politics. The Prime Minister has made it quite clear to the Queen that if Eddy is to take a seat in the House of Lords – something he is, apparently, very keen to do – then it is necessary for him to be a peer of the realm. And a prince is not a peer. Only a duke – and of course earls, marquesses, viscounts and barons – are peers. I expect,' she added, 'that within the family we will still always refer to dear Eddy as "Prince Eddy", and not as the "Duke of Clarence and Avondale", which is the title the Queen has decided upon.'

Later, when she was on her own, May tried saying the title

aloud. It seemed very cumbersome, and her private opinion was that either 'Duke of Clarence' or 'Duke of Avondale' would have been better than a double title, especially when the only historical Duke of Clarence she could remember was the duke who had so ignominiously drowned in a barrel of Malmsey wine.

In July there came a bright spot: an invitation to cousin Marie-Louise's eighteenth birthday party, which was to be held in the Belgian Suite at Buckingham Palace.

'I imagine it will be a very small, informal party,' Princess Mary Adelaide said, 'for your Aunt Lenchen and Uncle Christian are not the world's best party-givers. Both of them are homebodies. The only contribution Christian makes to any social activity is to take his glass eye out and replace it with one of a different colour. I remember ten years or so ago, at Osborne House, he showed Ducky, Missy and Alicky his entire glass-eye collection. Aunt Marie told me Missy had nightmares for weeks.'

In reply to a letter May sent to Alicky, telling her of Eddy and Hélène's romance, of Eddy's new title and of Marie-Louise's imminent birthday party, Alicky had written:

Dearest Kindred Spirit,

So glad you told me Eddy has found happiness with someone who truly loves him and that he isn't going to have to settle for one of Granny Queen's loveless arranged marriages. I know it caused a lot of hurt to his confidence when he carried out Granny Queen's wishes and proposed to me, and when I didn't accept him.

As for Uncle Christian and his glass-eye collection, I remember that incident so well! It was at that particular Osborne family get-together that you and I became Kindred Spirits – and that we became Kindred Spirits with Willy, although I have to admit that the Kindred Spirit thing with Willy is very hit-and-miss and I haven't seen him since last year, when Irène and Heinrich's baby boy was christened.

Marie-Louise sent me an invitation to her birthday party and although I count her a very dear friend and would have loved to come to England and meet up with her (and with you), it just isn't possible, as Papa is not very well at the moment and relies on me very heavily.

And now I want to let you into a very great secret. I have made friends with a lady who can contact those who are in the spirit world, and she has contacted my mama. Mama has sent a message to me asking that I never forget my confirmation vows, and so I have now become a very good Lutheran and go to church through the week, as well as on Sunday; and, as Mama did, I visit local hospitals and orphanages and give what help I can to the poor. I am so happy knowing that, in doing so, I am pleasing Mama.

The letter had gone on to say that Ernie was under increasing pressure to find a suitable bride; that Alicky knew, with all her heart, that Nicky was her one true love; and that so far Waldemar – Irène and Heinrich's little boy – was showing no signs of having inherited the family bleeding disease.

That Alicky, who always carried her enthusiasm to extremes and was far too fey and fatalistic for her own good, was now dabbling with spiritualism deeply disturbed May. She had been eleven when Alicky's mother had died, and she remembered her Aunt Alice as being very practical and full of brisk common sense. Not at all the sort of person who would have thought it helpful to be sending messages to her highly susceptible daughter from beyond the grave.

* * *

The spacious Belgian Suite was on the ground floor of Buckingham Palace's north-facing Garden Wing. Entering it with Dolly, May heard music playing and saw at once that as well as Toria, Looloo and a shockingly pale Maudie, there were cousins she hadn't seen for quite a while: Ducky and Missy – Missy looking alarmingly sophisticated for a soon-to-be fifteen-year-old – and Ernie Hesse, and Ernie and Alicky's eldest sister, Vicky.

With a slam of her heart May saw Eddy standing by one of the French windows that led into the garden. Hélène was with him and, even though his father was only yards away, in conversation with Marie-Louise's father, Eddy's arm was around Hélène's waist.

There couldn't have been a more public statement that they were a couple, and that their romance had his parents' blessing. Before they should see her looking towards them, May looked swiftly away, intending to cross the room towards Maudie.

Ducky forestalled her. 'I thought that eye-catching Romany-looking brother of yours might be here, May, but Marie-Louise says he's in disgrace over something or other and has left the country. Is it true? I don't want this party to be a complete waste of my time.'

She was thirteen and whereas Missy, only a year older, could have passed for being seventeen or eighteen, Ducky was still every inch a plain, awkward-looking adolescent.

Trying not to look as taken aback by Ducky's bluntness as she felt, May said a little stiffly, 'If you are referring to Frank, he's abroad improving his foreign-language skills.'

Ducky looked glum. 'I don't suppose he would have taken any notice of me, even if he had been here. It's always Missy who gets all the male attention.'

Looking across to where Missy was fluttering her eyelashes at a bemused Louis of Battenberg, May absolutely believed her. She looked round to see where Georgie was and, although he had been in the room when she had entered it, couldn't see him anywhere. Wondering if Maudie had got it right about Georgie being in love with Missy, she said, 'I understand Missy is quite smitten by Georgie.'

Ducky made a rude snorting sound. 'If all Georgie's wishes came true, she would be. Missy just enjoys teasing him and making him think she's smitten by him. He's so dull — and for the last couple of years has stayed with us on Malta so often – that Missy says it was the only way of relieving the tedium of his company. Missy,' she added, 'can be very naughty when she wants to be.'

May didn't doubt it and was quite relieved to see that Vicky had now joined Missy and Louis, and that Vicky had slid a hand proprietorially through her husband's arm.

'Mama wants Missy to catch the eye of a good marriage prospect, now that she's fourteen, going on fifteen,' Ducky continued, showing no desire to walk away and startle someone else with her racy conversation, 'and so she's wasting her time flirting with Louis of Battenberg when he already has a wife.

'Your mother must have been hoping she would accept a proposal from Georgie.'

'Lord, no! Mama says it was bad enough her having married into Granny Queen's Saxe-Coburg-Gotha clan, without Missy or me doubling up her error, although she *might* have made an exception where Eddy was concerned – I think Mama would quite like for Missy to be an empress one day as well as a queen. As it is, it looks as if Eddy is taken and I know that, even if he wasn't, Missy wouldn't fancy him in a month of Sundays. She likes men with Russian *chutzpah* and masculine aggressiveness. Eddy Wales is too polite to excite Missy.'

In an adjoining room, where the carpets had been rolled back, dance music was now playing.

'Goody!' Ducky brightened visibly. 'Now I have to find someone I can bully into dancing with me. Have you seen Ernie Hesse anywhere? Ernie is always good fun. If Missy had any sense, she'd marry Ernie.' And she darted off in search of him, leaving May wondering if it was their half-Russian blood that made the Edinburgh sisters so unnervingly uninhibited.

She looked across to the French windows, but the little group that had been standing there was there no longer. Maudie, too, was no longer anywhere to be seen and, remembering her party manners, May went in search of Marie-Louise.

'Darling, *darling* May!' An elated Marie-Louise almost squeezed the breath out of her. 'Thank you so much for the little book of poems by Elizabeth Barrett Browning. I shall treasure it always. Isn't it a shame that darling Alicky was unable to come? She's very much her papa's hostess, now that she's the only daughter left at home. Dear Vicky is here, though, and so that is some compensation, but not Irène.' She lowered her voice and said confidingly, 'I believe Irène is expecting another happy event.'

Georgie Wales came up to them. 'I don't do dancing,' he said to Marie-Louise, red-faced with embarrassment, 'but I've been told it would be awfully remiss of me not to have a birthday dance with you.'

Marie-Louise giggled. 'Thank you, Georgie. I'll make it as painless as possible.'

Dolly then asked May to dance and, after Dolly, she had a satisfying number of other dance partners, including an uninspiring older German cousin of Marie-Louise's, who never spoke a word to her and smelled unpleasantly of pear drops.

Because the dancing was taking place in a room far smaller than a ballroom, she was always aware of who else was on the makeshift dance floor. Missy seldom left it; even Uncle Bertie danced with her. Eddy had one dance with Marie-Louise and then danced only twice, both times with Hélène. After their second dance together they disappeared in the direction of the main drawing room.

After her dance with Uncle Christian, and feeling in need of a breather, May went in search of a glass of lemonade and Maudie. After a lot of looking, she found her standing at the set of French windows that Eddy and Hélène had been standing by earlier in the evening.

Maudie gave her a sad smile. 'My poor broken heart doesn't know how to mend itself. Do you know where Frank has gone, May? Have you heard anything from him?'

May shook her head. Frank had always been a poor letter-writer, but his not having let their distraught mother know where he was, or for how long he intended to be away, suggested a thoughtlessness that she wasn't going to forgive lightly.

'From as far back as I can remember, I always imagined I would one day marry Frank,' Maudie said bleakly, 'and now that I know that's not going to happen, I don't think I'll ever marry anyone. Have you ever felt that way about anyone, May? Have you ever met someone you absolutely knew you could build your life around?'

May hesitated, and then she said slowly, 'Yes, I have.' She couldn't possibly reveal that person as being Eddy, but there had been someone else who, although she had never had a crush on him, she knew she had liked and admired enough to have built her life around. That had been Thaddeus. She confessed, 'It was someone I met when I was living in Florence. He was only a few years older than I was, and very attractive and talented. I always loved spending time with him, and for quite a while after my return to England I missed him enormously.'

Maudie's jaw dropped. Nothing – absolutely nothing – could have amazed her more than that May, always so very correct and proper, had had a secret romance in Italy that no one knew anything about.

Frantically she tried to think of eligible Italian royals, but her knowledge of the Italian royal family was sketchy and the only name she could think of was that of Vittorio Emanuele, the Prince of Naples. But as he was only twenty and it had been seven years since the Teck family had been banished to Florence, May's secret romance couldn't possibly have been with him. Florence was, however, a very popular destination for sun-starved Russian royals.

The idea of May having had a secret romance with a hot-blooded Romanov was so mind-boggling that Maudie simply couldn't get her head around it. She remembered that although all Granny Queen's grandchildren had more than a generous dash of German blood in their veins, May was all-German, something that was easily forgotten, when she had been born and brought up in England.

'Was he a German royal?' she asked. 'Or perhaps a Russian royal?'

'Good heavens, no! He wasn't royal at all. And he was Irish.'

'Irish?' Maudie put a hand on the back of a convenient chair to steady herself. '*Irish?*'

'Yes.' Having gone so far, May didn't see why she shouldn't go the full hundred yards. 'And he was – is – an artist.'

It occurred to Maudie that she was having her leg pulled. 'You're teasing me, May. You have to be.'

'No, I'm not. And we didn't have a romance, although I think we came very close to having one. We still keep in touch by letter.' She paused and then added, 'He's married now and living in America.'

Through the wide-open doors leading into the adjoining room they could see chairs being laid out for a game of Musical Chairs.

Maudie said. 'Have you ever told anyone else, May?'

'Absolutely not. And I shan't.'

Maudie understood. Just as the truth about how far things had gone between her and Frank was something she knew May would never, ever speak about to anyone, so May trusted her with her secret.

The game of Musical Chairs was apparently only for girls, and as Marie-Louise, Vicky, Toria, Looloo, Ducky, Missy and Hélène began racing like mad things around the chairs to music from a phonograph, Eddy strolled back into the principal drawing room and looked around, as if searching for somebody.

May looked away from him quickly, but not quickly enough. Their eyes met and, with a relaxing of his shoulders, he began threading his way through knots of relatives to where she and Maudie were standing.

'Oh dear,' Maudie said. 'Eddy's going to do the caring-brother thing and ask me why I'm not joining in with anything.'

He didn't. Instead, when he reached them, he said to May, 'I was hoping you would be here tonight. I expect you've heard the good news about Hélène and me, but I wanted to tell you myself.'

It was so unexpected, and she was so overcome at his having sought her out in such a way, that all May could manage in response was to say stiltedly, 'I'm very happy for both of you.'

'I knew you would be.' He smiled the slow, languid smile that turned her knees to water. 'I remember unburdening myself to you about my love life when everyone expected me to marry Mossy, and when I was determined not to. You were a very good listener, May. I appreciated it. I also know that when I talk to you, nothing I say goes any further.'

May was aware that Maudie had moved away and they were on their own. With her heart feeling as if it was beating somewhere up in her throat, she said, 'When will there be an official announcement?'

'When the Queen has given us permission to marry – and we can't ask her for permission until the Roman Catholic thing is got out of the way.'

May said faintly, 'Roman Catholic thing? Is Hélène Roman Catholic?'

'Yes. I expect that was why, when Granny Queen was match-making, she never added darling Hélène's name to her list of possible brides. It was a silly oversight, when the RC thing can so easily be sorted.'

'Can it?' May frowned, and then said in puzzlement, 'Then why couldn't Georgie marry Julie?'

'Oh, that was completely different. Julie was a commoner. Hélène is a royal princess.'

The game of Musical Chairs had come to an end and the breathless participants were making their way back into the drawing room.

As Eddy saw Hélène walk into the room, arm-in arm with Marie-Louise, he said, bringing their conversation to an end, 'Hélène's father has written to Cardinal Manning informing him of our forthcoming engagement, and so you see, May, there is no need for any anxiety. Manning is the Archbishop of Westminster and the highest Catholic authority in England. Once he gives his approval – and the Count of Paris is certain that he will – everything will be straightforward.'

And with an aching heart and all her pleasure in the evening extinguished, she watched him cross the room to Hélène's side and slide his arm once more lovingly around her waist.

Chapter Seventeen

AUGUST 1890, MARLBOROUGH HOUSE

'I simply can't feel the same about Maudie, after the way she has broken poor Frank's heart and driven him out of the country with grief,' Princess Mary Adelaide said emotionally to May a few days later, as they travelled by train from Richmond into central London in a private carriage. 'And why you are spending even more time with her now than you did before she turned down Frank's proposal of marriage, I can't imagine.'

There were times – and this was one of them – when May was sorely tempted to tell her mother what the true situation had been, and of how dishonourably and appallingly Frank had behaved towards Maudie. Again, she thought of how devastated her mother would be if she were to know what the true situation had been, and so she fought the temptation. Far better that her mother was disappointed in Maudie than that she ever learned the truth about Frank's treatment of her, and of his involvement with a much older, married woman.

As her mother popped a mint humbug into her mouth and mercifully fell silent, May wondered if the nameless woman in Frank's life had perhaps joined Frank abroad, although she couldn't possibly have joined him immediately, because when they finally received a letter from Frank, it was one telling them he was staying with some of their father's Württemberg relations who had a summer villa in Switzerland on the south side of Lake Constance.

A few weeks later had come a postcard from Cannes, and then one from Monte Carlo.

'Monte Carlo,' her father had gasped, poleaxed, and had fallen ashen-faced into an armchair. 'Blackjack, baccarat, roulette! The boy is going to be ruined! And if we have to pick up his gambling debts, *we* are going to be ruined.'

When May had given Dolly an unedited account of what had led to Frank's exile, his reaction had been simply to say, pale with shock, 'God, what a fool Frank is! If he'd married Maudie, she would have been the saving of him. As it is, he's ruined his life – or is well on the way to doing so.'

It had been an opinion that May had fully agreed with.

On her arrival at Marlborough House, and escorted by a footman, May made her way to a small, little-used drawing room that Maudie had made her own.

As soon as she entered it, Maudie ran towards her and hugged her hard. 'You're a life-saver, May Teck. Just the fact that, when I'm with you, I don't have to pretend not to be heartbroken is worth its weight in gold. You have no idea how tiring pretending can be.' They moved across to a chintz-covered sofa and, sitting down, she said, 'What's the latest news from Frank, May? Is he still in Cannes?'

'No. His last postcard was from Monte Carlo.'

'Monte Carlo?' Maudie managed a wry smile. 'I'm glad he's somewhere it's easy to imagine him being. Frank and Switzerland were never an obvious match.' Adjusting her ankle-length skirt, she curled her legs beneath her. 'I know you think my continually talking about Frank, and asking where he is, is no help to my getting over him, and so I promise I'm going to stop asking you about him. I'd like to tell you some good news now, but all I have is bad news.'

She gave May a few seconds to steel herself for what she was about to tell her and then said, 'Irène and Heinrich's little boy, Waldemar, has inherited the family bleeding disease. They were both so certain that he hadn't, for there had been no long period of bleeding from his navel after birth, as happened with Irène's brother, Frittie, who bled to death when he was three. After first having believed that Waldemar was free of the family curse, Irène and Heinrich are devastated.'

May's heart went out to both of them, but especially to Irène, who would see herself as responsible for having transmitted the disease to Waldemar. The Queen had been the first person in the family to be a known carrier, and although the disease bypassed three of her four sons, her youngest son, Leopold, had inherited the disease and had died of it. That only females were carriers of it, and that only males ever suffered from it, was the most sinister aspect of haemophilia and caused a great deal of anxiety among the women in the family, fearing they might pass it on to any children they had. It was a fear that only May – a second cousin to the Queen, and not a direct descendant – was mercifully free of.

'And if that news isn't bad enough,' Maudie continued, 'Granny Queen has said that because of Hélène's Roman Catholicism, under no circumstances can Eddy marry Hélène, which really doesn't seem fair, when both Papa and Motherdear are so happy at the thought of having Hélène as a daughter-in-law, and when Hélène's parents are equally happy at the thought of having Eddy as a son-in-law.'

May's instant reaction was to be appalled at how crushed and shattered Eddy must now be feeling. Her second reaction was total mystification that such a reaction from the Queen hadn't been anticipated by Eddy's father. She could only assume that, like Eddy, the Prince of Wales had been under the impression that Hélène's royal status meant the religious barrier was one that could be overcome.

Maudie said, 'Eddy and Hélène are discussing the situation with Papa now and, when they have finished doing so, they will be joining us. Eddy says you are so clear-sighted he thinks you may be able to suggest a way round their difficulties. Have I to ring for some tea and biscuits? Or, as it's such a hot day, would you prefer iced lemonade?'

Suppressing with difficulty the longing for a small whisky, May said, 'Lemonade would be lovely, Maudie.'

When she had rung for the footman and asked for iced lemonade, Maudie uncurled her legs, saying, 'The only shred of good news is that Granny Queen is being very supportive of Georgie's intention to ask for Missy's hand in marriage, the minute Missy turns sixteen.'

May remembered how flirtatious Missy had been at Marie-Louise's birthday party, and how Ducky had ridiculed the idea of Missy feeling about Georgie as he did about her.

'I think,' she said cautiously, 'that Aunt Marie may have other plans in mind for Missy.'

'Well, if she has, they won't count for much. It's Granny Queen who has the last word where royal marriages are concerned.'

As Maudie finished speaking, Eddy and Hélène walked into the room, arm-in-arm and pale-faced.

Maudie sprang to her feet. 'I told May you would be joining us. I'll ring for more lemonade.'

May stood up and Hélène slid her arm from Eddy's and walked quickly across to her.

'Dear May, it's so very nice to see you.' She took both of May's hands in hers and squeezed them tightly. 'Eddy thinks you may have some ideas as to what we must do, in order to persuade the Queen to allow us to marry.' Her blue, black-lashed eyes glittered with tears that she was trying to hold back. 'Eddy and I love each other so very much and we are willing to do anything – anything at all – in order that we can marry.'

May had never before felt herself to be in such an embarrassingly difficult situation. Because of her own secret feelings for Eddy, she wanted to do everything she could to further his happiness, and nothing was more certain than that marriage to Hélène would achieve that aim. It was obvious Hélène genuinely loved him and wouldn't be marrying him out of a sense of duty, as would Mossy, or any other royal candidate the Queen might propose.

Her problem was that she didn't want him to marry at all. While he was still single she could cherish the daydream of Eddy one day having romantic feelings for her. And if she wanted to continue with that daydream, she should now say that she couldn't think of anything that could possibly help them. But at the sight of Hélène's distraught face and the despair in the set of Eddy's shoulders as he walked over to the drinks cabinet, she knew, even as the thought came, that it was one she would never act on.

Eddy poured himself a shot of brandy and said, 'The letter Hélène's father wrote to Cardinal Manning received an unoptimistic reply, May. According to him, the law that prevents an heir to the throne from marrying a Catholic could only be overturned with the agreement of both Houses of Parliament – and according to my father, that is as likely as pigs flying.'

An emotionally drained Hélène sank exhaustedly into a nearby armchair. 'And so, short of changing my religion, or Eddy stepping out of the succession, we don't know what to do next. Eddy thinks you may be able to help us, May, for he says you are wonderfully sensible and clear-sighted.'

It wasn't the mundane way in which May wanted to be thought of by Eddy, but it was better than him not thinking of her at all.

'What did the Queen say, when the two of you told her you wanted to marry?' she asked, struggling to think of a way out of the impasse.

'We haven't spoken to her ourselves.' Eddy downed his brandy and walked over to Hélène's chair, then put an arm lovingly around her shoulders. 'Once I told my father I wished to marry Hélène, he was so pleased he took it upon himself to tell Granny immediately.'

May's disbelief was total. 'But you have to speak to her yourselves! Once she sees how deeply in love the two of you are, she may well speak to the Prime Minister and some kind of a solution might then be found.'

'Do you truly think so?'

'Yes. I truly think so. Beneath her stern exterior, the Queen is very sentimental, and your father speaking on your behalf wouldn't have touched her heart in the same way that the two of you going hand-in-hand to speak to her would do.'

'Then that,' Eddy said slowly and with renewed hope, 'is exactly what we're going to do.'

Maudie went on, 'Granny Queen is at Balmoral. It's an awful long way to go.'

'No, it isn't. If I thought it would result in my being able to marry Hélène, I'd happily walk barefoot to the ends of the earth.'

'You look extraordinarily tired, pet lamb,' her mother said, when May returned home to White Lodge. 'I really don't think it does you any good seeing so much of Maudie. However, Papa has exciting news for you. It's so exciting that I think you should sit down and take a couple of deep breaths before he joins us and tells you it.'

May was in no mood for news, exciting or otherwise. Accepting that Eddy was in love with Hélène had been one thing. Hearing the intensity in his voice when he'd said he'd walk barefoot to the ends of the earth to marry her had been quite another, and all she wanted was to go to her room and get her feelings under control in private.

Removing her hat and taking off her gloves, she sat down at the large table around which so many family discussions had taken place – not least the discussion as to where, on the continent, they should move to, in order to fulfil the Queen's request that they live more cheaply. Although they hadn't realized it at the time, Florence had ended up being the happiest decision that, as a family, they had ever taken. She closed her eyes, overcome by the longing to be back there, living a carefree life within sight of the Arno once again at the golden-walled Villa I Cedri.

'There you are!' Her father erupted into the room as if he had been out scouring the country for her for hours. 'And you are already sitting down? Good. Good.' He seated himself opposite her, far more flushed in the face than was usual. 'I have here,' and he took a letter bearing a royal crest that May was unfamiliar with from his waistcoat pocket, 'a formal request for your hand in marriage. Now, what do you think of *that*, May? Isn't that a turn-up for the books?'

It certainly was. The blood drummed in May's ears. Who on earth was it who had asked for her hand in marriage? No one she could remember meeting had made any kind of over-ture towards her – and, intriguingly, the crest had most definitely been foreign.

'Who is it who wants to marry me, Papa?' She was filled with such hope she could hardly get the words past her lips, for it had to be someone uncaring of the fact that she had no dowry, and who was indifferent to her semi-royal status.

'It is someone who will most certainly have your Aunt Queen's approval and who, because of his nationality, has my approval also.'

'Yes, Papa. But please. A name.'

The Duke of Teck smoothed his hand across the heavy cream-coloured paper of the impressively crested letter. 'He is a German prince, May. Ernst Gunther, Duke of Schleswig-Holstein.'

She stared at him blankly. Among all the vast ramifications of European royalty, it was a name totally unknown to her.

Seeing her bewilderment, her father said helpfully, 'Ernst Gunther is the Kaiser's brother-in-law. It is a very suitable match, Pussy-cat.'

'And he is a nephew of Uncle Christian's,' her mother said. 'Dolly tells me you danced with him at Marie-Louise's birthday party.'

As fast as they had been raised, May's hopes crashed and died. She now knew who Ernst Gunther was. He was the uninspiring dance partner who had spoken not a word to her, and who had smelled unpleasantly of pear drops. If she accepted his proposal, she would no longer be an outsider in the royal European family circle, for she would become an integral part of Kindred Spirit Willy's family life. Empress Dona would be her sister-in-law. She would have a home of her own, probably several of them. Her financial future – and her parents' financial future – would be secure. In all likelihood she would have children.

But for all of these blessings she would pay a very high price. She would live out her life with a partner she didn't love. There would be marital intimacies to be endured with a man she found repellent.

She remembered the passion in Hélène's voice when she had said that she and Eddy loved each other so very much they were willing to do anything – anything at all – in order that they could marry.

It was how she wanted to feel some day about someone; and she wasn't going to settle for anything less. She pushed her chair away from the table and rose unsteadily to her feet. 'Please thank Prince Ernst for his proposal, Papa, and tell him it is one I will not be accepting.'

And ignoring her parents' stunned disbelief, well aware that she had turned down the only marriage proposal she was ever likely to receive, May walked from the room, her only consolation being her certainty that she had made the right decision.

Chapter Eighteen

'I want to know everything that happened in detail, right from when, having acted on your suggestion, Eddy and Hélène spoke to Granny Queen themselves.'

Alicky and May were seated in a quiet corner of Windsor Castle's gardens. It had been a long time since they'd had the opportunity to exchange news and gossip face-to-face and even though they had kept in touch with each other regularly by letter, Alicky wanted a verbal account of Eddy and Hélène's year-long battle to be able to marry.

'But why?' May was mystified. 'You already know the final outcome.'

'Yes, and you've been very good at keeping me up to date on all the family news, but it's a lot different being told what happened, from simply reading about what happened. What was it Eddy and Hélène said that changed Granny Queen's mind?'

It was a scorching hot day and even though they had sought a patch of shade beneath a tree, both of them had their parasols open. May adjusted hers on her shoulder a little more comfortably.

'According to Eddy, they went in to see her hand-in-hand, and he told the Queen very directly that they were devoted to each other, that they wished to marry and hoped she would help them.'

'And all this after she had told his father that such a marriage was absolutely impossible?'

'Yes.'

'Goodness.' Alicky was deeply impressed. 'Whoever would have thought Eddy would have so much backbone? I doubt if even Granny Queen's prime minister would have the nerve to persist in such a way, after first having received a very definite royal refusal. And so was it then that Granny Queen changed her mind about things?'

'No. She only changed her mind about consulting the government when Hélène said she would forsake her religion and become a Protestant if, in doing so, it meant she and Eddy could marry.'

'I thought that very extreme of her.' Alicky could be annoyingly self-righteous at times. 'Totally committed as I am to Nicky, I would never give up my religion for him. When Mama contacted me from beyond the grave, she asked me never to forget my confirmation vows and it is something I will never, ever do, and Nicky would never ask it of me.'

'Eddy didn't ask it of Hélène, but the poor girl was so desperate, it was the only thing she could think of that might enable them to marry.'

'I still wouldn't have done it. Being a Lutheran is far too important to me.'

Having known Alicky for so long, May knew there was no give in her at all, once she had taken a stance on something. She also knew, from Alicky's letters to her, that since her visit to St Petersburg, when she had decided that Nicky was the love of her life, there had been no opportunity for the two of them to meet again, and that no formal question of their marrying had ever been broached. If it *was* broached, Alicky being Lutheran when Nicky was Russian Orthodox would – unless Alicky was willing to adopt Russian Orthodoxy – be just as much of a stumbling block to their marrying, as Hélène's Roman Catholicism had been, when it had come to her and Eddy wanting to marry.

Deciding that nothing would be achieved by pointing this out to Alicky, May went on, 'And although the Prime Minister still found objections to raise, permission might have been granted, but when Hélène's father was told of what it was she was intending to do, he said the idea was impossible and that he wouldn't give his consent to a marriage made under those conditions. And under French law, Hélène can't marry without his permission until she's twenty-five.'

'And so Hélène went to Rome and threw herself at the Pope's feet?'

'And came away from the Vatican utterly defeated. Eddy had proposed that he relinquish his succession to the throne, marry Hélène, who would still remain a Catholic – all on the understanding that any children they had would be brought up Protestant and would retain their rights of succession. The Pope utterly vetoed the idea of children of a mixed marriage being brought up Protestant, and so that was the end of all their hopes. On her return to England, Hélène broke off their engagement and her parents have taken her abroad. I don't think they'll return with her until Eddy has reconciled himself to a royal duty marriage with someone of the Queen's choosing – something he now has no option but to do.' With difficulty, she kept her relief that Eddy wouldn't be marrying Hélène from showing in her voice.

'Poor Hélène, and poor Eddy.' Alicky's sympathy was genuine. 'It's a Georgie-and-Julie-Stoner scenario all over again.'

From where they were seated they could see Marie-Louise

and her recently acquired fiancé, Prince Aribert of Anhalt, strolling arm-in-arm in their direction. Royal engagements were never lengthy and their wedding, which was to take place in a few days' time in Windsor Castle's chapel, was the reason Alicky and family from Denmark and Germany were already gathered there. Alicky was to be one of the bridesmaids and, before Marie-Louise and Aribert came within hearing distance, she said fiercely, 'I hate being a bridesmaid. You're so lucky not always having to be one.'

'No, I'm not.' That Alicky could be crassly unperceptive, as well as self-righteous, was something May had long ago got used to. 'Not when the reason I don't get asked is because no one wants an unmarried twenty-four-year-old following them down the aisle.'

'I would. When I marry Nicky, I *definitely* want you as one of my bridesmaids. And my marriage to Nicky will be a love match. Ernie says that although Marie-Louise is in love with Aribert, he doesn't think Aribert is in love with Marie-Louise – and Ernie should know, because Aribert is a close friend of his. Not that Ernie had anything to do with arranging the marriage. It was Kindred Spirit Willy who did the arranging. Marie-Louise's father and Willy's wife's father are brothers, and I think Willy enjoyed trumping Granny Queen in the family matchmaking stakes.'

Because of living so close to Windsor, May and her family didn't stay at the castle, but they did spend most days there, as her parents wanted to seize every opportunity of meeting up with their German relations. Frank was quite naturally spoken of, but only in the sense of what a pity it was that, because of his language studies abroad, he was unable to attend the wedding. To May's intense relief, Ernst Gunther wasn't there, either.

'Poor Ernst is suffering from ear trouble,' Marie-Louise's

mother said to May. 'It's so disappointing, as I understand he is looking for a wife and this would have been such a wonderful opportunity for him to cast his eyes over any still-unmarried members of the family.'

Eddy was duty-bound to put in an appearance at the activities leading up to the wedding, but at each event, with dark shadows beneath his eyes and looking ill, he arrived as late as possible and left as early as possible, speaking to no one he didn't absolutely have to speak to, not even May.

Georgie, on the other hand, was in great spirits, constantly at Missy's side.

'Missy is sixteen in October,' Ducky said, seeking May out as she always did at family get-togethers. 'I've never seen anyone so optimistically heading towards calamitous disappointment as Georgie. Even if Missy *was* interested in him as prospective husband material – which she isn't – Mama would never agree to her marrying him. She has no high opinion of any of Pa's side of the family. The only comfort she's ever taken from marrying into it is that, being the only daughter of a tsar, she outranks so many of Granny Queen's brood and has jewels even more fabulous than theirs. I think I'm going to shock everyone now by lighting up a cigarette in public. They're Sobranie Black Russians. Do you want one?'

May had been smoking ever since her father had introduced her to the habit when she'd been eighteen, but she had no intention of smoking in public.

'No thanks, Ducky,' she said as Ducky lit up with practised ease. 'So who is it your mother has eyes on, as a prospective husband for Missy?'

'Anyone who is Russian will do, Cousin Nicky preferably, for then Missy will one day be an empress. However, Ma says there's little chance of her marrying Nicky, as Russian royals aren't allowed to marry first cousins. She does have someone else up her sleeve though. Nando Hohenzollern. If Missy marries Nando, she'll be Queen of Romania when his uncle, King Carol dies, and for some reason the thought quite pleases Ma.'

The wedding went off without a hitch. Eight bridesmaids followed Marie-Louise down the aisle – none of them a day older than her. Granny Queen wore her habitual black bombazine and if she was miffed that the groom wasn't one of her choosing, she didn't allow any displeasure to show. As always when Willy was in her company, she made a great fuss of him, for although his behaviour often caused him to be in her bad books – and he'd been in them for several days, when she had been told of the part he had played in Marie-Louise and Aribert's engagement – he was also her firstborn grandchild and, to lots of people's irritation, she was never displeased with him for long.

Willy and Dona were combining their presence at the wedding with a state visit. Since he'd become Kaiser, there was always tension where Willy's visits to England were concerned, for his mood and temper could never be counted on. He was either full of hearty bonhomie or explosive indignation at some imagined slight. He always thought he knew everything, and whereas his ministers rarely summoned up the nerve to tell him he was often wrong – and his wife never did – his family weren't so intimidated. And when they weren't, sparks flew.

On this visit, taking centre-stage as the person responsible for the matchmaking that had resulted in the wedding, and having enjoyed enthusiastic cheers and shouts of 'Good Old Willy!' and 'God bless the Kaiser!' on his carriage rides through London's flag-bedecked streets, Willy, to his family's relief, was full of goodwill to all men.

On the evening of the wedding, when the dancing began, Willy came up to May and said, 'I'd like the chance of a private word about the Ernst Gunther debacle, and the only way of managing one is if we take to the floor.'

In a state of high tension, May allowed him to lead her out onto the floor. For a man who only had the use of his right arm, Willy was a surprisingly good dancer and, as he skilfully ensured they were always as far away from other dancers as it was possible to get, he said, 'Lord knows that, for your own sake, I didn't want to see you married to my *Dummkopf* of a brother-in-law, May, but by refusing his proposal, you caused me to be at the receiving end of huge domestic tantrums.'

'Why on earth?' It wasn't at all what she had been expecting and she almost missed a step as they negotiated a far corner of the ballroom.

'Because of you not being *ebenbürtig*.'

'But I didn't accept Ernst Gunther's proposal! Surely Dona should have been pleased that I wasn't going to become her sister-in-law, not having tantrums about it.'

Willy snorted with laughter. 'But don't you see, May? Dona's indignation was caused by someone not of equal birth receiving a marriage proposal from her precious brother and then having the effrontery to turn him down. God in heaven! I thought the insult was going to be the death of her!'

May didn't share his amusement. As far as she was concerned, it was Dona's response to her having rejected Ernst Gunther's proposal that was the real insult.

'Truth to tell, Kindred Spirit May,' Willy continued, 'Dona may be a good woman, but she is also a very difficult one. No one knows what I have to put up with. My dear friend, Phili zu Eulenburg, thinks me a saint.'

May was tempted to respond that Phili zu Eulenburg was

the only person in the world who could possibly think so, but thought better of it.

Twelve years ago on the beach at Osborne, she, Willy and Alicky had shared confidences about their feelings of never truly fitting into the family, and they had done so in a way they had never done with anyone previously or, she was certain, since.

Alicky had declared that their conversation that afternoon had made them Kindred Spirits, a fact sealed by the blood-pact they had made. The surprising results of her childish play-acting had been a long-standing friendship between her and Alicky, and whenever she met up with Willy – which was far more rarely – he always referred to her as 'Kindred Spirit May' and was as informal with her as he had been that day at Osborne. She never forgot, though, that he was the German Emperor, and that liberties with his dignity would end their friendship in a flash.

His last words as the music came to an end were, 'Nicky Romanov wants to marry Alicky. It's a match I'm in favour of. I'd like the future Empress of Russia to be a German. However, Nicky's parents aren't in favour of it and are doing all they can to take his mind off her. The latest distraction they have put in his path is Mathilde Kschessinska, a ballerina with the Russian Imperial Ballet.'

Alicky's letter to May that July contained no reference to Mathilde Kschessinska, but even though it was now two years since Alicky's last meeting with Nicky in St Petersburg, her letters were still full of how frequently he wrote to her, and of how certain she was that they were destined for each other.

Eddy's Hussar regiment was now stationed in Dublin and, after several months' official leave, he left England in August to resume his military duties in Ireland. Looloo, Toria, Maudie and May all missed him, but only May was unable to voice quite how much.

In September, May's industrious round of charity work continued. She organized the sorting of several hundred items being sent in to the Needlework Guild and arranged for their distribution. She made weekly visits to hospitals and orphanages, and she helped out on an almost daily basis at the many soup kitchens that her mother sponsored. On top of that, she also continued acting as her mother's lady-in-waiting, accompanying her to an industrial exhibition in the East End that Princess Mary Adelaide opened; to a function at Finsbury in aid of factory girls; and to a concert given in order to raise money for soldiers' widows.

In October, May and her mother spent a few days with her mother's close friend, Lady Wolverton, whose home, Coombe Wood, was at Kingston-on-Thames and near enough to White Lodge that travelling to it was no hardship, and yet far enough away to make a pleasant change.

Sitting around the breakfast table, making plans for the day, they were interrupted by Lady Wolverton's butler. 'Forgive the interruption, Your Ladyship,' he said apologetically, 'but a letter from the Queen has just this minute arrived from Balmoral for Her Highness Princess Mary Adelaide.'

'A letter for me?' May's mother's knife and fork fell with an unladylike clatter onto her plate. 'From Balmoral?'

That the Queen had written to her at Coombe Wood, instead of waiting until she was again at home at White Lodge, indicated that the letter's contents were of unusual importance, and she practically snatched the letter from the butler's tray.

Within seconds of opening it, a hot flush flooded her cheeks and she pressed a hand to where, beneath a mountain of flesh, she assumed her heart to be. 'Oh, my goodness, May! The

Queen is asking that Dolly accompany you on a ten-day visit to Balmoral. For a *private* visit!'

It was such an unlikely request that May's immediate reaction was bewilderment. Informal family get-togethers took place at Osborne House. More formal get-togethers took place at Windsor. No get-togethers of any kind took place at Balmoral. When the Queen was in residence there – which she was every year from late summer to early winter – she kept very much to herself. Invitations for family to join her at Balmoral were virtually unheard of.

She was suddenly gripped by the fear that the only possible reason for the invitation was that the Queen was angry at her having rejected Prince Ernst Gunther's marriage proposal and wished to see her, to tell her how foolishly she believed May had behaved.

'What reason is given for the invitation, Mama?' Knots of tension had formed in the pit of her stomach. 'There must be one. Is it about the marriage proposal I turned down?'

'Goodness, no! She says only that she would like to get to know you a little better. This could be the beginning of Aunt Queen taking a much greater interest in you, May – something I have been hoping for, for a long time. I must write and accept, without a moment's delay. Do you think my not being asked to accompany you and Dolly was just a little forgetfulness? Perhaps I should include a delicate reminder about the omission?'

'If Aunt Queen didn't include Mama in the invite she sent, it was because she had no wish for Mama to accompany us,' Dolly said when, back home at White Lodge, May had been able to talk to him about the oddity of the invitation. 'It's true that invites to Balmoral are as rare as gold dust, but there was a time when Alicky was invited there quite often.'

'That was when Aunt Queen was trying to bring about a marriage between Alicky and Eddy.'

'Perhaps your having received a marriage proposal from Ernst Gunther – and having turned it down – has brought home to Aunt Queen that if she wants to continue her passion for matchmaking, her next project should be finding a husband for you?'

'But is she likely even to attempt that, when I'm not of equal birth? Perhaps she is simply going to say that I had an opportunity to marry and that, as another opportunity is unlikely to come my way, I should resign myself to spinsterhood and make the best of it.'

'And if that's the case?'

'Then it will be the perfect opportunity for me to tell her that, since Ernst Gunther's unwelcome marriage proposal, I have given a great deal of thought about my future and I have decided to do something I have longed to do for a long, long time.' There was a determined set to her chin and her eyes had narrowed in deadly seriousness.

'And what is that?' Dolly asked, hoping to goodness that she wasn't thinking of entering a convent.

'I'm going to live in Florence. The friends I still have there – friends like Belinda Light – will make me very welcome. And in Florence no one will speak the hateful *ebenbürtig* word to me ever again.'

Chapter Nineteen

Willy returned home from his state visit deeply disgruntled. Visits to his English family always unsettled him. One half of him – the English half – longed with fevered intensity to be accepted by his English relations as if, as well as having an English mother, he had been born there. The other half of him – the Prussian half – wanted nothing more than to hammer home to them how superior and powerful he, and the country of which he was Emperor, was.

He was, after all, far more powerful than his grandmother. She had to pay heed to her ministers. Since the day he had been proclaimed Emperor, Willy had never paid heed to anyone. Not even to Bismarck, a statesman the world held in deep respect and whom, with a click of his fingers, Willy had sacked when the Chancellor had overstepped the mark by insisting that Willy pursue a policy he was opposed to. Since then everyone in a high ministerial position had been recommended to him by Phili, and none of them had ever taken such an unforgivable liberty.

None of them, however, felt about England as he did. Damn it all, he *loved* England. His earliest memory was of being a toddler at Osborne and of being swung in a napkin by his grandfather, Prince Albert.

If only Albert hadn't died when he had still been a child, what a team they would have become! His German grandfather would have understood him. He would have made sure that his English family gave Willy the love and respect he deserved. And more than anything else, love and respect was what he craved from his English relations. His grandmother loved him of course, as he did her, but she didn't show respect to him, by coming to him for political advice. And there were times when he felt she was sorely in need of such advice. On one recent occasion, when a French admiral had been a guest at Buckingham Palace, the band had played the 'Marseillaise'. To his absolute horror, as this most incendiary hymn to revolution and the overthrowing of kings and emperors was being played, his grandmother had not only risen respectfully to her feet, but had remained standing throughout it! Even the memory was enough to make Willy shudder.

Republican France had never been a friend of Germany's, and the last thing he wanted was England forming an alliance with France or, for that matter, forming an alliance with any country other than his own. It had to be England and Germany or – as Germany already had a triple alliance with Austria– Hungary and Italy – it had to be England, Germany, Austria–Hungary and Italy. It was something he didn't have a single doubt about. Any cosying up of England to France smacked of disloyalty, and yet Uncle Bertie – England's next king – spent more time in France than he did in England.

At the thought of Bertie, Willie struggled not to hurl the first precious object that came to hand against a wall. His forty-nine-year-old uncle was too urbane, too sure of himself, too easy in his own skin. He could charm the birds off the trees – and anyone he wanted into his bed. Willie loathed him.

He didn't loathe Eddy and Georgie, for neither of them took after their father, in terms of personality. Although one trait Eddy did share with his father was being effortlessly charming and attractive to the opposite sex. Other than that, Eddy was too lacking in the kind of dominant forcefulness that, in Willy's estimation, any heir to a throne should have.

As for Georgie . . . He could be peppery-tempered, although he'd more sense than to be so with Willy, and on a recent occasion he had magnanimously awarded Georgie the Order of the Black Eagle, the highest order of chivalry that Prussia possessed. The trouble with Georgie was that he was dim and had no intellectual interests. All he was interested in was shooting and stamp-collecting. Willy was anything but dim, and he had a passion for all kinds of technological advances. A German designer and engineer had recently discussed with him his vision of a petrol-engine airship. Willy hadn't been able to get the prospect of such a glorious machine out of his head and had enthusiastically begun showing drawings of the proposed airship to Georgie. Even for politeness's sake, Georgie hadn't shown the slightest flicker of interest.

On many of his trips to England – visits that were merely family ones – Dona didn't accompany him. Nothing about England appealed to her and, for Dona, their state visit to England had been a duty, not a pleasure.

It had also been the scene of one of their most bitter marital rows. And as was the case with most of their rows, it had been about the amount of time he spent with Phili.

'But he is my best and closest friend,' Willy had protested, wanting to tear his hair out with frustration. 'Of course I spend time with him! God in heaven, who else would I spend time with?'

'With me. *With me!*' she had screamed, pummelling him in the chest, tears streaming down her face. 'I am your wife! *I* should be your best friend.'

He was an autocrat; an emperor who ruled the largest

country in Europe with an iron fist; a man who had sacked, without a second thought, the Chancellor who had forged a score of tiny weak principalities and duchies into a strong empire. And yet faced with his out-of-control wife, Willy was at a loss as to how to deal with her. He could hardly spell out to her that friendship – any friendship – had to have a common basis; that she bored him nearly to the point of insanity and that, in contrast, his dear, artistic and multi-talented Phili never bored him.

Phili was a poet, a playwright, a composer and a singer. The hours he spent turning the pages for Phili as, accompanying himself on the piano, he sang Nordic ballads of his own composition were hours that Willy could only describe as sublime. How could he ever feel such mental and spiritual unity with Dona, who didn't have an artistic or intellectual bone in her body? The answer was that he couldn't.

It mystified him that Dona couldn't see how her scenes and tantrums only resulted in his wanting to spend even less time with her, not more. He couldn't imagine Ella behaving in such a way, no matter what the provocation; or the calm, cool and collected May Teck. All in all, he felt himself very badly done by. So much so that the mask of all-powerful arrogant and boastful confidence behind which he permanently hid was, during rows about Phili, in danger of slipping – and he couldn't let that happen. Not when he was with Dona. Not when he was with anyone.

At the moment Phili was at Liebenberg, his family estate in Rhine-Westphalia. Reliving his last hideous scene with Dona had done Willy no good at all and, in desperate need of Phili's reassuring presence, he decided that Liebenberg was where he needed to be without a second's delay.

'Westphalia!' he roared to his clutch of long-suffering and always present aides-de-camp. 'We leave instantly.' He slammed his fist down on his desk and ink-pots clattered and pens rolled. 'Don't just stand there, dolts! Action! Action!'

Not for one second did he expect to find Phili alone at Liebenberg. Phili was far too popular for that to be likely. Phili would be surrounded by friends – always male – who, like him, all regarded themselves as being artistically inclined. Their nickname was 'the Liebenberg Circle', and all Willy's moments of happiness and relaxation occurred when he was counted amongst their number. He relished the applause the Circle gave to the practical jokes he loved playing; jokes that were always, of course, played by him, and never on him. He loved the masculine horseplay that was indulged in, and the hilarious, near-to-the-knuckle skits they all took part in. But first, of course, he and Phili would have time together privately; time to talk about matters the rest of the Circle were not privy to; time for Willy to bare his heart to Phili about the misery of his married life.

'She is killing me with her tantrums and her demands!' he said, a break in his voice and on the verge of tears. 'Truly, Phili, I do not think the woman is in her right mind.'

'Then if she isn't, my dear Kaiser, perhaps a sanatorium?'

'But the children? She is so kind and good to the children. If she was to go into a sanatorium, the children would never forgive me.'

Phili nodded, knowing the real reason his suggestion hadn't been taken up was that Wilhelm would have been unable to cope with the shame of having his wife publicly branded as mentally ill – especially as they both knew she wasn't. In public he spoke of her as being the most wonderful of wives, someone who made it possible for him to carry the tremendous burden of empire. When visiting a young men's army corps in Bonn, an army corps he had belonged to as a university student, he had told them that the smile their Empress had bestowed on them had ennobled their lives.

That she had never ennobled his was something to which only Phili was privy.

'Her jealous rages over our friendship utterly consume her,' Willy said, sinking deeper and deeper into self-pity. 'She flies into hysterical rages over the most trivial matters. She makes terrible scenes when I travel around Germany without her, but how can I take her with me? I wouldn't have a moment's peace! She is quite capable of weeping through an entire night.'

'Then my advice,' Phili said firmly, 'is that you lock the doors of all your private rooms against her, so that in the Marble Palace at Potsdam, or the Charlottenburg Palace in Berlin, or in any of the other royal palaces, she cannot gain access to you. That way, perhaps, you will be spared her senseless rages and undignified tantrums. And now, before we join the companions who share our individuality, shall I play some soothingly lovely music of my own composition?'

Later, while Willy and other members of the Circle rocked with laughter at one of their number cavorting to music from *Swan Lake* in tights and a pink tutu, one of those watching took Phili to one side and said, 'How long is it to be before the Kaiser realizes that everyone here, whose company he so enjoys and is so much at home with, is deviant? For how much longer do we have to be careful not to bluntly speak the word "homosexual"?'

'And bring home to him his repressed sexuality? Not ever, I hope, and so the pretence of jolly good but not always clean fun and romps, which he so enjoys, must be kept up, without him ever being aware of the undertones. There is a prudish side to our dear Kaiser that would never allow him to face up to what he would regard as the shameful truth about himself. If faced with it, he would sever all ties and the political power that we now enjoy would be gone in the twinkling of an eye. I would no longer be his minister at Munich. Moltke would no longer be Chief of the General Staff. Bülow would no longer be Head of the Foreign Office. And you, dear Bernard, would not be a Secretary of State.'

As he finished speaking there were fresh roars of laughter, this time obligatory ones. Willy had just cut through his Reich Chancellor's braces with a penknife, and Caprivi's trousers lay humiliatingly around his ankles.

Phili sighed. Showing hilarity at the Kaiser's schoolboy jokes was compulsory, even for the victim. Overall it was, though, a small price to pay for high political office, and he had the comfort of knowing that not only had he never been the butt of one of the Kaiser's practical jokes, but he was certain he never would be. The Kaiser loved him far too much ever to want to offend him. That he loved Phili more than he loved anyone was a declaration he'd had the satisfaction of receiving from the Kaiser's own ruby-red lips.

Chapter Twenty

NOVEMBER 1891, BALMORAL

May had never known her mother to be as flustered as she was the morning she and Dolly left for Balmoral.

'You must remember,' she said for the umpteenth time, as she and the Duke accompanied them to Euston station where they would catch the night train to Scotland, 'Aunt Queen lives very quietly and to a very strict routine. And she doesn't like noise. You must move around the castle like little mice. And she keeps early hours. You, Dolly, must be sure to remember that. Oh, my goodness! What on earth can be Victoria's reason for wishing to see you, May? I do wish I knew. I shall be in a frenzy until you are able to let me know.'

'The reason Aunt Queen wishes to spend time with May,' Dolly said, 'is the one she set out so clearly in her letter. She wishes to get to know May a little better.'

Privately their mother thought this might well be true. However, she didn't want it to be true. Her precious daughter had never been given one of the heart-to-heart talks that her cousin had always gone out of her way to have with grand-daughters and grandnieces when they were approaching marriageable age. At twenty-four, May was, of course, way past the age when such talks usually took place. All the same, try as she might she couldn't help fervently hoping that the reason for May's summons to Balmoral was because Victoria had a husband in mind for her.

The question most tormenting her was, if that was indeed the reason, who was the intended bridegroom? In not accepting Prince Ernst, May had shown she was unwilling to marry for marrying's sake and was only prepared to marry someone with whom she felt herself to be compatible, and for whom she felt the kind of affection in which, once married, love and respect could grow.

They reached the station in the evening darkness. Beneath the dull yellow glow of gas lamps, its cavernous interior was a hive of deafening activity. Porters dashed hither and thither with trolleys loaded high with luggage; departing passengers thronged the concourse; cloth-capped men hustled wives and children in the direction of third-class carriages; top-hatted men accompanied by elegantly dressed wives heading unerringly for first-class carriages. News-boys were hollering that they had papers for sale. A shawl-wrapped, toothless woman was selling flowers. A man was shouting that he had roasted chestnuts for sale.

To May's vast relief they didn't have to attempt to thread their way through the throng, for the station manager, wearing the gold-braided uniform he always wore when greeting arriving or departing royalty, was waiting to meet them. Within seconds a clutch of railway personnel had cleared a pathway towards the carriage reserved permanently for royal use.

'Be sure you remember to wrap up warm all the time you are there, May,' their mother said anxiously, as the door to May and Dolly's carriage was closed. 'Dolly, make quite sure she does so. It's so easy to catch pneumonia at Balmoral. I've only been a guest there once and I thought I was going to die of the cold. Even in the depths of winter, Aunt Queen insists on windows being left open. She believes it to be healthy, and maybe it is, for her. It certainly isn't for anyone else.'

A whistle blew. As the train began moving slowly out of the station and final goodbyes were waved and kisses blown, she called out in last-minute agitation, 'And don't forget both to be on your very best behaviour! The next few days could be so important. So very, very important.'

'Poor Ma,' Dolly said, when they were finally so far out of the station that they were able to close the window and make themselves comfortable. 'If her hopes – and we both know what her hopes are – don't come to fruition in a satisfactory way, are you still set on scandalizing everyone by making a life for yourself in Florence?'

'Yes.' May's ankle-length mauve coat had a fur collar that had been dyed to match, as had the fur hat she was wearing and the muff she was carrying. She laid the muff down on the seat beside her. 'What is the worst thing that can happen to me, if I do?'

'Well, for starters, Aunt Queen will never see or speak to you again.'

'Which is something I will be sad about, but not so sad I'm going to change my mind.'

'Ma will miss you.'

'And I will miss her – but she adores Florence, and I'm sure she'll begin visiting it for months on end once I am living there.'

'Maybe, but how can you afford it?' he persisted. 'Frank's latest gambling debts have got Pa and Ma strapped for cash again.'

'I'll be able to live in a modest way on the money Mama's mother left me, and at least I will be living life on my own terms.'

'With staff and a chaperone?'

'With a small staff and a chaperone companion.'

Coming from a sister he had always regarded as being wonderfully level-headed, it was a project so pie-in-the sky as to be madness. Dolly was certain it would never come to pass, for although an elderly woman might get away with living in such a way, for a single young woman of any respectable class to do so was unheard of. And May wasn't just any single respectable young woman. She was royalty, even if, like him, only second-class royalty.

Deciding it was best to let the matter drop, he changed the subject.

'Ma's secret hopes as to why your company is wanted at Balmoral might well be valid, May. Perhaps Aunt Queen is up to her matchmaking tricks again.'

'Why would she be, when she still has granddaughters who aren't yet matched up? Ducky is approaching marriageable age. Toria is still spectacularly single and, since Frank treated her so abominably, so is dear Maudie.'

'Toria is still single because Aunt Alix is totally opposed to her marrying anyone. She's chronically possessive about all her children – and that includes Eddy and Georgie. Georgie once showed me one of her letters to him, when he was serving aboard a ship in the Mediterranean, and it started off, "To my dear darling little Georgie boy." Where Toria is concerned, Aunt Alix doesn't want her ever to leave home. She wants her as her permanent companion, just as Aunt Queen keeps Beatrice as her permanent companion.'

'But at least Aunt Bea is her permanent *married* companion.'

'Only because Henry agreed to Aunt Queen's demand that he and Beatrice make their married home with her. And to do that, the poor devil had to give up his career in the Prussian Hussars. Aunt Queen,' he added darkly, 'can be viciously selfish when she wants to be.'

* * *

Later, when they were having a meal in a private dining carriage lit by oil lamps – the Queen allowed no gas lighting in any of her carriages – and furnished with a deep-piled wine-red carpet and matching silk-covered dining chairs, Dolly said, 'Doesn't something strike you as odd about this invite to Balmoral?'

'*Everything* about it strikes me as odd. Which aspect of oddness are you thinking of?'

'The apparent urgency. It's now the first week of November. The Queen's routine is to be at Osborne from the beginning of July until the end of August, Balmoral from the beginning of September to the beginning of November, and then Windsor until well after Christmas.'

'And?' May was unable to see what he was getting at.

'And as it is already the first week of November, she would, in normal circumstances, be back at Windsor within a week – two weeks at the most. If she wants to spend time with you, why is she not doing so somewhere that is only a hop and jump away from White Lodge? Why the urgency about seeing you immediately, when she is over six hundred miles away?'

May had no answer. It was something she hadn't thought of, and Dolly was right, it *was* odd.

In the end she said, 'I expect it was a whim and, when it occurred to her, she sent the message to Mama without thinking it through.'

Something else occurred to Dolly, but he didn't mention it until, an hour or so later, May told him she was going to bed. 'When Aunt Queen was hoping to make a match between Alicky and Eddy, and when she summoned Alicky to Balmoral, didn't she also invite Eddy at the same time?'

'Yes. I think she was hoping an engagement announcement could be made while they were still with her.'

'Well, this is just a thought, Sis. Max of Baden is on a visit to England. If we find him in residence when we arrive at

Balmoral, it can only be that Ma's hopes are about to be fulfilled and you have been invited so that he can look you over.'

'And the moon is made of green cheese. Goodnight, Dolly. And stop speculating. It's no help whatsoever.'

Despite the gentle rocking motion of the train and the rhythm of its wheels on the track, May didn't sleep well. Prince Maximilian of Baden was a very different kettle of fish from Prince Ernst of Schleswig-Holstein. She knew of him only by repute, but everything she had heard about him was encouraging. He was somewhere in his mid-twenties and had studied law and politics at Leipzig University. She had once overheard her Uncle Bertie say that if Willy had a brain in his head, he would make Max his Reich Chancellor, which meant there were no doubts as to Max's intelligence and ability; and she had heard Toria say that Max was handsome enough to die for.

Could Dolly's assumption possibly be correct? Was her summons to Balmoral in order that Max of Baden could meet her to see if they were compatible? And if so, why her? Why not Toria or Maudie? If he married Toria or Maudie, his father-in-law would one day be King of the United Kingdom and Emperor of India. Why, then, would he be allowing Aunt Queen to steer him in the direction of May Teck, who could bring nothing to a union but second-class royal status and a history of shameful family bankruptcy?

The last question she posed herself, as the train steamed further and further north, was whether she would accept Max's proposal if Dolly's reading of the situation was correct? Her head told her that out of respect for her parents' happiness, she should accept, but her heart didn't sing at the thought and when she finally fell into a troubled sleep, her dreams were not of Max of Baden, but of Eddy: heartbroken over Hélène, and miles away across the Irish Sea, drilling his soldiers on a Dublin parade ground.

The next morning they were met at Ballater station by a kilt-clad Henry of Battenberg and his equerry. 'So very good to see the two of you again,' Henry said with friendly cheerfulness as he escorted them out of the station to where carriages were waiting. 'Shame about the weather. There's a sniff in the air that indicates snow could be coming. We've never been snowed in yet at Balmoral. We're usually well tucked up at Windsor before the first mid-November blizzards. However, there's always a first time for everything and, if there is, views of the castle and the countryside around it will be satisfyingly pretty.'

It was too late in the year for wild flowers to be seen, but the rolling hills covered in a haze of heather and thick copses of fir and pine, and mountains in the not-too-far distance, gave a wild, romantic feel to the landscape and May could well understand the Queen's great love for her Highland home.

'Are there any other guests at the castle this week, Henry?' Dolly asked, not wasting any time in resolving the question uppermost in both his mind and May's.

'No, and within a day or two of you and May returning home, the Royal Household will also be leaving. Balmoral is a feast for the eyes in September and October, when all the mauve Michaelmas daises in the castle gardens are out, but when October comes to an end it begins losing its charm. Any minute now you'll catch a glimpse of the castle's turrets. We're nearly there.'

May's appreciation of beauty was deeply satisfied as, not long afterwards, their carriage rounded a bend in the track and, beyond the glittering gleam of the River Dee, the castle lay in front of them, its white stone glistening in the pale

November sunshine, its fairy-tale turrets, towers and battle-ments rising against a background of steep pine-covered hills, a mountain peak soaring wild and romantic in the near distance.

'It's spectacular,' she said to Henry. 'And much bigger than I'd expected. 'I'd imagined it as being smaller; almost on the scale of White Lodge.'

Henry shot her his attractive Battenberg smile. 'The original Scottish castle was very wee, as they say in Scotland. What you see in front of you is Prince Albert's rebuilt and far larger creation, and we need to be grateful to him. Comfortable amenities in the original castle would have been nil. Thanks to Albert, Balmoral is stuffed with water-closets and there are more than enough bathrooms.'

'I'm glad to hear it.' Dolly was thankful he could look forward to a hot bath after the long hours of travelling up from London. 'Am I going to be able to bag a stag while I'm here, Henry? A Balmoral stag would be a real feather in my cap.'

'Absolutely. In November, stalking is obligatory for male guests, as are kilts. You'll soon find yourself wearing one, even if you haven't brought one in your luggage.'

On arrival they were greeted by Beatrice, and by two of Beatrice and Henry's four young children.

'Mama will greet you in a little while, when you have had time to freshen up,' Beatrice said as a housekeeper whisked May's maid and Dolly's valet away and the luggage was taken care of. 'The children have been so looking forward to your arrival. Drino, Ena, say hello and shake hands nicely with Uncle Dolly and Aunt May.'

As five-year-old Alexander and four-year-old Ena shyly did as they were bid, May wondered why so many of Aunt Queen's tribe were christened with one name and then known only by a shortened version of it or a nickname, and of how bewildering to a child the habit of referring to members of the family as Aunt and Uncle was, when the relationship was one of distant cousinship.

'When you are rested, May, and when you have seen Mama, I'll take you on a visit to the nursery to see Leopold and baby Maurice,' Beatrice said, accompanying them to their rooms. 'They are both such little sweethearts, May. I'm sure you are going to utterly adore them.'

May had never understood the raptures so many women went into when confronted with a small mewling infant, much preferring children who were older and could be talked to. She knew, however, that this view wasn't one she could happily share with Beatrice, who had given birth to Maurice only weeks ago.

'Maurice is a very healthy little boy,' Beatrice said, answering the question that hovered over all of Aunt Queen's grandsons, adding with a new note in her voice – a note of anxiety – 'but Leopold is more . . . delicate. It is something we are hoping he will grow out of.'

'If he's a haemophiliac, it isn't something he's likely to grow out of,' Dolly said bluntly an hour later as they headed in the direction of the Queen's drawing room. 'This decor is a bit over-much, don't you think? Tartan, tartan everywhere. Tartan-patterned carpets, tartan-patterned curtains. I bet you anything that the chairs and sofas in the drawing room will be covered in tartan. What the Prime Minister must make of it all when he comes up here for his meetings with her, I can't imagine.'

May didn't respond. She was too nervous. Would Aunt Queen come straight out with whatever it was she wished to speak to her about, or would she keep her in suspense? And what if her nervousness was unnecessary and the Queen merely did want nothing more than to get to know her a little better?

The way she was greeted eased her nervousness, for immediately after she had risen from her curtsey to her, the Queen – who was scarcely five foot tall – stood on tiptoe, kissed her on both cheeks and said, 'What an elegant young lady you have become, May. I do hope you and Dolly had a pleasant journey. I have always enjoyed travelling on a train, although I prefer it if the train doesn't go too fast. If it does, I always send a message to the driver that he is to slow down.'

Her voluminous black silk dress was relieved by white lace at the neck and cuffs. Over her hair, which was worn in a bun, was a widow's white cap decorated with two satin streamers. With only minor variations, it was the way she had dressed ever since her beloved Albert had died. Frank had once joked – well out of her hearing – that she could easily be mistaken for an elderly and arthritic housemaid.

He was wrong, of course. Small, plump and plain as she was, Aunt Queen oozed imperial regality.

'In a moment we will go into the dining room for lunch, and then afterwards Henry will walk with Dolly to nearby Ballochbuie, where there is a cairn that marks his marriage to Beatrice.' She gave May a surprisingly shy smile. 'And I would like you to accompany me on my afternoon carriage ride, May. The Scottish air is so pure and invigorating that I go out once in the morning and again in the afternoon, no matter what the weather, for I find it very *erfrischend*.'

The carriage was a comfortable four-horse open one. With a plaid rug over their knees and without being accompanied by a lady-in-waiting, or by Beatrice, they set off, with May steeling herself for what she was certain was going to be one of Aunt Queen's matchmaking chats.

As they left the castle's grounds behind them, the Queen said, 'It was on just such a lovely late-autumn day over forty years ago that Albert and I first saw Balmoral – the original Balmoral, that is. We had often talked of buying a Highland home, and Lord Aberdeen had inherited Balmoral from his late brother and had no wish to keep it. When he asked if we might like to buy it from him, we immediately came north to view it. There was no train line then to Ballater from Aberdeen. It was horse-drawn carriages to Banchory, and then a change of horse and on to Aboyone. The nearer we drew to Balmoral, the prettier and prettier the countryside got, until at last we crossed the River Dee and looked upon the castle for the first time. We knew at once that it would become ours; that Balmoral had simply been *waiting* for us.'

She clasped her mittened hands together tightly in her lap. 'We were always so *happy* here. We rode ponies deep into the glens. We climbed the hills and Albert would spend days stalking stags with his ghillies, while I sat with my attendants and sketched and painted. Nowhere were we freer of the burden of royalty than here. Not even Osborne could match it. Albert said the glorious Highland scenery reminded him of the countryside around his beloved Coburg. As a family, we are all so very much more German than we are English. Unlike dear Willy, who is constantly torn between his German parentage and his English parentage, Albert was *all*-German, and how I loved him for being so. Although, like you, I was born at Kensington Palace, it is pure German blood that flows in my veins, and your blood is German, too. I know from your dear mama that you have always spent part of every year visiting relations in Mecklenburg-Strelitz and Württemberg and that you speak German fluently and love the country dearly.'

May was at a loss as to how to respond. Technically, of course, her blood *was* German, but she had never, ever *felt*

German. She thought of herself as being English through and through, and yet quite obviously this was not what the Queen wanted to hear.

'And I know you also speak French fluently and have more than a little Italian,' Victoria continued, saving May from having to think up a response that would be adequate and yet, at the same time, truthful. 'That is very admirable. All royalty should be fluent in as many languages as possible. Since Ella's marriage to Sergei, I regret very much that I have no Russian. However, all my children have excellent German, French and Italian. Bertie could speak all three languages fluently by the time he was six, and yet his children's French and German are deplorable, and Georgie and Eddy's Italian is next to non-existent. It is something I cannot understand at all.'

The horses broke into a trot and she continued, 'I believe you are an excellent secretary to your dear mama. Lady Wolverton tells me your mama's many charities benefit greatly from your clear-sighted input when committee meetings take place. Talents such as these mean that when you make a suitable marriage, you will be a very great support to your husband, and he will need such support, for the life of a royal prince can be a very stressful and lonely one. Now, look over there to the left, May. The peak you see is that of Lochnagar. A hike up its lower slopes is very invigorating and is an expedition you may well enjoy embarking on with Dolly and Henry later in the week.'

'And was that it?' Dolly asked when, after dinner, they were finally on their own. 'No hint as to which royal prince she could have been referring to?'

'No, but with all the emphasis on how German I was, and how I was able to speak German and had grown up visiting

Germany regularly, I can only assume you're right in thinking it's Max of Baden that Aunt Queen has in mind.'

'Then why aren't you punching the air? There isn't an unmarried princess in the family – or outside it, for that matter – who wouldn't happily accept a proposal of marriage from Max.'

'But I haven't met him yet. And if, when I meet him, I don't feel I will be able to live happily with him, then even if he does propose to me, I won't accept him. And no one – not even Aunt Queen – will persuade me to change my mind.'

For the next eight days there was no further hint that match-making plans were being made for May. The basic routine of the house never varied. The Queen breakfasted at ten and then went for a carriage drive, always taking May with her. Lunch was at two and then there was another obligatory carriage ride, the conversation never again touching on marriage, no matter how obliquely.

'Lord only knows how poor Henry survives the tedium,' Dolly said glumly as the days passed. 'I couldn't. I'm sick to death of going out on the hills with him, his equerry and half a dozen ghillies. By the end of the day I'm frozen to the marrow.'

Although Dolly was bored nearly out of his mind, May wasn't. She was fascinated by the diligent way the Queen attended to her red despatch boxes; by how state duty was carried out daily, even in the remote fastness of the Cairngorms. The house intrigued her as well. Nowhere was there a clear surface. Every desk, sideboard, occasional table and writing table held a galaxy of silver-framed family photographs. Cheek-by-jowl were bronze casts of small, chubby hands. One was of Beatrice's hand, made, according to its label, when she had been three. Another was of the childhood hand of Leopold,

Aunt Queen's youngest son, who had suffered from haemophilia and had died from it seven years earlier. Every wall was thick with antlers or paintings, and sometimes both. Everything made of wood had a thistle carved into it.

May would have loved to know what Thaddeus would have made of the glorious hotchpotch garishness. They hadn't exchanged letters in more than a year, but knowing how delighted he would be to receive a letter on Balmoral stationery, she had written to him during one long, empty afternoon when Dolly had been playing billiards with Henry and everyone else, apart from the Scottish household staff, had been resting.

The day before they were to return to London, the Queen announced that only May would accompany her on her afternoon carriage ride.

'This is it, May,' Dolly said, when no one was near enough to hear him. 'This is when the mystery will be over and we'll get to know who it is she has in mind for you.'

The weather next day was breezy and bitterly cold. 'It is,' the Queen announced as the carriage horses set off at a brisk trot, 'what the Scottish call a ve*rr*a raw day.'

She was suitably swathed in a black cloak of heavy warm wool, a black bonnet tied firmly beneath her chin. May had her coat collar up, her fur hat pulled over her ears and her gloved hands tucked deep inside her muff.

'I take all my guests on this particular carriage ride before they leave Balmoral,' the Queen continued. 'It gives glimpses of the memorial cairns that, as a family, we have built over the years. I am far too old and lame now to leave the carriage and climb up to them, for they have all, of course, been built on high crags, but I like to have sightings of them from the road. The first cairn we will come to is on the top of Craig Gowan and was built to celebrate our buying of the estate. I placed the first stone, then Albert laid one and then all the children laid a stone, in accordance with their ages. After that, everyone who had climbed up to the crag with us laid a stone. When the cairn was eight or nine feet high, Albert climbed to the top of it and, to cheers, my darling laid the last stone in place.'

Not for the first time May was struck at the intimate freeness of the Queen's reminiscences. When sharing her experience of seeing Albert for the first time she had said, as if she was a young girl sharing a close confidence, 'And I loved him at first sight. It was a *coup de foudre*, instant and undeniable, for Albert was more than handsome. Albert was *beautiful*.'

After Craig Gowan the next two cairns, Lenchen's and Louise's, were sited almost within sight of each other. 'Although the plaque says Helena, not Lenchen,' the Queen said. 'The German form of Helena would not have been suitable on a plaque such as this, which was built to mark her marriage to dear Christian.'

As the carriage rocked to a halt at the best viewpoint, she said, 'Christian is a prince of Schleswig-Holstein, and seeing his and Lenchen's cairn has reminded me that Prince Ernst of Schleswig-Holstein made a proposal of marriage to you a little while ago; a proposal that, to my very great surprise, you did not accept. Was your refusal because, as an only daughter, you had no wish to live so far away in Germany?'

May's tummy muscles tightened. She could let the Queen believe her assumption was correct, or she could tell her the truth. She took a deep, steadying breath. 'I had met Prince Ernst some time ago at Marie-Louise's birthday party and I . . . I felt no attraction for him and was sure we were not compatible. That was the reason I didn't accept his proposal.'

The Queen pursed her lips and was silent for so long that May was terrified she was going to be asked to step down from the carriage and walk all the way back to Balmoral.

Not until they had covered the short distance to where there was a glimpse of the cairn marking the marriage of Aunt Queen's fourth daughter, Louise, did the Queen say, 'Then, on reflection and considering your unfortunate position as a Serene Highness and your consequent lack of any previous royal marriage proposals, I think you showed great strength of character, May. And strength of character is always commendable.'

Once again there was no comment that May could suitably make, and she was deeply grateful when the Queen changed the subject and asked her what it was she had enjoyed best about her years of living in Florence.

'And it was then that the dear girl absolutely *blossomed*,' the Queen said later that evening to Beatrice. 'There was such enthusiasm in May's voice as she spoke of her visits to the Uffizi and the art-history classes she had attended, and she spoke of her preference for Donatello over Michelangelo in a way that has almost led me to think like her. As well as being clear-headed, sensible and possessing beautiful natural dignity, May is highly educated, has experience of living in a continental country – something I think is *so* important – and, above all, she is *cultured*. It is no wonder her dear mama praises her so highly.'

Beatrice laid her embroidery in her lap. 'So I take it your tentative wedding plans for her are tentative no longer, Mama?'

'Absolutely not. And if, when I pass on my opinion to the prospective bridegroom, he accepts my judgement, then I see no reason why dear May's engagement should not take place at the very latest by Christmas, and the wedding by Easter.'

Chapter Twenty-One

NOVEMBER 1891, LUTON HOO

'I wonder,' Dolly said, as their train steamed across the border into England, 'if we are likely to find Max of Baden waiting for us at Euston.'

May made a dismissive motion with her hand. Such a speculation was highly unlikely – and one she didn't even want to think about.

As it turned out, the only people waiting to greet them were their parents and their brother Alge, who, now seventeen, had just been accepted at the Royal Military College and looked, all of a sudden, enormously self-assured and grown-up.

Back home at White Lodge, May gave her parents a detailed account of what had happened at Balmoral and, like Dolly, her father immediately seized on the fact that the very eligible Max of Baden was currently in London.

'It is a very interesting coincidence, *nicht wahr?*'

'I don't think so, Papa.' May was tired from the journey, and tired of the subject. 'Aunt Queen may well have Max in mind for me, but if she has, I doubt if Max is aware of it. And if I'm wrong about that, then I'm not interested in a suitor who has spoken to Aunt Queen about his interest in me and yet has still not troubled to meet me.'

And on that deflating note, she excused herself from the table and went to bed.

At breakfast next morning she was greeted by the news that Maximilian of Baden's visit to London had been swiftly curtailed, as a close relative had died and he was, by now, already on his way back to Germany.

'And according to your Uncle Christian, who was with Max when he received the news, he left unfinished business behind him,' her father said, a meaningful tone in his voice. 'In two weeks' time, *Liebling*, he could well be back.'

May felt neither relief nor disappointment, but she did wish that, when talking to Aunt Queen about Florence, she had told her how much she would like to live there. As she wrote in her next letter to Alicky:

> *But I just didn't have the nerve, not when Aunt Queen had given lots of hints that my reason for being at Balmoral was so she could assess my suitability for whatever matchmaking plan she may be hatching. As it is, I have decided I have no wish to be party to an arranged marriage, for so few of them ever end happily.*

A little while later she began another letter, this time to Belinda Light, telling her of how she was thinking of returning to Florence with a chaperone-companion. She also asked if there was any likelihood of Belinda's aunt being able to make I Cedri available to her, if she was to do so, and she added:

> *Please tell your aunt that all this is in the strictest confidence, for as yet no one but you and Dolly is aware of my plans.*

* * *

For the next couple of weeks, acting as her mother's lady-in-waiting and secretary, May was grateful to be kept so busy. There was no reply from Belinda, but it was too soon to reasonably expect one. Neither was there any gossip to indicate Max of Baden was about to return to England and attend to what Christian had described as his 'unfinished business'.

What that unfinished business was no longer interested May, for she had made up her mind that if Max ever did propose to her, she was going to treat his proposal in exactly the same way as she had treated Prince Ernst's proposal. She was not going to accept it. How could she, when she felt about Eddy as she did? Her other resolution was that once the coming new year got into its stride, she was going to tell her parents what her plans were and, despite the avalanche of objections she knew she would meet, she was determined to go ahead with them.

Alicky's reply to her letter came quickly:

Dear Kindred Spirit,

I think you should think again, where Max of Baden is concerned. He is extremely eligible and is the number-one hope of lots of European princesses, so if it is Max that Granny Queen has in mind for you, don't reject him without seeing him, as you could well be making a very big mistake.

As for me, it is all horribly tragic, for Nicky's parents are absolutely opposed to his marrying me. They say I do not have the right qualities to be Russia's future Tsarina and want him to propose to Hélène of Orleans, who is still, as we know, desperately in love with Eddy. Nicky, of course, is going to do no such thing, but that isn't the worst of it. The worst of it is that even if his parents changed their mind and gave their permission for him to marry me, I WOULDN'T BE ABLE TO DO SO, for although Ella

*was able to marry Sergei without changing her religion
from Lutheran to Russian Orthodox, it was only because
Sergei isn't top of the list in the Romanov line of
succession. Nicky, of course, is. To marry him, I would
have to renege on all the solemn vows I made when I was
confirmed in the Lutheran Church and convert to Russian
Orthodoxy – AND BECAUSE OF MY PROMISE TO
MY LATE MAMA, THAT IS SOMETHING MY
CONSCIENCE WILL ABSOLUTELY NOT ALLOW
ME TO DO! Poor Nicky is heartbroken and I am
heartbroken, for truly, May, Nicky is the other half of my
soul.*

    Your unutterably wretched Kindred Spirit, Alicky

*PS: Kindred Spirit Willy has just announced that he has
made occult contact with the spirit of Frederick the Great. I
believe him, for the spirit world is all around us, although it
is only a privileged few who can make contact with it. Ernie
says Willy is certifiable, but I don't think he is, for, as you
know, I too often feel guided by unseen powers.*

It was a letter that troubled May, as she had become aware
that Alicky's religious zeal had begun verging on the extreme,
and she found the way Alicky talked of being guided by unseen
powers unhealthy and deeply unsettling.

At the end of November, May and her parents were invited
to a house party at Luton Hoo, in Bedfordshire. Their host
was Christian de Falbe, the Danish Minister at the Court of
St James's, and as Aunt Alix was Danish, a close family friendship had sprung up between the de Falbes and the Prince and
Princess of Wales. It meant that some members of the Wales
family were bound to be at Luton Hoo, although not Georgie,

who was at Sandringham recovering from typhoid; and not Eddy, who was now stationed at the Hussar barracks in York.

May enjoyed house parties. There would be twenty or thirty fellow guests and, as it was winter, there would be shooting for the men in Luton Hoo's acres of private woodland and companionable walks for the ladies in parkland and gardens designed by Capability Brown. In the afternoon there would be charades and whist and other card games and, for the more daring, the never out-of-date fun of sliding down a magnificent staircase on a tea-tray. Best of all, in the evening there would be dancing.

The first person she ran into, even before she had reached the bedroom she had been allocated, was Maudie.

'Goody,' Maudie hugged her tight, 'I was hoping you would be here. Let's find a quiet corner and have a glass of champagne and a chat. I want to hear all about your invite to Balmoral. What was it all about? When Toria heard Granny Queen had invited you there for ten days and that no one else had been invited, apart from Dolly, she was so jealous she practically spat nails.'

Once they had found a quiet corner, May said, 'I have no more idea than you have, Maudie, as to why I was invited. There were times when I thought I was there to be given one of Granny Queen's matchmaking chats, but no name was ever mentioned, and now I think I was reading too much into things. I think she was just a little lonely and wanted someone with whom she could reminisce about your dear departed Grandpa Albert. I heard all about how she had fallen in love with him at first sight and, on the day she took me to his memorial cairn, how she is looking forward to being with him again after she dies. All in all, it was a bizarre few days.'

'Well, if that was it, I'm crushed with disappointment. Someone else who is crushed with disappointment is Georgie.

In October he finally made his long-planned-for proposal to Missy – and she turned him down! And what she said when she did so is a corker, for she told him they could still be chums. Chums! It's an expression I must remember, if I ever find myself in a similar position. Rumour is that Aunt Marie has long had Nando Hohenzollern in mind as a husband for her daughter, and at the thought of Nando being preferred over Georgie, Mama and Papa are so livid that they are no longer on speaking terms with any of the Edinburghs. Not that Aunt Marie will care. Being Russian, she enjoys emotional fireworks.'

She paused for breath, and then said, 'Jollier news is that the de Falbes are patrons of the County Ball and it is being held here tomorrow night. Because he has typhoid, poor Georgie is going to miss out on it, but Eddy isn't. He will be arriving later today. Have you heard that Marie-Louise's marriage to Aribert is a disaster? Georgie says it's not surprising, seeing as how Aribert is a pansy. I've never really understood about pansies, have you? What is it they do? No one will tell me. Not even Georgie.'

May didn't know, either, and at the moment her curiosity about it was nil. All she could think of was that within hours she would see Eddy again and that, as there was to be a full-scale ball tomorrow evening, he would almost certainly dance with her, even if only out of good manners.

It was late afternoon when Eddy arrived. Seeing May across a crowded room, he gave her an acknowledging nod and then, dashingly handsome in his Hussar uniform, strolled off in the direction of the billiard room in the company of Christle, Marie-Louise's brother.

Nothing could have shown her more plainly that, with his battle to marry Hélène over, she was of no further interest to him and, to her horror, tears stung the backs of her eyes. Appalled and aware that she needed privacy fast, May walked swiftly out of the room, heading in the direction of the conservatory. It was a pretty place, full of hothouse flowers and potted palms and twittering birds in wicker cages.

With hot tears glittering on her eyelashes, she sat down beneath a palm tree in one of the conservatory's many cane chairs, telling herself she was a complete fool. Twenty-four was far too old to be still in the throes of a first crush, especially when it was such a hopeless one. All she could be thankful for was that no one knew about it, not even Maudie.

Why, she asked herself, should she have hoped that Eddy would immediately seek her out? It had been idiotic of her. What she had to do was accept the situation as it was – and the sooner she did so, the better.

Only after she had smoked three cigarettes did she return to the drawing room, looking so perfectly composed that no one could have guessed how her pleasure in the weekend had ended the moment Eddy had barely acknowledged her and then turned his back on her.

The next day she didn't accompany the shooters, for she disliked seeing birds shot for sport, but, accompanied by Maudie and several other female guests, she did join them for lunch. If Eddy was aware of her presence, he showed no sign of it and she told herself she was beginning not to care.

Her determination not to care didn't, though, prevent her from taking extra time over her toilette that evening. Maudie had opted to get ready for the ball with her, rather than doing so in the room she was sharing with Toria. As their maids fussed around them, lacing up whaleboned corsets to give them fashionable hourglass figures, Maudie said, 'Toria is unbearable these days. A few years ago she was always talking about the day when she would be a queen and now, with Motherdear insisting it is Toria's duty to remain at home with her, that day is growing less and less likely. Toria is now so desperate that if only Motherdear would agree to it, I'm sure she would settle for marriage to a member of the aristocracy, as Looloo did. And you remember how scathing Toria was when Looloo accepted Fife's non-royal proposal.'

May did remember. Toria's unkind tongue was the reason she never sought her company.

Twenty minutes later they were both securely fastened into their ballgowns. May's had been made in Paris and was one her mother had insisted on buying, even though the cost had been astronomical. Looking at herself in the mirror, May was, for once, glad of her mother's recklessness with money. The gown, made of rose-pink silk, was beautiful and made her look beautiful too, instead of just passably pretty. The heavily beaded bodice had a low neckline that showed the creamy rise of her breasts; the sleeves were short and flamboyantly puffed; her hand-span waist was emphasized by a wide sash; and the shimmering skirt fell into a train edged in luscious double ruffles.

'You look spectacular, May,' Maudie said truthfully, pulling on elbow-high white kid evening gloves. 'When you walk into the ballroom you're going to be the centre of attention.'

May only wanted to see admiring attention in one pair of eyes – Eddy's. She had, though, no intention of telling Maudie that.

Picking up her evening bag, she took one last look in the mirror. Her wheat-gold hair with its hints of auburn was worn as she always wore it: pulled back high and close to her head in tight waves, and with a low fringe of small, crisp curls that Toria had once said made her look like a poodle. Whether it did or not, it was a style that both suited her and was distinctive, and that was what mattered.

Satisfied that she had made the very best of her appearance, she followed Maudie out of the bedroom. As they headed in the direction of Luton Hoo's main staircase – and despite all her intentions that, where Eddy was concerned, she was never going to allow it to happen again – her body began betraying her, her heart pounding in her chest.

As the ball wasn't a normal house-party ball, but a County Ball, the ballroom was even more extravagantly decorated than usual and, instead of a band, there was a small orchestra.

For the next hour May danced with a wide selection of partners, always aware of the person with whom Eddy was dancing.

Breathless after a polka danced with Christle, she had just decided to catch her breath by sitting out the next dance, when Eddy finally began walking towards her.

Swiftly she looked down, smoothing an evening glove that didn't need smoothing, for what if she was mistaken and he wasn't heading towards her, but towards someone else? How humiliating if she had happy anticipation on her face, and he walked right past her.

He didn't. Stopping in front of her, he said with disturbing seriousness, 'I'd like to talk to you, May.'

It wasn't the invitation to dance she had been expecting. Fighting a crushing disappointment she said, certain of his answer, 'About Hélène?'

'Yes.' He looked deeply unhappy. 'About Hélène.'

She rose to her feet and, as the orchestra began playing a waltz, followed him from the ballroom, expecting him to come to a halt in the corridor leading away from it. Instead he led her up to the first floor, opening the door of a small sitting room. It was a woman's room, filled with vases of flowers and mirrors and delicate china ornaments. There was a fire in the grate and the room's purple-velvet curtains were drawn.

He said, 'This is Madame de Falbe's boudoir. She has given permission for me to speak with you here.'

May's throat tightened in something close to panic. What on earth was he about to say that had to be said in such privacy? Had he decided to relinquish his rights to the throne and turn Catholic, in order to marry Hélène? Had Hélène's parents arranged for her to marry someone else, and had she agreed to do so?

Eddy's gold-flecked eyes held hers. 'You do know how very much I love Hélène, don't you, May? And that I will never, ever be able to love anyone else?'

'Of course I do. And I know how much she loves you. What is it? What has happened? Had the two of you been given fresh hope, and has it come to nothing?'

'There has never been fresh hope. Worse, I've been told by Granny Queen that I can't fudge the issue of marriage any longer. Unless I take matters into my own hands, she will be announcing my engagement to Mossy at the end of the month.' He hesitated and then said, 'Do you remember how, five years or so ago at Marlborough House, I told you about the Queen's list of possible brides for me? It was the first really personal conversation we ever had and was, I think, the start of what I like to think has become friendship – and you have been just as good a friend to Hélène as you have been to me.'

The fire crackled and spat. Eddy cleared his throat. 'And so it occurred to me, May, that it would be much better for me to marry someone I like, and someone who is a friend, than it would be for me to marry someone who would never understand about my love for Hélène. And so I have brought you here to ask if you will marry me.' He dropped down on one knee in front of her. 'Will you, May? Believe me when I say I'd be most awfully grateful if you would.'

The blood drummed in her ears. Her heart slammed against

her chest. The ground felt as if it was slipping away beneath her feet. Was it a cruel joke? The kind of joke his father was so infamous for playing? The kind of practical joke Georgie had played so often on her, when they had been children? Were fellow guests now on the other side of the door, about to fall into helpless giggles if May Teck – a Serene Highness not royal enough to marry a royal – made a fool of herself by taking his proposal of marriage seriously?

Time stood still as she waited for him to realize that she had seen through the ruse, her disappointment in him for being a party to it so deep that she didn't know how she was going to come to terms with it.

But he didn't rise to his feet, saying, 'Sorry, May. You've seen through the joke.'

He remained where he was, in front of her and on one knee.

'Please, May.' There was an emotional break in his voice. 'If you don't accept me, I shall have no alternative but to marry Mossy. The Prime Minister believes there could be no better match dynastically than a future Queen of England who is also the Kaiser's sister. But nice though Mossy is, she isn't what I want. She would depend on me too much, and I need someone that *I* can depend on. That person used to be Georgie, but Georgie is nearly always on the far side of the world these days and, to tell the brutal truth, I'm not such great shakes, left to my own devices. I'm always on the brink of getting into trouble. I need a wife whose views I respect, who will keep me on the straight and narrow, and with whom I can share my anxieties. In short, I need you, May. Please don't turn me down.'

It had been a long speech and during it, although blood was still drumming in May's ears and her heart was still slamming against her chest, the reasons for their doing so had changed dramatically.

He was serious. Eddy, Duke of Clarence and Avondale, heir

presumptive to the most powerful throne in the world, was asking her to marry him. If she accepted him, she would not only be marrying someone she was certain she could be happy with, but she would be ensuring her family's future financial stability. On marriage, she would become a royal duchess. When Aunt Queen died and Eddy's father became King, Eddy would inherit the title Prince of Wales and she would be the Princess of Wales. And when Eddy's father died, Eddy would be King of the United Kingdom and Emperor of India. And she would be his Queen and Empress.

It was all too much to take in: too swift, too sudden.

And had Eddy forgotten that she wasn't 100 per cent royal?

She said through dry lips, 'The Queen and her prime minister will never agree to it. My paternal grandparents' marriage was morganatic. I'm a Serene Highness, not a Royal Highness. I don't know of a Serene Highness who has married the heir to a throne. It's something Aunt Queen and the Prime Minister are simply never going to allow.'

'But that is where you are wrong, May! I'm proposing to you with the consent of both of them. It is why Granny Queen invited you to Balmoral. She wanted to make quite sure I had made the right decision and, as I do, she thinks you are an exceptional girl and is willing to overlook your Serene status. She would like our engagement to be announced as soon as possible and for us to be married at Easter. So please, *please*, May. Will you marry me?'

The moment was so fantastical that she wanted to laugh and cry at the same time. She wanted to shout from Luton Hoo's rooftops, 'Yes, Eddy! Nothing would make me happier than to marry you. It's all I've ever, ever wanted.' But he wasn't asking her to marry him because he was in love with her, and such a shamelessly enthusiastic response would be embarrassingly inappropriate.

Instead, although joy was flooding through her from the top of her head to the tips of her toes, she said with great restraint, hardly able to believe she was awake and not dreaming, 'Yes, Eddy. I would be honoured to accept your proposal.'

Sagging with relief, he rose to his feet. Pulling a small jewellery box out of his trouser pocket, he took from it a magnificent ruby-and-diamond ring. Taking hold of her left hand, he slid the ring onto her fourth finger, saying as he did so, 'Thank you, May darling.' And then, a sudden note of uncertainty in his voice, 'You don't mind my calling you "darling", do you, May?'

She shook her head, too full of emotion to speak.

'I believe,' he said, his voice thickening, 'that on such occasions it is customary for the gentleman to kiss his fiancée?'

She flushed scarlet. It was the first time they had been alone in a room together. It was the first time they had held hands and Eddy was quite certain that, when he kissed her, it would be her first kiss. Aware that, under the circumstances, it was tenderness and not passion that was needed, when he drew her into his arms, he did so with great gentleness.

A tremor ran through May, and for a hideous moment he wondered if it was caused by her reluctance to be kissed, and then her arms slid up and around his neck, her fingers tightening in his hair.

With her heart beating fast against his, he lowered his head to hers. Her lips were warm and soft and, to his pleasure and stunned surprise, they parted beneath his, her body bending into his as if doing so was the most natural thing in the world.

The following moments were among the most pleasurable he had ever experienced and, when he finally lifted his head from hers, his eyes were dazed by the discovery that beneath his fiancée's always cool, self-possessed composure lay a passionate hidden fire.

He took hold of her hands and, as their fingers locked tightly, he said unsteadily, 'I think this arrangement is going to work out amazingly well, May.'

'Yes.' There was shy and joyful certainty in her voice. 'It is. And how surprised people are going to be!'

Chapter Twenty-Two

Her parents' reaction to the news that Eddy was about to become their son-in-law was one of near-hysterical rapture. 'There will be no more nonsense about May being second-class royalty now!' her father declared, so red in the face with triumph that May was terrified he was going to have a heart attack. 'And it isn't only May who will be elevated from being a Serene Highness to a Royal Highness. As her father, surely I will be given the title of Royal Highness as well?'

Her mother's concerns had been of a far different nature. 'Where will the wedding take place, May? Will it be at St Paul's? As Eddy is heir presumptive, it should be at St Paul's. And who will be your bridesmaids? Royal protocol being what it is, I doubt we shall have much say in the matter, although Toria and Maudie certainly, and Looloo and dear Marie-Louise as maids of honour, but you must have at least ten bridesmaids, and care must be taken that no one feels snubbed at not being asked. And then, of course, there is the question of your wedding gown. And of where you will live. Has darling Eddy mentioned yet where you will be setting up home? Perhaps St James's Palace?'

May wrote the next morning, on Luton Hoo headed note-paper:

*And so, Alicky, I am engaged to Eddy. Can you believe it? I
am certainly having trouble in doing so! An hour ago we had
our official engagement photograph taken in Luton Hoo's
garden, and Eddy has now left for London and Windsor to
break the news personally to his parents and to get the
Queen's official sanction for our marriage. Dolly has been
telegrammed and is already on his way here. I wish you
could have seen the reaction when I walked into the ballroom
arm-in-arm with Eddy and with a ruby-and-diamond
engagement ring on my finger!*

Alicky was the only person within the family that May wrote
to personally. She did, though, write to Thaddeus, telling him
that he would soon be receiving a very unexpected wedding
invitation. She wrote in a similar manner to Belinda Light,
adding that she no longer needed to trouble her aunt about
the availability of I Cedri and telling her how much their
long-standing friendship meant to her.

The next day a public announcement was made. All the
daily newspapers carried their engagement picture, and
congratulatory telegrams began arriving at Luton Hoo in
shoals. May's happiness was dizzying, and not even Toria's
rudeness dimmed it.

'I don't see why you are looking so happy,' Toria had said.
'Everyone knows Eddy isn't in love with you, or you with him,
and I think he has been very self-sacrificing in asking you to
marry him. Don't think for a minute he has done so because
he truly wants to marry you. He's asked you to marry him
because, for some unfathomable reason, Granny Queen has
insisted on it – although how she can have forgotten all about
you not being truly royal, I can't even begin to imagine.'

Under normal circumstances, rudeness was something May
never indulged in, but white-hot indignation got the better of

her. 'As you can't begin to imagine it,' she snapped back, 'don't bother attempting it! You're making a very good job of trying to spoil my happiness, Toria, but you're not succeeding one little bit.'

Toria's eyes narrowed. 'I truly believe you've schemed your way into this engagement, May Teck, and while other people may conveniently forget your Württemberg heritage, it's something I will never do.'

'And neither will I, Toria, for it's something I have never been ashamed of. And as you have finally expressed your feelings about me so bluntly, if you choose to opt out of being one of my bridesmaids, I will quite understand.'

Toria sucked in her breath. For her not to be a bridesmaid, at a celebration as important as Eddy's wedding, was unthinkable. She didn't truly think May would be able to exclude her, but it wasn't a risk she was prepared to run and she finally clamped her lips tight shut.

Coming from Toria, the spitefulness hadn't been unexpected. What was unexpected was Maudie's muted reaction to the news that May was about to become her sister-in-law.

'Why you, May?' she had said, genuinely bewildered. 'I simply don't understand it. Whose idea was it? Granny Queen's? Papa's?'

'I like to think it was Eddy's idea, although he had to get the Queen's permission and his father's permission before proposing to me.'

Maudie had looked more puzzled than ever. 'But you, of all people, know how deeply in love Eddy is with Hélène. And because she and Eddy once asked you for advice, Hélène's going to be doubly heartbroken that his duty-marriage is to be with you.'

'I hope not. I hope Hélène will be relieved that he is marrying someone with whom he is already friends, and someone who understands and respects the feelings that she and Eddy still have for each other.'

To May's intense disappointment, Maudie still hadn't looked convinced.

When Dolly arrived, and as soon as the door of her room had closed behind them, he said, 'You don't have to go through with this if you don't want to, Sis. Don't marry Eddy just to make Ma and Pa happy. Don't be dragooned against your will into one of Aunt Queen's matchmaking fiascos.'

She hugged him. 'I'm not being dragooned into anything, Dolly. Although not many people are aware of it, Eddy and I are friends and, although I've always been careful not to let anyone become aware of it, I've had a crush on him ever since I was twelve. Trust me when I say I think myself the luckiest and most fortunate young woman in the whole wide world, and that nothing – absolutely nothing – could make me happier than I am at this moment.'

Dolly still didn't look as if he believed her and, to show him how truthful she was being, May picked up her skirts and, laughing with sheer joy, waltzed round and round the room, saying as she finally collapsed into an exhausted heap on the sofa beside him, '*Now* do you believe that I'm deliriously happy, Dolly?'

Two days later, accompanied by Dolly and her parents, May travelled by train from Luton to St Pancras station. When she had departed from it less than a week ago there had been no one to see her and her parents off, for they were, after all, only minor royals leaving to attend a house party in Bedfordshire.

Their arrival back into London was far different. The station concourse was thronged with members of the public, all

wanting to wish her well. Although she couldn't see it, somewhere a brass band was playing. The people of London were
never shy of vocalizing their feelings and as she stepped down
from the train there were cries of 'Good on yer, Princess May!',
'God bless you, Princess May' and, cheekily from several of
the women, 'Give Prince Eddy a kiss from me, May!'

It was her first experience of being in such public focus,
but she had her mother's lifelong example at how to react to
public adulation. As she was handed a bouquet of flowers from
a top-hatted, tail-coated director of the station, May waved
exuberantly to the crowd with her free hand and, with all her
mother's infectious spontaneity, continued smiling and waving
all the way to their waiting carriage.

It took them straight to Marlborough House, where Eddy
and his parents were waiting for them and where they were
to have lunch.

To May's disappointment, there was no opportunity for a
private reunion and, in the presence of his parents and future
in-laws, Eddy's kiss merely brushed her cheek.

His mother's greeting was far more relaxed. 'Dearest May,'
the Princess of Wales said, taking both her hands in hers. 'I
can't tell you how happy it makes me that the person I am losing
my darling boy to is yourself, and not some foreign princess.'

As May was well aware that Eddy's mother had been
fervently in favour of Eddy being allowed to marry Hélène, it
occurred to her that she shouldn't believe everything her
charming mother-in-law-to-be said.

Where Eddy's father was concerned, May had, like her
mother, always been wary of him, not liking his unkind and
embarrassing 'chaffing'. On this occasion he was, though, on
his best behaviour and seemed sincerely pleased that the
long-standing question of Eddy's marriage had finally been
satisfactorily resolved.

'Though you must keep Eddy up to the mark,' he said, as if Eddy wasn't present. 'He's been in need of a good, sensible young woman for a long time, and the country is going to expect a great deal from both of you.'

Eddy's face was expressionless, and for the first time May became uncomfortably aware that there were underlying tensions between him and his father. She had been a regular visitor to Marlborough House ever since she had been a child, but she had always been there as a playmate for Looloo, Toria and Maudie. Until now, her interaction with his parents had been limited to a polite 'hello' or 'goodbye' at large family parties. She had never before dined with the family on such intimate terms and although, to her relief, her future father-in-law was being pleasant towards her, he was constantly disparaging whenever he spoke to Eddy.

Her Aunt Alix's attitude towards her son was entirely different, but even more unsettling. As they walked into the dining room, she lifted Eddy's arm and placed it so that it rested around her neck. Throughout lunch she frequently laid her hand on his. Whenever she spoke his name it was preceded, or followed, by a lavish endearment.

Eddy neither looked comfortable nor uncomfortable at such excessive physical attention from his mother. Instead his expression remained unreadable; almost disinterested. Whatever the Waleses' private family life was like, before lunch was over, May was certain it was nothing at all like the uncomplicated, affectionate, happy-go-lucky family dynamic that she had grown up with at White Lodge.

Hard on the heels of lunch at Marlborough House had come a summons for them to make their way to Windsor, where the Queen wished to congratulate them on their engagement.

Again, there was no opportunity for May and Eddy to be on their own, for her parents accompanied them.

At Windsor, the Queen told them how happy she was at their betrothal; how the day would come when, as King and Queen and Emperor and Empress, they would both bear unimaginable responsibilities. 'But I am sure,' she said, clasping May's hand tightly, 'that the two of you will find strength in each other, as I and my darling Albert did.'

There was an obligatory visit to Prince Albert's mausoleum, in order that they could receive his posthumous blessing.

'It's traditional whenever any of Grandpa Albert's children and grandchildren marries,' Eddy whispered, when May looked slightly alarmed by the idea. 'It makes Granny happy.'

Before they left Windsor, the Queen insisted that, as May was so soon to be her grandchild by marriage, she should no longer refer to her as 'Aunt Queen', but as 'Granny Queen'.

'For that is how I think of you now,' she said. 'Eddy is a dear boy, who has experienced a lot of heartache. I sense that your feelings for him are deep and sincere and that any heartache, for both of you, is now blessedly at an end.'

'What did Granny Queen mean by your "heartache"?' Eddy asked when, for the first time since Luton Hoo, they finally had a little privacy together, walking arm-in-arm on a frosted path in the garden of Marlborough House. 'God knows, my own heartache has been public enough, but I didn't know that you'd experienced heartache as well.'

May was tempted to tell him of the seemingly hopeless crush she'd had on him for so many years, but was too unsure of how he might react to do so.

She said, 'I suffered a great deal of heartache on my mama and papa's behalf, when their financial difficulties were such that the bailiffs were called in and many of our family possessions were sold at public auction.'

'That period of time must have been an utter nightmare for you.' There was deep sympathy in his voice. 'I wasn't in England when it was all taking place, I was in Lausanne, attempting to get to grips with French, but my mother wrote to me about it.' He took hold of her hand and gave it a comforting squeeze. 'What was the immediate aftermath?'

It was the first physical touch of affection he had shown her since he had left Luton Hoo to inform his parents and the Queen of their engagement.

Weak with relief, she summoned up the nerve to give it an answering squeeze. 'And then, at the Queen's request, we left England in order to live somewhere that wouldn't stretch our finances too much. After a short stay with some of Papa's Württemberg relations, who have a villa on Lake Constance, we moved on to Italy and settled in Florence.'

'Florence? Wasn't that deathly dull?'

Having always known how badly educated all the Waleses were, May was more amused than shocked by his response. 'No,' she said, looking forward to all the things she was going to open his eyes to. 'Florence is wonderful. I'd like for us to go there together.'

'It would be nice to do so on our honeymoon, but I'm afraid there's no chance. The powers-that-be have decreed our honeymoon destination to be Sandringham.'

It was a disappointment, but not an unexpected one. Royal honeymoons were always spent in one or other of the many royal palaces, or in the stately home of a friend. When her parents had married, her mother's friend, Lady Alford, had made her family home, Ashridge, available to them for their honeymoon. Eddy's parents had spent their honeymoon at Osborne House. That she and Eddy would be spending their honeymoon at Sandringham – although hopefully not when the rest of the family were in residence – wasn't much of a surprise. The word 'honeymoon' had, though, rendered her speechless with embarrassment.

Aware of it, knowing the reason for it and feeling more than a little embarrassed about it himself, Eddy said, after the silence between them had stretched for a full minute, 'The honeymoon could be a little tricky, May, seeing as how we've only held hands a couple of times and shared one kiss. The extraordinary thing is, though, that I feel completely at ease with you, and I hope you are beginning to feel at ease with me.'

'I am.' Her throat was suddenly dry.

He cleared his throat. 'During the year when Hélène and I were struggling to get permission to marry, opportunities to be alone together without a chaperone being present were few and far between, and it was Looloo and Fife who were our salvation. They regularly invited us to Sheen Lodge and, as a married woman, Looloo took on the role of chaperone and did so in a way that discreetly gave us time together alone.'

He stopped walking, giving her his slow, heart-stopping smile. 'Looloo and Fife don't look like a couple of romantics, but they are, and I think it would be a good idea if they were to offer some hospitality again, don't you?'

Blushing furiously, May nodded in agreement and this time, when Eddy lowered his head to hers, his kiss wasn't to seal their engagement; it was simply because it seemed a most natural and pleasant thing to do.

Shortly after May's return to White Lodge, a messenger arrived from Windsor with news of the wedding date.

'It is to be the twenty-seventh of February and is to take place in St Paul's Cathedral,' her mother announced, giddy with excitement. 'Goodness, but what a lot of arranging is going to have to take place in such a short space of time! A wedding gown to be made. A trousseau to be created. Flowers to be decided upon. All the furnishings and decor of your married home to be agreed upon. And on top of all that, there is Christmas.'

For the next few weeks May's feet scarcely touched the ground. When not being fitted for her wedding gown and trousseau, plus an entire new wardrobe appropriate for her new role in life, she was out and about in London with Eddy. They went to the theatre several times, always to see a musical production and, because they had enjoyed it so much, going back a second time to hear *Cavalleria Rusticana*. They visited the 'Venice in London' exhibition at Olympia, where they floated around a replica of the Grand Canal in a gondola; and they chose wallpapers for the spacious apartment they were so soon to be moving into at St James's Palace.

On the day they received the news that Hélène's parents had taken her abroad so that she wouldn't have to endure being in the country when it was their wedding day and that, as a family, they would be making Spain their home for the foreseeable future, Eddy's voice had been unsteady.

'It's so hard to have loved someone so much, and to have lost them,' he'd said with deep feeling, 'but you have been a godsend to me, May. I wouldn't be coping if it wasn't for you.'

A week before Christmas, when they were playing a game of bezique in front of a roaring log fire at Sheen Lodge, while Looloo and Fife were out walking their dogs, Eddy laid down his cards and said, with surprise in his voice, 'I've been able to talk to you about so much I've never been able to talk to anyone else about. How I hated being at sea all those years. How, although there are some aspects of the Army that I like – the camaraderie, for instance – I find other parts of it, the endless drill and the jogging round and round the riding school day after day, pointless and tedious beyond belief. I haven't even admitted to Georgie how unenthusiastic I am about the Army.' He stood up, drawing May to her feet and into his arms. 'Please believe me when I say I'm happier than I ever thought I could be, and that it is all thanks to you, darling May.'

Until now his kisses had been warm and tender, but never passionate. Now, as he looked down at her, there was something new in his eyes; something she had never seen before; something that made her heart begin beating in sharp, slamming little strokes that she could feel even in her fingertips.

'I think I've begun to love you, May,' he said thickly. 'Do you think you could possibly begin to feel the same way about me?'

'I already do.' She felt as if her heart was about to burst. 'I have done for longer than you could possibly imagine.'

That she was speaking the truth was evident in her voice, and in her eyes.

Eddy drew in an unsteady breath. No one would ever believe they were a love match. And it didn't matter. All that mattered was that they knew differently.

Although she was virginal, as a Hussar officer, Eddy was far from being so and this time, when he lowered his head to hers and kissed her, he did so long and slow, and deeply. Holding her close against him, his free hand moved up over the shiny silk of her high-necked gown to cup her breast caressingly.

For May, it was a moment when she recognized in herself emotions and longings that she had never suspected existed; when she knew exactly why Maudie had been unable to resist Frank's lovemaking; and why, having loved her Albert so passionately, Granny Queen so strongly discouraged long engagements.

Chapter Twenty-Three

Darmstadt was glistening white under a blanket of snow, and *en fête* in readiness for Christmas. Every stall in the little town's market place was draped in swathes of holly and colourful paper decorations. Mistletoe was hanging at heights convenient for girls to be kissed beneath; horse-drawn sleighs, not carriages, thronged the narrow streets; and although Christmas Day wasn't for another two weeks, carol singers were out in full force.

May's letter to Alicky had taken longer to arrive than usual, because ships carrying mail across the English Channel had been disrupted by bad weather, and it was only now that Alicky, curled up in a wing-chair before a crackling log fire, was eagerly writing back to her:

Dearest Kindred Spirit,

When you wrote me of your engagement to Eddy, I thought at first it was a tease! Papa told me it wasn't, as at the same time your letter arrived, letters for him, informing him of your engagement, arrived from both Granny Queen and Uncle Bertie. I think it is the most amazing, wonderful news, and I can well imagine how truly happy and over the moon you must be. Eddy is the sweetest person in the world, and I just know that the two of you are going to be incredibly happy together.

*I don't have much news. In a letter that arrived along
with yours, Irène has written that, in Berlin, Kindred Spirit
Willy has infuriated his mother by sending you and Eddy
unqualified congratulations on your engagement and by being
totally uncaring that his sister has, yet again, been passed
over. Poor Mossy. I do feel for her, but, like Cousin Willy, I
am very, very happy for you. All the unlikeable members of
our vast family – those who have never let you forget your
Serene Highness status – will now have to behave very
differently towards you. Where some of them are concerned,
it is something I would very much like to see!*

Alicky started another paragraph:

*Granny Queen has now turned her matchmaking passion to
poor Ernie, who is ducking and diving and so far showing
great resilience at not falling in with her plans. He is twenty-
three now and, as Papa's heir (and being the only boy), even
Papa is anxious to see him suitably married and safeguarding
the family line and title by producing a son (and, Papa says,
preferably producing more than one son). In my wildest
imagination, I cannot imagine Ernie ending up the father of
a platoon, as Willy and Dona have. As their tally of boys is
now six, I think it is safe to say that the throne of the
German Empire has been well and truly secured!*

She laid her pen down. The prospect of Ernie marrying
wasn't one she was looking forward to. With all three of her
elder sisters married and living their lives far from Darmstadt
– Vicky in whatever British naval base Louis was stationed at;
Ella in a palace in Russia; and Irène in a palace in Berlin – she,
Alicky, was First Lady of Darmstadt, and it was a title she
would lose when Ernie married.

Having acted as her father's hostess ever since Irène's marriage to Heinrich, and having become accustomed to giving and presiding at dinner parties and receptions and at the balls that regularly took place in the New Palace's white-and-gold ballroom, the thought of having to hand over all such responsibilities to Ernie's bride was not a pleasant one.

More importantly, it wasn't pleasant when she had finally accepted that, much as she loved Nicky, and much as he loved her, she was never going to be able to marry him – and that if she couldn't marry Nicky, she was going to remain single until her dying day.

She picked up her pen again:

I wish I had good news to send you where I am concerned, but nothing has changed.

Once again she stopped writing, for her last few words were a lie. A few weeks ago Ella had made a surprise visit to Darmstadt to tell their father that she was finally converting to Orthodoxy. That announcement alone had shocked Alicky to the depths of her being, but it hadn't been Ella's only bombshell.

When they had been alone together, Ella had said urgently, 'Nicky has asked me to tell you he still loves you very, very much, Alicky; that you are the dream and the hope he lives for every day. You mustn't give up hope of marrying him, for although his parents are as opposed as ever to the thought of you as his bride, Sergei is constantly trying to persuade them to change their minds. He wants to make them see what a wonderful Tsarina you would one day make.'

Alicky's response had been to clasp her hands tightly together in her lap. 'Even if they do change their minds about me, I can't abandon my religion for Orthodoxy. I just can't do it, Ella. I can't. I can't.'

Ella, always infinitely loving and patient, had said gently, 'It really isn't such a dreadful thing to do, Alicky. Orthodoxy and Lutheranism have lots of things in common, and I truly believe Orthodoxy would be far better suited to your highly religious, highly emotional temperament.'

Alicky had been about to tell Ella of the sacred promise she had made to their mama when Ella said, 'Unless you begin thinking differently, Alicky, you will lose Nicky.'

'No, I won't.' Her response had been immediate and without a shred of doubt. 'Nicky and I are soulmates. We will be soulmates forever and ever.'

Forced to play her last card, Ella said, 'Nicky has taken a mistress. Her name is Mathilde Kschessinska. She is a ballerina in the Russian Imperial Ballet.'

Alicky had ceased to breathe.

A ballerina. It was something of a joke that having a ballerina as a mistress was an essential requirement for a member of the House of Romanov. Sergei probably had a ballerina, too, but it wasn't something she was going to ask Ella about. Slowly she had sucked air back into her lungs. What did Mathilde Kschessinska matter, when it was her – Alicky – that Nicky loved? When she knew from his letters that he was going to love her forever and ever and throughout all eternity?

A great calm had come over her and she had known that Mathilde Kschessinska wasn't going to affect the love she felt for Nicky. What she did feel was sad. Sad that Nicky had become so lonesome that he needed another woman in his life. Sad that even if Nicky's parents eventually gave permission for him to marry Alicky, rigid Russian royal protocol would not allow her to do so as a Lutheran.

She looked down at the letter she was in the middle of writing. If May had been with her, she would unhesitatingly have told her all about Nicky's ballerina, but putting the words in a letter was different. She would be seeing May in the not-too-distant future, for May and Eddy's wedding was in February and she was to be one of the bridesmaids. There would be plenty of time then to confide in her about Mathilde Kschessinska.

She picked up her pen again:

Missy and Ducky and their mama are with us for a few days en route from Geneva to London, where they will be having a family Christmas at Clarence House. Missy is full of high spirits, as always, and Ducky is down in the dumps. She's fifteen and in love with one of her Russian first cousins, Kyril Vladimirovich. Her reason for being down in the dumps is that nothing can ever come of it, as Romanovs are not allowed to marry first cousins. Can you imagine if the same rule applied to Granny Queen's tribe? Her eternal match-making would be shot to pieces (and, come to think of it, she would never have been able to marry Grandpa Albert!).

That's all for now, as the ice on the palace pond is hard enough to skate on and Ernie is showing off his skating skills to Missy and Ducky. (Although, as Missy and Ducky spend such a lot of time visiting their relatives in St Petersburg, I think he may find their skating skills outshine his. Winters in St Petersburg last for at least six months of the year.)

Love and all best – and until your February wedding – Kindred Spirit Alicky

'I think your brother is a hoot,' Ducky said late that night as, in nightdresses, the three of them sat cross-legged on Alicky's bed eating Marie biscuits. 'Not even Kyril has whizzed me around the ice so fast.'

'That's because Kyril Vladimirovich is so steady as to be almost stationary.' Missy brushed some crumbs from her chest. 'When it comes to men, Ducky, you really do need to raise your sights. It's bad enough that Kyril is so low down in the Romanov line of succession, without him being as dull as ditch-water into the bargain.'

'I don't find him dull, and at least he's good-looking and doesn't have sticky-out red ears, like Nando.'

Missy smiled serenely. 'Ah, but Nando will be the King of Romania one day and, when he is and I'm his queen, I'm not going to mind about his sticky-out ears.' She uncrossed her legs and, pulling her knees up to her chest, hugged them with her arms. 'And it's all a done deal. Nando has officially offered for my hand and, on my behalf, Papa has accepted. The only fly in the ointment at the moment is Granny Queen. She doesn't think Nando is good enough for me. She's still hoping Mama will change her mind and consent to me marrying Georgie-Porgie.'

Alicky, who didn't often have the opportunity to share in such interesting girl-talk, was riveted.

She said, 'Once your engagement to Nando is announced, will the wedding follow quickly?'

Missy's pansy-dark eyes were thoughtful. 'Probably not. Probably not until at least a year afterwards. One doesn't like to look too keen.'

'Personally, I wish you'd marry him as soon as possible.' Ducky was always blunt. 'I want to know all about *IT*, and I've never found anyone willing to tell me. Mama tells me I'll find out soon enough, and that into every life a little rain must fall – and what she means by that is anyone's guess. You have three married sisters, Alicky. Have you ever got any of them to spill the beans as to what actually happens on the wedding night?'

Alicky shook her head. The *IT*-thing was something never spoken of to unmarried young girls. It was as if, if you were told, nothing on God's earth would ever get you down the aisle.

'Well, whatever it is, I'm quite looking forward to it.' Missy reached for another biscuit. 'I like new experiences and I enjoy being kissed and touched. Cousin Christle is a great kisser and toucher. It's odd, isn't it, how you wouldn't mind at all some men taking liberties. Eddy Wales, for instance. Hélène of Orleans is still absolutely potty about him and, with those gold-flecked eyes and slow, sensual smile, I can quite see why. All I can say is: lucky May Teck. For a semi-royal with an embarrassing family past, she's scooped the jackpot.'

She looked at the biscuit she was holding and giggled. 'Do you know, Alicky, that Marie biscuits are named after Mama? They were made to commemorate her wedding to Papa, and her indignation at having a biscuit named after her knows no bounds. I swear it's the reason Granny Queen has all her royal palaces stocked full of them and has reared all her vast family on them. It means Mama cannot go anywhere without a plate of them appearing at teatime, and her knowing people are inwardly sniggering every time they pop one in their mouths. It's very naughty of Granny Queen, don't you think? But then Granny Queen and Mama are old sparring partners – and all in all, Mama generally scores most of the points.'

After the Edinburghs had departed for England, Alicky's father said to her, 'I've never known Ernie get on with anyone in the way he has with Victoria Melita over these last few days. They got on splendidly, don't you think?'

'Victoria Melita?'

'Ducky. Though why she's been saddled with such an un-ladylike pet name, I can't imagine. However, she has certainly solved a problem for Granny Queen. I have already sent a tele-gram saying there could no better match for Ernie than Ducky.'

Alicky liked Ducky. Like Missy, her shockability factor could be very entertaining. However, meeting up with her on family occasions was one thing; Ducky becoming a future Grand Duchess of Hesse and by Rhine and usurping her – Alicky's

– position as First Lady was quite another. And besides, although it was true Ducky and Ernie had enjoyed a lot of fun together, it was because both of them were reckless risk-takers on the ice and because they shared a taste for practical jokes. Alicky couldn't see either fact indicating that a marriage between them would be a marriage made in heaven.

'Why the hell can't Papa leave well alone?' Ernie said explosively, when she broke the news to him that, thanks to their papa, Granny Queen now thought him and Ducky an ideal marital match. 'Ducky is great, but I don't want her as a wife. I don't want *anyone* as a wife.'

'Then tell Papa that, before Granny Queen begins setting a wedding date.'

He clenched his teeth. At twenty-three, he might be able to get away with putting marriage off for another handful of years, but time was running out and soon his obstinacy in remaining single would have tongues wagging. It might be best to take the bull by the horns and prepare his father for the news that he wasn't going to like, by putting him in the picture now.

His father's reaction was exactly as Ernie had feared it would be.

'A pansy?' he had roared. 'A *pansy*? No son of mine is a bloody pansy! All you need, boy, is a stiff purge of castor oil. A bloody pansy, indeed!'

'And so I might very well marry Ducky,' Ernie said later to Alicky. 'At least she's fun, which counts for something. But I'm not going to do so until I absolutely have to. There's no sense in running to meet disaster.'

And, shoving his hands deep in his trouser pockets, he went off in search of the latest new groom, in order to have a little fun and cheer himself up.

Chapter Twenty-Four

JANUARY 1892, SANDRINGHAM

May was fizzing with happiness. It was early January and, accompanied by her parents, she had just arrived at Sandringham to help celebrate Eddy's twenty-eighth birthday, which was in four days' time. London had been freezing when they had left it, but there had been no snow. In Norfolk the ground was covered by it.

'The good news,' Eddy said, within minutes of welcoming her, 'is that the lake is frozen solid and there's to be a game of ice-hockey on it this afternoon. The bad news is that flu is rife. Both Toria and Maudie have taken to their beds with it, and my equerry, who is a demon at ice-hockey, is so ill he's not going to be able to play.'

'What about Georgie? He's still convalescing from typhoid. If anyone should take care not to catch flu, it's Georgie.'

'Georgie hasn't a trace of a sniffle. Let's find a room with a roaring log fire where I can tell you some truly exciting news.'

Arm-in-arm they began walking in the direction of Sandringham's little-used library. Hugging his arm, May said teasingly, 'Is your news a change of plan and we are to go to Florence for our honeymoon?'

'I'm afraid not. It's something even better. Ireland.'

Her eyebrows flew nearly into her fringe of wheat–gold crimped curls. 'Ireland? For our honeymoon? Why on earth?'

'Silly minx, of course not for our honeymoon. When we are in the library I'll tell you, although you must keep it to yourself, as it's highly confidential. Even Motherdear and Georgie aren't in the know yet.'

Deeply intrigued, she remained silent until they had reached the library and Eddy had closed the door behind them.

Without sitting down or suggesting that May sat down, he took both her hands and said, 'The Prime Minister has suggested that I be appointed Viceroy of Ireland and Lord Lieutenant of Dublin Castle, and Granny Queen has agreed to it.'

May gasped, her eyes widening.

'After a lifetime of having no choice but to do things I have no liking for, such as being at sea for years on end, this is something I know in my bones I will be able to do well. Or at least I will be able to do it well with your help, because as well as all the socializing that goes with being a viceroy, the position also needs organizational skills, which is something I struggle with. However, I know you are ace at that kind of thing. Motherdear is always saying how you manage all the paperwork involved with your mother's charities, and how you write all the reports and often chair committee meetings.'

May was about to protest that the work she did for the Needlework Guild was hardly preparation for organizing the workload of a viceroy, but before she could do so, he continued, 'As Viceroy and Vicereine, we'll make a splendid team, May; and in a vicereine's robes and coronet you are going to look superb. And so what do you think? Isn't it just the most staggering news?'

It certainly was. May's head was spinning. Four weeks ago her future had been so bleak that she had been planning to leave England for Florence and embark on a life completely outside the royal circle. Now, she would not only be Her Royal Highness the Duchess of Clarence and Avondale, and a future Queen of England and Empress of India, but she had the prospect of being Vicereine of Ireland to look forward to. It was a dizzying thought.

Another soon followed. The Irish Sea conveniently separated Dublin Castle from Marlborough House, Sandringham and her future mother-in-law. Until now she had always regarded her Aunt Alix with affection, but that had been before she had witnessed how unnaturally possessive she could be with Eddy. The sea would ensure it was a possessiveness that she wouldn't have to endure too often.

'It's wonderful news, Eddy.' She squeezed his hands tightly. 'I've never been happier. Not *ever*!'

Sliding his hands around her waist, he kissed her with passionate gratitude, knowing the only reason he wasn't utterly daunted at the prospect of becoming a viceroy was because, when he did, May would be at his side. And with May at his side, he knew he would not only have a loving wife, but a friend who would always be there for him and would never let him down.

When they left the library and entered a drawing room thronged with New Year guests, Georgie immediately sought her out for a private word. It was their first meeting since his recovery from typhoid, and his usual ruddy complexion was pale.

'Can't begin to tell you how happy I am, May, that you will soon be my sister-in-law. Granny Queen has plagued Eddy for years about the necessity of marrying. Although he quite rightly has always held out not to marry someone he didn't feel he could genuinely learn to love. How long till the wedding? Six weeks? Seven? It doesn't matter. Either way I'll be fully fit by the twenty-seventh of February and will make a quite presentable best man.'

'That's a huge relief, Georgie.' May hugged him. 'It's impossible to imagine our wedding with anyone else as best man.'

'And equally impossible to imagine my ever needing a best man.' As well as looking pale and weak, Georgie looked distinctly glum. 'Not that my getting married has the same urgency as it's had for Eddy.'

Despite having known him all her life, May could only remember having had one personal conversation with Georgie, and that had been when he had told her of wanting to marry Julie Stoner, the daughter of his mother's lady-in-waiting, and of his distress at being unable to do so. As a child and a young adult she had been in the habit of avoiding him, as Georgie took after his father in his love of playing unkind jokes on people. Once, when she had been eight and reading a book, he had dropped a mouse into her lap; and when she had been fourteen and proudly wearing a new dress to an afternoon party in Windsor Castle's gardens, he had squirted her with dirty water from a bicycle pump.

Putting such memories behind her and seeing how despondent he was, she said, trying to cheer him up, 'Of course you will be married before too long, and of course Eddy will be your best man. You're third in line to the throne, and that makes you very eligible.'

Georgie didn't look remotely cheered. 'It didn't make me very eligible in Aunt Marie's eyes. Or Missy's. Aunt Marie reacted as if I was a baker's boy, when I asked for Missy's hand in marriage. And Missy didn't attempt to change her mother's mind. She simply told me she was about to become officially engaged to that long streak of uselessness, Nando Hohenzollern. I thought she felt about me the way I felt about her, but she obviously never did. And that's the trouble with girls, Cousin May. A fellow can't possibly tell what's going on in their heads. They give you encouragement and then make you look an utter ass, when you mistakenly think they feel the same way about you as you do about them.'

'Not all girls, Georgie. That wasn't the case with Julie. You didn't read Julie wrongly.'

'No.' She was appalled to see his eyes glitter with unshed tears. 'Did you know that my darling Julie married last year?'

She shook her head.

'Her husband is French. Julie is now the Marquise d'Hautpoul de Seyre and all I can do is hope she'll be happy, because I can't bear the thought of her not being so. And although I did think I could have made a go of it with Missy, I doubt I'll ever bother trying to do so with anyone else. As far as I'm concerned, romance is overrated. But I'm glad for you and Eddy. I didn't think he'd ever be truly happy, after being unable to marry Hélène, but since his engagement to you he clearly is.'

That evening a dance was held in Sandringham's ballroom. As well as members of the family staying as guests, there were lots of Bertie's and Alix's non-royal friends staying in the house. They were the only members of the family to have such friendships, for Bertie liked mixing with bankers and members of the government and diplomats, and it always gave invitations to Sandringham an interesting and exciting edge.

Later, in her diary, May wrote:

I don't believe any young woman in the entire history of the world has ever been as happy as I am now – and it's all thanks to darling Eddy and the wonderful life we are about to embark on together. As we said goodnight to each other, he

gave me the white camellia he had been wearing in his
buttonhole, and I am going to press it within this page so
that it will be a reminder of this glorious evening for ever
more.

And before she did so, she pressed the flower tenderly to
her lips.

In the morning, as they sat side by side at a large desk, writing
letters expressing gratitude for congratulations and gifts, Eddy
suddenly said, 'A few weeks ago I would have regarded this
as tedious, but doing it together is fun. When we move into
Dublin Castle I'm going to arrange that our writing desks are
in the same room and next to each other. Then we can always
attend to our paperwork side by side, just as Granny Queen
and Grandpa Albert did.'

His mention of Dublin Castle sent a delighted shiver of
anticipation down May's spine. It was still a secret, with only
the Queen, the Prime Minister, Eddy's father and themselves
in the know.

'And that is the way it has to stay, until after the wedding
and until everything is ratified,' her future father-in-law had
said to her. 'I can't tell you how pleased I am, May, at the
change in Eddy, now that he has you by his side.'

It was typical of the way the Prince of Wales habitually
spoke of Eddy, and May was irritated, for she found it belittling
and unfair. She was just wondering how, without damaging
her new-found relationship with him, she could tell him so,
when he said, 'And you mustn't let Lenchen's and Vicky's rude
remarks about your engagement to Eddy and the unsuitability
of it – as you are a Serene and not a Royal – distress you.
They both have unmarried daughters, and Lenchen would
have liked to see Thora as Eddy's bride, and Vicky would have

liked to have seen Mossy as his bride. Their disappointment is something they'll soon get over. You can rest assured that, by the time of your wedding, their attitudes will have changed.'

May hoped he was right. Until now she had been totally unaware of Aunt Lenchen's and Aunt Vicky's feelings. Aunt Vicky didn't matter too much as May rarely met up with her and, knowing of the dead-hare and iron-machine cruelties she had put Willy through when he'd been a small child, she had never had any desire to know her any better. Aunt Lenchen, however, was another matter, for May was very fond of her; and that her affection was not at the moment being returned hurt her.

Later in the day Looloo and Fife arrived to join the birthday guests.

'Although I was very doubtful about doing so, when I learned how influenza is rampaging through the house,' Looloo said nervously to May. 'I haven't visited Toria and Maudie's sick-beds, as I don't want to catch it from them. You don't feel unwell, do you, May?'

'No,' May said, fighting down the temptation to pretend to sneeze.

That evening a skating party was held on Sandringham's frozen lake. The lake and the little island in the centre were lit by coloured lamps and by the flickering flames from dozens of burning torches. There was much hilarity as girls were sent skidding and shrieking across the lake's glitteringly hard surface on skating chairs – fun that even the Princess of Wales took part in. Scalding-hot baked potatoes were passed round, as were hot toddies of port and lemon, dusted with nutmeg. The only person who didn't take to the ice was the Prince of Wales, who stood on the hard-packed snow in a beaver-collared overcoat, puffing on a cigar and bellowing with laughter when anyone lost their balance and went slithering on their bottom across the ice.

May found skimming across the ice at night with Eddy's arm firmly around her waist even more romantic than waltzing with him, as there were areas on the lake that the lamps didn't reach and, whenever they skated into darkness, he immediately took advantage of it by dropping kisses on to the top of her head.

Her rapture in the evening was marred when his mother tucked her hand through Eddy's free arm, even though Eddy still had the other arm around May's waist, saying, 'The party may be far from over, but I've had enough of skating for one evening. Escort me indoors, if you will, Eddy darling.'

Eddy shot May an apologetic look and, suppressing a sigh, she removed her arm from his.

As Eddy and his mother disappeared into the band of darkness that lay between the lamplit lake and the house, Looloo said, 'I doubt you will see Eddy again this evening, May. Motherdear will want him to stay with her and have a game of bezique. Her possessiveness, where Eddy is concerned, is something you will have to get used to. We have had to.'

'We?'

'Toria, Maudie and I. Not Georgie. Motherdear is nearly as possessive about Georgie as she is about Eddy. Her possessiveness is why you will be living at Sandringham after your marriage. Motherdear doesn't intend your marriage to cause the slightest change in her relationship with Eddy.'

May's gloved fingers dug deep into her palms. If that was Motherdear's vision of the future, she was going to be disappointed, for thanks to Aunt Queen and the Prime Minister, she and Eddy wouldn't be living at Sandringham when they married; instead they would be far away across the Irish Sea, in Dublin.

The next morning was spent in the billiard room with Eddy, Dolly, Alge and Christle.

'You won't be too bored, will you, sweetheart?' Eddy asked, when telling May of his plans for the day and assuming she would be a spectator.

'No, but we're going to be an odd number, aren't we? If we play each other, and Dolly and Alge play each other, who will Christle play?'

He chuckled. 'Billiards isn't a card game, May. It isn't a game for ladies.'

May had been playing billiards since childhood with Dolly and Frank, and she opened her eyes wide and said in feigned innocence, 'Oh, but I would love to give it a try. Please say I can.'

'All right.' He smiled down at her indulgently. 'Before we men start playing, I don't see why you shouldn't pot a few balls if it will amuse you.'

When they gathered in the billiard room Eddy announced, 'May wants to try her hand at potting a few balls.' Alge's eyebrows rose and he was about to protest that May didn't need to 'try her hand' when Dolly dug him hard in the ribs. Handing May a cue and joining in the joke, he said, 'The table is all set up, Sis. Do your best. It isn't as easy as it looks.'

At the thought of a woman trying to come to grips with a billiard cue, Christle folded his arms and prayed for patience. Eddy stood at the head of the billiard table, in case he needed to give May a little help.

May chalked the end of her cue and then, appearing a little nervous, hesitated about where to set the cue ball on the table.

Eddy positioned it for her. Then, as she lined her cue up

for a shot, he said helpfully, 'You need to break up the triangle of red balls at the far end of the table, but try not to hit the pink ball at the top of the triangle or you'll lose points.'

'Thank you, Eddy.' May was all demureness. And then she steadied her cue, lined up her shot and cracked the cue ball into the side of the reds.

They scattered. The pink ball rocked slightly, but otherwise didn't move.

Eddy's eyebrows rose in admiration. 'Wonderful beginner's luck, May. Well done.'

May lined up her cue again, concentrated and then slammed a red ball straight into a bottom pocket. Even more spectacularly, the cue ball came to rest exactly where she had intended it to, which was in a position perfect for potting the black.

Before either Eddy or Christle had got their breath back, May potted it and then, still with the cue in her hand, turned her back on the table and, with a wide grin on her face, said to a dazed Eddy, 'Sorry for the tease. I just couldn't resist it. I've been playing billiards since I was old enough to hold a cue. Do you think the two of us could play against Christle and Dolly, or Christle and Alge?'

'I most certainly do, May, but you're a naughty girl and, as a penance, I want to see you play the same joke on my papa.'

At midday, news came that although Toria and Maudie were slightly better, two other guests and another member of the household were now suffering from influenza, and Eddy's mother had developed a severe cold and was keeping to her room.

'It's a bugger. The house is beginning to resemble a hospital,' Georgie said at lunchtime. 'If it wasn't for Eddy's birthday the day after tomorrow, I'd be packing my bags and heading straight back to Marlborough House.'

'Cheer up.' Christle threw a pellet of his bread roll across the table at him. 'It's out with the guns in the morning. A bit of fresh air in our lungs will keep the influenza bugs at bay.'

Following the guns wasn't one of May's favourite activities and she arranged to meet Eddy at the Sandringham estate home of Sir Dighton Probyn, where the shooting party was to have lunch. Sir Dighton was a longtime equerry to the Prince of Wales, and thirty years ago, as a young cavalry officer, had won the Victoria Cross for outstanding bravery during the Indian Mutiny. He always had a fund of entertaining stories to tell and, although she was a little shy of him, he was someone May greatly liked.

Georgie hadn't felt up to a morning's shooting in the bitterly cold weather, and so they walked the short distance to Sir Dighton's home together.

'Since your engagement, dear old Eddy has gained a whole new lease of life,' he said as they scrunched companionably over the snow-covered ground. 'Papa is in great good humour over it. He says you are going to be the making of Eddy.'

May stopped walking.

After continuing another step or two, Georgie halted and turned round. 'What's the matter, May? Is it too cold for you? Do you want to turn back?'

'No.' She remained where she was, her hands tucked deep into her fox-fur muff. 'It's just that I don't understand why your father speaks of Eddy in such a derogatory way. Whenever he speaks to me, whatever he says is always interjected with "You must keep Eddy up to the mark, May," or "See that Eddy does this, May" or "Make sure Eddy does that." It's all so unnecessary. Why does he never concentrate on Eddy's good points? On the way that Eddy doesn't possess a fiery temper, as he does? On how he is the best whist-player in the entire family, which in this family is saying an awful lot? On how he's a first-class and utterly fearless polo player? And on how he speaks Danish far more fluently than anyone else in the family apart, of course, from Motherdear? And last but by no means least, on how he's the sweetest-natured, kindest, most charming, amiable and well-loved member of the family there is?'

She was on the point of saying that even if his father didn't have a high opinion of Eddy, the Queen and the Prime Minister had, and that Eddy would soon be Viceroy of Ireland. Remembering that no one – not even Georgie or his mother – was to be told this until after the wedding, she finished by saying, 'So why does your father always go out of his way to belittle him?'

On hearing his father spoken of in such a manner, Georgie stared at her, open-mouthed with shock, and it occurred to May that perhaps she had gone a step too far.

'It's just . . .' Georgie floundered. 'It's just that dear Eddy keeps himself so much to himself. It . . . it *exasperates* Papa.'

May didn't find this a satisfactory answer, but knew it was as good an answer as she was likely to get. She also knew it was a subject that she shouldn't have brought up, and one it would be wisest not to pursue.

Beginning to walk again, and as Georgie fell into step beside her, she said, 'How long do you think it will be before you'll be well enough to re-join your ship?'

Georgie fumbled in his overcoat pocket and withdrew a bag of sweets. 'I've no idea. To tell the truth, I'm quite enjoying being on dry land. Would you like a bullseye, May? I never go anywhere without them.'

Luncheon was a buoyant affair, for Sir Dighton had the table in fits of laughter with tales of India and of how, when wandering unarmed from his tent one evening for a quiet smoke, he had come face-to-face with a tiger and had eyeballed it and yelled, 'Be off, sir!' and the tiger had immediately cut and run. The only person not in high spirits was Eddy.

May looked at him in concern, suddenly aware of how little he seemed to be enjoying himself. He was abnormally flushed, and she said with a frown, 'Are you feeling all right, Eddy?'

'No. Truth to tell, May, I feel damned peculiar. I think I've caught a chill.'

The second that luncheon was over, May sought out Georgie. 'Eddy isn't well,' she said, 'and I think he has a temperature. Would you help me walk him home? He needs putting to bed before he gets any worse.'

'This is very kind of the two of you, but you're both fussing far too much.' Eddy's words, as they walked him home, didn't hold conviction, for he had a raging headache, was dizzy and his legs clearly felt like jelly.

'Sodding influenza!' Being a sailor, Georgie's language was constantly peppered with swear words. 'Why couldn't it have waited another few days before laying you low? It's going to bugger up tomorrow's birthday party.'

'As I feel at the moment, Georgie, I couldn't care less about my birthday party. I'm just upset that the day will be spoilt for May.'

'Then don't be, for all that matters to me is you feeling better again.' May was all brisk efficiency. 'Georgie is going to put you to bed and I'm going to arrange for hot-water bottles and hot lemon barley-water to be sent to your room.'

As they stepped over Sandringham's threshold, Eddy said, 'I'm not in my own bedroom, May. There are so many people here this week that my room is being used as a guest room, and at the moment I'm in a little room next to the one Georgie and I once used as a study.'

As Georgie began steering Eddy in the direction of the

main staircase, May headed off to the drawing room to ring for a maid. When that task was completed, she went in search of Manby, the local doctor who had been resident in the house ever since the first of the house guests had fallen ill.

Later, after Manby had seen Eddy, May went with Georgie to sit with Eddy for a little while. Her first reaction, on entering his temporary bedroom, was at how truly small and poky it was.

'Goodness!' She seated herself on the only chair the room possessed. 'You weren't exaggerating, Eddy. You couldn't swing a cat in here.'

The idioms she used always amused him and, with a grin, he said, 'I must admit it's a bit cramped, sweetheart. If I stretch my arm out, I can touch the fireplace.'

Their eyes held. It was the first time she had ever seen him in his nightshirt and in bed, and her cheeks warmed at the thought that soon the sight would be one that would be as natural to her as breathing.

He took hold of her hand and gave it a reassuring squeeze. 'Sorry to be so out of sorts, May. It's foul bad luck, but I'll be up and about in no time. Manby says Toria and Maudie are already back on their feet.'

'What's Manby's diagnosis?' Georgie asked. 'A chill or influenza?'

'Influenza, and although it pains me say this, May, you mustn't kiss me when you leave. I don't want to infect you with it.'

Aware that he needed to rest, they didn't stay with Eddy for long, and when they left May's kiss was one that she lovingly blew from the room's doorway.

The next morning Dr Manby informed the Prince and Princess of Wales that Eddy's temperature had risen to one hundred and three degrees and that, even though it was Eddy's birthday, he should remain in bed throughout the day.

When May visited him, in the company of Georgie, she was disturbed to find him much worse.

'Sorry, May darling,' he said croakily. 'Not up to one of our companionable little chats, I'm afraid. I'm feeling very ropy indeed.'

'But that's the way of influenza.' Dr Manby was reassuring when giving the Prince and Princess of Wales, and Georgie and May, his daily report. 'It has to reach a peak before it begins to subside. As it's his birthday, I don't think any harm will be done if he spends an hour or so downstairs this evening.'

Supported by Georgie, Eddy manfully tottered downstairs long enough to open his birthday presents and thank everyone for them, before apologetically, and again with Georgie's assistance, climbing back to the claustrophobic little cell that was serving as his bedroom.

Early the next day, after his morning visit to Eddy, Manby said he suspected that Eddy had pneumonia. The Prince of Wales summoned his own physician, Dr Laking, so that Laking could assist Manby. Then he telegraphed for Dr Broadbent, who had so recently and successfully treated Georgie for typhoid.

In the afternoon May sat by the side of Eddy's bed and read to him. Propped up on pillows, he managed to talk to her about their wedding and how fortunate it was that he'd fallen ill now, and not nearer their wedding date, when the wedding might well have had to be postponed.

With Laking and Broadbent's arrival, pneumonia was diagnosed and the following morning, when May went with Georgie to visit Eddy, it was to find that a screen had been erected around his bed and they could only see him by standing on their tiptoes and looking over the top of it.

For the first time it occurred to her that Eddy was not just out of sorts, but ill. The same thing had occurred to the rest of the birthday party and, wanting to give the family privacy at such a time, house guests began leaving discreetly, all saying that it wouldn't be long before they would be meeting up again at the wedding.

Having fought off her cold, his mother was now also visiting Eddy for long periods throughout the day, and the room next to the bedroom, which had previously been used as a study, was now turned into a sitting room, so that his close family had no need to keep navigating the narrow corridors that led to his room from the main part of the house.

The doctors reported on Eddy's condition regularly to the Prince of Wales, and when May asked her future father-in-law why, with the guests gone, Eddy couldn't be returned to his own comfortable bedroom, he said, 'The doctors don't recommend such a move, May. Not yet, although maybe they will do so in a few days' time when Eddy has turned a corner and is on the mend.'

May was now spending nearly all her time with Georgie, peeping over the barrier of the screen as Broadbent, Laking and Manby hurried in and out of the room; or taking short walks with him in the grounds to get a breath of fresh air.

'I don't know what I would have done without you,' Georgie said to her on one of their walks. 'Motherdear won't believe Eddy is seriously ill. She sent a telegram to Granny Queen this morning that read: *Thanks so much for best wishes. Poor Eddy has influenza. So tiresome.* She simply won't allow herself to believe in the pneumonia diagnosis. Toria is nearly as bad. Looloo is just the opposite. Every time I try and speak with her, she dissolves into floods of tears. Maudie isn't so bad, but even she doesn't have your inner strength, and I'm very grateful for that strength, May. Truly I am.'

Four days after first feeling unwell, Eddy's temperature soared to one hundred and eight degrees, there was congestion in both lungs and he had developed a hacking cough.

What should have been a wonderfully happy and carefree week celebrating his birthday was fast turning into days of ever-increasing anxiety as, instead of 'turning a corner' as his father had put it, Eddy's condition grew slowly worse. He began drifting in and out of consciousness, sometimes recognizing May and sometimes staring through her with glazed eyes, as if she was someone he didn't know.

Princess Mary Adelaide was in a state of near-collapse. 'I do hope the wedding day isn't going to have to be postponed,' she said time and again. 'If it is, it will take us into Lent, and how can a wedding that will be the cause of national celebration take place during Lent? It can't. It simply can't. And so that means the wedding will be delayed until Easter!'

'And if it is, it won't be the end of the world, Mama.' May didn't care how far in the future a new wedding date might be, as long as Eddy recovered his health. As Dolly kept reminding her, he would recover, for he was young and strong, and pneumonia was fatal only in those who were old and fragile.

By dawn the next morning a second hard-backed chair had been squeezed into the room, so that the Princess of Wales could sit on one side of the bed, sponging Eddy's brow, while the nurse who had been called in sat on the room's original chair.

Whenever the nurse needed a break, May took over from her and, despite her inner distress and deep anxieties, did so in such a calm and competent way that all three doctors regarded her presence in the room an asset, not a hindrance.

The Prince of Wales came into the room for a few minutes

every hour, on the hour, and May heard Laking say to him, 'I think, sir, a public bulletin should be posted on the gates of Marlborough House.'

There was a taut silence and then Bertie said unsteadily, 'And the wording?'

Laking's voice was nearly as unsteady as Bertie's. 'Sandringham, nine-thirty a.m. Due to symptoms of great gravity, his Royal Highness the Duke of Clarence is critically ill.'

May felt as if all the air had been sucked from her lungs. There was no hint in Dr Laking's summing-up of Eddy's condition that, having reached a critical point, the next stage was slow, but certain recovery. She clenched her hands so tightly together that the knuckles were white. Eddy had to get better. He *had* to. Any other prospect was too horrific even to think about.

That afternoon he became delirious, shouting for Fuller, his childhood valet, as if he was in the room, and holding a conversation with his grandmother as if she, too, was with him.

Fuller was summoned urgently to Sandringham. Queen Victoria, who earlier had stated her wish to be at Sandringham at this time of great anxiety, and who had been persuaded not to make the long journey, was not there.

'Dear God, no,' Bertie had said when it had been suggested that the Queen should be sent for. 'It would only ratchet up the distress levels even higher.'

With Toria and Maudie now having recovered from flu and, like their mother and Looloo, either sitting in the hastily fashioned sitting room or in the sickroom itself – and all constantly in floods of tears – May didn't see how the distress levels could rise any higher.

Throughout that night she alternated two hours on and two hours off with the nurse. Toria, who felt she should now be the one to take on a nursing role with Eddy, gave vent to her feelings by saying waspishly that Hélène and her family should have been summoned to Sandringham, once it had been realized how dangerously ill Eddy was.

'It isn't,' she said to anyone who would listen, 'as if May loves Eddy as poor, dear Hélène loved him, and I'm sure it isn't May of Teck whom Eddy wants to see at his bedside. I'm sure he wishes it was Hélène sitting there.'

No matter what Toria might say, May knew differently. For in the early hours of the following morning, Eddy turned his head on the pillow and, looking towards her, said without the least trace of delirium, 'There you are, May. Sweet May. Lovely May.'

And then Manby and Broadbent bustled in, as did the nurse in order to take over from her. Exhausted after nights of broken sleep and certain that Eddy was at last on the road to recovery, May went into the sitting room. Curling up in one of the room's easy chairs, she fell into the first restful sleep she'd had in days.

She was woken four hours later by Georgie, saying, 'Eddy's delirious again, May.' His face was sheet-white. 'He doesn't recognize anyone – not even Papa and Motherdear.'

During the rest of the day Eddy, drenched in perspiration, tossed and turned, shouting orders at the top of his voice to his regiment, the Prime Minister, his horses. He shouted for Hélène; for his long-dead Grandpa Albert; for the Archbishop of Canterbury. Time and again he thought he was still aboard the *Bacchante* and climbing the rigging.

Throughout the entire nightmare his distressed mother remained at one side of the bed and May, dazed with horror, at the other. The screen was removed, so that Georgie, Toria, Looloo and Maudie could squeeze into the room without anyone first having to leave it.

That evening, flanked by Dr Manby and Dr Broadbent, Dr Laking informed the Prince of Wales that they feared the worst.

'Are you,' Bertie asked hoarsely, 'telling me my son is dying?'

Laking, for years his personal physician, said with compassion in his eyes, 'Yes, sir. There can no longer be any hope.'

It was the moment when the family's sick-visiting turned into a vigil, as all through the long, agonizing night Eddy fought for life.

As the first rays of morning seeped into the room, he said in delirium, 'Something terrible has happened! My darling brother Georgie is dead!' And then, panic still in his voice, 'Who is it? Who is it?'

Her voice thick with tears, May said gently, 'It's May, Eddy darling.'

A great calm came over him. Weakly he squeezed her hand and then, so faintly his mother claimed never to have heard it, he took his last breath and, with love in his voice, died with her name on his lips.

PART THREE

CHOICES

Chapter Twenty-Five

As she sat at a desk that looked out onto a garden thick with summer roses, May wrote:

Dearest Alicky,

Forgive the far-too-short notes I have been sending you so far this year. Until now I haven't been able to bring myself to relive the morning of my darling's death and the months that have passed since then. Now, however, I feel I can at last do so.

In the hours before he passed away I was seated at the side of his bed, holding his hand. Eddy had no awareness of my being there, or of anyone else – even of his mother and Georgie being there – but just before the end he squeezed my hand ever so weakly, and I know that he knew it was my hand that he was squeezing. Moments later he passed away and all that was left for me to do was to kiss him goodbye. As I kissed his dear brow, I was so crushed by all that I had lost I could scarcely comprehend the enormity of it. Even now, six months later, it is still difficult to do so.

At the funeral (which took place at Windsor), my father handed Uncle Bertie my bridal wreath of orange-blossom and Uncle Bertie laid it upon the coffin. How I lived through the service and the next few days and weeks, I do not know. To have been on the verge of having so much, and then to have lost not only Eddy, but everything that would have gone with marrying him – royal status, financial security for my family, the satisfying prospect of being a helpmate to Eddy – all to be snatched away and with nothing to replace it, has been an enormity too difficult to come to terms with. I have, however, slowly begun doing so.

Immediately after the funeral Uncle Bertie, Aunt Alix, Georgie and the girls stayed as guests of the Duke of Devonshire at Compton Place in Eastbourne, for none of them could face returning home without darling Eddy. From there they went to the South of France where, for several months, they stayed at Cap Martin.

Mama's friend, Lady Wolverton, had leased a villa further along the Riviera at Cannes, and she kindly invited us to spend the spring and early summer with her. Although we were seventy miles or so distant from Cap Martin, Uncle Bertie and Georgie visited us on their yacht. I used to be very chary of Uncle Bertie, but I am so no longer, for despite his own terrible grief, he has been kindness itself to me and I now see him in a quite different light.

She paused and laid her pen down. Did she write and tell Alicky of how, at Cannes, a sense of embarrassing constraint had entered her relationship with Georgie – and the reason for it – or did she not? In the end she picked up her pen and wrote:

Ever since darling Eddy's death, Georgie's marriage has become a question of priority for Aunt Queen and, so the newspapers say, for the country as well. Do you remember the story behind Nicky's parents' marriage? How Aunt

Minny had been engaged to Uncle Sasha's brother, the Tsesarevich? And how, when his brother died, Uncle Sasha then became engaged to Aunt Minny and married her? Some people – my father, I'm sorry to say, being one of them – are saying that as I am in exactly the same position as Aunt Minny once was, it is a precedent that should be followed here, in England. As you can imagine, such a suggestion is desperately embarrassing for both me and Georgie. At Cannes we did our best to laugh it off, but weren't very successful.

She paused once again, hot with remembered embarrassment, and then began a new paragraph:

We stayed in Cannes for two months and then went to Stuttgart for a lengthy stay with Papa's Württemberg relations. While we were there, Aunt Queen conferred a dukedom on Georgie, just as she did on Eddy when he was second in line to the throne, and so Georgie is now His Royal Highness the Duke of York, Earl of Inverness and Baron Killarney.

Three days ago we finally returned to England – something I did reluctantly, owing to all the speculation about Georgie and me.

I now have to settle back into my former lifestyle, helping Mama with her many charities and caring for Papa who, since his stroke, is quite an invalid. It is, of course, nothing like the life I thought I was about to embark upon, or like the life that, immediately before Eddy's proposal, I had been planning privately (which was a life for myself in Florence). Even before my engagement, that project would have been difficult to achieve, but as darling Eddy's bereaved fiancée, it is now not even remotely possible.

So there you are. I have brought you quite up to date and
I hope you will keep me up to date with all that is happening
in your life and in dear little Darmstadt.
   All my love, May

She put the pen down and reached for an envelope and
then, before putting the letter inside it, reached for her pen
once again and wrote:

PS: I forgot to tell you that in the days after Eddy's death,
Willy sent me a very tender letter of condolence, quite out of
keeping with his usual bombastic and brash style. There are
times when I don't mind at all our once having regarded him
as a Kindred Spirit. xxx

In September, Georgie received a letter from his grandmother
saying she wished to see him before she left for her autumn
stay at Balmoral. He didn't need to speculate on what it was
that she wanted to see him about. He knew what it would be
about. It would be about how nice it would be if he were to
ask May to marry him.

In any other set of circumstances, he would not have found
the suggestion objectionable. Even when he had been much
younger he had always had a secret pash on May, but her
reserved manner, coupled with his own crippling shyness, had
ensured that the only way he'd felt safe in attracting her
attention had been by playing practical jokes on her.

Those days, of course, were back in the days of their childhood, but his admiration of her had continued, and it had
increased a hundredfold during the harrowing week of Eddy's
illness and death.

Everybody else in the family was, he knew, under the impression that Eddy and May's feelings for each other had

been those of a practical nature, the same kind of feelings that attended all royally-arranged marriages, and while that may have been true in the beginning – at least where Eddy was concerned – he knew that by the time of his death, Eddy had developed a feeling of great affection for May; and May, Georgie suspected, had felt even more than affection for Eddy.

How could he possibly marry someone who, he was certain, was mourning his brother just as deeply as he was? The answer was that he couldn't. And wouldn't.

'So that is how I feel, Granny,' he said two days later as he stood nervously before her, trying to ignore his Aunt Beatrice, who was seated at her side, knitting. 'I believe Cousin May's feelings for dear Eddy went far deeper than is generally realized, and I believe it would be wrong and insensitive of me to suggest to her that she now marries me.'

His grandmother had never thought of Georgie as possessing a great deal of sensitivity, and it pleased her that she had been wrong on that score. It wasn't, however, going to change her mind about what she was now about to say to him. Turning to Beatrice she said, 'I would like to speak with dear Georgie alone, Beatrice.'

With her knitting still in her hands, Beatrice hurriedly left the room – something Georgie would have given a king's ransom to have been able to do.

'Two years ago, Georgie, typhoid fever threatened your life.' The Queen's double chin wobbled with emotion. 'If something similar was to happen to you again, and this time you were tragically taken from us – as dear Eddy was so tragically taken from us – I would like you to think of the situation as regards the throne.'

Georgie struggled to do so.

'As the eldest of your father's remaining children, Looloo

is next in line to the throne after your father. And it is my opinion, and the opinion of my ministers, that the position of Queen and Empress is one Looloo is totally unfitted for.'

She waited for the enormity of what she was saying to sink in and then said, 'There is another crucial reason why a situation with Looloo as heiress presumptive cannot be allowed to happen, and that is Fife. Fond of him as I am, he is *not* royal. He is a subject. As I am sure you can see, the political ramifications of a queen and empress with a commoner husband do not bear thinking about.'

It didn't. Georgie loved all his sisters, but with the best will in the world, he could see that Looloo – highly strung, nervous and dim – was not the best person to succeed to the throne.

'It is for all these reasons, Georgie,' his grandmother continued, 'that it is *imperative* you marry soon and have a family, and I can think of no one who would make a more imperious and dutiful future Queen of England and Empress of India than dear May. I would like you to go home now and give very serious thought to all I have said to you.'

With the words lodged in his throat, he told his grandmother he would do as she asked. Then, suffering from palpitations, he returned speedily to Marlborough House, locked himself in his room and opened a large bottle of brandy.

At the end of November, the Teck family were invited to Sandringham to celebrate the Princess of Wales's birthday with her. It was the last thing in the world May wanted to do, for their visit would run into the beginning of December and the anniversary of her engagement to Eddy.

'The memories will be hard to bear, sweetheart,' her mother said sympathetically, 'but they are something you will have to endure.'

May had enough self-knowledge to know not only that she

was good at enduring, but that she was good at keeping her feelings to herself while doing so. It was something she had learned the hard way as a child when being constantly reminded that, as a Serene Highness, she was not truly royal and so not really part of the family. It was an ability she had relied on at the time of her parents' bankruptcy when, with a broken heart, she had watched the contents of her family home being sold at public auction and she and her family had so humiliatingly been sent into exile. Her agony at the shame of it all had been intense, but she had not allowed it to show, for she believed deeply that intense emotion was cheapened by public display.

Her week at Sandringham was just as difficult as she had anticipated. Her Uncle Bertie's and Aunt Alex's kindness to her was as unstinting as it had been in the days immediately after Eddy's death, but she'd had to suffer being taken by Aunt Alix into the room in which Eddy had died and which, now filled with flowers, was kept as if his death had never taken place. A fire burned in the grate of the little fireplace that Eddy had once said he could touch, even from his bed – a bed now covered with a large Union Jack. There was soap in the soap dish, and his hairbrush and comb were laid out as if, at any moment, he would be picking them up to use them. Also in the room was the hard chair she had sat on for so many long, heart-breaking hours, and once again she could see Eddy's head turning on the pillow towards her and hear him saying huskily, 'There you are, May. Sweet May. Lovely May.'

That afternoon, pleading a migraine, she had kept to her room and cried and cried into her pillow until she was exhausted.

The next day, the Waleses had taken her to Sandringham church so that she could view Eddy's memorial window, which had been given by Eddy's brother-officers of the 10th Hussars. It depicted Eddy as St George in shining armour and was exactly the way she would have wanted him depicted. For in looks, Eddy had always reminded her of Donatello's marble statue of St George in Florence.

At Christmas, Georgie sent her a present of a brooch, and she sent him a small pin. In the card accompanying the brooch he addressed her as 'Dear Cousin May', and she addressed him as 'Dear Cousin Georgie'. The embarrassment, although not as intense as it had been, continued, not helped by newspaper headlines such as 'Will next year be the year Princess May becomes the Duchess of York?' and 'Buckingham Palace prepare to announce the engagement of the Duke of York to Princess May'.

'It's all bosh,' May said whenever she was asked if there was any truth to the rumours. 'Newspapers simply make up any outlandish story they think will sell copies.'

In mid-February 1893, Queen Victoria again summoned Georgie into her presence. 'Have you,' she asked, black satin-slippered feet on a footstool, a small Pomeranian dog in her arms, 'thought any more about the conversation we had in September?'

'Yes, Granny.' Georgie's discomfiture was intense, but he was determined to stand his ground. 'And I thought that perhaps, in time, I might find a German Protestant princess I could propose to.'

'Then if that is what you want, propose to May!' The Queen's patience – something she never had much of – was being sorely tried. 'May's bloodline is *wholly* German and she is Protestant to her backbone. As for finding another German Protestant princess to propose to, there *are* no other suitable German princesses of the right age, in good health and in their right minds!'

Georgie tried to think of a response, and couldn't find one.

His grandmother tried a different approach. 'Think of all dear May's excellent qualities, Georgie. Although because of her father's morganatic bloodline she is only a Serene, on her mother's side she is, like you, a direct descendant of King George III. She has a strong sense of royal duty, is sensible, even-tempered, highly intelligent, cultured and, although not beautiful, is exceedingly pretty. And no one can deny that she possesses great natural dignity – something that is essential in someone who, if you propose to her, will one day hold the highest position there is.'

Georgie had no intention of attempting to deny May's natural dignity and he knew that if he was going to marry – and it was obvious he had no choice but to do so – then he would far prefer his bride to be May than anyone else.

He replied, 'In two weeks' time I am leaving with Darling Motherdear, Toria and Maudie on a long-arranged trip to Greece. We will be returning at the end of April and, when we do, I will propose to May.'

'Thank you, Georgie.' His grandmother beamed at him. 'An engagement announcement in the month of May, for a bride-to-be named May, will be most suitable. And,' she added, 'so will a summer wedding, in either June or July.'

A month later, with Georgie still in Greece, it was May's turn to be summoned to Windsor. The Queen regarded her thoughtfully, aware of how changed she was by Eddy's death. There was a new gravity and maturity about her, and the twinkle that had previously lit up her cornflower-blue eyes was still sadly absent.

After saying that she thought May looked very fetching, dressed in the half-mourning colour of deep lilac, the Queen asked May to sit beside her. 'I wish,' she said, taking hold of her hand, 'to speak with you about your present unhappy situation, May, and of how it can best be resolved.'

For a wild moment May wondered if exile was again going to be suggested as a solution to a Teck 'unfortunate situation'. Instead her Aunt Queen said, 'Before Georgie left for Athens, I had a long talk with him and, when he returns in a couple of weeks' time, he will be speaking to you in order that your position can be rectified in a way beneficial to you both.'

Certain of what was now about to come, May caught her breath, her eyes widening in alarm.

Seeing her reaction and ignoring it, the Queen said firmly, 'You must be realistic, May. Your position as Eddy's bereaved fiancée renders it impossible for anyone of lesser rank to make you a proposal of marriage. The only suitable person is Georgie, and so the newspapers are quite right in thinking that marriage between the two of you will be the best possible outcome, from what has been a terrible tragedy.'

'But surely my marrying Georgie would be wrong?' There was a pain in her heart so deep she could scarcely breathe.

The Queen's fierce eyes were stern. 'It would *not* be wrong, May. It would be your royal duty, for the qualities that would have made you such a supportive Queen Consort for Eddy are the same qualities Georgie will be in need of. Despite their being so different in looks and personality, there were strong similarities between them – the first being that neither of them was educated to an acceptable standard. The result has been a total lack of fluency in either French or German, languages *essential* for the monarch of a country as great as ours, and languages you have been fluent in since childhood.'

The grandfather clock in the corner of the room began striking three and the Queen paused until it had finished chiming.

'And despite their both having spent years at sea,' she

continued, 'neither of them have – or, in dear Eddy's case, had – any understanding or appreciation of foreign cultures, an accusation that cannot be levelled at you, after your years in Italy studying art and European civilization. And so, just as you would have for darling Eddy, you will be able to compensate for all that dear Georgie lacks, and I know of no one else of the right rank, religion, education and temperament able to do that in the way you will be able to. For that reason, May, when Georgie proposes to you – and he will be doing so on his return from Greece – I very much hope you will accept him.'

May's head whirled. The Queen believing it best for the country that she marry Georgie was very different from the newspapers thinking so.

'I must have time to think.' Her voice was unsteady. 'I cared for Eddy so much, you see.'

'And I am glad that you did.' Queen Victoria had a tender heart and it pained her to see how sincere May's grief was. 'But Eddy would be the first person to encourage you to move on with your life – and the only satisfactory way of doing so will be with Georgie.'

Two hours later and back home at White Lodge, May sat on the edge of her bed, a silver-framed photograph of Eddy in her hands. It had been given her by the Queen shortly after Eddy's funeral, and he was looking heart-stoppingly handsome in full Highland costume, a view of Balmoral behind him. Engraved at the foot of the silver frame were the words 'DINNA FORGET' and she knew for a certainty there wasn't the faintest chance of her ever doing so. But did that mean that she should never move on in her life? And was the Queen right in thinking that her only way of doing so was by marrying Georgie?

No matter how much she thought about things, she couldn't come up with what her answer was going be, when Georgie asked her to marry him, and she still hadn't done so when a couple of weeks later Looloo invited her for afternoon tea at Sheen Lodge. Looloo had not long since given birth to a baby girl who had been named Maud, after Maudie. May had only seen baby Maud once, at the christening, and was looking forward to seeing her again.

The first person she saw when she entered Sheen Lodge wasn't Looloo and baby Maud, but a desperately uncomfortable-looking Georgie.

'Hello, May,' he said, looking as if he wished himself anywhere but there. 'I only got back from Athens yesterday, and I thought I should start visiting family, especially as Looloo and Fife have had an addition.'

'Yes.' She made a valiant effort to recover her composure. 'How were Sophie and Tino?'

Sophie was one of Kindred Spirit Willy's sisters, and four years ago she had married Constantine, the heir to the Greek throne.

'They were all in the best of health. I like Tino, he's a solid, steady sort of chap, and Sophie is so easy to get on with. Not a bit like Willy.'

May was well aware that, apart from Alicky, she was the only person in the entire family who found it easy to get on with Willy, but she didn't say so. There had never been an awkward silence between her and Georgie when they had been at Sandringham, but there was now, and just as it began lengthening into one of acute embarrassment, Looloo came to their rescue by hurrying up to them and suggesting that they sat down to afternoon tea in the drawing room.

Aware of the reason for Georgie being there, Looloo and

Fife were almost as tense as their guests and the conversation was painfully stilted.

At last Looloo said, with something like desperation, 'Georgie, don't you think you ought to take May into the garden to look at the frogs in the pond?'

Scarlet in the face, Georgie rose to his feet and May had no option but to rise to hers.

This, she knew, was it. Once in the privacy of the garden, Georgie would propose to her and she would have to have her answer ready, and she knew what her answer was going to be. It was that she loved him as a cousin, but she didn't want their relationship to change into anything more.

There was a wrought-iron garden seat by the pond and, as they sat down, he took hold of her hand. Words had never come easily to Georgie, and they didn't come readily now.

'I would like . . .' he said, his face beetroot-red. 'I would be very honoured if . . .' He couldn't get any further. He took a handkerchief out of his pocket and mopped his brow with it, then said in a headlong rush, 'Dash it all, May. Will you marry me?'

For May, time stood still and halted.

She had had her answer all ready to give him, but now the words stuck in her throat. He looked so desperately in need of someone in his life who would be, to Georgie, what she would have been to Eddy that her heart went out to him. She had always been susceptible to male beauty. Irish good looks, as well as his talent, were what had attracted her so strongly to Thaddeus. It had been Eddy's good looks – which were not dissimilar to Thaddeus's – that had so attracted her when she was a young girl, and which had attracted her ever since.

Georgie was not remotely in the same category of handsomeness as Thaddeus and Eddy. Both of them had been tall and slim. Georgie was an inch or so shorter than she was – a difference that became apparent when she was wearing heeled shoes – and he had knock-knees and was slightly built. In looks he was, as the Queen had said so descriptively, 'homely'. He had no education to speak of – but then Eddy hadn't had any, either. Georgie also had a loud, abrasive voice, which she assumed was born out of having to bellow orders in rough, tempestuous seas. On the other side of the coin, he was dutiful, straightforward and it was impossible to imagine him ever being anything other than a faithful husband.

Most of all, though, as she looked into his very anxious face, she knew how much Georgie needed her. If she accepted his proposal, she would always be there for him, and she would always have a role in life; a role she suddenly felt had always been waiting for her; a role she was destined for.

'Yes,' she heard herself say. 'Yes, dear Georgie. Of course I will marry you.'

Chapter Twenty-Six

May's engagement to Georgie held no similarity to her engagement to Eddy. There was no laughter. No sense of ease and closeness. No animated conversations about how they would decorate their future home. No companionable choosing of fabric and wallpaper and visits to see popular musicals. With his proposal to her made – and her acceptance of it – it was as if Georgie felt he had done all that could be expected of him.

The companionship that had sprung up between the two of them in the days when she had been engaged to Eddy, and Georgie thought he was going to be her brother-in-law, was a thing of the past. He was stiff and shy with her and, because he was, May's own shyness and sense of awkwardness were crippling.

Almost immediately after the announcement of their engagement, and with no consultation with either May or Georgie, it was announced that their wedding would take place on 6 July.

'But that's only eight weeks away!' she had said in panic to her mother.

Her mother, for whom the wedding couldn't come soon enough, had gleefully replied that there was no time to be lost and they must immediately set about organizing her wedding gown and buying her trousseau.

So much had to be crammed into the eight weeks of their engagement that there was no time for her to be alone with Georgie – something May sensed Georgie was grateful for, and which only added to her pre-wedding nerves.

Georgie, too, was suffering from pre-wedding nerves and at White Lodge, with the wedding only days away, he and her mother had a most undignified falling-out. Princess Mary Adelaide's chatty exuberance and her constant interference with everything to do with the wedding had long been a source of intense irritation to Georgie and suddenly, when she was happily in full flow, his face flooded red and he shouted that he was tired of listening to her.

May's poor mother collapsed into a chair with shock. May was stupefied with horror. And Georgie speedily left the house.

A full day passed without an apology from him and May knew it was up to her to break the deadlock, if her wedding day wasn't to be one on which her mother and her bridegroom were not on speaking terms. So she wrote conciliatorily, and then a little untruthfully:

Dearest Georgie,

Mama has already quite forgotten your little spat of the other day. I quite sympathize with your outburst of temper. Mama can be very irritating, and at the moment things annoy us which we would not normally bother about. It is a very stressful period, and I am looking forward to the time after the wedding when we will be alone together.

She paused and then quickly, before she lost her nerve, she added:

*Forgive me for being so shy with you. I am trying hard not
to be, for it is too silly for us to be uncomfortable together,
when we are so soon to begin lovingly spending our lives
together.*

*Believe me when I say this little note comes with all my
heart, May x*

Ill at ease expressing his emotions verbally, Georgie much
preferred putting his feelings on paper. Ever since he had been
in his teens, his mother's deafness had been so profound that
writing to her had always been the way he expressed his love
for her; and it was to be the way, all through their marriage,
that he would most comfortably express his feelings for May.
He wrote back to her now:

*Thank God that we are able to understand each other so
well. I will try in the future to have patience with your
mother, who I know means well. I, too, suffer from being shy,
and my shyness may make me appear cold and indifferent,
and for that I can only apologize.*

Your husband-to-be, Georgie

The remaining days until the wedding were taken up with
receiving deputations of ladies from towns all over England,
presenting their wedding gifts; sitting to have her portrait
painted – wishing it was being painted by Thaddeus; attending
a dinner for two hundred, in her own and Georgie's honour,
at Marlborough House; going to command performances at
the Royal Opera House and the Theatre Royal; making the
obligatory trip to Frogmore to receive Prince Albert's posthumous blessing; and, most importantly, having fittings for
her wedding gown and trousseau.

The silk gown made for her wedding to Eddy had been

embroidered with mayflowers. The wasp–waisted, off-the-shoulder, cloth-of-silver wedding gown now being made for her was lavishly embroidered with roses and shamrocks. With it she would wear a wreath of orange blossom intertwined with myrtle and her mother's wedding veil, secured with a Rose of York diamond diadem, a present to her from the Queen.

All through the latter part of June and the beginning of July, London had sweltered in a heatwave, and May's wedding morning dawned bright and clear, with the same promise of heat in the air.

At eleven-thirty Georgie's mother and all the royal wedding guests left for St James's Palace and the Chapel Royal in open landaus, through streets crammed with cheering, flag-waving crowds. Fifteen minutes later, Georgie left the palace accompanied by his father, Next, in the state Glass Coach and to thunderous ovations, came the Queen accompanied by Princess Mary Adelaide. The Queen, dressed in black silk, wore the Riband of the Garter across her ample chest, and the diamond coronet she had worn at her own wedding was perched on top of her wispy, snow-white hair.

With rising tension, May watched every departure from a window of Buckingham Palace and then, accompanied by her father and Dolly, hurried downstairs to where her own carriage was waiting.

The route to the Chapel Royal took them up Constitution Hill, through Piccadilly and along St James's Street, and on every inch of the way she was greeted with the same kind of thunderous ovation that the Queen had met with.

At the Chapel Royal her bridesmaids were waiting for her. As they fell in behind her, the organist began to play the 'Wedding March', and as she walked down the aisle on her father's arm – hardly able to believe how her life was about to change – Georgie, handsome in naval uniform, looked towards her and made her a courtly bow.

Her mother cried when, four hours later and after the wedding breakfast, it was time for May and Georgie to leave for Liverpool Street station, where the train to Sandringham, at which they were to spend their honeymoon, was waiting for them.

'Life is going to be so quiet at White Lodge without you, May.' The words came from the bottom of Princess Mary Adelaide's heart. 'What on earth am I going to find to chat about, with only your papa for company?'

It was a question that, with the best will in the world, May had no answer for.

Liverpool Street station was thronged with relatives wanting to wave them on their way, and it was only when the train at last steamed out of the station that May was able to take off her hat trimmed with ostrich plumes and white rosebuds and collapse into one of the royal carriage's deeply comfortable armchairs.

'Thank God we don't have to smile any more,' Georgie said devoutly. 'You don't mind if I close my eyes and have a snooze, do you, May? It never occurred to me that getting married would be so exhausting.'

She didn't mind. She, too, was in dire need of a little peace and quiet. Until now she had refused to allow herself to think of anything other than the nervous tension of the ceremonial procession from Buckingham Palace and the wedding service. Now that those two hurdles were behind her, she had no excuse not to face what she had always known would be her biggest hurdle – Sandringham.

It was still so linked to memories of Eddy's agonizing death that it was the last place on earth she would have chosen for their honeymoon. She had hoped for Florence, or indeed anywhere that didn't have such painful memories. Instead, Georgie had chosen for them to spend their honeymoon at York Cottage on the Sandringham estate. Even worse, York Cottage, only a hundred yards from the big house, was where they were to make their home.

She bit her lip, knowing she had to forget the unhappy memories associated with Sandringham and think instead of how she and Georgie were on the threshold of making lots of new, happy memories there.

As the train steamed north-east out of London, May's thoughts turned to how the two of them were going to manage the coming night. Would Georgie know what to do? Had he had any previous experience?

She certainly hadn't, but her mother, a stranger to embarrassment, had told her what to expect.

'The first time isn't comfortable,' she had said frankly, when she had finished explaining the mechanics of what would take place, 'but you'll get used to it. You can get used to anything, given time. And Georgie is a gentleman,' she had added reassuringly. 'And that always helps.'

That evening in York Cottage they had a game of bezique and then several games of Halma. At last, as the drawing-room clock chimed ten o'clock, Georgie said, putting the Halma pieces back into their box and not meeting her eye, 'It's time to turn in, I think, May. It's been a long day.'

They walked up the stairs together and then, in their separate dressing rooms, changed into their nightclothes. Her nightdress, made of white silk lavishly embellished with French lace, demurely long-sleeved and high at the throat, fell reassuringly all the way down to her ankles. Dismissing her maid, she gave a last look in the mirror and, with her heart pounding, entered the lamplit bedroom.

A nightshirted George was sitting up in bed, waiting for her. 'You look very pretty, May,' he said, sounding as nervous as she felt, as she got into bed beside him. 'I like you with your hair unbraided.'

She lay down an inch or two away from him.

Georgie extinguished the lamp.

Several minutes went by and, in the deep darkness, she began to wonder if he had gone to sleep. Finally he said hoarsely, 'I'm going to have to lift the hem of your nightdress, May.'

Her mother had told her that when the moment came, it would help if she focused her mind on something else. She began mentally listing all the things that needed doing to York Cottage, if it was ever to be a comfortable home for the two of them. Georgie, whose only previous sexual experience had been with a prostitute in West Wickham to whom Eddy had kindly introduced him, proceeded to do what he always did. He did his best.

Within weeks May was pregnant.

'Let's hope it will be a boy,' Georgie said, cracking open a bottle of champagne. 'If it is, he will be Edward Albert Christian George Andrew Patrick David. Edward after Papa. Albert because Granny Queen will insist on it. Christian after Motherdear's papa. George after myself. And Andrew Patrick David after the three patron saints of Scotland, Ireland and Wales.'

May tightened her lips. Her own father's name was conspicuously absent and she knew why. Francis was quite simply not an English-enough-sounding name. There and then she decided that, if the baby was a boy, she would at least ensure that within the family he would be known by the name she liked best of the seven. He would be David.

Chapter Twenty-Seven

Alicky was at the Ehrenburg Palace in readiness for her brother Ernie's marriage to Ducky Edinburgh, although whether she was still Ducky Edinburgh, now that her father had succeeded a paternal uncle as the ruler of Coburg, she didn't know and didn't care.

And although I have always liked Ducky, I think our relationship might become difficult, once she moves into the Ducal Palace and takes over all the responsibilities I've taken care of for so long.

Alicky was in the middle of a letter to May:

The trouble with Ducky is that as well as being lively – something I truthfully don't mind – she is also, like her mama, assertive and bossy, and those are traits I do mind, and I know that living under the same roof as her is not going to be easy. As you are in a similar position with your mama-in-law, I know you will understand. How Georgie can bear living in such close proximity to Sandringham House – for a five-minute walk away on the Sandringham estate is no distance at all – I can't imagine, and to have

Aunt Alix calling in on the two of you without any warning, and even at breakfast time, would tax anyone's patience.

On a much different note, it is very nice seeing so many members of the family again, and all at the same time. Vicky, Irène and Ella and their husbands have already arrived in Coburg, and I cannot remember the last time we have all been together in such a way. Vicky and Louis have brought all three of their children with them, and Irène and Heinrich have brought Waldemar with them. He is five now, but as he has inherited the family blood disease, they cannot let him run about and be boisterous like other boys of his age. Ella and Sergei arrived yesterday, as did Vladimir and Paul, Sergei's Grand Duke brothers, and best of all – and oh, with what mixed feelings I write this – Nicky is due to arrive by train this afternoon. One part of my heart is singing with joy at the very thought of being with him again, while the other half is utterly broken at the knowledge that my Lutheran faith means I can never truly be his.

I do so, so, so wish that you had been able to travel and be here with me over the next week when Nicky is here, but fully understand that as your happy event is due in only a few weeks, it is utterly impossible for you to do so. Willy is going to be here and doubtless will have a handful of his sons with him. I don't know if Dona will also be attending the wedding, for if Willy can attend things without her, he generally does so.

And before I forget, Granny Queen and Uncle Bertie are expected at any moment. Coburg is such a tiny little duchy, and it has quite lost its head at the thought of Granny Queen gracing it with her presence. But of course, as Grandpa Albert was raised in Coburg, her attendance has never been in any doubt.

There came the sound of horse-drawn carriages entering the palace's cobbled courtyard and many feet running along corridors and down the stairs.

Putting her pen down, Alicky ran to the window in the hope that the carriages signalled her grandmother's arrival. She was just in time to see Missy step down from the leading carriage and, with Nando a few steps behind her, run into the arms of her loving mama.

It was time, as a sister of the groom, to socialize with her cousin and soon-to-be sister-in-law, and even though doing so was always torture for her, she had never found it difficult with Missy. Neither, according to Ernie, had many other people, including one of Nando's equerries, and an officer in his uncle, King Carol's, Imperial Guard.

In order to welcome Russia's Tsesarevich to Coburg, the city's small railway station was thick with bunting, streamers and white-blue-and-red Russian flags, the cheering populace kept at a distance by barriers and policemen. Two students were holding a giant home-made banner aloft on which was written WELCOME TO COBURG TSESAREVICH NICHOLAS. A military band was in place, ready to strike up the second Nicky and his entourage stepped from their imperial train, while a guard of honour was in place to escort him.

Alicky wasn't alone on the platform waiting to greet him, for the parents of the bride, her Uncle Affie and Aunt Marie were with her, as were many wedding guests who had arrived in the tiny principality earlier in the week.

As the train steamed to a halt, Alicky was oblivious to everyone standing around her. It was five years since they had said goodbye to each other in St Petersburg, and the world had narrowed down to just one person: Nicky.

He stepped from the train looking splendid in the full-dress uniform of the Imperial Hussars and, as the band struck rousingly into the Russian national anthem, his eyes flew to hers, and Alicky's chest felt so tight she thought it was going to burst.

There was no chance of private words together, for first Affie and Marie warmly welcomed Nicky, and then everyone else who had come to the station greeted him. The formalities took an age, but it didn't matter. From the moment their eyes had met, they had both known instantly that nothing about their feelings for each other had changed.

All that day and evening, surrounded by extended family, there was no chance for them to be alone together, and that night – the night of Nicky's arrival – the wedding party went en masse to an operetta.

Being able to have any private time together the next day was just as impossible, as Granny Queen arrived, accompanied by Uncle Bertie and a squadron of British Dragoons. As Alicky was the Queen's favourite granddaughter, the Queen never let her out of her sight.

Only on the second day did she and Nicky finally manage to speak together in privacy.

'And what I have been so bursting to tell you, Alicky darling, is that my parents have finally realized that I am never, ever going to marry anyone but you, and I can now propose to you with their full blessing!' He held both her hands tightly in his. 'Papa has not been well, and it has reminded him that he cannot live forever, and he wants to see me married and with sons, and the succession to the throne secured before he dies.'

He went down on one knee before her. 'And so dearest, darling, most wonderful Alicky, please say this changes your mind about not marrying me, and that you will marry me. *Please*, my darling, for I cannot face going through life without you. You are my sun, moon and stars. Please say you will marry me, Alicky.'

She shook her head. 'No, Nicky. I cannot.' Tears of despair rolled down her face, her voice so thick with tears it was barely audible. 'Truly, I cannot. When I was very young I made contact with my mama at a seance and she asked me never to forget my confirmation vows, and so, you see, I can never deny being a Lutheran. I cannot accept Russian Orthodoxy. It simply isn't possible, my darling, truly it isn't.'

Nothing he could say would change her mind.

All Alicky said in a whisper, time and time again and with her hands still held tightly in his, was: 'No, I cannot, Nicky. I cannot.'

Everyone in the palace was aware of the situation between the two of them, and the main topic of conversation was not Ernie and Ducky's wedding the next day, but whether or not Alicky would eventually change her mind and agree to marry Nicky.

'It's totally infuriating,' Ducky said crossly to Missy. 'Tomorrow is *my* day! *I'm* the bride. *I'm* supposed to be the centre of attention. And all anyone is talking about is Alicky and Nicky. Do you think she's holding out on him in order to spoil my wedding day? She doesn't want me to marry Ernie, I know that. She's been First Lady of the Duchy for too long to want me displacing her, but I have never, *ever* been the centre of attention, because I have never been the pretty one – *you* have always been the pretty one – and now, just when I could expect to be the centre of everyone's attention for a few days, it's all Alicky, Alicky, Alicky!'

Missy rolled her eyes. 'Goodness, Ducky, don't let Alicky rattle your cage before the wedding. It's going to be difficult enough when you are both living beneath the same roof. You're suffering from pre-wedding nerves, and the only cure is either several glasses of champagne or a long, hard horse-ride. So which is it to be? Personally, I'd opt for champagne.'

Ducky hadn't. With less than twenty-four hours to go before she walked down the aisle, she took her favourite stallion out for a long, breakneck gallop. With a stiff breeze stinging her cheeks, she knew she hadn't been truthful with Missy as to why she was in such a bad-tempered mood. True, it was annoying that when she should have been the centre of everyone's attention, she wasn't, and Alicky was, but that wasn't the reason she was so overwrought. The real reason was that although she liked Ernie an awful lot – and with good reason, for he was terrifically good-looking and great company – she wasn't head over heels in love with him. In fact, she wasn't in love with him at all. She was in love with Grand Duke Kyril Vladimirovich Romanov, Nicky's cousin.

That Kyril had never made a serious pass at her didn't matter. She had seen the way he looked at her and was certain that, if it hadn't been for Romanovs not being allowed to marry their first cousins, he would have made a pass at her years ago. She had never heard his name linked seriously with anyone – except with ballerinas, of course; ballerinas were de rigueur for all Romanov men. One had only to look at Kyril – six feet four, broad-shouldered, slim-hipped and oozing sex appeal – to know that he wasn't deviant, as Marie-Louise's husband, Aribert of Anhalt, so blatantly was.

On the brow of a hill she reined her horse in. A whole raft of Romanov relations had made the journey to Coburg for her wedding, but Kyril had not been among them. She knew why. It was because he'd had no desire to see her marrying Ernie.

But if he had come to Coburg, had taken her passionately in his arms, said that he loved her and couldn't live without her, that Romanov protocol forbidding first cousins from marrying didn't matter, and that even though it would mean exile from Russia, he would happily be exiled for her sake – if she had to ditch Ernie and run away to Paris with Kyril – she would have done so in a flash.

She was a tough young woman who rarely cried, but tears glittered on her eyelashes. There was going to be no Kyril in her life, but there was going to be Ernie, and she was just going to have to make the best of the cards she had been dealt.

With her heart feeling as if it was about to break, Ducky turned her horse's head around and headed bleakly back to the palace, doing so at a slow trot, in no hurry to arrive.

That evening a handful of the male wedding guests, Nicky and Willy among them, congregated in the billiard room to smoke and drink and pot a few balls. Nicky was in an almost suicidal state of depression.

'Alicky loves me,' he said, when Willy asked him how things stood between him and Alicky. 'She loves me with all her heart, Willy, but the dear girl simply cannot bring herself to forswear her religion for Orthodoxy. Ella has tried to get her to change her mind, for although Ella didn't convert when she married Sergei, she has converted since; and Sergei's mother was born Lutheran and she, too, converted when she married. So Alicky has two wonderful examples to follow, but neither Ella nor Aunt Miechen has been able to get her to change her mind and, as the Tsesarevich, I absolutely cannot marry her unless she does so.'

A tingling sensation ran through Willy's body. If he could get Alicky to agree to marry Nicky, he would be seen as the matchmaker par excellence in the family, while at the same time achieving a masterstroke of international diplomacy. For with Russia's future tsarina a German, Russia was never likely to be a military threat to Germany, which was becoming an ever-increasing concern on the international stage.

'Leave it to me.' He slapped Nicky hard on the back. 'I'll speak to Alicky the minute tomorrow's church service is over. I'll get her to change her mind.'

Nicky had no faith at all in Willy's confidence. He couldn't see how, if both Ella and Miechen had failed to change Alicky's mind, Willy would be able to, for it wasn't as if he and Alicky were close. He'd never even heard her mention Willy's name.

So deep in despair that he couldn't see how he was going to get through the next few days, let alone the rest of his life, he went to his room to write Alicky another desperately pleading letter.

The next morning, after Ernie and Ducky's wedding ceremony and in the interval before the wedding guests sat down to the wedding breakfast, Willy asked Alicky if he could speak to her privately, as a Kindred Spirit.

Alicky was too taken aback to say no, for although she and May had kept the Kindred Spirit bond affectionately alive between the two of them, Willy had long regarded it as too childish to be taken seriously and had thereby broken the blood-bond between them, and she was surprised he even remembered it.

'I want,' he said when the door of a small room had closed behind them, 'to speak to you about why you should no longer keep refusing Nicky's proposals of marriage.'

Alicky's eyes, red-rimmed from a night of crying, opened wide with shock. 'As Kaiser, you're Head of the German Lutheran Church! You, of all people, know why I cannot marry him!'

'And in that role, I can tell you that you will not be abandoning the Church of your birth if you adopt Orthodoxy. Instead, your adoption of Orthodoxy will enrich and deepen your Lutheran faith.'

It was far from being what he really thought and felt. A few years ago Willy had barred his sister Sophie from ever setting foot on German soil again, when she had married Tino of Greece and had converted to Orthodoxy. For the moment, though, it was convenient to convince himself that they were his real feelings; and when Willy wanted to convince himself of anything, he did so easily and with passionate – although temporary – sincerity.

'It is what both Ella and Miechen have found,' he said, having no idea whether or not this was true. 'And Nicky's mother, too, was a Lutheran until she married Nicky's father. A change of faith is really not such an unusual thing for a royal in your position.'

'No,' Alicky said, as she had said to Nicky. 'I cannot do it. I cannot.' Tears choked her throat. 'I have made a promise to my late mama that I will never forget my confirmation vows.'

Willy had the vision of a much-needed military alliance between Germany and Russia in front of him, and he wasn't accustomed to being thwarted.

'There is no need for you ever to do so,' he said, with what he hoped was God-like authority. 'The vows you took as a Lutheran are, in essence, the same as the vows taken at confirmation in the Russian Orthodox Church. And so, when you make your vows on becoming a member of the Orthodox Church, you will simply be reaffirming your Lutheran vows.'

Whether what he was saying was true, he didn't care. All that mattered to him was that Alicky married Nicky, and that the future Empress of Russia would be a German.

'Think of Nicky,' he continued, undeterred. 'He is a mild-mannered, gentle young man, not unlike late Cousin Eddy. And Granny Queen realized that when Eddy became King and Emperor, he would need a strong woman at his side to give him the strength and forcefulness his own nature lacked. That was why she arranged for a marriage between him and

Kindred Spirit May – and it is why, on his death, she didn't let such an admirable future Queen and Empress go to waste and saw to it that May married Georgie. When Nicky becomes Tsar, the responsibilities he will inherit are so vast they will crush him. If he is not to be dominated by his uncles – and make no mistake, Alicky, his uncles' intentions will be to dominate him and rule through him – he will need a wife who will be a strength to him; someone who will rule the largest country in the world alongside him, allowing no one else to influence him. And God's purpose for you, Alicky, is to be that person. It is,' he ended with an over-the-top theatrical flourish of his good hand, 'your royal duty and God-given destiny!'

Alicky stared at him, stunned. For a moment Willy thought she had stopped breathing. 'And will I truly not be breaking my promise to my mama if I become Russian Orthodox?'

'How can you be, when the vows to love God and to live in service to Him are the same, although expressed differently, for both Lutherans and members of the Russian Orthodox Church?' He was so convincing, he almost believed what he was saying.

Alicky certainly did so. Slowly, but very purposely, she rose to her feet.

'I need to find Nicky,' she said dazedly. 'I need to tell him I now see my way clearly. I need to tell him I have changed my mind.'

'You'll find him in the little snug outside Ernie's room, waiting for the outcome of my conversation with you,' Willy said, even more highly pleased with himself than usual.

He would have said more – that Nicky would be in a state of near-collapse waiting to know if she had, or hadn't, changed her mind – but Alicky had run from the room, the door swinging on its hinges behind her.

Ignoring dozens of her startled relatives, she sprinted in

the direction of the palace's main staircase. On reaching it, she scooped her skirt up in her hands, taking the wide steps at a run, narrowly avoiding knocking over a startled Louis of Battenberg, who was coming down them.

Breathlessly, her heart hammering, she ran in the direction of the set of rooms that were Ernie's. Almost sick with the fear that Nicky would no longer be in the snug, and gasping for breath, she flung open the door.

He had been standing facing the fireplace. At her entrance he spun round, every line of his body taut with tension.

With blazing happiness on her face she rushed across to him, throwing herself into his arms, saying, 'I will marry you, darling Nicky. I will, I will!'

With a sob of overwhelming thankfulness, he burrowed his face in her hair. 'Oh, thank God, sweetheart. My life would be nothing to me without you in it. I love you so much. My whole life is yours, Alicky. Always and for eternity!'

And his mouth came down on hers, hot and sweet, passion uniting them in a way that would never, to the end of their lives, fail them.

Chapter Twenty-Eight

'And the dear darling just burst into tears when I told him.'

Alicky was sitting with a heavily pregnant May in the garden of York Cottage, Sandringham.

'The family – and there were more than sixty of them gathered there – went wild at the wedding breakfast when we announced our news. Ducky was dreadfully miffed, but that couldn't be helped. We simply couldn't keep such tremendous news to ourselves, and it was perfect being able to tell everyone all at once.'

May, who was so physically uncomfortable she felt as if it was a baby elephant that she was pregnant with, eased herself into what she hoped would be a more comfortable position. It wasn't.

'And we had ten blissful, beautiful days before Nicky had to return to St Petersburg,' Alicky continued, 'and as I had already arranged to stay with Granny Queen for three months, I came to England. And Granny then invited Nicky to Windsor, so that she could get to know him a little better, and he is going to be with me for nearly the whole time I am here. I'm so happy, May! I never knew people could be this happy. Truly I didn't.'

May was sincerely glad Alicky was so passionately in love with Nicky, but she had some reservations.

Putting her foreboding into words, she said, 'Once you marry Nicky, you will constantly be the centre of attention. Have you thought of how you will cope with that? I know how much you have hated being a bridesmaid at family weddings, but family weddings are nothing in comparison to the great state occasions that are part and parcel of Nicky's life, and are now going to be part and parcel of your life also.'

Alicky had been reassuringly dismissive. 'There's no need to worry about me on that score, May. Uncle Sasha is only in his forties and is an enormously big, strong man. Do you know that he can bend an iron poker with his bare hands? It's going to be twenty or thirty years before Nicky succeeds him as Tsar, and until then Nicky and I are going to live in the same kind of quiet domesticity that you and Georgie so happily live in here, at York Cottage.'

May didn't flinch at the word 'happily', but it took a lot of her willpower not to do so. With fierce determination, she put all thoughts of her and Georgie's tortuous shyness and embarrassment in the bedroom – and their total incompatibility out of it, as well as in it – to the back of her mind. 'Quiet domesticity may be achievable in England, Alicky,' she said wryly, 'but I doubt it's a phrase much used in Russia. You and Nicky will be trailblazers!'

Their time together as an engaged couple in England was idyllic, but by September the idyll was over, and Nicky was back in St Petersburg and Alicky was in Darmstadt. As the fiancée of the Tsesarevich, she would be joining him for good in the New Year when, in preparation for a spring wedding, she would be accepted into the Russian Orthodox Church.

It was a day that couldn't come soon enough, for the harmonious atmosphere in the New Palace that had existed before Ernie and Ducky's marriage was harmonious no longer.

'Why did no one tell me?' Ducky demanded time and again, on the verge of hysteria. 'You must have known, Alicky! Why didn't you tell me Ernie is only interested in men? Why did you leave it for me to find out on my wedding night? And now I've found out, it seems that everyone else in the family knows of Ernie's preference for Hussar officers, valets and stable-boys – and yet no one, *no one*, thought it important enough to tell me!'

'You did return from your honeymoon pregnant,' Alicky had pointed out, trying to get Ducky to look on the bright side of things.

Ducky's dark eyes had flashed fire. 'Oh yes, that major miracle occurred! But only because Ernie becoming a father and having a son to inherit Hesse and by Rhine after him was the only reason he married me. And if he could have come to bed fully dressed and with gloves on to do the deed, he would have.'

In October, Alicky received an urgent telegram from Nicky: *Papa ill. We are at Livadia, in the Crimea. I need you, darling. Please come.*

If she could have flown there in an instant, she would have. As it was, and with the telegram still in her hand, she ran to her bedroom, calling out for her lady-in-waiting and for maids. She needed to pack. She had to leave at once, if she was to give the love of her life the support he so badly needed.

She travelled by train as far as Warsaw with her lady-in-waiting and with Vicky, who had been on a sisterly visit to Darmstadt. At Warsaw, Ella, who had travelled from the Crimea to meet them, took over as Alicky's escort, bringing with her no good news.

'Uncle Sasha is desperately ill,' she said as they settled into a compartment aboard the train that would take them to Simferopol, where they would be met by Nicky. 'He has nephritis. His kidneys are on the point of failing completely.'

'And when they do?' Alicky's heart was in her mouth.

'Then he will die – and the doctors say it is only going to be days before he does so.'

The blood fled from Alicky's face. How could Nicky's father die now, when Nicky had not anticipated succeeding him for many years? What would happen to the future that she and Nicky had been so eagerly looking forward to? How could a life of quiet domesticity be lived, once they became Tsar and Tsarina? The answer, of course, was that it couldn't.

Other questions came thick and fast. How would Nicky cope with so suddenly becoming the autocratic ruler of a great empire? How would she cope with the public display that came with being Tsarina? As question after question flooded her brain, Alicky struggled to think of an alternative scenario. Perhaps Ella was exaggerating. Perhaps the doctors had made the wrong diagnosis and were being unnecessarily fatalistic. Perhaps, even at this very moment, Nicky's father was beginning to regain strength, rather than continuing to lose it. Another thought came to her and she said, 'Who is in control of things at the palace, Ella?'

'No one. It's complete chaos. We all knew Uncle Sasha hadn't been well for some time, but no one imagined he was ill with something that would prove fatal. Nicky is in complete pieces, as is Aunt Minny.'

At Simferopol, Nicky was waiting to greet her, flanked only by a couple of equerries. Hugging her tightly, his voice breaking with emotion, he said, 'Oh, thank heavens you are here, Alicky. I couldn't have survived another day without you. And apologies that there is no reception party, and that no imperial train was waiting for you when you reached the border, but the minister whose job it is to arrange such things forgot all about doing so, in his anxiety about my father.'

'Reception parties and imperial trains are of no importance

at a time like this.' Alicky slid her hand into the crook of his arm and squeezed it, in loving reassurance. 'How is your papa? Has there been any change in his condition?'

'A little, but none that gives hope.' Nicky looked towards Ella, who, together with Sergei and his father's other three brothers, had been at Livadia for more than a week. 'He now only speaks when he absolutely has to, Ella,' he said to her as they stepped into a waiting carriage. 'I just hope and pray he is still able do so by the time Alicky arrives.'

Simferopol was a mountain town, and their carriage ride to Livadia took them through a high pass before heading down through heavily wooded hillsides towards the Black Sea. Beautiful as the scenery was, none of them were capable of appreciating it, their thoughts taken up with what they would find when they arrived at their destination.

What they found was the chaos that Ella had warned Alicky about – and it was chaos laced with panic. Government ministers and court officials ran like headless chickens up and down stairs and along crimson-carpeted corridors. Aunt Minny, usually so vivacious and dazzling, was white-faced and dazed with anxiety.

'Your father has insisted on being dressed, so that he can greet Alicky in the way the Tsar of Russia has always greeted a future Russian empress,' she said to Nicky, after she had given Alicky two hasty kisses on both cheeks. 'I tried to dissuade him, but he was adamant. Absolutely adamant.'

The vast bedroom smelled of sickness. There were oxygen bags in a corner of it, and a bedspread embroidered with double-headed eagles hid evidence that the bed had only recently been vacated. Seated in an armchair in the centre of the room was the waxen, wasted figure of what had once been an all-powerful bear of a man.

Minny moved to the side of his chair and rested a hand tenderly on a shrunken shoulder. Once, long ago, when the imperial train had become derailed and the roof of the carriage the family were travelling in had collapsed, her husband had taken the colossal weight of it on his back and had lifted it sufficiently to allow her and their children to scramble to safety. Now he looked as if a puff of air would be more than he could survive.

Fighting for breath between each word, he formally welcomed Alicky, telling her that although she was German by birth, on her marriage to Nicky she would become Russian by adoption. Just as his Danish-born wife had become Russian by adoption. And then, as she and Nicky kneeled before him, he had valiantly given them his blessing.

For the next few days Alicky rarely saw Nicky. That his distraught mother and his dying father needed his presence was something she understood. But it meant she had no one, other than Ella, to help her accustom herself to a foreign court – one that was in uproar and in a near-hysterical state of panic.

'Bertie and Alix have been sent for,' Ella said to her. 'Minny needs Alix at a time like this. As sisters, they have always been close. And Bertie will bring a sense of order to things.'

That it was going to be up to English Uncle Bertie to bring order to a disarrayed Russian court bewildered Alicky and she felt indignant, on Nicky's behalf, that Ella should think Uncle Bertie was needed.

It didn't take long, however, for her to begin seeing things differently, for although it was obvious to everyone that Nicky would be the Tsar within days – possibly hours – no one treated him with the respect that, as his father's heir, was his due. Instead of coming to him with the latest findings on his father's condition, the doctors bypassed him and gave their reports to Minny. Government officials also ignored him, bringing state papers to Minny and not to him. Even Sergei didn't seek Nicky out in the way Alicky felt he should have, and neither did the Tsar's other two brothers, Vladimir and Paul. Instead, the three of them were constantly to be found in close, secretive huddles, always falling silent if anyone walked too near them. Whatever Alicky had expected on her long journey to Livadia, it hadn't been that she would be sidelined when she arrived; and that Nicky would be equally sidelined shocked her deeply.

Her shock showed, as did her feelings concerning the doctor's attitude towards Nicky and his uncles' attitude towards him. Before long her presence at Livadia became very unwelcome and, as the Tsar's condition continued to deteriorate, the superstitious Russian household blamed Alicky, muttering amongst themselves that she had brought bad luck into the country with her.

Three days later, and without the doctor's attitude or that of his uncles towards Nicky having changed, Tsar Alexander kissed his wife, took a last agonized breath and slid from this world into the next.

If things in the palace had been chaotic before, they were even more chaotic now that the giant who had ruled Russia so ably was there to do so no longer. Nicky was shattered by grief and in despair. Over and over again he said, 'I'm not ready to be Tsar, Alicky. I've never wanted to become Tsar. I don't know *how* to become Tsar!'

'Yes, you do, my darling.' She was as firm as, only a few months ago, Willy had been with her. 'God's plan has always been for you to be Tsar. Becoming Tsar is your God-given destiny, Nicky. You must put your trust in Him, as I do, and all will be well.'

Uncle Vladimir burst in on them.

'There's no coffin!' he said explosively. 'For weeks Sasha has been slowly dying and yet there's no coffin and no embalming arrangements in place.'

As Nicky frantically tried to get his head around all the arrangements that it now seemed were up to him and not, as he had imagined they would be, up to the Minister of the Imperial Court, Uncle Alexis put his head round the door. 'Everything is ready for the oath of allegiance, Nicky,' he said tersely. 'The priests have had a field altar set up in the garden. Household staff, officials and courtiers are already assembled and the family are now on their way down.'

Nicky sucked in a deep, steadying breath. This was it – this was the moment he had dreaded all his life, and which he had hoped he wouldn't have to face for another couple of decades. His eyes met Alicky's and, drawing strength from the total love he saw in their blue-grey depths, and with her at his side, he walked out of the room and out of the palace.

It was twilight and, beneath a blood-red sky, priests in golden robes faced a large group of family and courtiers. From nearby Yalta came the sound of the guns of the Russian fleet booming a tribute. Livadia's church bells tolled.

Alicky came to a halt beside Minny. A white-faced Nicky took his place in front of Father Yanishev, his father's confessor. The guns fell silent and, as Father Yanishev administered the oath, Minny could be heard stifling a sob.

In deepening twilight Nicky repeated the words of the oath and as he was proclaimed 'His Imperial Majesty The Emperor and Autocrat of all the Russias!' distant thunder rolled far out at sea.

'Holy God,' Sergei muttered to Vladimir. 'A storm is coming. What an omen! The less said about it when we reach St Petersburg, the better.'

'And no pointing out that our new Tsarina will be heading to her wedding behind a coffin,' Vladimir added grimly. 'You know how superstitious people are. If that unpleasant truth takes hold, Alicky will never be seen as anything other than an ill-luck bride bringing bad fortune to Russia. And then where will we be?'

Chapter Twenty-Nine

For Alicky, the following week was made survivable only by the arrival of Uncle Bertie and Aunt Alix. Under Bertie's imposing, forceful direction the atmosphere at the palace changed, for no one, not even Nicky's uncles, wanted to appear panicked and inept in front of England's firmly capable Prince of Wales.

Within a few short hours of his arrival, order was once again mercifully established. Aware that Nicky was far too grief-stricken to make even the slightest of decisions and that no funeral arrangements were yet in place, he suggested that perhaps it would be useful if he, Bertie, began making them.

'Dear God, please do!' Nicky was fervently grateful. 'I'll be forever in your debt, Bertie.'

Wreathed in cigar smoke, Bertie organized the coffin, the embalming and the travel arrangements for the transportation of the coffin to Moscow. There it would lie in state for three days, before the onward travel to St Petersburg, where the funeral service and burial would take place.

While he was doing this, Nicky – inspired by Bertie's smooth efficiency – arranged that Alicky be received immediately into the Russian Orthodox Church.

'Because until you are, we can't marry.' He paused. 'And I

want us to marry here, at Livadia. I can't bear the thought of having to wait until the funeral has taken place in St Petersburg.'

Feeling the exciting hardness of his body against hers, Alicky was no more willing to wait than he was.

Nicky's uncles thought differently.

'Preposterous idea!' Vladimir said to Nicky, as if Nicky was merely a badly behaved nephew. 'A tsar's wedding is as great a national event as his coronation.'

Sergei and Alexis were equally adamant that marrying in the Crimea would be the very worst way for him to start his rule as Emperor and Autocrat of all the Russias.

It was only when Bertie said, 'Your uncles are speaking sense, Nicky. Go ahead with Alicky's confirmation, but wait to be married until you are in St Petersburg and then you can follow Romanov tradition by being married in the Winter Palace', that Nicky reluctantly abandoned the idea of a quiet Livadia wedding.

Alicky wrote in violet ink to May:

> But my confirmation into the Orthodox Church went ahead, with close family present and with everyone dressed in black. It was wonderful how utterly calm I was, and how sure I was that I was doing the right thing. Nicky's first official act as Tsar was to sign a decree confirming me in my new faith, along with my new name, which is Alexandra Feodorovna. Nicky has begun calling me Alix (but to friends and family I will always be Alicky).
>
> The transporting of Uncle Sasha's body from Livadia to St Petersburg took nearly two weeks, as the funeral train stopped at town after town so that city dignitaries could pay their respects. In Moscow, people filed past the open coffin all night long, with many people kissing Uncle Sasha's

embalmed lips. How Uncle Bertie survived it all, I don't
know, but he never let a hint of distaste or impatience show,
and I and Nicky will always be grateful to him.

Once in St Petersburg, there was another long procession
through snow-covered streets to the Cathedral of St Peter
and Paul. Ernie is here for the funeral, but he arrived
without Ducky, who is four months pregnant and continually
being sick. Kyril Vladimirovich (Nicky's Uncle Vladimir's
eldest son) asked after her. I thought it an odd thing for him
to have done, for he could hardly have expected me to update
him on her pregnancy! Nicky said their being first cousins
explained it, and that Kyril – who is by far the handsomest
of Nicky's many cousins – is a law unto himself. Like
everyone else, he is staying on after the funeral for the
wedding, which, at Nicky's insistence, is to take place in just
over a week's time.

There is no question but that I will once again have
thousands and thousands of pairs of eyes upon me, but I will
survive it by blocking everything from my consciousness,
other than my beloved Nicky and our vows, as we are bound
together body and soul for what I know will be eternity. I
only wish Granny Queen hadn't taken the view that there
were enough English royals leaving England for St
Petersburg, without you leaving your darling baby to add
to their number. Ever since Georgie has arrived, he has
looked as if he is missing you – as I know that, in similar
circumstances, my beloved Nicky would be missing me.

Just as Georgie and Nicky were constantly mistaken for
each other when we were in England in the summer, so the
same thing is happening now, here in St Petersburg. Because
of their being so alike – the same height, same build, same
piercing blue eyes, same hair colour, same identical
moustaches and trim Van Dyke beards – family we don't

meet up with very often, such as the Serbian royals and the
Swedish royals, regularly chat to Nicky, thinking he is
Georgie; and to Georgie, thinking he is Nicky. It leads
to all sorts of comical situations, which Nicky and Georgie
naughtily encourage.

And now I really must finish. A wedding that would
normally take months of preparation is going to take place in
eight days' time – and it is only because it falls on Aunt
Minny's birthday that court mourning will be suspended.

Lots and lots of love to you and to Baby, your loving
Kindred Spirit, Alicky

'There's no need to worry about Ducky, Alicky,' Ernie said, when they managed to speak together on their own without an army of relations chipping in and interrupting them. 'Wretchedly sick, of course, but the doctors say that will come to an end before very long.'

'And what about the bedroom situation?' Well-bred unmarried young women were kept in ignorance about the nuts and bolts of marriage until their wedding night, but thanks to Birds-and-Bees chats with their progressively-minded married sister Vicky, Alicky prided herself on being exceptionally knowledgeable.

'Dash it all, Alicky!' Ernie fumbled for his cigarette case and lighter. 'That's not the kind of thing a girl should be asking her brother. All you need to know – all anyone needs to know – is that I've done my duty and that, in a few months' time, Hesse and by Rhine will have an heir! And that is what you should be putting your mind to. Giving Russia an heir, not hounding me about Ducky.'

Next day Alicky stood by a weeping Nicky as his father's heavy coffin was lowered slowly into the family vault.

'And now that Nicky is Emperor,' Sergei said to her, as they stood on the hard-packed snow outside the cathedral, waiting for her carriage to roll up and take its place in the procession back to the Winter Palace, 'he is going to need all the help in ruling Russia that I – along with Vladimir and Alexis – can give him.'

Beneath her black mourning veil, Alicky's forehead creased in a frown. Sergei was the Governor-General of Moscow. Vladimir was Commander of the Imperial Guard. Alexis was the Grand Admiral of the Fleet. Paul, Nicky's good-looking youngest uncle, was only eight years older than Nicky, and his not holding an important position was presumably why Sergei hadn't mentioned him. She remembered Kindred Spirit Willy saying to her that when Nicky became Tsar, his uncles would try and dominate him and rule through him, and that Nicky needed her at his side to make sure they didn't succeed in doing so.

'Nicky will always be glad of your support, Sergei, and of Uncle Vladimir's and Uncle Alexis's, but the Tsar is answerable to no one but God and so needs no help in ruling. I remember you teaching me that when I was a child.'

It was so far from being the reaction he was expecting that Sergei's eyebrows shot up in surprise. Recovering himself swiftly, he said, 'Forgive me, Alicky, but you haven't yet been at Nicky's side long enough to appreciate how completely ignorant he is of anything to do with affairs of state. Sasha believed he still had decades left in which to introduce Nicky to the business of ruling. It's something he was tragically wrong about and, as a consequence, Nicky is totally unfamiliar with state papers and hasn't even headed a committee. He knows no more than a child about the business of ruling.'

Her carriage, in which traditionally – as a bride-to-be – she was to ride in unaccompanied, had come to a halt in front of them. 'Even though you are his uncle,' Alicky said, moving to step into it, 'that is not how you should now refer to Nicky. He isn't a child. He is twenty-six. And as he is the Tsar, God will help him with whatever it is that he doesn't yet know.'

And with great dignity, as if already an empress, she settled herself in the carriage. As it joined the long line of carriages now rolling away from the cathedral, Alicky kept her eyes fixed firmly forwards, resolutely not looking back to where Sergei was staring after her, a look of shocked disbelief on his face.

'Who the devil does she think she is?' Vladimir exploded, when Sergei told him of the reaction he had had from Alicky. 'Does she have a lust for power? Because God help Russia if she has! How can a young woman from a tadpole-sized duchy like Hesse and by Rhine imagine she can give Nicky the help he's going to need to rule the largest country on earth? The boy couldn't even organize a coffin for his father's funeral!'

Paul said mildly, 'You said you'd been laying the groundwork for this moment for years, Sergei; that if, and when, she became Empress, she would be eating out of your hand and that consequently Nicky would be, too.'

'And I believed it – and it's how things are going to be. I spoke without thinking and didn't gauge the moment right. Things will be different when she realizes how inept Nicky is.'

'They had better be!' Veins stood out like cords on Vladimir's bull-like neck. 'Nicky's as weak as water. Someone has to put some spine into him, and that someone isn't going to be an adoring wife who will never see past his charming good looks and their bedroom door. For the sake of Russia, it has to be me, you and Alexis. We have to be the power behind the throne! Not a chit of a girl from Darmstadt.'

* * *

'That our wedding ceremony is to take place in the chapel of the Winter Palace and not in St Isaac's Cathedral, as it would have if my father hadn't died,' Nicky said as he and Alicky snatched a rare precious moment of privacy together, 'means that although there will be a lot of the pomp and ceremony you so dislike, there won't be quite as much as there might have been.'

He hugged her tight, as mad with desire for her as she was for him.

'And am I to leave for the Winter Palace from Sergei and Ella's palace on Nevsky Prospekt and accompanied by your mama?'

'Yes, but not in your wedding gown. Being dressed in your wedding gown is a ceremony in itself and takes place in the Winter Palace's Malachite Hall. Mama has asked me to warn you how heavy everything will be, for a cloth-of-gold mantle is worn over the gown, and a train yards and yards long will be attached to your shoulders. And then of course there is the weight of the jewels you will be wearing. Mama said that on her processional walk from the Malachite Hall to the chapel her knees buckled more than once.'

Alicky fought down rising panic. Fiercely she told herself that if she did as she had decided to do, and blocked out of her consciousness everything but Nicky and the vows they would make to each other, then the ordeal was one she could, and would, survive – and oh, how worthwhile surviving it would be.

'Just think, dearest love,' she whispered, close and safe in the comfort of his arms, 'after the ceremony we will never need to spend a single night apart. No matter what each day brings, at the end of it will be the utter, utter bliss of lying in each other's arms in a vast soft bed in our own private world – and for that blessing I will pay any price.'

The heat in Nicky's eyes as he lowered his head to hers told her how passion-filled those nights would be.

Although there were a dozen maids fluttering around in Alicky's bedroom on the morning of her wedding day, it was Ella who was assisting her with her toilette.

'As you stayed beneath my palace roof last night, and as I am your older sister, there is no one who can tell me it is not royal etiquette for me to be doing so,' she said, applying a faint touch of rouge to Alicky's cheeks. 'And I want to do it. It reminds me of when, after Mama died, I did so much of the looking after you.'

A light dusting of powder followed the rouge. Ella stood back from her handiwork and surveyed it in the dressing table's large triple mirror. 'I think you should wear a little lip colour as well, Alicky. Not much. Just a smidgeon.'

A few seconds later she said, 'There, pet lamb. I have been very delicate.'

Alicky looked in the mirror. Was the face looking back at her the face of a woman about to become Empress of Russia? She didn't know, but she did know that she'd had years of practice in concealing her inner fears and anxieties. She resolved that whatever fears and anxieties she met with in the future, no one, apart from Nicky, would ever know of them; not the crowds that would always be wanting a glimpse of her; or the hundreds of courtiers in the Winter Palace, the Anitchkov Palace, the palace at Peterhof and the palace at Livadia.

As she rose to her feet to allow the maids to dress her in the silver-and-brocade gown that she was to wear to the Winter Palace, she vowed that from now on, no matter how turbulent her inner feelings, outwardly she would always be the very essence of imperial dignity. It was what her Granny Queen would be expecting of her, and what her beloved Nicky needed from her, and she wasn't going to let either of them down. Not now. Not ever.

A valet knocked on the door and gave a message to her lady-in-waiting. The Dowager Empress's carriage had arrived at the palace and it was time for Alicky to join her.

Alicky took one last look in the mirror, set her mouth in a determined line so that her crippling nervousness wouldn't be obvious to the crowds and then, draped in furs, turned and walked from the room. One part of her life was over. Another part – unimaginably, unbelievably different – was about to begin.

Chapter Thirty

Alicky wrote to May, her pen flying over the imperial headed notepaper:

> *And so I must apologize for barely keeping in touch with you over the last eighteen months, but I have been so busy helping my dearest Nicky with the crushing load of government papers he has to attend to every day – being an autocratic ruler, every last little detail of ruling Russia is up to him and the burden is almost intolerable. Also, being a new mama, I have been spending every other minute with my plump little Olga, who is now almost six months old.*
>
> *Coronation Day is now only a week away, and you ask why it hasn't taken place before now and how I shall survive the ordeal. The reason for the long time-gap between Nicky becoming Tsar and being crowned is that there was a twelve-month mourning period after his papa's death, and the remaining six months have been taken up with all the arrangements for it being made. As to how I shall survive it, I shall survive it as I did my wedding, and that is by focusing only on Nicky and the vows we will make. Nicky tells me that despite the thick snow and freezing weather – spring is very late in coming this year – the crowds on the*

337

processional route will be even greater than the crowds on our wedding day. Apparently my robes and crown will be even heavier than my wedding dress and nuptial crown were – something I find hard to believe, as my Russian-court wedding gown was so stiff and heavy with diamonds I could barely move in it.

Other things I remember are having a necklace once worn by Catherine the Great placed around my neck (it added immeasurably to the weight of everything else). Standing in front of the beautiful gold mirror that all previous tsarinas-to-be have stood in front of. Walking into the chapel with my maids of honour behind me and seeing Nicky, so handsome in his scarlet Hussar uniform, a fur-edged cape hanging from his shoulders. Nicky's younger brother, Misha, and his cousin, Kyril, holding our two wedding crowns; and the flickering candles that Nicky and I were given to hold. For the most part, though, it was a blur that I knew I had somehow to survive – and the coronation will be the same, but oh, how I wish it was already over and behind me!

The main things making such long ceremonial occasions an agony for me are my poor old legs. When I was a child I was playing catch with Irène and Ernie in the palace vegetable garden, and I tripped and fell through a sheet of plate glass that was protecting some plants. It took months for the deep lacerations on my legs to heal, and ever since my legs have never been strong. Standing for too long has always been an agony for me.

How blessed you are that, after only two and three-quarters years of marriage, you and dear Georgie have two sons! Nicky and I do not mind in the slightest that our firstborn is a darling little girl, but everyone else in the family seems to think it a great failing on our part not to have produced a son first time around. God willing, our next child will be a boy, and the heir everyone is so eager for.

I am writing this in my mauve boudoir at the Alexander Palace, Tsarskoe Selo. Tsarskoe Selo is an imperial village fifteen miles from St Petersburg (and so is a welcome distance from St Petersburg society, which, try as I might, I cannot feel comfortable in), and the Alexander Palace is where Nicky was born and is the palace we are happiest in. Although it is just as grand as all the other Romanov palaces, I have done as Granny Queen has always done and made our private rooms snug and comfy, doing so in the English style that I grew up with at Darmstadt. If you could see my boudoir, you would think yourself at Osborne House or Balmoral, especially as there is a large portrait of Granny Queen hanging on the wall above the fireplace.

My mother-in-law thinks me dreadfully bourgeois, but I don't care. I care only about giving Nicky surroundings that he can relax in, and that come as a welcome relief from acres and acres of gold leaf and marble.

Minny has asked that I call her 'Motherdear', which I obediently do, but privately I find it impossible to think of her as 'Motherdear', as she has made life difficult for me since the wedding. For months she refused to hand over certain pieces of the imperial jewels that it is traditional for a dowager to pass on to her successor, and it was only because of the uproar it would cause if I wasn't seen to be wearing them at my coronation that she finally parted with them. She would never have behaved so, if Nicky had married someone else; but for some reason I don't understand, she never wanted Nicky to marry me, and it was only because of his insistence that if he wasn't given permission to marry me, he would never marry at all, that she finally accepted me as her daughter-in-law. So there you have it. She doesn't approve *of me and, sad to say, has no genuine affection for me. I wish it were otherwise, but it isn't.*

What else? Thank you for your update on Kindred Spirit Willy. I am glad you and he are still on such easy terms. Nicky does his best with him, but Willy will harangue Nicky about Russia's relationship with France (Willy wants Russia to sever all ties with France, on the grounds of it being a republic and not a monarchy and therefore, as far as he is concerned, completely untrustworthy). All in all, Nicky finds a little of Cousin Willy goes a long way – as, of course, does nearly everyone else, apart from your infinitely patient self.

I'm beginning to feel the same way about Ducky as Nicky does about Willy. She says I am very unfeeling about her situation, but Ernie is my brother and so of course I see things from his point of view, as well as hers. It isn't as if he beats her, or ill-treats her in any physical way; and he has given her the most exquisite little daughter. She has told Ernie she wants a divorce. A divorce, can you imagine? The word alone is enough to give Granny Queen a heart attack. I sometimes wonder if Ducky and Missy are mentally quite the thing. (There are some very salacious rumours going the rounds about Missy's behaviour in Romania, but not ones I can put on paper!)

And now I must close, giving much love to you and Georgie and lots of precious kisses to little David and baby Bertie. (Wouldn't it be nice if, in another fifteen years or so, there was to be a romance between David and my darling little Olga? Not a royally arranged marriage, of course, just a natural and wonderful falling in love. How happy that would make Granny Queen, and what a couple of proud mamas we would be at the wedding!

Love, love, love, Kindred Spirit Alicky

Having finished her letter, she was about to hurry to the nursery to scandalize Olga's head-nurse by announcing yet again that she, and not the nurse, was to give Olga her morning bath, when there came a rumble of approaching carriages accompanied by what sounded like an entire regiment of outriders.

Her heart sank. Nicky was in St Petersburg for the morning, in deep discussion with his uncles over matters to do with the coronation. Ella, when she visited, never arrived with an ostentatious number of Hussars accompanying her. Her mother-in-law, however, always did. But why on earth was she visiting this morning, when she would know that Nicky was in St Petersburg, meeting his uncles? Had she come in order to spend time with baby Olga? Or had she come to demand back some of the imperial crown jewels she had been so loath to part with?

Minutes later, Minny – looking indecently young in a wasp-waisted, high-throated, trailing lace gown and a wide straw hat drowning in artificial flowers – was dropping air-kisses in the direction of Alicky's cheeks. 'Forgive me for this unexpected intrusion, Alicky, but I have been meaning to speak with you for some time and today, with Nicky in St Petersburg, seemed as good a time as any.'

They seated themselves on the French Regency sofas that faced each other a few yards apart. Minny made polite enquiries about baby Olga and then launched into the reason for her visit.

'I have come to believe that I have not been very fair to you Alicky,' she said, her voice apologetic. 'Because you were only in Russia days before you became Empress, you didn't have time to appreciate the great difference between court life in Russia and the court life you had previously experienced in Darmstadt and in England. As a result, and through no fault of your own, you started your reign on the back foot. A drawback I should have put to rights by explaining all the things that the Russian public – and the court – expect of their Empress. I was simply too grief-stricken over the loss of my beloved Sasha to do so, and you are not to be blamed for things that have begun causing disquiet.'

Alicky was confused. Was Minny making an apology to her for not having given her the guidance she had so badly needed, or was she about to launch into yet another tirade of criticism?

'The main duty of a Russian empress is to be seen, not to hide away, as you are doing here, at Tsarskoe Selo,' Minny said, answering Alicky's unasked question. 'The Empress is the undisputed leader of St Petersburg society. As such, you should constantly be seen at St Petersburg balls and parties and receptions. The public want to see you bowling down Nevsky Prospekt in an open carriage with a cavalcade of outriders in the summer, and in a sleigh with even more outriders in the winter. As it is, you shrink from appearing in public and the people barely know what you look like.'

'The people will know and love me for the things I am able to do for them,' Alicky said through gritted teeth, wondering for how much longer she was going to be able to keep her temper. 'I have no wish at all to be a frivolous example to them.'

Minny's eyes flashed fire. 'I hope you are not insinuating that, when I was Empress, I set a bad example?'

Alicky had been, but enraged as she was, she knew she couldn't possibly say so. 'No,' she said through gritted teeth, 'but your way of being Empress is not my way.'

Minny's dark eyes flashed fire. 'I've lived in Russia for thirty years. You have been in Russia barely two years. You might do me the politeness of acknowledging that I know what I am talking about. At the moment you are achieving the near-impossible. You are antagonizing not only the court and the public, but the family as well.'

And, sick at heart, she rose to her feet and, without giving Alicky the courtesy of a kiss goodbye, swept from the room.

'Did you tell her about the charity you will soon be launching?' Nicky asked, when Alicky told him of what had taken place between her and his mother.

It was late evening and they were in the cosy intimacy of her boudoir. She was seated on his lap, her red–gold hair unbraided and spilling in undulating waves way below her waist.

His arms tightened around her lovingly. 'About how it will be on the same lines as the Needlework Guild that Aunt Alix, Princess Mary Adelaide and Cousin May give such support to, in England?'

'Yes, and she was very crushing. She said Russia wasn't England, and that women of the nobility in Russia would never spend time making and embroidering articles of clothing to be given to the poor. But surely, Nicky, that is only because they have never been asked to do so?'

Nicky was never contentious and never took sides. 'It's time to forget Mama and her concerns, sweetheart. It's time for bed.'

Minny's hurtful remarks were immediately forgotten. It was only nine o'clock, but that didn't matter to either of them. As Nicky carried her in the direction of the bedroom, Alicky clasped her hands around his neck. There was a tiny bead of sweat on it and, as he closed the bedroom door behind them with his heel, she licked it away.

She loved the taste of him; the scent of him; the feel of his hair against the palm of her hand; the weight of his legs as they intertwined with hers. Most of all, she loved the rapturous feeling of utter, ultimate surrender. In bed there had never been any shyness or restraint between them. They were good lovers and successful ones, for although no one but themselves knew, she was several weeks pregnant – and this time, after weeks and weeks of praying in front of her favourite icon, she was absolutely certain that the child in her womb was a boy.

A week later and the morning of the coronation in Moscow dawned bright and clear. Once the capital of Russia, until St Petersburg had superseded it, the city was still a glorious sight. Its wide avenues were lined with palaces and mansions. Its skyline was a sea of steeply pitched red-and-green roofs, golden domes and glittering church spires and, at its heart, lay the forbidding medieval walls of the Kremlin, a city within a city.

In their apartment in the Kremlin Palace where they had spent the night after their ceremonial entry into the city, Alicky woke early, still clasped in Nicky's arms. Coronation Day. Not just Nicky's Coronation Day, but her Coronation Day also. As Head of the Orthodox Church, Nicky would crown himself, and then crown her. She wondered what her mother would have thought of her little girl one day being crowned Her Imperial Majesty The Empress of all the Russias.

The little girl who had been born and brought up in the small and modest court of Hesse-Darmstadt, being shown by her English mother how to make her own bed, darn her own stockings and mend her own clothes, seemed light years away.

As a child, and despite having been born in Germany and having a German father, Alicky had spoken English long before she had spoken German. She had grown up regarding Osborne House, Windsor and Balmoral as much family homes as the New Palace was her family home, and she had always thought of herself as being English. And now she would never again do so, for from today all her loyalties would be to Russia.

* * *

The dim interior of the Cathedral of the Assumption was lit by hundreds upon hundreds of candles. Beneath clouds of swirling incense, more than a thousand of Europe's royalty and nobility stood in the flickering light, squeezed shoulder-to-shoulder. Their eyes focused on the two slight figures who, beneath a purple canopy, were seated on diamond-encrusted coronation thrones.

'How many more hours do you think it will be before we can totter into the fresh air and sunlight?' Ducky whispered to Missy, hoping to ease her backache by transferring her weight from one foot to the other.

'An age. Nicky hasn't been invested with his regalia yet. Alicky hasn't ever been high on my favourite-cousin list, but I must admit she really does look the part. When it comes to imperiousness, no one does it better. Not even Granny Queen.'

From somewhere unseen, a choir began to sing.

Ducky stood on tiptoe, trying to give herself more height and catch a glimpse of Kyril.

Ernie, who was standing on the other side of her, said out of the corner of his mouth, 'Do stop fidgeting, Ducky. At least you're half-Russian and accustomed to all this kerfuffle. If Nicky has to crown himself, why doesn't he get a move on and get it over with?'

'Did you catch a glimpse?' Missy whispered from the other side of her, knowing full well what it was Ducky had been trying to do.

'Yes,' she whispered back.

'And how did he look?'

'Divine and unobtainable.' She wiped a tear away.

Thinking the tear was caused by the emotion of the scene, for a gold-robed priest had now begun investing Nicky with his regalia, Ernie was impressed.

'Buck up, Ducky,' he said. 'Only another few hours of this

droning on and we'll be on the home-straight and heading for the celebration dinner.'

'Alicky behaved magnificently,' Sergei said three hours later, as he and Ella took their places in the banqueting hall. 'Her unfortunate unpopularity of the last months will, now that the people can see how impressive she is on a great state occasion, soon be forgotten. I don't think even Catherine the Great could have looked as regal as Alicky did today – and she certainly couldn't have looked as beautiful.'

Ella flushed with pleasure, pleased at Sergei's praise of her little sister. 'She was faultless, wasn't she?' she said. 'And it can't have been easy for her. Her legs have begun troubling her when she becomes overtired, and if she wasn't overtired by the time today's ceremony was over, she must be now, poor darling.'

Both of them looked to where, by rigid tradition, Nicky and Alicky were dining apart, wearing their coronation robes and their crowns. Alicky still looked stunningly regal, but Nicky's gold crown had been made for Catherine the Great and sat far too low over his eyebrows.

Vladimir, who was seated on the other side of Sergei, said drily, 'Our Tsar looks like a small boy playing at dressing-up.'

Sergei grunted agreement. 'I have things other than Nicky on my mind at the moment. The day after tomorrow is the traditional coronation feast for the people. It's going to be held at the old military training field. Four hundred thousand are expected, and it's down to me to see that it goes off without any revolutionaries baying for an end to the monarchy – and for equal rights for everyone – causing trouble. I'm not going to relax until it's over.'

Vladimir grinned. 'That job is one of the penances of being

Governor-General of Moscow. And if you are expecting four hundred thousand, trust me when I say that, with free food and beer being given out, it's more likely to be seven hundred thousand. It's going to be mayhem. Make sure you have plenty of policemen there.'

Two days later, news of the tragedy came before it was even fully daylight.

'Forty dead! Possibly even fifty,' Vladimir announced grimly, marching in while Nicky was still having breakfast. 'I told Sergei he'd need every possible policeman there.'

'What? Where?' A totally bewildered Nicky stumbled to his feet.

'Khodynka Field. You and Alicky are due to make an appearance there this afternoon. With luck, the bodies will have been removed by then, but all the same . . . it's going to be seen as a bad-luck omen.'

'I still don't understand. How can forty or fifty people be dead?' The blood drained from Nicky's face. 'Was it a bomb, which was meant for me and Alicky and exploded early?'

'No. People had been allowed to gather there all through the night, and by dawn there were apparently more than a hundred thousand of them in the field, all wanting to be early and first in line for the beer and souvenir coronation mugs that were to be given out. Some fool said there wasn't going to be enough beer and mugs to go round, and a stampede started to be first in line for them.'

'Yes, but even so . . .'

'Being an old army training field, Khodynka is full of trenches and troughs. In the dark, people fell into them and then more people fell on top of them. Is there coffee in that pot? I'm glad it's all down to Sergei to sort out, not me.'

Fifteen minutes later the telephone rang. Nicky answered

it and Vladimir heard him say, 'More than two hundred, Sergei? *Two hundred?'*

'Holy Mother of God!' Vladimir blanched. 'You had better break the news to Alicky. Your visit to the field this afternoon is going to have to be called off.'

When Alicky was told of the disaster, her horrified reaction was that if more than two hundred people had been crushed to death in the dark, hundreds more must have been injured.

'What arrangements have been made for the injured to be taken to hospital?' she asked Vladimir, feeling sick at the horror of it all. 'Are the fire services helping?'

'Yes. No. Probably.'

'Probably?' The criminal enormity of his indifference to her question robbed her of breath. Knowing that she would never want anything to do with him ever again, she turned to Nicky. 'We must go down to the hospitals immediately. We must comfort the wounded.'

Nicky nodded in instant agreement.

Vladimir stared at them as if they had lost their minds.

A footman entered with a message on a silver salver, and Nicky snatched it and tore open the envelope.

Sergei had written only one sentence: *Death toll now over a thousand.*

Nicky sank down on the nearest chair. 'Dear God in heaven,' he whispered, showing the message to Alicky, his face ashen.

She laid her hand on his shoulder and said urgently, 'We can do nothing now for the dead, but we must waste no more time in visiting the wounded. They have to know how deeply we care. *Everyone* has to know how deeply we care!'

Nicky nodded, rose to his feet and swiftly they left the room, a mutual support group of two.

Vladimir stared after them in disbelief. The first action of any other tsar would have been to issue orders making sure the bodies were shunted into a mass grave. Then communicate that only a modest number were acknowledged as having been crushed to death, and that the day's celebrations would go ahead as planned. Instead, and thanks to Alicky, Nicky was on his way to visit the hospitals, bringing the most public attention possible to what had happened.

It was utter madness, and if he had ever doubted Alicky's influence over Nicky before, he did so no longer. To make matters worse, the French Ambassador was giving a ball that night in Nicky and Alicky's honour. Silver plate and tapestry had been shipped in from Versailles, as had one hundred thousand roses from the South of France. And from what he had just seen, Alicky would convince Nicky that, because of the death toll, it would be inappropriate for them to attend, which would be seen as a great insult by their French visitors.

He needed Sergei and Paul's help to change Nicky's mind. Together they would be able to hammer home to their nephew the necessity of acting as his late father would have done. But what of the next time Alicky gave Nicky bad advice? And the next time? And all the times after that?

He strode out of the palace, boiling with anger and frustration, hardly able to believe that Sergei had been such a fool as to think that he was going to have complete control over their new rulers. It was a belief that had been a mirage – and now, God help them, they were going to have to live with the consequences.

Chapter Thirty-One

JUNE 1897, YORK COTTAGE

May was seated in a basketwork chair on the lawn of York Cottage, a writing pad on her knee as she tried to catch up on her correspondence while at the same time enjoying the summer sun.

She was disturbed by George – her days of thinking of him as Georgie were long over – striding down from the house towards her, a telegram in his hand. 'News from Nicky.' He handed her the telegram. 'Alicky has had the baby. It's a girl. Tatiana. With all the pressure on them to give Russia an heir, he and Alicky must be crushed with disappointment.'

'Yes.' May was aware of prayers not answered. 'They must be.'

His errand accomplished, he said, 'Don't stay out in the sun too long. It will give you one of your headaches.' And having shown what he felt was husbandly concern, he stomped back to the house and his waiting stamp collection.

May closed her eyes. Another girl. The Russians would no doubt begin saying that Alicky was a woman who bred only girls, but they would be wrong. A letter from Alicky, written just over a year ago, meant that she, May, knew differently. It had been a letter stained with tears, which Alicky had written in shaky handwriting:

*I have to share this news with you, or I will go mad. I had
a miscarriage less than a week after the coronation – and
that I did isn't surprising, my coronation robes being so heavy
that I could barely move in them and, once I was crowned,
my crown was so heavy I thought my neck was going to
break. How I endured the weight of it all, I truly don't
know; and then afterwards there was a celebration dinner –
again hours and hours long – at which Nicky and I were
still wearing robes and crowns, and then a ball. It was
utterly exhausting for someone in my condition. Whether I
would have had the miscarriage four days later, even if the
Khodynka Field tragedy hadn't happened, I don't know, but
what I do know is that the horror was on such a scale – the
final death toll was more than three thousand – that it
will live with me until my dying day. Nicky and I went
immediately down to the hospitals, and oh, the sight of the
children, May. It would have broken your heart.*

*And then, on top of everything, the grand-uncles
(Vladimir, Sergei and Paul) absolutely insisted that Nicky
and I put in an appearance at a ball that had been arranged
in our honour at the French Embassy. We argued and argued
with them, but not even Sergei would have it any other way.
As we left it, our carriage was spat at in the street and then,
when we finally arrived back at the Kremlin Palace, I began
to bleed and half an hour later I miscarried what the doctor
(sworn on his life to secrecy) said was a boy.*

*The grief of it is almost more than I can bear. Please pray
that my next child will also be a boy, May. I have become so
unpopular (and unfairly so) that only if I give the country a
boy am I likely ever to have the chance of becoming the kind
of popular empress and tsarina I so long to be.*

Your more than heartbroken Kindred Spirit, Alicky

May stared at the dismal view in front of her. There was more lawn and then a small lake, or a large pond. Either description would have fitted. It wasn't a pretty water feature, being ringed on its near side by reeds and on its far side by thickets of laurel, its only decoration being a lead pelican.

It was, however, better than the alternative view, for if she sat facing in the opposite direction she would be looking towards the house. York Cottage – her home. Even after four years she wasn't able to look at it without a flinch of distaste, for the name 'York Cottage' was a complete misnomer. When Dolly had first seen it, he'd given her a fit of the giggles by saying it reminded him of three Merrie England pubs joined together. It had originally been built as overflow accommodation for Sandringham's male shooting-party guests, and although screened from the Big House by huge swathes of rhododendron, it was only a hundred yards' walk away from it. Without asking her opinion, and blind to York Cottage's architectural hideousness, George had asked his father if they could make it their marital home.

His reason for doing so had been that his mother now spent nearly all her time at Sandringham, her deafness so total that Marlborough House and London society had lost all charm for her. It meant that George could pop into Sandringham House and see her whenever he wanted, and that his mother could pop into York Cottage whenever the fancy took her. And it took her often.

May regarded such intrusions as both rude and insensitive. George was always simply overjoyed to see her.

If she had been given free rein in the decoration and furnishing of York Cottage – or even if she and George had been able to come to an agreement on how it should be decorated and furnished – she might well have begun to feel differently about it, but she had had no say in the matter.

Before their marriage, and without telling her, George had

supervised a decoration scheme of various shades of brown and tan, relieved only by the decor of his study, where the walls were covered in hideous dark-red cloth. Ignoring all the beautiful furniture he could have cherry-picked from royal store-rooms, he had ordered factory-built furniture from the Maples department store in Oxford Street. The real travesty, though, was that not one piece of the artwork he had chosen for York Cottage was original. In a family that owned as many original paintings as May's favourite galleries, George had opted for reproductions. Nothing else could have shown more clearly the difference in their tastes and interests. Hers were all cultural: art, music and books. His were shooting – it was another of the reasons he so liked living on the Sandringham Estate – and stamp-collecting.

'Cooee, May!'

At Ducky's familiar voice, May slid her half-finished letter into her writing case and sprang to her feet, happy to have an end to her depressing train of thought.

'I didn't know you were in England,' she said, turning to greet Ducky as, despite the narrowness of her ankle-length skirt, Ducky walked across the grass at remarkable speed.

'I'm an early arrival for Granny Queen's Diamond Jubilee celebrations. I wanted to speak with her before all the brouhaha starts. Unfortunately, we didn't part on good terms, and so I couldn't very well ask for Windsor bed and board. Uncle Bertie had been Windsor-visiting as well and, as he was leaving, he suggested that I keep him company and take the opportunity of a surprise reunion with Aunt Alix, Toria and Maudie. And yourself, of course. And so here I am, seeing you first, as you might well expect.'

They hugged and kissed each other on the cheek.

Ducky flopped down into one of the basket-chairs. 'While I was at Windsor a telegram arrived with news that Alicky and Nicky had had another girl. Because of the Ernie situation,

Alicky and I no longer get along too well – it's obvious her sympathies lie with her brother – but even so, I feel sorry for her. She's begun suffering quite badly from sciatica, and being pregnant so often doesn't help.' She quirked a glossy dark eyebrow and changed the subject. 'Do you know about Ernie's sexual preference for Hussars, footmen and valets?'

May wondered what it would be like to be as bluntly outspoken as Ducky, but found it too much of a stretch of her imagination.

'Yes, Ducky. You've been quite vocal about it. I think everyone in the family now knows.'

'As I want to have a divorce, I've had to be quite vocal about it. However, I'm not getting anywhere on that front.' She let her arms hang loosely over the basketwork sides of her chair and, with closed eyes, raised her face to the sun. 'It's why I so desperately needed to see Granny Queen. She was the one who was keen for me and Ernie to marry, and so you would think – her judgement having been proved so wrong, when it comes to my husband's suitability for marriage – that she would at least have the decency to allow me to divorce him. But she won't. She says Ernie will grow out of his "odd little ways" in time, and that I must be patient.'

For the life of her, May couldn't think of anything encouraging to say. Compared to Ducky's marital difficulties and Cousin Marie-Louise's marital difficulties – which were the same as Ducky's, except that Aribert was a nasty piece of work, something Ernie most definitely was not – her own difficulties with George were trifling.

Ducky sat up straight and opened her eyes. 'And I have been patient, May, but I can't be patient much longer; not when I'm still so in love with Kyril.'

'Oh, Ducky dear, I hadn't realized!' May's eyebrows flew so high they nearly disappeared into her fringe of tight curls. 'I thought that was over long ago.'

'No,' Ducky rummaged in the small beaded purse that hung from the waistband of her skirt and withdrew a slim silver cigarette case. 'My feelings for Kyril have never changed, May. They never will.' She held out the case so that May could take a Russian Sobranie. 'He's always had a pash for me as well, although it's only since I've been married to Ernie that he's admitted it.' She lit their cigarettes and blew a plume of smoke skywards. 'And if he had been quicker off the mark, it really wouldn't have made much difference – not when the Romanov ban on first-cousin marriage still holds.'

Ever practical, May said, 'And so what difference would a divorce from Ernie make?'

'We could marry, if we did so without Nicky's consent – which he would never give in a million years – and if we did so in a country where first-cousin marriage *is* allowed, and if we lived as exiles afterwards.'

'But, Ducky darling, even if you were able to get a divorce without her consent, Granny Queen would never agree to you marrying again!'

'Perhaps not, but she's seventy-eight and it can't be long before Uncle Bertie succeeds her and is King-Emperor. And with Uncle Bertie's long history of marital infidelity, he's bound to look at my situation sympathetically. And when he does – and when I have my divorce – Kyril won't waste his breath asking Nicky if he can marry me. He'll leave Russia and we will marry in Paris and live happily ever after.'

She stubbed out her cigarette. 'It's time I showed my face at Sandringham House – but only because I'd like to catch up with Maudie, who I'm assuming will by now have arrived there from Denmark, in readiness for the Jubilee celebrations.' Ducky rose to her feet. 'Is her marriage to Carl of Denmark a happy one? It would be nice to have one cousin – other than yourself, of course – who is happily married, and as her marriage to Carl wasn't one of Granny Queen's arranged marriages, I'm assuming it was a love match.'

'It was. It is. They share the same Danish grandparents, so there has never been a time when they haven't known each other.'

She began walking Ducky back to York Cottage and the path leading to Sandringham House, vividly remembering Maudie's happiness when she had confided in her that Cousin Carl had asked for her hand in marriage.

'I never, ever thought I would love anyone as much as I once loved Frank,' Maudie had said to her, 'and this is such a different sort of love, May, that at first I didn't recognize it for what it was. When I was in love with Frank, it was all fireworks and rockets going off, and feeling that every time we parted I would die if I didn't see him again soon. With Carl, it is all sweetness and security, and a feeling that when we are together all is right with the world.'

She had hesitated, two spots of warm colour flooding her cheeks.

'After he had asked me to marry him, and before I accepted his proposal, I told Carl of how I had once thought myself in love when I was much younger, and of how I was what is referred to as "damaged goods". He was quiet, and for so long that I thought I had destroyed all my future happiness. And then he took my hands in his and said how much my honesty meant to him; that it showed him, more than anything else could have, that there would never be any secrets between us – only pure, shining trust. And he said he hoped I would be forgiving of a couple of long-regretted incidents in his own past. I knew then how different the love we shared was from anything I had experienced before, and what a very, very special kind of person he was.'

When May had waved Ducky goodbye, she stepped into the coolness of the house. From the direction of the nursery came the sound of her eldest two children, three-year-old David and eighteen-month-old Bertie, playing under the watchful eye of their nanny. There was no sound from the direction of eight-week-old baby Mary's nursery, and she decided not to disturb the peace and quiet by looking in on her and perhaps waking her up.

Bypassing the closed door of George's stamp room, she walked upstairs to her own inner sanctum, her boudoir. It was what her German father would have described as *gemütlich* – cosy – and yet elegant at the same time. As was the habit among all Granny Queen's offspring, framed family photographs occupied every available surface.

Her desk faced the window and she sat down at it. On it stood a photograph of George in naval uniform. It had been a long time since George had captained a ship, but he still felt more comfortable in uniform than he did out of it. Next to it was a photograph of David, awkwardly clutching hold of Bertie.

There was a photograph of Dolly on his wedding to Margaret Grosvenor, and another of Alicky, Nicky and baby Olga that had been taken on their most recent visit to Balmoral. There was a photograph of her mother and, looking at it, May felt a flare of anxiety, for her mother had not been well of late. And there was a photograph of Granny Queen. On May's marriage to George, when the Queen had told her that she was no longer to refer to her as 'Aunt Queen' but as 'Granny Queen', that – of all the many privileges that had come with her marriage to George – was the one that had given her the most satisfaction.

Last, but by no means least, there was a photograph of Eddy. Not their engagement photograph; that lay in a box of memorabilia that no one but herself had access to. It was a photograph that had been taken of him in 1891, not long after he had been created Duke of Clarence and Avondale, and in which he was wearing his ceremonial gold-braided and bemed-alled Hussar uniform. Dashingly moustachioed, and with one hand lightly clasping the hilt of his sword, he looked splendid, but then – in May's eyes – he always had.

Her conversation with Ducky, and the memory of her conversation with Maudie, had put her in an odd, reflective frame of mind where her own marriage was concerned. Without a doubt, she knew there were aspects of married life that she would have found happier if Eddy, and not George, had been her husband. Intimacy with Eddy had been natural and easy, and although he had died without their having become lovers in the married sense of the word, she knew there would have been no embarrassed awkwardness between them, once their bedroom door had closed – as there had been, and often still was, between her and George. And Eddy would never have been so insensitive as to have not discussed with her how their home should be decorated and furnished. There would also have been much more companionship between them, for although Eddy had been as poorly educated as George, somehow they had always found things to chat and laugh about.

But would that happy state of affairs have continued?

In the years since Eddy's death, she had come to know a lot more about him than she had during the few short weeks of their engagement. She now knew that even when he had been so eager to marry Hélène, he had been writing love letters to Lady Sybil St Clair-Erskine, the nineteen-year-old daughter of the Earl of Rosslyn – and she knew that his having done so wasn't merely salacious rumour, for Sybil had shown the letters to many people, one of them being Dolly.

She had also discovered that Eddy had been just as much of a gambler as Frank. Due to the misery that Frank's gambling had caused – and was still causing – it was a vice she had no sympathy for.

Eddy's ability to be faithless and to lose heavily at the races, and to keep dubious company when playing baccarat for high stakes, were not aspects of his character that she would have been able to live with easily. In comparison, her disappointment that George was incapable of expressing his feelings for her verbally was one that she should have long ago come to terms with, especially as, in letters, he did assure her that he loved her.

In a letter he had sent to her some months after their honeymoon, he had written that although he hadn't been in love with her when they married, he had come to love her, and he had ended the letter by writing, '*And I am now utterly devoted to you, Sweet May.*'

In a letter he had sent her from St Petersburg when he had attended Tsar Uncle Sasha's funeral and then the wedding of Nicky and Alicky, he had written, '*I really believe I will become ill if I have to be away from you for much longer. Goodnight, Sweet May. God Bless.*'

Unlike Eddy, George would not have been writing letters to another woman at the same time he had been writing his letters to her.

George wasn't romantic, but he was very, very dependable and 100 per cent honourable. When he had written that he had come to love her, and was utterly devoted to her – and although he couldn't bring himself to tell her so – then she could rest assured it was the truth. Unlike so many other women in Granny Queen's vast family, she was married to a man who would never dream of being unfaithful to her; a man who, although he had a blunt manner and a peppery temper, would never treat her in the cruel way that Aribert of Anhalt treated Marie-Louise.

Another thought came to May, which was that her own shyness and reserve must have always been as off-putting for George in the bedroom as his deep shyness and reserve had been off-putting for her. The stiff politeness that still existed between them, even after the birth of three children, hadn't existed between them before their marriage. She remembered the Georgie who had wept in front of her when telling her how it had been explained to him that, as Julie Stoner was a commoner, he couldn't possibly marry her. She remembered how they had relied on each other for mutual support during the agonizing days of Eddy's illness, and of how they had instinctively known the depths of each other's grief when he had died. There had been no stiff politeness between them then. Instead there had been mutual, bone-deep grief and an unspoken understanding of what the other was suffering. Only when it had become apparent that an arranged marriage between the two of them was the inevitable outcome of Eddy's death had stiff politeness intruded on loving friendship. And for both of them, the stiff politeness had grown into a habit.

A feeling of resolution flooded over May. If she wanted to break down the unseen barriers between them, then she was going to have to take the first step, for she knew George was incapable of doing so. And if she was going to take the first step, there was no reason why she shouldn't take it now, immediately, by going down to the stamp room and putting her arms around him and telling him how very, very fortunate she felt herself to be in having him for her husband.

Abruptly pushing her chair away from the desk, she rose to her feet. Swiftly she left the room and then broke into a run; running along the landing to the head of the stairs and, to the alarm of two members of her household staff, running down them.

At the stamp-room door she came to a breathless halt and hesitated, but her hesitation was minimal.

'George?' With a fast-beating heart, she gave the door a sharp knock. 'George, it's May. There's something I'd very much like to say to you. There's something I simply must tell you.'

Chapter Thirty-Two

JANUARY 1901, YORK COTTAGE

It was the start of a new year, but just like last year and the year before, May wasn't in the mood to celebrate it. The last New Year she had truly enjoyed had been three years ago, before anxieties about what was happening in Russia and in South Africa had surfaced. In the June of that year, after Alicky had given birth to her second girl, Tatiana, the British Ambassador to St Petersburg had informed Granny Queen that there were rumours that if Alicky's next child was also a girl, Nicky's uncles intended removing him from the throne and replacing him with his younger brother, George.

Alicky hadn't mentioned such things in her letters to May – letters that were becoming more and more sporadic – but four months ago she had written that she was once again pregnant, and May was aware of how vitally important it was that this time the baby was a boy.

In South Africa long-term unrest between Dutch and British settlers had, a little more than a year ago, boiled over into war. And now, arriving back at York Cottage after three days in Wales, where she had attended the funeral of a young man who had died in the fighting, May was in a deeply depressed state of mind. The deceased had been the twenty-two-old son of one of her ladies-in-waiting, just one of thousands of British soldiers to have died since the beginning of the Boer War fifteen months ago – a war that showed no signs yet of coming to an end.

It was a war that was affecting hundreds of thousands of families in Britain, including her own, for all three of her brothers were fighting in the Transvaal. Dolly was a major in the 17th Lancers; Frank was a major in the 1st Dragoons, and Alge was a second lieutenant in the 7th Hussars and only two months ago had received the Distinguished Service Order for bravery in combat.

Almost as many men were dying from sickness in the in-hospitable climate as from battle wounds. One of her most engaging and likeable royal cousins, thirty-three-year-old Christle, Marie-Louise's brother, had served as a staff officer and had died of enteric fever. A telegram told his parents that Frank had been with him when he died. 'And so at least he didn't die amongst strangers,' Uncle Christian had said, his voice breaking in grief. 'He had a brother-in-arms who was also a much-loved cousin with him, and Frank ensured that Christle's funeral was carried out just as we would have wanted.'

Having Frank spoken of with appreciation made a welcome change, and May was still thinking about Frank when she walked into her drawing room – a room she had long estab-lished as her own by having its brown-and-tan decor altered to a crisp white, with pale-yellow touches.

Although the paintwork blessedly remained the same now, nothing else was as she had left it. All the furniture, every last little stick of it, had been rearranged. Pictures had been rehung – and not successfully. Framed photographs and *objets d'art* had been rearranged, and some of her most precious ornaments had been removed altogether.

She didn't need to ask who was responsible. It was the same

person who had been responsible for creating havoc when, without asking permission to do so, May now thirty-three, had had the temerity to have a small scented garden planted below her boudoir window.

No one she knew could keep control of her feelings as she did, but there were limits, and this was one of them. With all thoughts of Frank forgotten, she flung her muff down and, without even taking off her hat and her beaver-collared-and-cuffed coat, went in search of George.

'Why' she demanded when she found him, 'was Motherdear allowed to take it upon herself to rearrange *my* furniture in *my* home?'

Under the pretext of tamping tobacco into his pipe, George avoided meeting her eyes. 'She thinks it now looks much prettier, and thought it would be a nice surprise for you, darling. And it does look very pretty, don't you think? Having the display cabinet in one of the alcoves, and the bureau placed nearer to the window, means there is full daylight on it, which will make letter-writing so much easier on the eyes?'

'It does *not* look prettier than how it looked before, and the display cabinet loses its entire point when half-hidden in an alcove; and the bureau is exceedingly cumbersome so near to the window. And where have the things gone that have been removed from the room?'

'I don't know, May. I'm sure they're somewhere safe. And there can be no question of rearranging the room, now that Motherdear has gone to such an effort to improve it.'

May was saved from saying words she might regret by the telephone on George's desk ringing. It was there primarily for him to ring out on. Very few people, other than his father and Toria, ever had the temerity to ring him.

Grateful for any kind of an interruption to the present conversation, George snatched up the receiver. 'Yes?' he barked into it and then, seconds later, sat down so suddenly, and in such a state of shock, that May forgot all about the unwelcome changes to her drawing room.

He said numbly, 'It's Papa, May. He's at Osborne. Granny Queen is dying.'

On the other end of the telephone line her father-in-law bellowed, 'May? Pour Georgie a brandy, and then both of you need to leave for Osborne immediately. Do you understand?'

'Yes. I understand.' Her mouth was dry, her heart thumping with shock. A world without Granny Queen was unimaginable. Her indomitable presence and loving concern had been a comfort to her for as long as she could remember. Even when, eighteen years ago, Victoria had insisted that her parents leave the country in order to live more cheaply abroad, it had been a banishment made out of loving concern.

Hard on the heels of the grief she knew she would soon be feeling came the realization of how much change would come, if Granny Queen really was dying. For on her death, Bertie would become King; he and Motherdear would move from Marlborough House into Buckingham Palace; and George would be the heir apparent.

The biggest change of all, however, would be becoming accustomed to a world in which there would no longer be a short, squat figure in black silk tapping with her stick down royal corridors, and ruling an empire and a family that straddled every European royal court, and to whom she, May, owed everything. Without Granny Queen having taken an interest in her, she would still be an unmarriageable Serene Highness, facing a future of Needlework Guild charity work and being an aunt to Dolly and Margaret's children, and any children Frank and Alge might one day have.

The Queen had transformed her life by seeing qualities in her that no one else had seen. Identifying May's potential, she had decided that she would one day be England's Queen Consort.

From behind his desk George stumbled to his feet, distraught. 'How will the family manage without her, May? His protuberant blue eyes were full of tears. 'How will the country manage? How will the *Empire* manage?'

It was bitterly cold crossing the Solent, and by the time they arrived at Osborne House, snow was falling.

'She's still with us, thank God,' Louis of Battenberg said to George as he and May stepped into the house, 'but the doctors say there is little hope. Aunt Lenchen and Aunt Louise have been supervising her care over the last few days and are with her now. Aunt Vicky has been informed, but she's so ill she can't possibly travel all the way from Germany. My Vicky is here, of course. Alicky has been informed, but because she's pregnant she can't travel. Uncle Arthur Connaught was in Berlin, attending an anniversary celebration of the Prussian Crown, but left immediately he was telegrammed and is expected to arrive soon, which means that five out of six of Granny Queen's surviving children will be with her before the end. Willy is also on his way – much to your father's exasperation. It means he's going to have to leave Osborne and return to London in order to greet him.'

To May, he said, 'Beatrice and Aunt Marie are in the drawing room with Aunt Alix, Toria and Looloo. Maudie is en route. Irène and Heinrich have gone for a walk. Marie-Louise is here, as is Thora, and all three Connaught grandchildren are here. Ducky isn't here as she's caught tonsillitis. Ernie is on his way.'

All May wanted to do was rest from the rough crossing. Pleading a headache, she went immediately to the bedroom that she and George always occupied at Osborne, then wrote a short note to Louise asking when she could spend a precious few minutes with the Queen and gave it to a footman to deliver.

She'd no sooner done so than George burst in on her, his face flushed with temper.

'Bloody Willy!' he said vehemently. 'He's going to rub everyone up the wrong way with his theatrical posturing and, as if that isn't bad enough, Papa has asked me to accompany him back to London so that Willy can be given an appropriate royal greeting.'

'It would be disgraceful if he wasn't greeted by the two of you,' she said reasonably. 'And remember that Willy will be very, very upset. Granny Queen has always been the most important person in the world to him.'

'Bosh!' George said and, still wearing his hat and overcoat, left the room to face another stormy crossing of the Solent.

May found Willy energizing and, unlike many members of the family, always looked forward to meeting up with him. Under normal circumstances George, too, got on with Willy. On one of their visits to Berlin, Willy had bestowed on George Germany's highest honour, the Order of the Black Eagle. Last year Willy had stood as godfather to her and George's third son, Henry, and not long afterwards she and George had attended Willy's eldest son's coming-of-age celebrations in Berlin. It wasn't the thought of Willy that was the cause of George's bad temper. It was the thought of having to cross the Solent again – and not once, but twice.

Her thoughts were interrupted by Beatrice. 'Louise says now would be a good time to sit with Mama for a few minutes, May. Lenchen is catching up on some sleep. She and Aunt Marie sat with Mama all through the night, last night.'

May had never before been in the Queen's bedroom. Over the fireplace hung a painting of the Entombment of Christ, and the room was full of portraits and photographs of Albert. A large framed portrait of him hung over the canopied bedhead and, on the other side of the bed, looking pathetically small and fragile, the eighty-one-year-old Queen was lying with closed eyes against a bank of pillows, a shawl around her shoulders, a lace cap covering her wispy white hair.

Aunt Louise was seated at one side of the bed and May sat down on the other side, trying hard not to be reminded of the nightmare hours she had spent sitting beside Eddy when he had been dying.

May didn't know Louise well, for Louise, a talented sculptress, kept herself very much to herself.

Rising to her feet, Louise said, 'If you want to say a few last words to Mama, it's no use hoping for a time when her eyes open. My advice is to seize the moment and hope that you get a response when she hears your voice. The nurse will have to stay here with you, but other than that, I'm going to leave you on your own with her for five minutes.'

She left the room and, grateful for Louise's thoughtfulness, May took one of the Queen's hands in hers. 'It's May, Granny Queen,' she said, hoping her naturally low-pitched voice would be loud enough to rouse her. 'I want you to know how very grateful I am for all the things you have done for me, and that I will always strive to live up to your expectations of me.'

There was a long silence and then the Queen said weakly and uncertainly, 'Is that May Teck?'

'Yes, Granny. It is.'

The Queen's eyes fluttered open. 'Dear May.' She gave her hand a feeble squeeze. 'I have been thinking about you while I have been so ill.' She paused and then said with great effort, her once-silvery voice barely audible, 'I've been thinking how strange it is, our having being born in the same room at Kensington Palace, and in the same bed. It is a connection between us – and I do so believe in mystic connections.' She paused again and then said, her voice growing fainter, her eyes closing, 'I am so glad I have been able to tell you how satisfying it is to me that you will one day be Queen.'

Moments later Louise entered the room, 'Did Mama not wake? Never mind. If she had, she probably wouldn't have recognized you. There are times when she doesn't recognize either me or Lenchen.'

May rose to her feet. 'She did wake. And she did recognize me. All I wanted to say was said, and all she wanted to say to me was said, too.'

When Willy arrived – dressed in the uniform of a British admiral, an honorary position that he took very seriously – he was on his best behaviour. Even the Princess of Wales, who disliked him intensely, could find no fault in him after he had said that he would keep out of everyone's way, his only wish being to see his grandmother before she died.

A day later Maudie arrived, as did Ernie. Children and grandchildren took turns filing in and out of the bedroom, Louise telling her mother – who could now no longer see – who it was who was coming and going. At one point the Queen rallied enough to ask that her little dog, Turi, be brought to her, and he was laid on the bed so that she could place her hand on his soft fur and have the comfort of feeling him near her.

The day after Maudie and Ernie's arrival it was obvious that the end was near, and on her doctor's advice the bulletin 'The Queen is slowly sinking' was issued.

'I'd like to be with her,' Willy said to Bertie.

'You'll have to wait.' Bertie was under enormous strain. 'You had a couple of minutes with her when you arrived, and her Connaught grandchildren haven't spent time with her yet.'

May was standing nearby and she held her breath, certain Willy was about to erupt in indignation.

He didn't. Mindful of his grandmother's impending death, Willy, perhaps for the first time in his life, controlled his temper. Abruptly turning away from Bertie, he saw May and said, through clenched teeth, 'I'm going for a walk. Are you coming?'

May was only too willing to escape the tension in the crowded house, and ten minutes later she was walking with him across the snow-covered lower terrace.

'Damned arrogance!' he erupted, with such rage that the upturned ends of his stiffly waxed moustache trembled. 'I'm the firstborn grandchild and the favourite! If Grandmama wants anyone at her bedside, it's me.'

Where arrogance was concerned, Willy took some beating, but May thought what he had said was probably true. No matter how badly he behaved, the Queen always forgave him and reminisced as to how her late beloved Albert had once swung Willy in a napkin when he had been only a few months old.

'And it is only out of respect to my grandmother that I didn't publicly take Bertie to task for speaking to me as if he was an uncle talking to a nephew, when although I *am* his nephew, I am also the Kaiser and an emperor – and he is only the Prince of Wales! It's my opposition to the Boer War that he can't stomach. The Boers are Dutch. Why should the republics they founded half a century ago now come under British control, just because they are rich in diamonds and gold?'

May remained silent. It wasn't up to her to begin defending the Boer War. But as her father-in-law and Willy were going to be fellow emperors, and would then have to see eye-to-eye with each other over world events of great gravity, it seemed to her that her father-in-law should have injected a little more regret into what he had said.

Mercifully, and with characteristic speed, Willy changed the subject yet again. 'How's my godson?'

'He's nine months old and bald as a badger.'

Four children in seven years had shown May that, when it came to babies, she wasn't naturally maternal.

With a mood change as swift as his change of subject, Willy barked with laughter. 'You have three fine sons. I have six strapping sons. And poor old Nicky can't get a son to save his life.' His satisfaction at his own virility was blatant. 'Alicky and I don't get on well any more. All that Kindred Spirit nonsense ended long ago, where she is concerned. If you are still in close contact with her, you might tell her to put a stop to all this religious palaver with so-called holy men that she's begun resorting to, in the belief it will help her conceive a boy. My ambassador in St Petersburg says she's gone from being merely unpopular to being actively disliked. Hides herself away at Tsarskoe Selo, somewhere no member of the public can ever see her. Nicky should take her in hand, but he won't. I'm fond of Nicky – he's a splendid chap, but weak as water.'

At his mention of Kindred Spirit nonsense, May had come to an abrupt halt. As Willy came to a halt, too, waiting for her to catch up with him, she said dry-mouthed, 'Do you remember the Kindred Spirit blood-pact the three of us made years ago on the beach at Osborne? Alicky and I have kept it up, but you haven't, Willy. By regarding it as nonsense, you've broken it.'

The hairs on the nape of her neck prickled.

'Is that why bad things have begun happening, Willy? Alicky not being able to give Russia an heir? Me living in daily dread of receiving a black-edged telegram telling me that one, or maybe all, of my brothers fighting in the Transvaal has been killed? You not having the respect shown to you that, as Granny Queen's eldest grandchild, should be shown?'

He stared at her. Willy believed very deeply in portents and signs. And things were always going wrong for him. He was always being criticized in the British and German press for saying things that would have been better left unsaid.

'With regard to the blood-pact' – a pulse had begun throbbing at the corner of his jaw – 'if it's been broken, can it also be mended?'

'No. Blood-pacts and vows don't work like that.'

If Willy didn't want to believe something, he always found it very easy not to. And he didn't want to believe that bad things were going to happen to him, now that the blood-pact between himself, May and Alicky had been broken.

Regarding the matter as closed, he began walking again and, as May fell into step beside him and they reached the end of the terrace and the snow-covered steps leading down to the lawn, Willy said, completely out of the blue, 'Uncle Bertie doesn't like me.' At the bottom of the steps he continued with great feeling, 'When he becomes a fellow emperor, he's never going to take advice from me in the way dear old Nicky does. He's far too fond of France, and no good will come of Britain forming an alliance with France – or, for that matter, with Russia. If Uncle Bertie forges an alliance with France and an even closer alliance with Russia, Germany will be encircled and vulnerable. It doesn't bear thinking about. It isn't something that would happen with Georgie as England's King and Emperor, but how many years is it going to be, before he is? And by the time he is, the damage will be done!'

He came to a halt, carried away by his own passionate language, seeing himself as a Prussian St George in bronze helmet and breastplate, shield in one hand, sword raised gloriously aloft in the other.

May, aware that Willy was what George called 'theatrically posturing', turned and looked back at the house. How long had they been away and out of touch with what was happening? Ten minutes? Fifteen? Instinct told her that, however short the period of time, it had been far too long.

With a terrible sense of premonition she said urgently, 'It's time we went back.'

Willy blinked, reminded himself that when he was at Osborne it was his half-English side that was dominant, not his Prussian-German side, and immediately set off at a pace so brisk she could hardly keep up with him.

The crowded bedroom was tense with fearful expectation. The Queen's doctor, Dr Reid, was at one side of the bed, supporting her against her pillows, with Bertie on his knees beside him. When Willy moved forward, kneeling at the opposite side of the bed and sliding his good arm around his semi-conscious grandmother, supporting her as Reid was doing, no one, not even Bertie, protested.

The Dean of Windsor, who had been summoned a day earlier, began reciting the Queen's favourite hymn, 'Lead, Kindly Light'.

When he had finished Beatrice said, 'Mama always thought of Papa and Alice and Affie and Leopold, and of her longed-for reunion with them, whenever she sang the line, "And with the morn those angel faces smile, Which I have loved long since, and lost awhile".'

'And not only of your sister and two brothers,' Uncle Christian said gruffly. 'She would have been thinking of Christle and Eddy as well.'

A long, tortured hour passed, and then another one. Occasionally, having to obey the calls of nature, people left the room and then returned to it. Throughout it all Willy never moved by so much as an inch, even though, having only one useable arm, he couldn't take pressure off it by changing sides with Reid.

The January afternoon drew to a close; the sky darkened. The Queen's breathing changed in rhythm and Reid said gravely, 'It won't be long now.'

'Then let us call out our names to her,' Louise said. 'Her children first, then grandchildren and then other close family members.'

Amid floods of tears, and as Reid kept his thumb on the Queen's pulse, the emotional roll-call began.

As it ended, Reid made a slight motion with his free hand, for the Queen's face had taken on an expression of inexpressible peace. An awed silence fell. For a moment there was a faint movement of her lips, as if she was about to whisper a name, but all that came was a last long, slow exhalation of breath.

Reid lifted his hand from her wrist and gently laid it back on the coverlet. 'It is over.' His voice was raw with emotion. 'Her Majesty The Queen has peacefully passed from this life into eternity.'

Sobs that had been stifled were stifled no longer. Irène collapsed half-insensible with grief into Heinrich's arms.

Beatrice said, her voice thick with tears, 'The name she was trying to say was Papa's. I know that it was dear Papa's.'

'I'm sure you are right, Bea.' Louise hugged her close. 'And she will now be reunited with him. For forty years it is all she has longed for. We shouldn't cry for her. She wouldn't want us to. She would want us to be happy for her.'

Maudie gripped tight hold of May's hand, saying with tears streaming down her face, 'Without Granny Queen, nothing is going to be the same.'

'No, Maudie dear, it isn't.' Not since Eddy had died had May been so close to breaking down.

Bertie rose to his feet, saying unsteadily, 'With Arthur's help, I will lay Mama in her coffin.'

It was something Willy had wanted to do and he said, 'If I am not to perform that service for my grandmother, can I request that the coffin is draped with the Union Jack?'

Vastly relieved that Willy hadn't asked for it to be draped in a German flag and thankful for small mercies, Bertie said courteously, 'Yes, of course, Willy. The Union Jack.'

Looking at her father-in-law, May wondered what kind of a king he was going to make. When she had been a child, his habit of 'chaffing' had ensured that she'd always gone to great lengths to avoid him. Over the last few years – and as her father-in-law – his 'chaffing', where she was concerned, had become a thing of the past, although he did like to shatter her natural primness by telling her risqué jokes and convulsing her in laughter.

But a king who told risqué jokes in mixed company? A king who, for nearly all the years of his married life, had been openly unfaithful to his wife? A king who, as king-in-waiting, had never been instructed in the use of political power and whose entire existence had been a life of fashionable leisure?

Alicky often referred to Bertie slightingly as being an ageing playboy, and now the ageing playboy was King and Emperor, and not only would things never be the same for the family, but they most certainly would never be the same for the country and the empire.

May's last thought that night, before falling into an exhausted sleep, was that the Victorian age was over. A new, unknown age was about to begin under Bertie, and all anyone could do was to pray for the best.

PART FOUR

THE DARKEST NIGHT AND
THE GLORIOUS DAWN

Chapter Thirty-Three

It was the last day of July and the heat was suffocating. By her doctor's calculations, Alicky was due to give birth any day, and she was resting on a sun-lounger in the shade of one of the palace's many verandas. It would be her fifth child and so far she had only given birth to girls. With each failure to give birth to a son, her panicked anxiety had grown, for Russia's Salic law meant that none of her and Nicky's daughters could inherit the crown. Only a son could inherit and, unless she produced a male heir, the crown would pass to Nicky's younger brother.

Their four girls were their joy and deepest happiness, and Nicky had never blamed her when, time after time, the gun salute that announced the birth of a child to a tsar – firing out over St Petersburg one hundred times for a girl, three hundred times for a boy – only ever fired one hundred times.

As she waited for her pains to begin, fear ate away at her, crippling her with anxiety. This time it had to be a boy. It *had* to be! She loved Nicky with every fibre of her being, and not to be able to give him the one thing so essential to him as Tsar was such a monstrous cruelty there were times when she could scarcely breathe, her sense of failure weighed so heavily upon her.

She remembered the breaking of the blood-pact. Was that

the reason she only gave birth to girl after girl? That other people had boys and she couldn't? May now had four of them. Willy had six. At the thought of Willy, Alicky gritted her teeth. His badgering of Nicky was giving her husband migraines. No matter what the situation, international or domestic, Willy constantly showered Nicky with unwanted advice. Russia had been an ally of France for more than ten years, and the fact that she was an ally was a perpetual bee in Willy's bonnet. 'A monarchy allied with a republic?' he would thunder down the telephone line from Berlin. 'Stuff and nonsense, Nicky! We emperors must stick together. Germany and Russia, not Russia and France!'

Eight-year-old Olga ran out onto the veranda, saying as she ran over to her mother, 'Aunt Ella and Uncle Sergei have arrived, Mama. They are here to have lunch with us, and Papa says we are to dine al fresco.'

'Then you must be sure to wear a wide-brimmed sunhat – and so must your sisters. Will you tell them so for me?'

'*Naturellement*.' French was the language of the Russian court and Olga spoke it as easily as she did English and Russian. Throwing her arms around Alicky's neck, she gave her mother a kiss on the cheek and then scampered off to do what had been asked of her.

Although terrified of having a fifth daughter, Alicky loved the daughters she had, with all her heart, and counted her blessings that they were all healthy. Her eight-year-old niece Elisabeth – Ernie and Ducky's only child – had died of typhoid fever a little less than two years ago, shortly after Ducky had so shamefully insisted on divorcing Ernie. What had made her death doubly horrific had been that it happened when Ernie and Elisabeth had been on holiday with her, Nicky and their children at their Polish hunting lodge, and that Elisabeth had died before Ducky could reach her.

Irène, too, had lost a child. Her and Louis's little boy, Henry, had died from the family bleeding disease six months ago after falling and bumping his head.

As hard as she prayed that the child she was carrying was a boy, she prayed that if it was a boy, he would be free of the bleeding disease. Although Irène, the sister next to her in age, was a carrier of it – Henry's older brother, Waldemar, suffered from it, too – Vicky had two boys, George, who was eleven, and four-year-old Louis, and neither of them had inherited it, which indicated that Vicky wasn't a carrier. Whether Ella was, it was impossible to know, for she and Sergei had no children, but as Vicky was quite clearly not a carrier, then it was quite possible that Alicky was not a carrier, either.

Having eased her mind a little, and helped by a stick and her lady-in-waiting, she walked the short distance to where the luncheon table was set out, and where Nicky, Ella, Sergei and her little clover leaves – which was how she lovingly referred to her four daughters – were waiting for her.

Such a relaxed, informal luncheon would have been impossible if they had been living in the Winter Palace or any of the other palaces in St Petersburg, for there formal court protocol was set in stone. Only here, at Peterhof, and at the Alexander Palace at Tsarskoe Selo could she and Nicky live the informal family life she had grown up with as a child and that was so vitally important to her.

The conversation that had come to a halt as Alicky took her place at the table had been about the war that Russia was fighting in far-away Manchuria, against the Japanese.

Five months ago Japanese destroyers had attacked the Russian fleet at Port Arthur and war had been declared. Initially no one had been very worried, for it had been assumed that Russia's army and naval strength would soon bring the Japanese to their knees. It wasn't working out like that, though, and the war was beginning to cause a lot of anxiety. It had also hit very close to home. The battleship that Nicky and Sergei's cousin Kyril was serving on as First Officer was torpedoed, with the loss of more than seven hundred lives, and as well as nearly drowning, Kyril had suffered life-threatening injuries.

Aware that war was perhaps not a suitable topic for a woman about to go into labour at any minute, Sergei changed the subject by saying, 'How are your social projects managing, without you being able to be hands-on at the moment, Alicky? Which of them has precedence?'

'The nurse-training school at Tsarskoe Selo.' She smiled across at Ella. 'Do you remember how, when we were children, Mama once established a similar project in Darmstadt?' She turned her attention back to Sergei, 'Our mama was always trying to think of ways of improving people's lives. Once, she—'

She stopped speaking and, with the blood rushing to her face, pushed herself abruptly away from the table. 'I think the baby is coming! I'm sure it is.'

Her last two babies, Marie and Anastasia, had both come with wonderful speed and this one came even more quickly. Within an hour of Alicky leaving the table, the baby's head was crowning and minutes later, as Nicky gripped her hand so tightly it was bruised for days, a healthily plump baby boy slithered into the midwife's broad, capable hands.

'It's a boy, Alicky!' Nicky could hardly believe his eyes. 'Thanks be to God. *It's a boy!*' Tears of relief and gratitude poured down his face. They had a son! Russia had a Tsesarevich. The long, hideous years of torment were finally over.

Woozy from chloroform, Alicky didn't register the wonder of what had just happened. 'It's another girl, isn't it?' she said hysterically. 'It's a fifth girl, and Russia is never, ever going to forgive me!'

'It's a *boy*, Angel!' Nicky's voice was choked with tears of thankfulness. 'He's a big, healthy baby. Listen to him bawling. What a mighty tsar he will one day be.'

'A boy?' Her incredulity was total. '*Truly*, Nicky? *Truly?*'

'See for yourself, my darling.' Ignoring the ecstatic doctor and midwives, he helped her push herself up against the pillows. 'Isn't he a whopper, Alicky?' Their son was kicking his legs and clenching his little fists in indignation at his so–very–sudden emergence into the world. 'Isn't he the most magnificent baby boy you've ever seen?'

'He's a miracle!' Alicky's joy was so all–encompassing she thought she was going to faint with it. 'Oh, when can I hold him, Nicky? When will the cord be cut?'

'Soon, Your Imperial Majesty,' the doctor said, certain that, in gratitude for his last hour's work, his reward would be dizzyingly lavish.

Even before the cord was cut, Nicky gave orders for the news of his newborn heir to be made public, and for the first time he and Alicky were able to listen to the boom of Peterhof's saluting cannon fire in the joyous knowledge that the firing wouldn't stop at one hundred, but would continue all the way up to a glorious three hundred.

In St Petersburg the batteries of the Peter and Paul Fortress thundered similarly. Soon church bells were ringing all over Russia. The national anthem played in parks and public squares. Flags flew. At a time when the country was at war in the east, the glorious news of an heir was doubly, trebly welcome.

As Alicky wrote to May:

And so, dear Kindred Spirit, I am at last the very proud
mama of a beautiful and healthy baby boy. (You can
imagine what that word 'healthy' means to me!) I can't

*begin to tell you how magnificent he is! Like his papa, he
has the most beautiful blue eyes and his hair is the palest
gold you can ever imagine.*

*Shortly before I conceived him, I made a pilgrimage to
Sarov to honour St Seraphim, whose holy relics have
performed many miracles. Those in need of miracles bathe in
the Sarovka River, where St Seraphim bathed, and as at
night I waded into the icy depths, I prayed with all my
heart and soul that my next child would be a boy – and my
prayer has been answered! Although we gave our precious
son the name Alexei, after the tsar who was Peter the Great's
father and who is the tsar Nicky admires most, we had very
much wanted to name him Seraphim, but Nicky's mama and
his grand-uncles – even Sergei – nearly had heart attacks
when we told them. And so my little darling is Alexei
Nikolaevich, Sovereign Heir Tsesarevich, Grand Duke of
Russia.*

*Nicky and I are so pleased that Georgie agreed to be one
of his godparents, as did Willy (despite me no longer
thinking of him as a true Kindred Spirit!). My two eldest
girlies were absolutely splendid at his baptism ceremony. It
was the first time either of them had taken part in anything
so formal, and they looked absolutely delicious in traditional
Russian court dresses of deep-blue satin decorated with silver-
thread embroidery and little stiff headdresses decorated with
pearls.*

*You cannot begin to imagine, dear May, what a difference
Baby's birth has made to us. (Baby is our pet name for
Alexei.) Where once I was so unpopular, both with Nicky's
family (other than Sergei), and with St Petersburg society
(who are absolutely NOT typical of the real Russia), now I
can do no wrong. There has been some terrible unrest in the
country over the last several months – all caused by*

*troublemakers who fill the heads of the workers with unrealistic
expectations; there was even a general strike some months ago
in Odessa – but Baby's birth has shown how truly devoted to
us the country as a whole is. The peasants – who are the true
Russians of Russia – refer to Nicky as their 'Little Father',
and now I am 'Mamushka', their Little Mother. Outside St
Petersburg, at Ilinskoe, where Ella and Sergei have their
country home, we have only to appear and the people flock in
hordes from miles around and bow respectfully in their
hundreds to us. Some of them even fall on their knees, so do
not believe any rumours as to our unpopularity!*

*My last piece of good news is that Sergei is soon to be
relieved of the burden of his governorship of Moscow and is
to be recalled to another position here, in St Petersburg. I
will then see far more of Ella than I have for quite some
time, although she and Sergei were on a visit to Peterhof
when darling Baby was born.*

*Much love and huge hugs, your always Kindred Spirit,
Alicky*

That evening, as Alicky was leaving Marie and Anastasia's
bedroom after listening to them say their prayers and after
kissing them goodnight, one of Alexei's nurserymaids came
hurrying down the corridor towards her, an anxious expression
on her face.

Dipping a curtsey, she said, 'There is no cause for alarm,
Your Imperial Majesty, but there is a little spotting of blood
on His Imperial Highness's swaddling bands and—'

She got no further.

Alicky's hand had flown to her throat. To the nearest of the
footmen who lined every yard of every corridor, she said,
'Inform his Imperial Majesty his presence is needed in the
nursery.'

And then, struggling not to let her alarm show, she headed swiftly and with fast-rising fear to her precious son.

In the lamplight Alexei was lying in his cradle, freshly bathed, sweetly-smelling and nightgowned, cooing happily. There was no sign of him being even remotely distressed.

'The blood,' she said tightly to the head nursery-nurse. 'Where did it come from?'

'His navel, Your Imperial Majesty. And it was only a few spots. Hardly anything at all.'

With a thudding heart Alicky leaned over the cradle. As she lifted up Alexei's linen nightgown, the head nursery-nurse said, 'I swabbed the spots away. There will be nothing to see, but if you would like to see the swab?'

Alicky wasn't listening to her. She was undoing the safety pins holding Alexei's muslin nappy together. As the nappy fell away, there were fresh drops of blood on its inner folds. More drops were oozing from his tummy button.

The head nursery-nurse said, perplexed, 'But it had stopped, Your Imperial Majesty! I can show you the swab I used. I—'

She fell abruptly silent as Nicky strode into the room. Taking one look at the beads of blood, he said, white-lipped, 'Summon the doctor.'

As the nurse hurried from the room, Nicky said to the nurserymaid, 'Leave us.'

The girl did so, unable to imagine what all the fuss was about. Her mother had had twelve babies and would not have blinked an eye at a few spots of blood leaking from the navel. It was certainly nothing for the Tsar and Tsarina to worry about; and the doctor, when he came, would tell them so.

In the room behind her, Alicky and Nicky looked at each other with horror-filled eyes.

'Is it possible it is natural bleeding?' A pulse throbbed at the corner of Nicky's jaw.

Although he knew that one of Queen Victoria's sons had died from haemophilia and that Alicky's brother and Irène's little boy had, too, and that others in Alicky's family suffered from it, he had always been confident that his Romanov blood-line would ensure that the sickness wouldn't affect any son he and Alicky had. Now, however, he was filled with terrible doubt.

'Yes.' Her voice was unsteady. 'It could be natural bleeding. It *has* to be. But if it isn't? Oh God, Nicky! What if it isn't? God couldn't be so cruel as to have given him to us and then to have given us such a burden to bear, could he?'

Nicky didn't answer her. His birthday fell on the feast day of the Old Testament prophet, Job; and, like Job, he believed in fate and the impossibility of battling it.

The arrival of the doctor went some way towards reassuring him.

'It is just a slight leakage, Your Imperial Majesty,' he said to Nicky, after swabbing away the trickle of blood and beginning to bandage Alexei's tummy. 'The umbilical-cord stump probably dropped off a little too soon. His Imperial Highness is not in any distress. Tomorrow will show how little cause there is for anxiety.'

'Should we have told him the reason for our anxiety?' Nicky asked, when they were in their own room, lying in the darkness, clasped in each other's arms. 'How can he have made an accurate diagnosis, without being in possession of all the facts?'

'We can tell him tomorrow – if we have to. But pray God we don't have to, Nicky.' Tears rolled down Alicky's cheeks, falling onto his naked chest. 'Pray God his diagnosis is correct and that there will be no sign of bleeding tomorrow, and no sign of any sinister bleeding in the future.'

He pressed her hard against him and then, feeling her response, rolled her beneath him. Her lips parted, even before his mouth closed on hers. Lovemaking had always been their joy and comfort, and it was their comfort now. Tomorrow would bring reassurance. Tomorrow there would no longer be any anxieties about Alexei's health. Tomorrow, God willing, all would be well.

The next morning Alicky rose as dawn was breaking. If Alexei's navel had continued to bleed throughout the night, she wanted to know. She didn't want evidence being wiped away before she had seen it for herself.

The nursery was filled with soft early light. The nurserymaid was asleep on the night-sofa; the head nurse in her bedroom adjoining the nursery. Only Baby was awake, placidly blowing bubbles.

As she leaned over the cradle, her heart was slamming against her breastbone. '*Please let the bleeding have stopped. Please! Please! Please,*' Alicky whispered fervently, her whole heart in her prayer; her entire being in it.

With trembling hands, knowing the future of the monarchy rested in what she was about to see, or not see, she removed the covers to reveal the bandage the doctor had bound her precious son's tummy with. It was still neatly in place.

And it was saturated with bright-red blood.

Never again were her beautiful, classical features to be untouched by strain and anxiety. At thirty-two years old, Alicky began living with a tension that was palpable and, because people were unaware of its cause, unpleasantly disconcerting.

Her public appearances had always been rare, but now they became rarer still and, when she did appear in public, her lips were always set in a tight line and her complexion, once so flawless, was often stained with ugly red blotches. Her saving graces were the heavy, lustrous glory of her hair, and her figure, which, despite her many pregnancies and with the help of French corsetry, was still enviably slender.

Not until a couple of weeks into the new year of 1905 did she write to May. Sitting in her mauve boudoir at a walnut-inlaid escritoire that had once belonged to Marie Antoinette, she wrote:

Dearest May,

After six months we now know, without any shadow of doubt, that Baby has the family bleeding disease. Ella and Sergei know. Vicky and Irène know – how could I possibly keep it from Irène, when she has already lost a child to the disease and another child is a semi-invalid through suffering from it?

Sergei has said – and in this I agree with him, as does my poor, darling Nicky – that no one else must know. Not his mother or his brothers, or, other than Sergei, his uncles. With the war in Japan going so disastrously wrong and dissatisfaction in the country so rampant, if it became public knowledge that the Tsesarevich had a disease that could mean him not living long enough to inherit the crown, the country might well turn into full-scale revolution. As it is, the threat is so real we have to be guarded in a way inconceivable to you and Georgie in nice, cosy England. Only recently a government minister was assassinated, and in Moscow Sergei receives death threats on a daily basis.

She laid her pen down. There had always been civil unrest in Russia. It was why the country could only be governed by a strong, autocratic tsar. Sergei said it was the speech Nicky had given to the leaders of local governments, shortly after his father's death, when he had said he regarded their hope of representative government as being a 'senseless dream', that had given birth to the Social Revolutionary Party. Another, smaller organization, going by the name of the Bolsheviks, was run by a man called Lenin, who was living in exile in Geneva.

It was the Social Revolutionary Party and the Bolsheviks who were demanding an end to autocracy – and not only an end to autocracy, but to the monarchy as well – and who were behind all the bombings, the government minister's assassination and the death threats that Sergei was receiving. With a heavy sigh, Alicky picked up her pen again:

Today we received news of a Workers' March that is to take place tomorrow in St Petersburg. According to Uncle Vladimir (who is now the city's Governor-General), the march is to culminate at the Winter Palace, where the leader of the march intends handing a petition listing all the workers' grievances to Nicky. As Nicky isn't in St Petersburg, but is here, at Tsarskoe Selo, this is clearly an impossible outcome, and it is to be hoped that Uncle Vladimir makes this clear to them and that, even at this late date, the march is called off without there being large-scale public disturbance.

So many things are so very grim, and I often think back to those golden, far-off days when we were young girls enjoying family get-togethers at Osborne, or Balmoral, or even, sometimes, at Windsor. When Granny Queen was alive there was always such a sense of safety! Ella often talks of the days when you and she were best friends and always shared a bedroom at get-togethers and sat up in bed, talking for hours on end and eating Garibaldi biscuits. Even I can never see a Garibaldi biscuit without being overcome by the memory of dear Granny Queen, so small and squat in black silk and her little white lace cap, with its long chiffon streamers, and the wonderful faint scent of orange blossom that she so loved to be surrounded by.

Alicky put her pen down. That, because of her pregnancy, she hadn't been able to be with Granny Queen when she died was something she knew she would always regret. She had been Granny Queen's favourite granddaughter. Had her grand-mother asked after her, as she lay dying? No one had said she had, but then it had never been something that – fearful of not receiving the answer she so wanted – Alicky had ever asked about.

She picked up her pen again and wrote:

Enough. I must end. Ella and Sergei will be here by the end of the month, and then at least I will have one sister always close by. Irène and Vicky visit as often as they can, but Tsarskoe Selo is such a long, long way from both of them.
    All my love, your secret Kindred Spirit, Alicky

PS: When Vicky was last here, she told me it is widely believed by some members of the family that I am so conscious of your Serene Highness background that I have little time for you! As the truth is so very different, I found it very funny, and hope you do, too. xxx

Three weeks later, in Moscow, Ella was still trying to come to terms with the appalling death toll on what was now spoken of as 'Bloody Sunday'. According to Vladimir, it was the Preo-brazhensky Guards who had opened fire on the marchers as they approached the Winter Palace, but they had not done so under his instructions. Some reports said hundreds had died; others that the death toll was more than a thousand. Whatever the truth of it, the blame lay heavily on Vladimir's shoulders, as Governor-General of the city. However, where the country was concerned, the blame was entirely Nicky's.

'And he knew only that a peaceful march was intended,'

Vladimir said over the telephone, 'and that, as he wasn't in the city to receive the petition, it was a march that would be called off. He's the most pacific person – far too pacific – that I know, and now the shouts on the streets are of "Nicholas the Bloody" and "Nicholas the Murderer". Until now, revolution was only a possibility. Now, God help us all, we're on the brink of it!'

Due to the strikes in Moscow, the atmosphere was electric with tension, as if a thunderstorm was about to break. Ella, packing for their move back to St Petersburg, lived in constant fear for Sergei's safety. She had always known that her marriage was a mystery to both their mutual families and to the court, and that it was generally believed that Sergei was a harsh husband – and one who, it was suspected, had homosexual tendencies. The reality of their relationship was known only to them, but when she had insisted to Granny Queen that she was perfectly content with Sergei, it had been the truth. There was more than one kind of love, and if theirs was different from most people's, what did it matter? All that mattered was the strength of the bond that existed between them.

The city was deep in snow and Sergei had just left the Kremlin for his government office. It would be his last visit there, for he had been relieved of his position as Governor-General twenty-four hours earlier and all that was left for him to do was a little tidying-up.

She was thinking what a comfort to Alicky it would be, when she and Sergei were again living in their palace in St Petersburg, when there was an explosion so deafening it was as if every mighty wall surrounding the Kremlin had been blasted into atoms.

She screamed, knowing instantly who the bomb had been meant for, and then she began to run.

Running down the wide stairs with her heart in her mouth,

she left the palace and crossed the snow-covered courtyard. She was dimly aware that people were both racing after her and towards her, all of them trying to stop her; all of them trying to prevent her from seeing the horror that awaited.

She would have none of it. With the strength of a madwoman she fended them off, racing towards the smoking remains of what had been Sergei's carriage.

And then she came to a sudden, rocking halt, unable to take in what it was that she was faced with. There was no injured Sergei. There wasn't even Sergei's body. Scattered far and wide across the bloodied snow were simply bit and pieces of him. A leg here. An arm there. His boots had been blown clear off his legs, his feet still in them. There was no trace of his head, or his shoulders. She stumbled over a severed hand.

His rings. She must take his rings. Sergei would want her to do so. She was on her knees amongst bones and cartilage, retrieving from pulverized flesh the icon that Sergei had always worn around his neck. 'A stretcher,' she said, time after time, like a mantra. 'A stretcher. We must have a stretcher. We must take his remains to the monastery and lay them before the high altar.'

A stretcher was brought. Other hands beside hers gathered up bloodied body parts and placed them on it. A blanket was brought to cover them.

Still wearing her blood-soaked dress, still clutching his rings and the icon that Sergei had never been without, Ella stumbled behind the stretcher as it was carried into the Kremlin's Chudov Monastery. And there, this time in prayer, she fell on her knees again to cry.

Chapter Thirty-Four

It was mid-morning and Willy was on the ground floor of the Neues Palais, standing legs astride in the little-used Grotto Hall. Encrusted with shells and with a marble floor decorated with sea-urchins and marine plants, the Grotto Hall reminded him of his grandmother's sketching alcove at Osborne and was where he always came when, as now, he didn't want to be disturbed.

Nothing at the moment was going his way, and that it wasn't was not his fault. It was all the fault of that arch-Satan: his Uncle Bertie, King Edward VII, King of England and Emperor of India.

He breathed in hard, his nostrils flaring, the upward tips of his moustache quivering. Who would have ever thought that womanizing, pleasure-loving, surely-not-very-bright Uncle Bertie would have turned into such a competent, hands-on king? He was a constitutional monarch, for God's sake. He was supposed to leave political conniving and real government to his ministers, not jaunt behind their back, forming alliances with other nations as easily as if he was playing bridge. Queen Victoria had never done so! When he thought of his much-missed grandmother – and of how different European politics were without her – Willy felt so emotional he had to ball his good hand into a fist to stop himself from weeping.

He had, of course, had another bad night; a night when the recurring nightmares that he had never quite outgrown seized hold of him with such power that he'd thought, on waking, he was going to lose his reason. Now, in the Grotto Hall, he was trying to get a grip on himself. The person who had already lost their reason – the person who had begun playing the diplomat as if he were an autocratic ruler, not a constitutional monarch – was Bertie.

Almost immediately after the Boer War had ended, Bertie had made what, on the surface, was yet another of the personal pleasure trips to Paris that he had been making for more than forty years; a trip that appeared to have no political ulterior motive.

Except that it had, for devious Bertie had been laying the groundwork for an *Entente Cordiale* – a close, committed friendship between England and France. On his 'pleasure trip' he made impromptu public speeches (always, of course, in his fluent, flawless French) saying how he had always felt himself so very much at home in France. Everywhere he went – at a state banquet, at the races, at the theatre, at the Élysée Palace – he gave off-the-cuff speeches in his relaxed, affable manner. His charm-offensive and effortless bonhomie resulted in the Parisians cheering him to the rafters.

It was the kind of popularity that Willy constantly craved for himself, and the sight of arch-Satan Uncle Bertie achieving it with such effortless ease had made him want to vomit. A year later, when the *Entente Cordiale* had been formerly signed in 1904 and England was firmly allied with Germany's enemy, France, he had wanted to vomit even more, for it meant there was now no possible hope of an alliance with England.

Bertie's action had carved Europe in two, with England,

France and Russia in one camp, and Germany, with her long-standing allies Austria–Hungary and Italy, in the other. And what use, Willy thought savagely, staring up at the Grotto Hall's painted ceiling, would Italians be, when the chips were down?

It was at fraught times like this that he needed his close friend Phili and the distractions of tomfoolery that his company provided. But Phili was hundreds of miles away, writing Nordic ballads on his Liebenberg estate.

To his intense irritation, he heard footsteps approaching, and seconds later his eldest son walked apprehensively into the Grotto Hall, a newspaper held in a trembling hand.

'Apologies for disturbing you, Papa, but I very much need to show you something.'

Willy's jaw tightened. Wilhelm was twenty-four, had been married for little more than a year and had already begun whingeing that he found his delightful young wife boring.

'What is it now?' he snapped, too concerned with Germany's future safety to be bothered with Wilhelm's gripes about married life.

'The newspaper *Die Zukunft*, Papa.' His voice was unsteady, his face unnaturally pale. 'It is hinting that Count zu Eulenburg and the friends close to him – the members of what he calls his Liebenberg Circle – are . . . are . . . are homosexual.'

Willy's jaw dropped. 'Homosexual? *Homosexual?*' His eyes nearly popped out of his head. 'What libel and utter nonsense! Phili is a married man. He has eight daughters. I'll demand a retraction immediately. I'll have the paper shut down. On dear Phili's behalf, I will demand a very public apology. Who is the editor?' He snatched the newspaper from Wilhelm's hand. 'Harden? I'll have him castrated! That my poor, dear Phili should be so publicly and wrongly maligned . . .'

The very thought brought tears to his eyes.

Wilhelm was at a loss. It had never occurred to him that his father might be unaware of Phili zu Eulenburg's sexual preference. His father had, after all, counted Eulenburg his closest friend for the past eighteen years. Eulenburg and members of his Liebenberg Circle had been his father's guests aboard the imperial yacht countless times. Several times a year they went on hunting trips together. Several times a month they met up for evenings of drinking and practical jokes. How could his forty-seven-year-old father not have known?

'Because your father is an innocent!' his mother said to Wilhelm when, after Willy had blundered into his study to telephone Phili, her son had shown the newspaper article to her. 'He takes people at face value. Your dear, dear papa never *thinks*! What other horrible things are now going to be printed?'

On the telephone a near-hysterical Willy was saying agitatedly to Phili, 'That it is all lies, beloved Phili, doesn't matter. They are lies that *must* be refuted. You must sue for libel! You must emerge from this farrago of nonsense with your reputation intact.'

Stunned, Phili said he was going to take court action immediately, and Willy collapsed in relief – but it was relief that was short-lived.

Dona, thick-waisted and stout, stared at Willy disbelievingly. 'And you think the threat of a libel action will put an end to these rumours about yourself and Philipp zu Eulenburg?'

'*Gott im Himmel!*' He wanted to tear his hair out in frustration at her stupidity. 'There *are* no rumours about me. The filthy, lying rumours are all about dear Phili.'

'But they are *NOT*!' There were times when Dona found her husband's inability to see the wood for the trees almost unendurable. 'Your name is not mentioned – how could the Kaiser's name be mentioned? But it is implicit in every line that, if Count Philipp zu Eulenburg and his close circle of friends are all . . . are all . . .' she struggled to say the word 'homosexual' and couldn't bring herself to utter it, 'are all *deviant*, that *you* are deviant as well. The accusation of unholy, illegal practices isn't being levelled solely at Phili. *You* are the person at whom the accusations in *Die Zukunft* are truly being levelled. And the only person who doesn't realize it is you!'

Willy had thought her certifiably mad. It was his sister-in-law, Irène, who matter-of-factly pointed out to him that if Phili was homosexual, then, as his closest friend, it was only to be expected that people assumed he was well aware of it.

But he hadn't been, and he did what he always did whenever he was faced with something utterly unpalatable and hadn't the slightest idea how to deal with it. He shut himself away in his rooms in a state of nervous collapse.

This time his period of collapse was a long one. Phili's original court case led to the public disclosure of several liaisons, the most salacious being an ongoing relationship with Count Dietrich von Hülsen-Haeseler, who, on Phili's recommendation, Willy had made chief of his military Cabinet, and whose private performances in a pink tutu he had always, in the past, so innocently enjoyed.

'When and where is it all going to end?' he said piteously to Irène, as one court case led to another and *Die Zukunft* revealed that the Liebenberg Circle had feminine nicknames for each other and that his, the Kaiser's, was 'Sweety'.

Irène had had no answer for him, for by now there could be no doubting the truthfulness of the insinuations that were being made.

The country was scandalized. Willy was thunderstruck.

'How could I have known?' he said pathetically time and time again. 'I thought only that we were all the best and truest of friends – and the horseplay we indulged in was surely only the horseplay that all men indulge in, when no ladies are present to be offended?'

Despite his love of risqué jokes and coarse horseplay, he was essentially a prude, and the revelations as to the true nature behind all the good times he had so enjoyed not only embarrassed him, but appalled him – and they did so because he knew how very near the truth the hints about his own sexuality were.

He had always preferred the company of men to the company of women. Although as a youth he had indulged in a couple of paid sexual encounters with women, he had done so more out of curiosity than desire. The only woman he had ever felt genuine love for was Ella, and Ella had rejected him for Sergei – the irony being that, up until the day of his horrific death, rumours about Sergei's sexuality had been rife.

Other than Ella, women had never held any great emotional appeal for Willy. Dona, who had been pretty as a young woman and was reassuringly admiring and docile, had been a momentary aberration, and one he had grown bored and exasperated with even before their honeymoon was over.

He had always been happiest amongst his Hussars. And then he had met Phili – old enough to be a father-figure, debonair and sophisticated, creatively gifted, highly cultivated – and his entire world had changed. The huge social gap between them had meant nothing. In Count Philipp zu Eulenburg he had met his soulmate and, like the soulmates in the medieval poetry that the two of them so enjoyed, the union between them had never descended into coarse carnality. It had been a thing of spiritual beauty. And now, thanks to the editor of *Die Zukunft*, all the beauty had been destroyed and he, Germany's All-Highest, had been made a laughing stock.

He had been unable to bring himself to bear the pain of seeing Phili again and, coward-like, had ended their relationship by letter. All connections with the Liebenberg Circle had been severed. All the prestigious high public and political appointments that he had, at Phili's suggestion, showered on his former friends were terminated.

It was over, and his heartbreak was so extreme that his ministers began speculating that the damage caused to his arm at birth had not been the only thing that had been damaged. They suspected his brain had also been damaged, and it wasn't long before gossip as to the Kaiser not being quite right in the head spread to the courts of England and Russia.

Alicky was far too worried about Alexei's terrifying bleeding episodes to care about unkind gossip about Willy.

May, however, let everyone in Marlborough House know exactly how she felt about such gossip. 'Bosh!' she said forcefully, using one of George's favourite expressions.

Privately, though, and knowing Willy as she did, she wondered if there was any truth in the gossip and, on Willy's behalf, felt deep concern.

Chapter Thirty-Five

It was the end of April and Paris was at its best. In the Champs-Élysées the chestnut trees were thick with blossom and flower-sellers were out in full force, the scent of tulips and anemones filling the air, as sweet and spicy as a drug.

Accompanied by Margaret, Dolly's wife, May was strolling down the avenue des Champs-Élysées on her way to the art exhibition that was the purpose of her visit. At forty-two, she still had a neat figure and, beneath her pleated silk hat, her hair, although no longer possessing a coppery glint, was still wheat-gold and she wore it the way she had always worn it – high and tight at the sides and with a distinctive poodle fringe.

'And was the artist whose works we are going to see a very great friend of yours when you were a girl and your mama and papa lived in Florence?' Margaret asked as they turned out of the Champs-Élysées and into the narrow but elegant rue Saint-Honoré, where the gallery was situated.

'Yes.' And then, mindful of the crush she had had on Thaddeus when she was seventeen, and not wanting her sister-in-law to guess at it, she added, 'A very great *family* friend. When we knew him, he went by his birth name of Henry Thaddeus Jones, but he later changed it to Henry Jones Thaddeus – the

399

surname Thaddeus being much more memorable for an artist, don't you think?'

'Oh, much!' May was so knowledgeable about things artistic, Margaret wouldn't have dreamed of disagreeing with her.

As they approached the gallery May was pleased to see that the exhibition was being very well attended. The gallery hadn't been advised of her visit beforehand – something that was her habit when visiting small galleries, otherwise she would have to suffer the annoyance of being formally met and escorted from picture to picture, instead of being able to wander at will and browse undisturbed.

The pictures were of a variety of subject matter. There were pastoral scenes and European landscapes – May recognized Lake Trasimeno in Italy and Lake Garda in Switzerland. There were Orientalist paintings: one of a gateway in Samarkand, another of a street market in Cairo. There was a historical painting of a Scottish family being evicted at the time of the Clearances, and then last, but by no means least, there were the portraits.

As they moved out of one of the gallery's small rooms and into another room, May was just telling Margaret how, many years ago, Thaddeus had painted portraits of her parents, and of how the portraits had been exhibited at the Royal Academy, when they walked straight into Ducky, arm-in-arm with an exceedingly tall and good-looking gentleman whom May knew could only be Kyril Vladimirovich.

May gasped in surprised delight. Ducky gave a squeal of joy. Kyril looked bemused, and Margaret, who had never previously met either Ducky or Kyril, was very quickly introduced.

'Dearest, darling May! How long has it been?' Ducky said rapturously, uncaring that their little group was causing disapproving heads to turn. 'It must be ten years at least since we last met. You and Georgie were living at York Cottage, and I was still married to Ernie!'

As more heads turned in their direction, Kyril gave a mean-ingful cough.

Ducky removed her hand from his arm and linked arms with May, saying to Margaret, 'Do forgive me, but I so want to have a long family chat with May, and here is quite obviously not the place to do so. Would you think it horrendously bad-mannered of me if I suggested I stole her away for half an hour?' Without waiting for a response, she said to May, 'The Hotel Bristol is only a few yards down the street, and we can catch up over tea and cakes while Kyril escorts Margaret around the rest of the gallery.'

Kyril, accustomed to Ducky's lack of regard for accepted etiquette, proffered Margaret his arm. 'It would be my pleasure,' he said disarmingly, and before Margaret could agree or disagree, she found herself being escorted by a Russian she had heard of, but had never previously met, towards a large painting bearing the ominous title: *A Woman Led Astray*.

'Goodness, this is fun,' Ducky said as, in the Hotel Bristol, they settled themselves in a small lounge that gave them complete privacy. 'What subject shall we hit on first, before Margaret and Kyril decide they have had enough of each other's company and come to join us? My divorce from Ernie and marriage to Kyril? Your having become the Princess of Wales? The children we have had since we last met? Alicky, and the disaster she is making of being Tsarina? Ella having become a nun? It's your choice, dear May. But let's do it over champagne. I only mentioned tea and cakes when we were at the gallery in case your very proper-looking sister-in-law thought me too outrageously fast.'

'Let's start with your divorce and marriage to Kyril.'

A waiter deferentially approached. Champagne was ordered.

Ducky, whose olive skin and raven-dark hair made her look

stunningly exotic, leaned back in the red-velvet armchair she was seated in and said, 'Once Granny Queen had joined Grandpa Albert in a Happy Land Far, Far Away, the divorce was easy. We didn't get married immediately, though. Kyril takes his time over things. However, once Russia had so thunderingly lost the war with Japan – Kyril nearly died once from war injuries, and then a second time from shame – we married in Paris, without even troubling to ask for Nicky's permission, which we knew he would have refused.'

Their champagne served, Ducky said, 'Nicky's reaction to Kyril marrying a divorced woman was typically petty. He stripped Kyril of his titles and honours and his naval decorations for bravery, and said that neither of us would be allowed to enter Russia again, but what Nicky had forgotten was how close Kyril is to the throne. Since his father's death, Kyril is third in line. It finally gave Nicky pause for thought, and last year we were invited not only to live in Russia again, but to be given a house at Tsarskoe Selo within spitting distance of the Alexander Palace. So there you are. That is number one on the list taken care of. What was number two?'

Number two had been her present title of Princess of Wales, and as May didn't want to waste precious time talking about herself, or discussing subject number three, which had been the children they had had since their last meeting, she took a drink of her champagne and jumped straight to subject number four. Alicky.

'Alicky?' Ducky groaned. 'She made a poor enough Tsarina before Alexei's birth. Why, being so naturally antisocial and disliking mixing with anyone but close family, she thought she could make a good job of being Tsarina, I can't imagine. Now, with Alexei a victim of the family bleeding disease, things have gone from bad to worse. She is rarely seen – and neither, of course, is Alexei. Her entire life is bound up with caring for him and living the lie that there is nothing seriously wrong with him. The outside world no longer has any meaning for her. If people were to know the reason for it, they would, I think, have some sympathy, but they don't know and so the sympathy is nil.'

She took a deep drink of her champagne and said, suddenly no longer full of *joie de vivre*, but deathly serious, 'As doctors can offer Alexei no relief from the pain he suffers whenever he has an internal haemorrhage, she has turned to religion in the hope of a cure and, tragically for Russia, religion has come in the form of a so-called holy monk, Father Grigory Yefimovich Rasputin. According to Alicky, he can bring the bleeding to a halt and, whether he can or can't, Alicky believes he can, so Rasputin has become part and parcel of life at Tsarskoe Selo – and part and parcel of every brothel in St Petersburg as well, if what is said about him is true.'

She took a Fabergé cigarette case out of her handbag and, after they had lit-up gold-tipped Sobranies, said, 'Now who shall we talk about next? Saint Ella or Sinner Missy?'

'Ella. I used to be very close to her, but we lost touch almost completely after she married Sergei.'

'As did nearly everyone else. Sergei was a mystery I think only Ella ever really understood. Did you know his head was found days after the explosion, on a nearby roof?'

May gasped and Ducky said apologetically, 'Clearly you didn't. Would you like a brandy?'

'No.' May's voice was unsteady. 'Has Ella really become a nun, or has she simply moved out of the palace and into a convent? I've heard so many bizarre stories I don't know what is true and what is rumour.'

'Then I'll tell you what is true.' Ducky waited while a waiter refilled their glasses before saying, 'Within days of Sergei's death, Ella began getting rid of all her worldly goods – which, let's face it, were considerable. Then she began spending all her time caring for the poor and the sick. Up to that point the family simply thought she was in shock and would begin acting normally again, given time. It was only when she began divvying up her Romanov jewels that alarm bells began ringing.'

She gave a despairing lift of her shoulders and elegantly blew a thread of blue smoke into the air. 'Then she bought land, built an orphanage, a hospital for the poor and a convent that she named the House of Mary and Martha. When the Church granted the convent official recognition, Ella took vows of poverty, chastity and obedience, created herself Abbess of the Order and has worn nothing but a rather fetching pearl-grey habit and wimple ever since. The people regard her as a saint. The family think she's barking mad, but then perhaps religious madness lurks in her bloodline. Little sister Alicky is proving to be just as barmy, when it comes to religious fanaticism.'

'No one could accuse Vicky, Irène and Ernie of religious fanaticism.'

'That's true and, as siblings, they are all still very close. All three of them regularly visit Tsarskoe Selo and, when they do, Vicky and Irène always stay at the far side of the imperial park with Kyril and me. Ernie visits Alicky as well, but when he does, he doesn't cross the park and visit me. A husband visiting an ex-wife would be seen as very bad form. Kyril puts up with a lot, but even for Kyril that would be a step too far.'

'And then who should walk in on us but Margaret, Kyril and Thaddeus!' May said later to George, when she was back at Marlborough House. 'I do so wish you had been there to meet Thaddeus, George. He was born in Ireland and we had what he calls "great crack" together – meaning much fun and laughter – before we all said goodbye to each other.'

'I'm glad you and Margaret had a splendid three-day jaunt, but I'd prefer it if you didn't have another one for quite a while, May. I miss you when you're not here.'

It was rare that George put his feelings into words. In all the years of their marriage there had only been a few occasions when he had told her that he loved her, although it was obvious to her that he did.

'And when I'm away from you, I miss you,' she said truthfully. 'But I did so want to see Thaddeus's Paris exhibition, and you know how you hate being dragged around an art gallery.'

'God, yes.' George shuddered. 'I don't know which I would have hated more. The gallery or finding myself in France.'

She fought down the desire to say that if in the past he had troubled to learn French, then visits to France would be much more pleasurable for him. From the day they had married, she had always been careful not to remind him of how inadequate his education had been, and to constantly remind herself of all George's good qualities. Basic decency was one of them; dogged steadfastness another. As Prince of Wales, he didn't have many official duties, but those that he had he performed with painstaking care. Also, and unlike his father, he was a reassuringly faithful husband.

That he was so mattered to her, for something rather wonderful had happened between them, when they had been six years into their marriage. George had been performing his marital duty – something he was rather keen on – and May had been wondering how long it would be before he collapsed with perspiration from his efforts, when she had begun experiencing the most bizarre, pleasurable sensations. They had grown and grown until she had lost all control of herself and had given herself up to the most indescribable, all-engulfing pleasure.

'Well, May,' he had said minutes later, pushing himself up

on his elbows and looking down at her with great satisfaction, 'that was a turn-up for the books.'

'Yes, George,' she had said, blushing rosily. 'It was rather, wasn't it?'

A week after May's return from Paris, the King cut short a holiday he had been enjoying in Biarritz with his long-standing mistress, Mrs George Keppel. For a long time he had been suffering from frighteningly severe bronchial attacks and breathing difficulties.

'But this one is by far the worst,' an anxious George said to May, after having visited his father who had taken to his bed in Buckingham Palace. 'Motherdear has informed Maud, and Maud and Carl are already on their way to London.'

Over the next few days the King's breathing difficulties became worse, not better, and other members of the family began congregating at the palace. Looloo and Fife travelled down from Scotland with both of their daughters. Irène and Heinrich arrived from Germany with one of their two sons. Vicky and Louis arrived from the Isle of Wight. Lenchen and Christian visited daily from Kew. Louise returned from a visit to Nice. Russian Aunt Marie came all the way from Coburg. Marie-Louise came and, signalling how serious Bertie's condition was, so did the Archbishop of Canterbury, Book of Common Prayer in hand.

On 6 May, sitting by his father's bedside, desperately wanting him to take a turn for the better, George said, 'I have some news that will please you, Papa. Your horse, Witch of the Air, has won at Kempton Park.'

Bertie's bulky figure was propped up on a mountain of pillows and he attempted a cackle of pleased laughter, and then began gasping for breath. Doctor Laking, who had been his doctor for more than a decade, held an oxygen mask over his nose and mouth.

When he removed it and Bertie was again wheezily breathing unaided, Alix took Laking to one side and said in a low voice, 'Please tell me when the end is near, for there is someone not here whom I know my husband would like to see before he dies.'

'Then in my estimation, Ma'am,' Laking said gently, 'the person in question should be contacted immediately.'

Ashen-faced, Alix turned to Louis of Battenberg. 'Would you please send for Mrs Keppel, Louis.'

And then in explanation, to a stunned-looking George, 'It is the last thing I can do that will make your dear papa happy. He will want to say goodbye to her.'

On Alice Keppel's arrival at the palace, everyone other than Alix left the bedroom, heading for the nearest drawing room or smoking room.

Aware of how close to a breakdown George was, May said, 'I think the library is the best place for us, George.'

Once in its blessed privacy, he held onto her like a drowning man holding onto a rock. When he could finally trust himself to speak, he said, 'I've lived every day since dear Eddy's death dreading the moment when I would not only lose the best father there ever was, but would become King. Now that hideous moment can only be days – possibly hours – away.' He held her even tighter. 'But when it happens, the burden won't be mine alone, will it, darling May? You will be here to be my strength and comfort?'

'I will always be that, George.' It was a promise as solemn as a vow. 'And when the moment you so dread arrives,' she said firmly and with great conviction, 'you will, I know, handle it superbly. No tears. Tears can come later, when we are on our own. At the moment of kingship you must be in full command of yourself.'

He nodded, knowing that he would never be able to manage without her and that, thank goodness, he would never have to, for she would always be at his side as his queen.

A thought so glaringly obvious that he couldn't imagine why it had never occurred to him before was: what would May's title be then? It couldn't be Queen May. May was her family pet name. And it couldn't be her first Christian name, because that was Victoria, and as Granny Queen had only been dead for nine years, for May to become known as Queen Victoria would be highly insensitive and unpopular. It would have to be one of her other Christian names, and he couldn't for the life of him remember what they were.

'What Christian names do you have, other than Victoria, May?'

'Mary Augusta Louise Olga Pauline Claudine Agnes. But why on earth?'

'Because the instant I become King, you will become Queen and you will have to have a name, and for obvious reasons it can't be Victoria.'

'I always sign letters and official papers as Victoria Mary. Surely Victoria Mary wouldn't cause offence? It is how I have always assumed I would be known.'

George frowned. He didn't care for double-barrelled names, and he didn't much care for the thought of her second name becoming the name she would be known by. The last queen called Mary had been nicknamed 'Bloody Mary', for her habit of having Protestants burned at the stake. It had been four hundred years ago, but Englishmen had long memories.

Mentally he went through the other options. Augusta was too old-fashioned. Queen Louise might work – or might have, if Aunt Louise's reputation with men wasn't so well known.

Olga was far too Russian. Pauline wasn't stately enough. Claudine was too French. And a Queen Agnes would quickly become known as Queen Aggie.

By a process of elimination he was back to Mary, a name that did at least have the benefit of being straightforward and one it was impossible to shorten.

'Mary,' he said, anxious to get back to his father's bedside, Mrs Keppel or no Mrs Keppel. 'You will be known as Queen Mary, May.'

And sixteen hours after his father had died peacefully in his sleep, and when, at the Court of St James's, George had officially been proclaimed King George V, May, for the first time, answered to her new title of Queen Mary.

Born a Serene Highness not royal enough even to have been marriageable until Queen Victoria had come to her rescue, it was a very sweet moment. As a very old lady, she remembered it as being the sweetest moment of her life, for in becoming a queen and an empress she knew, without any apprehension or uncertainty, that she was fulfilling what had long been her destiny – and she was determined to be the most regal queen and the most imperial empress England and India had ever had.

Chapter Thirty-Six

Alicky looked at herself in the gold-framed mirror hanging in
her mauve boudoir. Although she was now forty, her willow-
slim figure, superb bone structure, the English-rose complexion she had inherited from her mother and her gloriously thick
red-gold hair ensured that, even in maturity, she was still beautiful, but it was beauty without radiance. How could she ever
look or feel radiant, when she lived every hour of every day
with such terrible fears and anxieties?

For seven years Russia had lived on the edge of full-scale
revolution, but she couldn't remember any time being as bad
as it was now, for there was violence in every single corner of
the country and assassination was an ever-present threat. She
thought of what had happened to Sergei and was seized by a
fear that was crippling in its intensity.

Making the situation a dozen times worse than it was already
was her dear darling's inability to be the kind of strong and
forceful Tsar that his father had been. Nicky was too gentle,
too kind. Desperately trying to do his best and never to hurt
anyone's feelings, he often made situations worse by dithering
over decisions and then, having finally made one, changing
his mind about it.

Her most overriding terror was that he would be assassinated. Exactly a year ago, and while Nicky was at the Kiev Opera House, his Prime Minister, who had also been attending the performance, had been twice shot in the chest and had died as a result of his wounds.

On top of her ever-present terror that, despite all the security that permanently surrounded him, Nicky, too, would die at the hands of an assassin, there was the non-stop nervous strain of keeping Alexei safe from any falls, knocks or bumps that might result in a life-threatening bleeding episode.

He was now eight and, like any small boy of that age, Alexei loved to run and play, to have games of tag with his sisters and kick balls and ride a bike. And every time he did so, her heart was in her mouth. Two sailors were always on hand in case of any accidents, but if and when an accident happened, their usefulness was nil. All that could be done was for Alexei to be carried to bed and for the vigil to begin. Some bleeds were not as agonizing as others – although they still could end in death. The most crippling bleeds were when the blood flowed into a joint, and that joint became excruciatingly deformed. She then had to endure the agony of hearing Alexei shrieking, 'Please, Mama. Please take the pain away. Please, Mama! Please!'

Night after night, week after week and month after month she had knelt on the cold stone of the chapel in the imperial park and prayed for the bleeding episodes to come to an end. They never had, but five years ago God had answered her prayers. He had sent her Father Grigory.

Father Grigory Yefimovich Rasputin had arrived in St Petersburg from Siberia, a self-styled *starets*, or holy man, who had the reputation of being a faith-healer. When Alexei had injured his leg while playing at bunny-hops, Alicky, in utter despair and remembering what she had heard of Father Grigory, had sent for him.

In his mid-thirties, tall and muscular with an unkempt beard, night-black hair hanging to his shoulders, ingrained dirt in his hands and nails, deep-set eyes of a disturbing intensity and wearing knee-high boots and the ankle-length coat of a peasant, he had been brought from St Petersburg to Tsarskoe Selo. Once in Alexei's bedroom in the Alexander Palace, Father Grigory had shown not a flicker of awe or intimidation at finding himself in the presence of the Tsar and Tsarina of All the Russias, and had addressed them not as their Imperial Majesties, but as '*Batyushka*' and '*Matushka*' – Little Father and Little Mother. Then he had raised his hand, made the sign of the cross, knelt by the side of Alexei's bed and begun to pray.

Throughout his long prayer Alexei's whimpers of pain came less and less often, and then at last Father Grigory had risen to his feet. 'Your pain is going away, my child,' he had said in a hypnotically soothing voice. 'You will soon be well. Thank the good God for healing you, and then sleep.'

That Alexei was able to do so was proof to Alicky that she hadn't summoned Father Grigory in vain. Although it wasn't until the next morning, when the hideous swelling showed every sign of reducing in size and there was no recurring pain, that she had known without a shadow of a doubt that Father Grigory had been sent to her by God.

Since then, both she and Nicky had come to regard Father Grigory as a miracle-worker they couldn't do without. He alone was able to halt Alexei's haemorrhages, and he did so with nothing more than his presence and his prayers.

To the doctors and blood specialists who had been in attendance on Alexei since he had first been diagnosed with haemophilia, there was no rational explanation for how the presence of the *starets* brought the bleeding to an end. With his filthy hands and dirty clothes, he was an affront to their profession and they labelled him a fraudster, accusing the holy man of being able to judge when an internal bleeding episode might end of its own volition and taking advantage of that moment.

Not knowing of the dreadful disease Alexei suffered from and that it was the reason for Rasputin's presence at Tsarskoe Selo, Nicky's family were equally outraged by his presence at the palace. For as well as having a reputation as a healer, Rasputin also had a reputation for depravity.

When Nicky's ministers had come to Alicky with police reports detailing Rasputin's visits to St Petersburg's brothels, she had refused to believe them and then, over time, she had begun ignoring them. Not even the report of his having raped a nun could shake her faith in him, or her need of him. Only Rasputin could bring an end to the agonies Alexei suffered, and that he could accomplish that miracle and relieve Alexei's suffering and keep him alive was all that mattered to her. Anything else she treated as wicked lies.

A human whirlwind burst into the room.

'Mama! Mama! Aunt Ella has arrived and, when the two of you have finished talking, can I show her the new puppies?' Alicky's eleven-year-old daughter Anastasia threw her arms around her mother's waist. 'Please do say I can, for perhaps she would like to take one of them back to Moscow with her?'

'I don't think nuns are allowed to have dogs.' The nerves in Alicky's stomach had tightened, for she knew why Ella had come from Moscow to speak to her. 'But if Ella would like to see the puppies, then of course you can show them to her.'

'Thank you, beautiful Mama!' Anastasia hugged her fervently. 'Thank you. Thank you! Thank you!'

Alicky's heart filled with fierce maternal love. Anastasia was a force of nature. Everything was either wonderful or dreadful. There was no in-between. She was also a tomboy. Whereas her older sisters would never dream of climbing the imperial park's tallest trees or, when at Livadia, swimming way out of their depth, Anastasia relished such challenges. She was rumbustious and naughty and endlessly entertaining, and if there was any light in Alicky's life, a very great part of it was because of Anastasia.

When Anastasia had exited the room at her usual hurricane speed, Alicky steeled herself for Ella's arrival. A week ago the girls' governess, Sophie Tiutcheva, had made what Alicky judged to be an uncalled-for complaint about Father Grigory and the outcome had been her dismissal. The indignant governess had returned to her home in Moscow and given her version of events to Ella, and now here was Ella, paying her a sisterly visit – and it wasn't hard to guess the reason for it.

That Ella was as disapproving of Father Grigory as Nicky's family were mystified Alicky, for unlike them, Ella knew the nature of Alexei's disease. How could she not, when so many of their relatives had either suffered or died from it?

If anyone should have been as grateful as she and Nicky were, for Rasputin's ability to keep Alexei alive, that person was Ella. That she wasn't lay quite beyond Alicky's under-standing. There were also other things about her once-favourite sister that had begun to irritate, not least Ella's conspicuous display of devoutness and the way people had begun referring to her as a saint.

When Ella entered the room she did, though, give her sister a welcoming smile. Perhaps, with a little skill, the subject of Father Grigory could be avoided. Perhaps they could talk about Ernie, and how fast the two children he'd had with his second wife were growing. And if not Ernie, perhaps they could talk about Irène and Vicky. Or she could even, although she didn't want to do so, talk about herself and how, under the constant strain she lived with, her health was now so bad as to render her an invalid at times.

'I love coming into this room,' Ella said as the doors were closed behind her. 'It so reminds me of how Mama's room used to look when we were children, and of Granny Queen's rooms at Osborne, Windsor and Balmoral.'

As always, she was dressed in her specially designed pearl-grey habit and veil.

Alicky said, 'There were no icons in Mama's room, or Granny Queen's rooms.'

'No, but there was always lots of English chintz and, after Mama's death, Granny Queen always had the same photograph of her that you have, and it hung on her boudoir wall in the same prominent position as it is here.'

The wall was covered in mauve rose-patterned silk, and opposite the photograph of their mother was a portrait of Queen Victoria. The many small occasional tables in the room were covered with silver-framed family photographs and *objets d'art*, just as their mother's room and Granny Queen's rooms always had been, and the overall effect was a mix of Russian and English cosiness that was a world removed from the ornate grandeur and splendour of the rest of the palace.

Alicky, who had risen to greet her sister, seated herself back down on a velvet-upholstered chaise longue, while Ella settled into a nearby chintz-covered armchair. There were no ladies-in-waiting present, and the two gigantic Nubian bodyguards whose sole function was to open and close the double doors to Alicky's boudoir had, after opening them for Ella, remained outside the room.

They were on their own in complete privacy, two sisters who, for different reasons, both knew deep heartache and who, when younger, had meant the world to each other.

Wondering how she could lead into what she knew was going to be a difficult conversation, Ella said, 'Ernie intends visiting Moscow later in the year. It would be nice if the three of us could get together.'

Despite the fact that it had also been her intention to start their conversation off with family matters – and family matters that revolved around Ernie – Alicky now had no patience with such prevarication.

'You haven't travelled all the way from Moscow to chat about Ernie, Ella. You are here because of the lies Sophie Tiutcheva has filled your head with.'

Ella sucked in her breath. How did Alicky know that Sophie Tiutcheva had spoken to her? Even as she thought the question, the answer came. Alicky knew because the secret police kept her and Nicky informed of everyone's movements – especially the movements of discontented, dismissed staff. In Nicky and Alicky's world, no one could be trusted; everyone was regarded as a potential assassin, or the aider and abettor of a potential assassin.

'I do not think Sophie Tiutcheva has filled my head with lies, Alicky.' Ella did her best to sound calm and reasonable. 'She was deeply distressed when she came to see me.'

'And she came to see you with false stories about Grishka.'

'Grishka?' Grishka was a pet diminutive of the name Grigory, and that Alicky was using it as if Rasputin was a much-loved relative appalled her.

'And whatever she told you would be nothing but vicious lies.' Angry colour flushed Alicky's cheeks. 'Grishka is a holy man of God. He is Nicky's friend and my friend.'

Ella took a deep, steadying breath. 'Sophie Tiutcheva has been a very diligent governess to the girls for several years, and I know from the way the girls have always spoken of her that she cares for them a great deal, as they do for her. Why, then, would she have come to you with such disturbing concerns, unless those concerns were valid?'

'Her concerns?' Alicky's eyes flashed fire. 'Her concerns were that she had seen Grishka in the girlies' bedrooms – and if he was in the girlies' bedrooms, it was with my knowledge. He is their friend, as well as our friend. Tatiana and Olga are fifteen and sixteen and are old enough to regard him as a confessor and a confidant, and he gives them good and true spiritual advice, as he does to Nicky and myself. And there – unless we are to fall out very seriously – is an end of it.'

Ella had known the conversation was going to be difficult, but she hadn't realized quite how difficult. Determined not to leave until she had said everything she had come to say, she pressed the point, 'Sophie Tiutcheva saw Rasputin in the girls' rooms while they are getting ready for bed, Alicky. She has seen him sitting on their beds and behaving with indecent affection towards them.'

'Just as you and I would sit on their beds and be affectionate towards them! The only difference being that he says their prayers with them. You, of all people, should understand and respect such devout holiness.'

Sick at heart, Ella knew there was nothing left but to be starkly blunt. 'Other talk on the streets is that Nicky never appoints his ministers without first taking Rasputin's advice, and the ultimate end of such a practice will be demands for Nicky to abdicate.'

For a second she thought Alicky was going to hit her. '*Abdicate?* Nothing will ever induce a God-appointed tsar to abdicate! How could he do so? Being Tsar is not something Nicky has chosen to be! It is something God has chosen him to be. And what better advice could Nicky ever take, in ruling Russia, but to take the advice of a holy man of God?'

Knowing she had failed miserably in what she had set out to do, Ella said, 'Your blindness, where Rasputin is concerned, will be your downfall, Alicky. And not only your downfall,

417

but the downfall of the entire monarchy. Everyone at court and in the government wants to see Rasputin banished – not only for the way he has brought the monarchy into disrepute, but for the influence he has over yourself and Nicky. A tsar taking advice from a theatrical upstart peasant? It's insanity, Alicky. If you want the dynasty to survive, you *must* get rid of him.'

White with fury, Alicky sprang to her feet. 'You may be the sister next to me in age, Ella, but never, *ever* speak to me again as you just have!'

Overcome by a sense of defeat, Ella stood up. 'You have to listen to sense from someone, Alicky. Rasputin isn't a man of God. He is the opposite. He is a charlatan who possesses the evil power to make you and Nicky believe anything – and, in doing so, he is even more of a threat to the country than the Marxist revolutionaries.'

'I want you to leave.' Alicky's hands balled into fists. 'I want you to leave now! Immediately! And until you can make apologies for the wicked words you have just said about a holy man of God, I don't want to see you again.'

Ella walked towards the door. On reaching it, she turned and said, so distraught and despairing she could hardly breathe, 'I love you, Alicky. All I want is your safety – and your family's safety – and in continuing to receive Rasputin as openly as you do, you are putting that safety in the most terrible jeopardy.'

In a moment that Ella was never to forget, Alicky turned her back on her.

'You did the right thing in speaking to Ella as you did, sweetheart.' Nicky held Alicky so close it was as if their two hearts were beating as one, 'but she may be right in that we should put some distance between ourselves and Our Friend.'

She sucked in her breath, pressing her hands against his chest so that their eyes could meet.

He said reluctantly, 'I received a deputation of ministers today. The newspapers have accused you of being Our Friend's mistress, and they have done so in the grossest and most degrading way. It was the deputation's view that the only way to stop such hideous lies being printed is if we are seen to disassociate ourselves from him. The suggestion was made that I banish him to his home village in Siberia.'

'But you cannot give in to such demands!' The horror in her eyes nearly undid him. 'What if Alexei has a fall and needs him? How can Father Grigory put an end to any bleeding if he is in Siberia?'

'Alexei hasn't had a devastating bleed for some time now. The doctors think he could be growing out of them. And the banishment would only be for a few months; just until these appalling accusations about you and Our Friend are a thing of the past.'

Vehemently she shook her head. 'No, Nicky. It would be giving in to the demands of people who know nothing of the true situation.'

'And who can't – without us making the situation even worse than it presently is – be told of it. The revolutionaries are jumping on this latest untruth and, unless we do something to end the lies, there is no telling what the outcome will be. Our Friend will understand, when the situation is explained to him. And in a few months' time he will return and, when he does, we will meet him in one of Tsarskoe Selo's minor palaces; not here, at the Alexander Palace.'

Alicky's heart was hammering so hard she thought it was going to burst, but when she thought of the unspeakable vileness of what was now being printed in the press about her and Father Grigory, and of how much Nicky must be hurting on her behalf because of it, she understood why he was suggesting that Father Grigory leave St Petersburg for a little while.

'All right, lovey,' she said at last. 'Just for a few months – but only for a few months. Do you promise?'

'I promise.' The relief in his voice was vast.

And fighting down her fears, wanting to give him comfort, she slid her arms up and around his neck, her lips parting for the reassurance of his kisses.

In the weeks after Rasputin had left for his home village of Pokrovskoe in western Siberia, Alicky was even more vigilant than usual concerning what she allowed Alexei to do. He wanted to swing on the rope that one of his sailor-attendants had, at Anastasia's request, tied to the branch of a tree, so that she could hurl herself through the air while hanging onto it. When she had learned of the existence of the rope swing, she had immediately ordered it to be removed.

Alexei wanted to play tennis, something he was usually allowed to do, but which she didn't dare risk when, if he fell and a bleed resulted, there would be no Father Grigory to bring it to a swift end.

A high-spirited child, Alexei grew fractious, kicking his sailor-attendants in frustration, shouting that he wanted to be a normal little boy; that he wanted to do the things normal little boys did; that he was bored, bored, *bored*.

'You won't be bored for much longer, for we go to Spala in a week's time,' Nicky said to him encouragingly, 'and you know how much you enjoy being there.' Spala, the family's favourite hunting lodge, was a large wooden-built palace set in the middle of a forest in a remote area of Russian Poland, and was somewhere the family always enjoyed holidaying.

'It's September,' Nicky continued, pleased to see that

Alexei's face had already brightened. 'There will be black-berries to pick and lots of wildlife to see. Do you remember how last time we saw both wolves and wild boar?'

The following week Alicky began to visibly relax as the imperial train made its way on its long journey towards Spala. Her health had never been robust, for even as a girl she'd had sciatic pains in her legs and she was regularly plagued by migraines and shortness of breath. On holiday trips away from St Petersburg, at Livadia or on the royal yacht, or at Spala, these ailments rarely troubled her.

'It is anxiety that is the root cause of Her Majesty's ill health,' Dr Botkin, the royal family's doctor, had said to Nicky. 'If the anxiety could be removed, Her Majesty would, I think, enjoy perfect health.'

Dr Botkin was part of the large number of people accompanying them to Spala, for wherever they travelled, all key members of the royal court travelled with them. As did many guests, invited to make up the required numbers for hunting parties. As Alicky didn't hunt, she had invited Irène, and Irène's son, Sigismund, to join them. Irène would be a companion for her while Nicky was out hunting and the girls were enjoying exhilarating horseback rides down forest paths, and Sigismund would be a playmate for Alexei.

While they were all happily en route to Spala, and while playing catch with his sisters down the corridors of the train Alexei fell, banging his thigh hard. Dr Botkin examined him and found a slight swelling just below his groin, but there was no discoloration that indicated internal bleeding and only slight soreness, and none of the usual agonizing pain that followed such a knock.

By the time they arrived at Spala, Alexei seemed to be in full recovery, and Nicky was buoyant, convinced that his son was beginning to grow out of his disease. When he arranged a mushroom-foraging expedition for the next morning, Alexei and Sigismund were included in his plans. Or they were until Alicky heard of them.

'No, my sweetheart,' she said to a deeply disappointed Alexei. 'Wait another few days before scrambling about on your hands and knees. Instead, come with me on a carriage drive into the forest. We can take our cameras and get some wonderful nature shots of animals.'

Mollified, for he liked taking photographs, Alexei agreed, but only on condition that when they returned, he and Sigismund could go boating on a nearby lake.

Alicky was happier than she had been for a very long time as they set out together on their carriage ride. It was a beautiful September day and the novelty of being out alone with Alexei, with no one else within sight but the carriage driver, was such a rarity to her as to be a gift from heaven. She loved the sounds and scents of the forest: the rustle of the leaves; the birdsong; the fragrance of wild mint and marjoram; the tranquillity. She loved knowing that the great ancient swathes of oak, hornbeam and lime stretched not for a few miles on either side of them, but for untrammelled scores of miles. And she loved sharing in Alexei's pleasure as, in sun-dappled forest clearings, they caught glimpses of majestic, huge-antlered bison or clusters of deer.

As they bowled down the narrow sandy paths she was reminded of long-ago carriage rides with her Granny Queen whenever, as a small child and then as a young girl, she had visited her at Balmoral or Osborne. For Granny Queen, an afternoon carriage ride had been obligatory, no matter what the weather; and the colder it had been, the better Granny Queen had liked it.

Alicky was so deep in happy memories of the past that when Alexei said suddenly and with a catch in his voice, 'I'm getting a tummy-ache, Mama,' she didn't at first take much notice of it. Absent-mindedly she patted his hand, her thoughts full of Balmoral and its nearby mountains at sunset. He squeezed hold of her hand tightly. 'I'm getting a tummy-ache *fast*, Mama.'

This time he had her attention and, when she turned her head towards him, her heart nearly failed her. He was as white as a sheet and trembling.

'Oh, dear God,' she whispered. 'Oh, dear, *dear* God!' And then, to the driver, 'The Tsesarevich has been taken ill. We must return to the lodge immediately.'

The carriage slewed around so abruptly that Alexei fell against her. 'I have a pain at the top of my leg, Mama,' he said, clinging to her. 'At the top of my leg, where I banged it.'

Both of them knew what it signified – and the only doctor at Spala was Botkin, who was efficiency itself when it came to coughs, colds and childish ailments, but totally out of his depth when it came to haemophiliac bleeds.

The forest pathways were bumpy and uneven, jolting the carriage almost continually. With every abrupt rocking movement, Alexei screamed in pain. Despite the urgency of reaching the lodge in the quickest time possible, Alicky kept calling out for the driver to slow down and then, whenever the sandy path grew a little smoother, demanding that he speed up.

As she held Alexei in her arms, all she could think of was the distance that still had to be covered until they reached the hunting lodge – and when they did reach it, what then? The only person who had ever brought Alexei relief from his pain, and put an end to his internal bleeding, had been Father Grigory, and they were in Poland while Father Grigory was thousands of miles away in Siberia.

By the time the hunting lodge came in sight, Alexei was moaning in agony and only semi-conscious. Wrapped in a blanket, he was carried inside and up to his bedroom and Dr Botkin was summoned.

It was a nightmare scenario and one that the very diligent Botkin had lived in dread of. With no other doctor there for support, how could he possibly handle a situation in which the heir to the throne could quite possibly die? A careful examination told him that the previous small swelling in Alexei's groin – a swelling that had been healing satisfactorily – had ruptured on the bumpy carriage ride and begun bleeding in earnest, the trapped blood forming a swelling the size of a grapefruit in Alexei's groin.

After ordering for ice-packs to be applied, he sent a telegram to Dr Federov and Alicky's blood specialist in St Petersburg, Dr Derevenko, telling them of the situation and of how their presence was urgently needed. He sent a similar telegram to Alexei's paediatrician, Dr Ostrogorsky. Then all he could do was to do what everyone else at Spala was doing, which was pray.

Without Irène, Alicky doubted if she would have been able to get through the next few days. Irène had lost one child to haemophilia, and Sigismund's older brother, Waldemar, suffered from the disease. If anyone could sympathize with the torment she was suffering, it was her sister, and Irène was also able to stand in for her when it came to acting as a hostess to the many Polish nobles who had descended on Spala. For appearances of normality had to be kept up, regardless of the hideous drama unfolding in secret in the Tsesarevich's bedroom.

On their arrival at Spala, Dr Derevenko, Dr Fedorov and Dr Ostrogorsky were all in agreement that blood was seeping into Alexei's groin and lower abdomen and that, with every passing day, it was finding new places in which to form fresh haematomas. The pain Alexei was in was dreadful. As he writhed and thrashed and screamed, Alicky never left him. Day and night she remained by his bed, trying to give him what comfort she could, her red-gold hair turning whiter by the minute.

'Help me, Mama!' he gasped time and time again, and then, 'When I'm dead it won't hurt any more, will it? I want to die, Mama. I want to die!'

On the sixth day the doctors told Alicky and Nicky that Alexei's stomach had begun to haemorrhage and that Alexei couldn't be saved. Bulletins were issued to prepare the public for the Tsesarevich's death. A priest came to perform the last rites.

Swaying with fatigue and almost insensible with grief, Alicky said, 'If Alexei is dying, then Father Grigory has to be told, so that he can pray for his soul.'

In the early hours of the morning, and thousands of miles away in Siberia, Rasputin responded to her telegram:

> GOD HAS SEEN YOUR TEARS AND HEARD YOUR PRAYERS STOP DO NOT GRIEVE STOP THE LITTLE ONE WILL NOT DIE STOP DO NOT ALLOW THE DOCTORS TO BOTHER HIM TOO MUCH STOP

Peace and certainty flooded through Alicky. It was going to be all right. Incredibly, miraculously, even from a hamlet in far-distant Siberia, Father Grigory had been able to perform a miracle and save Alexei's life.

When she told the doctors and showed them the telegram, they looked at her with pity in their eyes. Alexei had by now received the last rites and there could be no further hope. As if to prove it, over the next few hours nothing in Alexei's condition changed.

But then came the dawn, when, to their utter disbelief, Fedorov, Derevenko, Ostrogorsky and Botkin saw that not only – against all their expectations – was Alexei still alive, but the haemorrhage had stopped. From the very brink of death he had begun to make a recovery, and it was a recovery they had no explanation for.

Their stunned bewilderment wasn't shared by Alicky. She knew it was Father Grigory's prayers that had saved Alexei's life; that, incredibly, he hadn't had to be with Alexei for his prayers for him to be answered; that in far-away Siberia all he had needed to do was go down on his knees and pray.

And she knew something else as well. Father Grigory's banishment was going to come to an immediate end and, no matter how loud and insistent the complaints from Nicky's ministers, or the demands of the newspapers and the Russian people, she and Nicky were going to continue to rely on him, not only for the way he kept Alexei alive, but for advice in every other area of their lives – political as well as personal. Any alternative was unthinkable.

Chapter Thirty-Seven

Willy was buoyant. Everything was going his way. The hideous period in his life when Phili and other members of the Liebenberg Circle had – because of a mountain of evidence to the contrary – been unable to defend themselves against claims of homosexuality was now in the past. By the skin of his teeth, and because he had instantly severed all ties with Phili, never meeting or speaking with him again, he had managed to escape the scandal that had followed. The void in his life afterwards had seemed bottomless, but he had survived.

Now, about to give his precious only daughter, his last child Princess Viktoria Luise, in marriage to Prince Ernst August of Hanover in a few days' time, Willy couldn't have been happier. Not only was it a love match, but Sissy – the only name Viktoria Luise had answered to since she'd been a child – had assured him of that, as had the groom. Ernst's pedigree was impeccable. Via his Danish mother he was both Georgie and Nicky's first cousin and was closely related to the Norwegian and Greek royal families as well. It meant the wedding guest list was going to cover every royal court in Europe, as well as Russia.

It was going to be the biggest, most spectacular royal wedding in decades, and Willy's only disappointment about it so far was that, although Nicky would be attending, poor health meant that Alicky would not.

It was a disappointment he had overcome. Alicky was rumoured to be mentally unstable, antagonizing Nicky's family by her habit of rarely appearing in public and by her bizarre, insistent friendship with a depraved, mystic monk who was equally *bekloppt*, or, as English Georgie would say, barmy.

As well as Sissy's wedding giving him the opportunity to appear in a wide range of military uniforms – Willy would, of course, wear his British admiral's uniform when greeting Georgie and May, while an equally splendid Russian military uniform would suffice when meeting Nicky – there were also lots of other heavily gold-braided and bemedalled uniforms that he could don when greeting other guests.

The Danish contingent, for instance, would be very large, considering that the groom's mother was Danish. Norway, too, was going to be represented, as his English cousin Maud, who had married Prince Carl of Denmark, had, by a bizarre turn of events eight years ago, found herself Queen Maud of Norway, after Norway had separated from Sweden. Wishing to establish its own monarchy, the country had offered the throne to her and Carl. While Maud had retained her Christian name, Carl had changed his to the Norwegian Haakon. Willy had found it a disturbing way of establishing a monarchy, but the deed was done and Maud was, after all, a first cousin.

Politically, of course, the new King Haakon was of no importance whatsoever. His brother-in-law Tino, the newly crowned King Constantine of Greece, was in a different category, Greece being in such a close geographic position to the Balkans.

Just thinking about the Balkans gave Willy pause for thought. There was always trouble in the Balkans, an area where two great empires, Austria–Hungary and Russia, had opposing interests. The problem with that, of course, was that as Germany had an alliance with Austria–Hungary, and Britain had an alliance with Russia, if Austria–Hungary and Russia went to war over their differences there, Germany and Britain would find themselves on opposing sides; and for half-English Willy, such a thing was unthinkable.

Sissy's wedding was a heaven-sent chance to discuss the matter with Nicky and Georgie. All three of them were emperors. If they got their heads together, surely they should be able to come up with a solution that would pacify Austria–Hungary and ensure peace in Europe.

He gave himself a shake. War – why the devil was he thinking of war, when he was about to play host at such a joyous event as Sissy's wedding?

Throwing off all thoughts of war as easily as throwing off a cloak, he shouted for his valet, in the tones of an English sergeant-major shouting for a squaddie. He needed to be dressed in his British admiral's uniform. Georgie and May would be arriving later that morning and although, among his hundreds of guests, Nicky was the most important, being not only a fellow emperor but one who ruled as an autocrat, Georgie and May were the guests Willy was always most pleased to see.

Even as children, he and Georgie had always got on well, and he had sincere affection for May. Even if it hadn't been for the childish Kindred Spirit nonsense all those years ago, he would have singled her out as one of the few women whose company he enjoyed and whose intelligence he respected.

His late beloved grandmother had known what she was about, when she had ensured that May would one day be Queen of England – and the proof of her being so single-minded about it was the way, after his Cousin Eddy's death, that she had simply arranged for May to marry Georgie instead.

And Willy counted Georgie a very fortunate man, for May

had all the qualities his own wife lacked, chief of which were common sense, intelligence and, above all, the ability to remain in command of her feelings at all times. No matter what the situation, it was impossible to imagine May being reduced to hysterics. Dona, on the other hand, gave way to hysterics at the slightest provocation. There were even times when he wondered if, like Alicky, she was a little touched in the head.

To her credit was her deep devotion to him – although, with all his wonderful qualities, why wouldn't she be devoted? And she was also devoted to all seven of their children, even Eitel, whom he could barely stand. There was also a natural stateliness about Dona, something he thought was largely due to her magnificent yard-wide, ostrich-feathered and flower-bedecked hats, which often had the addition of a small stuffed bird tucked amongst the foliage, and all of which he had designed.

May rarely, if ever, wore anything a yard wide. Mindful of her tightly curling fringe, she nearly always wore a toque, pleated and ruched to resemble a turban and adorned with a spiky Hussar plume or a small, jaunty ostrich feather.

No one, though, could wear jewels in the same way May could – and certainly no one could get away with wearing so many items of jewellery all at the same time. A tiara would be worn with a pearl-and-diamond choker twelve strands or more deep, which in turn would be worn with ropes of pearls hanging to her waist, brooches, bracelets and earrings of emeralds, or rubies or sapphires – and sometimes a collection of all three stones at once – and always a selection of fabulous rings. Why she didn't look like an overdressed Christmas tree he didn't know, but she never did. Instead, with her superb posture, she always looked the epitome of imperial glamour.

In many ways he thought her entirely lost on Georgie, whose only nod to flamboyance was to wear a white gardenia in his lapel, and who looked more like a well-to-do country solicitor than a king and emperor.

Willy had decreed that Dona and all six of their sons were to accompany him to the station where, as Georgie and May stepped from the train, a brass band would launch into the British national anthem. He and Georgie would then ceremoniously inspect a Guard of Honour before, in open carriages, making a state procession through crowded, banner-decorated streets all the way to the Neues Palace.

Tomorrow morning there would be a repeat performance for him, as he met Nicky from the train, the colossal difference being that where Georgie and May had travelled with a modest entourage, consisting primarily of Georgie's private secretary and his equerry, plus the usual valets and ladies-in-waiting, he had been informed that Nicky would be travelling not only with his always very large entourage, but with more than a hundred policemen on an armour-plated train.

If Willy was riding high on a wave of elation, the same was true for May. George rarely travelled abroad. As a sailor, he had seen enough of foreign lands to last him a lifetime, but even he had been happy to cross the Channel for Sissy's wedding. May relished any opportunity for a change of scene – and this change of scene was a very special occasion, for it would be an opportunity to meet lots of family she either rarely saw or hadn't seen for some time.

Even before she stepped inside the palace she was greeted by more than a dozen of her German relatives, who came chattering and laughing down the palace steps and into the courtyard to greet her carriage. There were Mecklenburg-Strelitz cousins, Württemberg cousins and even a barely remembered Schleswig-Holstein cousin, and there was much kissing on the cheeks and heel-clicking.

That evening at dinner she and George were seated centrally on the top table with Willy and Dona. All in all, it was a dazzling array of European monarchy, and May's satisfaction at being such a very prominent member of it was deep. It was at moments like this that she remembered how, for her, it could all have been so very, very different.

Willy, who was much enjoying having May seated next to him, dug her in the ribs with his good arm, saying jovially in German, the language they always spoke together, 'I think we should have a toast to Kindred Spiritship, May.'

'I quite agree.' She shot him a warm smile. She had always had a weakness for a handsome man and, for all his faults, Willy was very handsome. As well as his magnificent up-twirling moustaches, his strong, regular features and his still-thick dark hair tamed by Macassar oil, he had a forceful vigour that, when he was at his best, as now, was very attractive.

Nicky's arrival the next day completed the two-hundred-and-fifty-strong family guest list, and Willy almost immediately took the opportunity for a private conversation with him in regard to the situation in the Balkans. Nicky listened to him with resigned passivity, saying only what he thought Willy wanted to hear. A little later Willy had a similar conversation with Georgie; and afterwards, when Georgie had managed to escape from him, Georgie was able to tell Nicky that Willy believed all three of them were now in complete agreement regarding the Balkan states.

Nicky said that if they were, it was news to him; and the two of them moseyed off to enjoy a game of billiards together and chat about nothing more controversial than whether or not Nicky and his family would be attending the Cowes Regatta in August, aboard their imperial yacht, the *Standart*.

That evening there was another grand state banquet. Willy,

wearing the full dress uniform of an English Royal Dragoon, and with the Russian Order of St Andrew emblazoned across his breast, led May into dinner, while Georgie, wearing the uniform of the Prussian Dragoons, escorted Dona, and Nicky escorted Willy's elderly aunt, the Dowager Grand Duchess of Baden.

For May, dressed in a shimmering white gown beaded with diamonds, with more diamonds at her ears, throat and wrists, and wearing Queen Victoria's spectacular wedding tiara, it was a never-to-be-forgotten moment. One that in those long-ago days in Florence and after Eddy's death, she could not even have imagined.

Out of the corner of her eye she saw Looloo and Toria. Looloo was looking at her with a slightly dazed, bewildered expression. The look in Toria's eyes would have curdled new milk, and May knew why. As a girl, Toria had always taken it for granted that she would one day be a queen and that she, May – being only a Serene Highness – would remain an unmarriageable spinster. That it had turned out so very differently was something Toria bitterly resented, but her jealousy and animosity May had long ago come to terms with.

She caught a glimpse of Maudie, who not only gave her a matey wink, but also, at waist level, a thumbs-up sign. The corners of May's mouth twitched. Although she had drawn a short straw where two of her sisters-in-law were concerned, Maudie was pure gold and always had been.

Later that evening she would catch up with Maudie, and with the other members of the extended Royal Mob to whom she had always been closest: Vicky and Louis; Irène and Heinrich; Russian Aunt Marie; Marie-Louise and Ducky. And she would get over her disappointment that the two people she would have most liked to spend time with – Alicky and Ella – were absent.

'Alix sends you her love,' Nicky said in his quiet, gentle manner when they had a few minutes' conversation together. He always called her Alix, never Alicky. 'Her health isn't good, as I believe you know – and she doesn't enjoy this kind of event. She is much happier when the family group is small and intimate – as it was last year when we visited you and Georgie at Balmoral with the girls and Alexei.'

'George tells me we may well see you in August, at Cowes?'

It was polite small talk, and not at all what May wanted to say to him. She wanted to ask about Alexei's health, but knew that, even coming from her, it was a question Nicky would find quite unacceptable. Equally unacceptable would have been the riveting subject of Rasputin.

'And that's the problem with Nicky,' she said much later that evening, as she and George shared a whisky nightcap together, 'he is always exquisitely well mannered; always on the surface so very amiable and agreeable, but when it comes down to it, you can never have a truly honest conversation with him. He's as inscrutable as a sphinx. Do you know what his attitude will be, if Emperor Franz Josef continues stirring things up in the Balkans, or haven't you asked him?'

'I haven't asked him. I left that up to Willy. And as Willy seems happy enough with Nicky's attitude, so am I. Now are you coming to bed so that I can turn the light off?'

'Yes, and yes.' She slipped into the giant canopied bed that dominated the cavernous room they had been allocated. Sliding her hand into his, she said, 'I shall be wearing a gown of embroidered Indian cloth of gold and a crown, not a tiara, tomorrow. And the rest of my jewellery – earrings, choker, necklaces, brooches and bracelets – will all feature Teck family emeralds.'

'You'll look magnificent, darling. No woman there will be

able to hold a candle to you. I can't begin to tell you what a lucky chap I think I am.'

She squeezed his hand tightly. 'Goodnight, George. God bless.

He squeezed it back, a deeply contented man. 'Goodnight, May darling. Pleasant dreams.'

Despite the huge number of guests – the all-in complete number, counting all the minor royalties from the kingdoms, duchies and principalities that made up Germany's empire, was nearly a thousand – the wedding ceremony and celebrations were carried out with typical Teutonic efficiency. At five o'clock in the afternoon Sissy and her retinue walked in stately procession towards the palace chapel, followed by Ernst and his retinue. Inside, the chapel was packed to capacity, with several of the wedding guests not even able to squeeze inside.

There were emotional tears in May's eyes as Sissy and Ernst made their vows and George whispered gruffly, 'No need for tears if their marriage proves to be as happy as ours is.'

He often said such things, and she always thought of how they could be even happier if only they shared the same interests. George, however, was quite uninterested in art and books, and even his own family history, something she found fascinating, was, to George, jaw-droppingly boring. George only had two interests. The first was his stamp collection, and the second was tramping through woods, or over moors, with a shotgun tucked beneath his arm. And just as he couldn't share her interests, she couldn't share his. Like Toria's cattiness, it was something she had come to terms with, but she did sincerely hope that Ernst's and Sissy's meeting of hearts was also a meeting of minds.

The wedding vows were concluded. Sissy and Ernst were

man and wife and the organ began to play the opening bars of one of Luther's greatest hymns.

'*Lobe den Herren, den mächtigen König der Ehren*,' every wedding guest but one sang in faultless German.

'Praise to the Lord, the Almighty, the King of Creation,' George, who had barely a word of German, sang in a deep tenor.

After the end of the wedding breakfast that followed the church service, Ducky sought her out.

'It's been ages since I've seen you, May.' she said, kissing her affectionately on both cheeks. 'And I love the crown. Pearls and diamonds together. So pretty. Was it one of Granny Queen's?'

'It was. It's the State Diadem, and I wear it at State Openings of Parliament and when attending foreign coronations and, although a wedding isn't a coronation, I thought Sissy and Ernst deserved no less.'

'Quite right – and why be satisfied with wearing a tiara when you have a closetful of crowns to choose from? Where can we go to have a little privacy?'

'The palace is so crowded – nowhere but a bedroom. The one George and I have been allocated is quite near, and I could do with a break from the crush.'

'And so,' Ducky said fifteen minutes later as she made herself comfortable on a sofa with a glass of champagne in one hand and a cigarette in the other, 'first things first. Alicky. Do you hear from her often?'

'Not as often as I used to, but we do still write to each other.'

'About Alexei?'

'Yes and no. She writes about him in the same way she writes about Olga, Tatiana, Marie and Anastasia. Family doings.'

'And never mentions his disease?'

'She told me about it when it was first realized he had it, but no, she never mentions it in her letters, and neither do I. How can I?'

'You can't, but it is the source of all the problems the Russian monarchy is facing – because if it wasn't for the family disease, Alicky and Nicky wouldn't be hiding Alexei away at Tsarskoe Selo; Alicky would probably be behaving as an empress should behave and wouldn't be so very, very unpopular; and there would be no need for Rasputin. And if it wasn't for Rasputin, there wouldn't be the widespread belief that he is ruling the country through Nicky.'

May stared at her, shocked. 'I knew things were bad in Russia. George says that unpleasant man Lenin is at the bottom of the unrest in the country – but surely no one can believe a faith-healer is influencing the decisions Nicky makes?'

'You'd think not, wouldn't you? But they do. Six or seven months ago it looked as if Nicky appreciated the danger Rasputin was posing, even if Alicky didn't, and he banished him to his home village in Siberia. It made a huge difference. Even Aunt Minny and Nicky's Uncle Paul, and his brother Misha, thought the danger was over; and then Nicky and Alicky took the girls and Alexei to Spala.'

She paused, not at all the usual bouncy, vital Ducky that May was used to.

'Did Alicky tell you about Spala, May?'

'Yes. They go there every year, and she said she was looking forward to spending time there and getting away from the almost unbearable pressure of St Petersburg.'

Ducky put her untouched glass of champagne down. 'I think I'd rather have a Scotch, if you don't mind, May.'

May walked across to the drinks cabinet and said, with a deep sense of foreboding, 'What happened at Spala?'

'Alexei had a bleed. Botkin, the doctor who accompanies them everywhere, sent for Alexei's blood specialist and his paediatrician and they came hot-foot to Spala, but of course there was nothing they could do.'

May had poured two tumblers of Scotch, one for Ducky and one for herself. Handing one of the tumblers to Ducky, she said, 'And what happened? Quite obviously Alexei didn't die.'

'No. He didn't. Alicky sent a telegram to Siberia asking Rasputin to pray for Alexei's soul. Rasputin sent a telegram back telling her that Alexei wasn't going to die, and within hours the haemorrhage had stopped and Alexei was on the road to recovery.'

Ducky took a drink of her whisky.

'It means Rasputin's ability to stop Alexei's haemorrhages isn't down to the laying on of hands or, as been suggested, to hypnotism, because this time when he stopped the bleeding he wasn't even with Alexei.'

She stubbed her cigarette out and lit another one. 'After Spala, Nicky finally told his mother, his brother Misha, who is next in line to the throne after Alexei, and his one surviving uncle, Uncle Paul, the truth about Alexei's disease, although that hasn't made things any better. Instead of them finally feeling sympathy for Alicky, they hate her for having brought the disease into the family. Plus Misha doesn't want to be heir to the throne. His mistress, with whom he has a child, has finally obtained a divorce and, only weeks ago, after breaking his promise to Nicky that he wouldn't do so, Misha married her. And if Misha falls by the wayside when it comes to inheriting the throne, the next in line is Kyril – a thought I don't particularly want to dwell on. Ernie, whom I am once again on good terms with, says it's a pig's ear, and he's right.'

There was simply nothing positive May could think of to

say about the situation and, changing the subject, she said, 'And Ella?'

'Ella is the same darling she has always been, but her relationship with Alicky has suffered since she tried to speak sense to her about Rasputin.'

Ducky looked down at her dainty pendant watch. 'We've been closeted up here for far too long, May. It's nearly time for the Hohenzollern Wedding Torch Dance, and you can't be absent for that. As the only empress here as a guest, you'll have a main part to play.'

The Torch Dance was to take place in the white- and silver-decorated White Hall. Historically it was a polonaise that was always danced – apart from the first dance by the bridal pair – in groups of three.

Troops in scarlet-and-gold uniforms lined the walls of the hall and, as Sissy and Ernst opened the dance, the troops began passing flaming brands from hand to hand. Then Sissy made a second circuit of the floor, this time dancing with her father on one arm and her father-in-law on the other, and Ernst followed, dancing with his mother and with Dona. Then it was Nicky and George's turn to accompany Sissy, and May and Willy's sister danced with the bridegroom.

Forming similar groups of three, all the Royal Highnesses present joined in and the floor was a glorious, ever-shifting tapestry of European royalty.

When the dance finally came to an end, Heinrich, Irène's husband, said to May, 'If you have been worrying about a European war breaking out over the Balkans, you can stop doing so. You've only to look around you, to see why. When the rulers of the countries who would be involved are family, war is impossible. Any talk of it is tosh. Utter tosh.'

Chapter Thirty-Eight

Archduke Franz Ferdinand, heir to the Austro-Hungarian Empire, and his wife, Sophie, were on the last day of a short official visit to Bosnia, a Balkan country that was part of the empire. Its neighbour, Serbia, believed that it should have sovereignty over Bosnia and, because of the royal visit, tensions were high.

In the intense heat of the afternoon the couple were being driven in an open-topped car through Sarajevo's narrow streets towards the governor's palace, where they were to have lunch. At a corner so tight the car had to slow almost to a halt to negotiate it, a young Serb stepped from the pavement and fired two shots. Sophie died instantly. Franz Ferdinand died half an hour later in the palace where the lunch prepared for him still lay on the table.

Willy was at a racing regatta in the city of Kiel and was aboard the *Hohenzollern* when an Admiralty launch pulled alongside and an officer shouted that he had a most urgent telegram for him.

Willy wasn't interested in receiving it. What he was interested in was how well his racing yacht, *Meteor*, was performing.

The officer, knowing that the result of not getting an urgent message to Germany's All-Highest would probably be a court-martial, folded up his despatch, put it in his cigarette case and lobbed it aboard the *Hohenzollern*.

'What the devil?' Willy said in annoyance, when a member of the crew nervously came to him with the cigarette case.

'There's a despatch inside it,' the unfortunate crew member said apprehensively. 'It is, perhaps, of some importance.'

Impatiently Willy ripped it open and then, seconds later, staggered. Assassinations were not uncommon – but they usually took place in Russia. Regicide! And so much closer to home than Russia! Fear and rage roared through his veins. He and Franz Ferdinand had been more than fellow royals; they had been close friends, and genuine grief added to his fear and rage.

The fear was for his own safety, for one royal assassination could very easily lead to another. The rage was at the thought of his friend and his gentle-mannered wife meeting their ends in a filthy Bosnian street.

'Lower the imperial flag to half-mast!' he thundered. 'Head back to port.'

He needed to be in Berlin. He needed to be at the centre of things. And however Emperor Franz Josef, the Archduke's uncle, decided to handle the matter, Willy needed to tell him that, whatever action he took, it was action that would have his full support.

Nicky was aboard his yacht, the *Standart*, enjoying a summer cruise off the coast of Finland with Alicky, Alexei and the girls. Both he and Alicky took the news of Franz Ferdinand and Sophie having been shot in a Bosnian street far more stoically than Willy had. For one thing, assassinations were regular occurrences in Russia and something they were desensitized to. For another, they had a far greater calamity to worry about, for they had just received news that Rasputin had been stabbed in the stomach by a madwoman and was fighting for his life in a Siberian hospital.

A telegram of condolence was sent to Emperor Franz Josef and their cruise continued, with Alicky praying several times a day for Rasputin's recovery.

When Georgie received the news, his first instinct was to share it with May.

'Terrible new, May dear,' he said, disturbing her as she labelled gold teaspoons that dated from George IV's reign. 'Archduke Franz Ferdinand and his wife have been shot and killed in Sarajevo.'

May gasped, the blood leaving her face.

'The telegram I've received from Vienna says they were on the last day of a short official visit. Shot down, May, like animals in the street.' His voice cracked and broke. 'It doesn't bear thinking about. Their poor, dear children. And poor Emperor Franz Josef! What a dreadful, dreadful shock for him.'

May pushed her chair away from her desk and rose unsteadily to her feet.

George said, 'I must order a week's court mourning and send a telegram to the Emperor immediately.'

May nodded agreement. 'And it would be a caring gesture if you were to make a condolence visit to Ambassador von Mensdorff at the Austrian Embassy.'

'I'm not sure about that, May. Doing so would be a breach of protocol.'

'Which is why it would mean so much. Von Mensdorff is a cousin of a kind, because his grandfather was married to one of Granny Queen's aunts. I think such an action on your part would be much appreciated by him.'

Trusting her judgement, George had done as she suggested and Ambassador von Mensdorff had been deeply touched by the gesture, as May had known he would be.

For nearly a month the usual trouble in the Balkans caused more tension than normal, but nothing too dreadful happened.

Willy was happy with the blank cheque of support that he had given Emperor Franz Josef, the day news of the assassinations had broken. In the following weeks he did a good deal of strutting about in military uniform, wearing a ferocious-looking spiked *pickelhaube* helmet and spouting inflammatory phrases such as 'Serbia must pay for this cowardly, detestable crime!' as he sabre-rattled to his heart's content. For he was safe in his belief that Austria–Hungary could give the Serbs a short, sharp shock without risking Serbia's friend, Russia, coming to her defence, for how could Russia do so?

'Russia isn't braced for war,' he said confidently, standing with his legs apart and twirling his moustaches, 'and Cousin Nicky hasn't the balls for one.'

He was right in thinking that war with Austria–Hungary – or with any other country – was the last thing on Nicky's mind. The attack on Rasputin had been so life-threatening that he was still hovering between life and death, which was of very great concern to Alicky.

Nicky's mother, whose one fervent hope was that Rasputin would shuffle off to hell and never be seen again, announced that she was giving a ball at the Anitchkov Palace.

'And I'm doing so for the enjoyment of Olga and Tatiana,' she said waspishly to Nicky. 'At their ages, they should be attending balls several times a week, not only once in a blue moon. And if Alicky is too sick, too tired, too bored, too busy saying prayers for that fiend Rasputin to attend the ball with them, tell her I quite understand.'

Although a ball given by Minny was the very last thing she wanted to attend, Alicky gritted her teeth and, for Olga and Tatiana's sakes, accepted the invitation. The girls were ecstatic at the prospect of it, and between his concerns for Rasputin and looking forward to seeing his two eldest daughters knock St Petersburg society for six, the present upheaval in the Balkans barely entered Nicky's head.

Georgie, too, had more pressing matters on his mind than how Emperor Franz Josef was, or was not, handling the aftermath of the assassinations of his nephew and his wife. Whereas Nicky's chief concern was Rasputin's long battle for life in far-off Siberia, Georgie's was the threat of civil war in Ireland.

'Ireland,' he said to his private secretary, Lord Stamfordham, 'is a bugger. How many more hundreds of years are we to go on being plagued by it?'

'This time it is a question of the geographical limits that Ulster is to be given, sir,' Stamfordham said, trying to sound soothing. 'Not least in relation to Fermanagh and Tyrone.'

If Stamfordham hadn't been present, George would have torn his hair out. He hadn't the slightest desire to begin struggling with the political issues of Ireland. All he wanted to do was retreat to his stamp room and slam the door behind him.

'Tell me again,' he said, feeling a much-persecuted man, 'the specific details as regards to Tyrone.'

On 23 July, almost a month after the assassinations, Austria–Hungary sent an ultimatum to Serbia and the focus shifted once again to the Balkans, and did so sharply.

'An ultimatum? What kind of an ultimatum?' Willy

demanded, once again aboard the *Hohenzollern* and realizing too late that if it was a war ultimatum, it was one that he would have to disassociate himself from fast, for Russia would come to Serbia's aid and might be more braced for war than he had previously given her credit for.

'The ultimatum states that the assassination plot was one that had been hatched in Belgrade,' his private secretary said, reading the long cable with great care, 'and that Serbian officials had been actively involved in it.'

Relief swept through Willy. Those facts had been obvious right from the beginning, and if it had taken the Austrians just shy of a month to set them down on paper, then he was panicking over nothing. The four weeks since Franz Ferdinand and Sophie's deaths had taken the edge off his initial reaction to them and, volatile as ever, his instinct now was to disassociate himself from the situation.

With that decision made, he waved his private secretary away. He had heard enough, and this time he wasn't going to hare back to Berlin. He was going to continue with his cruise up the coastline of Norway.

Unlike Willy, Nicky read every last dot and comma on every piece of official paper that crossed his desk, and he certainly did so when he was handed a copy of Austria's ultimatum. He read the opening accusation about the plot having been hatched in Belgrade and of Serbian officers being involved, then read on to where it stated that all Serb nationalist publications were to be banned, all Serb nationalist societies disbanded, all agitators rounded up, all those involved in the plot brought to trial, and that Austrian officers were to be allowed to enter Serbia and conduct their own investigation and Austria was to oversee all legal actions.

Thinking he must be hallucinating, he read it again and

then a third time. The demands were outrageous. No sovereign state could agree to them, and when Serbia didn't do so, what was Austrian reaction going to be?

Even before he spoke to his Prime Minister, Nicky picked up the phone to speak to Willy, only to be told that the Kaiser was aboard the *Hohenzollern* and out of telephone contact. He sent a cable asking Willy for his thoughts on the ultimatum. Back came a cable saying that he knew nothing about it, and that the matter was between Austria and Serbia and was nothing to do with Germany. He also sent love and best wishes to Alicky.

The Austrian Ambassador to St Petersburg's reading of the situation was equally low-key. 'Austria is simply trying to teach Serbia a lesson,' he said to Nicky. 'It is a rap on the knuckles; nothing more serious than that.'

Georgie didn't believe the ultimatum was a mere rap on the knuckles. No self-respecting country could accede to the demands Austria was making, and Austria would be well aware it couldn't. And what would happen when Serbia didn't accede to them? His answer to his self-imposed question was immediate. Austria would use it as an excuse to declare war on Serbia and, when it did, Serbia's friend, Russia, would come to her aid. And when Russia came to her aid, what nightmarish spot would Russia's allies be in?

It was all too dreadful to even think about, and so he didn't think about it. Instead he went down to his stamp room, poured himself a stiff tumbler of whisky and began rearranging stamps of Australia and New Zealand, all of which reassuringly bore his own image.

The next morning came news that Serbia had replied to Austria's ultimatum and that, except for an unimportant point, the Serbs had agreed to every demand. The relief in Potsdam, London and St Petersburg was overwhelming. Austria now had no excuse for declaring war on Serbia and consequently there was no danger of Russia, Germany and England being dragged into the Balkan mire.

Nicky went down to the tennis courts and, in hot sunshine, played an energetic match against Tatiana. Willy ebulliently fired off a congratulatory telegram to Emperor Franz Josef, saying that Serbia's agreement to all Austria–Hungary's demands was a great victory for Vienna; that it did away with any need for war and was an outcome on which Emperor Franz Josef was to be congratulated. Accompanied by his equerry, a vastly relieved George took his favourite horse for an energetic gallop across Windsor's parkland, giving private thanks to God that the world was a safe place again.

The next morning Austria–Hungary declared war on Serbia and, from the far side of the Danube, Austrian gunboats began shelling Belgrade.

Willy was poleaxed. Always all front, his sense of insecurity and fearfulness that he kept so deeply buried beneath the swagger and bombastic bluff and bluster was terrifyingly laid bare. If Russia came to Serbia's aid, he would have to carry out his thoughtless promise made in the aftermath of Franz Ferdinand and Sophie's murders and stand shoulder-to-shoulder with Austria. And if he did that, he would most likely find himself not only at war with Russia, but with Russia's long-term ally, France – and for Germany, because of her geographical position, that would mean war on two fronts.

It was a prospect that filled him with crippling panic, and he immediately sent off a telegram to Nicky saying that he was about to exert his utmost influence with the Austrians to arrive at a satisfactory understanding, and that he hoped Nicky would help in smoothing over any difficulties that might arise.

Nicky replied that Austria's attack was an outrage, and the next day he mobilized his army along Russia's border with Austria.

'It's just in case events escalate even further,' he said to Alicky truthfully. 'It's only a precaution.'

Distraught, Alicky sent a telegram pleading for advice to Rasputin, who was still in a Siberian hospital bed. The cable she received back was starkly blunt: *Let Papa not plan war, for with it will come the end of Russia and of yourselves, and you will lose to the last man.*

Appalled, Alicky ran to show the telegram to Nicky, who, in a meeting with his ministers and military leaders, did something previously unthinkable for him, where advice from Rasputin was concerned. He ignored it.

Other telegrams began flying thick and fast between the Foreign Office Departments of St Petersburg, Berlin and London and, on a personal level, between Nicky, Willy and Georgie.

Willy cabled Nicky, demanding that he halt his mobilization.

Nicky responded that it was technically impossible for him to do so, but that as long as conversations with Austria were not broken off, his troops would not take the offensive.

Willy replied that he had gone to the utmost limits in his efforts to keep the peace; that he wouldn't be the one to bear responsibility for the disaster now threatening the civilized world; and that if the Russian mobilization of troops was halted, a general war could still be avoided.

It was a telegram that his government followed up with an ultimatum. Unless Russia halted mobilization within twelve hours, Germany would have no alternative but to mobilize also.

When the deadline arrived and Russia had not replied, Willy carried out his threat and, as there was still no response from Nicky, on 1 August Germany declared herself to be at war with Russia.

Denmark, Sweden and Norway hurried to declare their neutrality.

France mobilized.

On 3 August, Germany declared war on France, and Belgium refused permission for German troops to pass through its country en route to France. As if he had no memory of King Albert and Queen Elisabeth sitting alongside him at Sissy and Ernst's wedding breakfast in close family harmony, Willy signed an order that sent his troops marching through Belgium anyway.

It was too much for the British government. On 4 August, George signed the document declaring that Great Britain and all her Dominions over the seas were now at war with Germany.

When they were alone together, George said, ashen-faced, 'There was no alternative, May. Belgium is a neutral country, and for Willy to have ignored that . . .' His voice shook. 'We had to come to King Albert's aid, but that it should have come to this, May.' Tears streamed down his face. 'War with Germany. What on earth would Granny Queen have said?'

Knowing the kind of response he needed, she said robustly, 'Granny Queen would have said it is none of your fault, George, and she would have been heartbroken, as we are, and as all the rest of the family are.'

An hour later she stood next to George on the balcony of Buckingham Palace, in front of a vast cheering, flag-waving crowd that stretched from the palace gates all the way down The Mall to Admiralty Arch and beyond. It was a sea of thousands, all wanting to show loyalty to her and George, and all exultant at the thought of a war that would show the bullying Germans what was what. It took all of May's iron self-control to keep her own, very different emotions from showing.

She hadn't been exaggerating when she had said that she was heartbroken. Only fifteen months ago, at Sissy and Ernst's wedding, the Royal Mob had been united in close family togetherness; now it was difficult even to know on what side of the conflict some members of the family stood. For nearly all of them had either married Germans or, like herself, had far more German blood in their veins than English blood.

Irène and Willy's sister, Sophie of Greece, had been holi-daying together at Eastbourne and were now, she knew, desperately trying to return to the other side of the Channel – Irène to Germany, where her English-loving husband Hein-rich was commander of the Baltic Fleet, and Sophie to Athens.

Irène's sister Vicky, whose husband Louis of Battenberg was First Sea Lord of the Royal Navy, had been visiting Ella in Moscow, and Vicky had sent a cable saying she was now on her way back to England and was praying she would meet with no difficulties when it came to crossing Germany, the land of her birth.

As Grand Duke of Hesse, their brother Ernie had no choice concerning where to place his loyalty.

'Willy will have him commanding troops within days,' George had said when May had mentioned Ernie, 'and the same applies to newly married Ernst. What other choice will either of them have?'

Nicky's mother was in England visiting her sister, Georgie's mother, at Sandringham.

Russian Aunt Marie had shocked George deeply by declaring that she was siding with Germany and would be in Coburg for however long the war took, until it was over and everyone regained their senses. This meant her daughter Ducky, married to a Romanov and with homes in St Petersburg and Tsarskoe Selo, was now technically her enemy.

As the crowd of thousands on The Mall began singing the national anthem, May's mind was full of thoughts of her two eldest children. Twenty-year-old David was already in the Army, having joined the Grenadier Guards in June; and Bertie, who, like his father, had been a naval cadet, was at present serving as an officer aboard HMS *Collingwood* in the Mediterranean.

'And our boys will fulfil their duty splendidly, May,' George had said to her. 'We shall be able to be proud of both of them.'

As the crowds rousingly and deafeningly roared, 'God save great George our king! God save our noble king! God save the king!' tears stung the backs of May's eyes. Of course she would be proud of David and Bertie. She couldn't, in a million years, imagine being anything else. But oh, how she wished things were different, for so many of England's enemies had a place deep in her heart – and always would have.

Chapter Thirty-Nine

DECEMBER 1916, PETROGRAD

One of the first acts Nicky had taken after war with Germany had been declared had been to change the Germanic-sounding name of St Petersburg to the more Slavic 'Petrograd'. It had been a change Alicky had fully supported. Half-English and half-German, she had now utterly repudiated the German side of her heritage and had become as fiercely anti-German as every other Russian. All her loyalties were to Russia; all her prayers were for an Allied victory.

As for her former Kindred Spirit, Willy – she now thought of him as the devil incarnate, for it was Willy who had broken the blood-pact he had sworn to decades ago at Osborne. She remembered as if it were yesterday May asking what would happen if the pact was ever broken, and she recalled her own reply: that to break it would be to bring about something more terrible that could ever be imagined; something so terrible it would be like the end of the world.

She was in her mauve boudoir, counting off the hours until Nicky and Alexei arrived home from the Stavka, the Russian Army Headquarters situated in the deep forest of Poland, halfway between Moscow and Warsaw.

When war had broken out, Nicky had appointed his cousin, Grand Duke Nikolai, as Commander-in-Chief of the Army, and for the first weeks of the war Russia had enjoyed exhilarating victories, but the victories hadn't lasted. When Russia began suffering a series of defeats, Nicky had dismissed Nikolai and taken overall command himself. It hadn't been a popular move within the family, but both she and Nicky were long accustomed to receiving criticism from his family, whatever it was they did.

Even though it meant the agony of long separations between the two of them, Alicky had been fully supportive of Nicky's action. He was the Tsar and, as Tsar, his rightful place was to be in overall command. She had even been supportive when he had suggested that Alexei spend time with him at the Stavka. 'He will enjoy feeling part of the Army that will, after all, one day be his army,' Nicky had said, adding sheepishly, 'And he will also be able to sleep in my quarters and be company for me.'

Nicky's new role had also meant a new role for Alicky – one she had undertaken with great uncertainty in the beginning, but which she now felt quite at home in. At the Stavka, Nicky couldn't fulfil his autocratic task of governing the country and so, with his blessing and with Rasputin by her side to offer advice, she had begun doing it for him. Doing so exhilarated her. Her darling Nicky had always been too hesitant when it came to changing ministers; he didn't possess her inner certainty and iron will. Now in a position where she could bring about change, she had set about doing so and had earned her darling Nicky's gratitude.

Olga ran into the room. 'Word has come that Papa and Alexei are on their way here from the station. Their cars will be arriving any minute!'

At the outbreak of war, Alicky had turned the Catherine Palace at Tsarskoe Selo into a military hospital, and a wing of the Alexander Palace into a surgical unit. Then, along with her two oldest daughters, she had trained as a Red Cross nurse. By now all three of them were qualified and highly competent and Olga, having just come off-duty, was still in her nurse's uniform.

Alicky sprang to her feet. Every day that she and Nicky were apart she longed for their reunion, and especially for the nights they would once again share. To be in Nicky's arms in the darkness, to feel his lips on hers and his hands on her body was the very breath of life to her. Having been married now for twenty-two years, for both of them the passion and the rapture never faded.

This time, though, their reunion didn't bring joy in its wake, for when Nicky walked into the palace, Alexei wasn't at his side. He was being carried, and Dr Fedorov was hurrying alongside him, holding great pads of blood-stained bandages to Alexei's nose.

Alicky screamed and broke into a run.

Nicky said tersely, 'It started with a sneeze. At first it didn't seem as if it was going to be a serious bleed, but by this morning I knew I had to get him home.'

Over the top of the blood-saturated pads, Alexei's eyes flickered open. 'I'm sorry, Mama,' he whispered, and then his eyes closed, his face deathly white.

'Grishka!' she said through a sob, running after Nicky and the officer who was carrying Alexei as they headed at top speed up the grand staircase towards Alexei's bedroom. 'Have you contacted Grishka?'

'I've sent word. He's on his way.'

By the time Alexei was propped up on pillows on his bed, Dr Botkin was with them and not long afterwards Rasputin entered the room at a run, snow clinging to his long hair and knee-high boots. Ignoring Botkin and Fedorov, he strode to the side of the bed and, as Alicky dropped to her knees to join him in prayer, he stood silently, as he always did at times like this, his head bowed.

For several minutes he prayed and when he finally raised his head he said in his deep, soothing voice, 'Do not be alarmed, Little Mother, Little Father. Nothing bad is going to happen' and then he turned and left the room – and the palace – with the same speed with which he had entered it.

Exhaustedly, Alicky rose to her feet and sank into the chair by Alexei's bed. 'The bleeding will end,' she said to Fedorov and Botkin. And then, to Nicky, 'And this Man of God who holds our son's life in his hands is the man your family wants you to banish? It must never happen, Nicky! Never!'

Fifteen miles away, in the Vladimir Palace in Petrograd, a royal family conference was taking place, chaired by Miechen, Vladimir's widow.

'Desperate situations call for desperate measures,' she said grimly, looking around at the small group of people seated in her opulent drawing room. 'We are all agreed, aren't we, that something has to be done?'

'Absolutely.' Tall, and with the ramrod-straight bearing of a man who had been a soldier all his life, the Grand Duke Nikolai was standing sentry-like near the door. 'But how do we do anything that will make Nicky see sense? In the past I've stood in front of him and threatened to shoot myself, if he didn't change his tune and grant the kind of reforms Russians are desperate for, and what response did I get? He simply tapped ash off his cigarette, gave me that damned enigmatic smile of his and wished me good day.'

Nicky's Uncle Paul was sitting on the arm of a chair, a glass of vodka in one hand. 'Nikolai is right.' He ran his free hand over still-thick hair. 'It's impossible to reason with Nicky, and we all know the obstacle. Alicky was bad enough before Nicky acted like a madman and took over from Nikolai as Commander-in-Chief of the Army, but now that she's begun governing the country while Nicky is at the Stavka for months on end, we're going to hell in a handcart. Six Ministers of War in as many months. Three Ministers of Food and Distribution. Two Prime Ministers. How can a country at war be run in such a manner? It's insanity!'

No one in the room – Miechen, Nikolai, Misha, Ella, Paul, Paul's twenty-five-year-old son Dmitri or Prince Felix Yusupov, who was married to one of Nicky's nieces – disagreed with him.

Misha said, 'It's Rasputin who is behind every governmental change she makes. Alicky does nothing that her mad monk hasn't suggested and approved of – and the people know it. There are queues a mile long every day outside his flat in Gorokhovaya Street, all people who want a favour, a position, all knowing that it lies in his power to see to it that their wishes are granted – if, of course, they give him what he wants.'

'And when it comes to the women, we know what that is,' Felix said, looking as richly dressed as if for an imperial ball and wearing a delicate touch of blue eye make-up.

It was a crudity that Miechen and Ella didn't even blink at. Everyone knew of Rasputin's reputation with prostitutes, and with the aristocratic women who thronged his flat, all wanting the thrill of being able to say that the Tsarina's mad monk had indecently pleasured them.

Paul drained his glass and said, 'Every last person in Russia believes Alicky is his mistress and, when Rasputin is constantly in the bedrooms at the Alexander Palace and Nicky is hundreds of miles away in Russian Poland at the Stavka, you can't blame them for thinking that. There are times when I've come damn near to thinking it myself.'

'The last time she showed her face in public, people began shouting "*Niemetzkaia bliad*".' There was a raw edge to Misha's voice, 'Because her Russian has never been more than basic, she didn't understand they were calling her the German whore. But that isn't the really serious stuff, is it? The serious stuff is that it's obvious from despatches that the military secrets Nicky shares with her, she then shares with Rasputin.'

Miechen looked towards Nikolai for confirmation and he nodded. 'It's true, Miechen. There are rumours sweeping the country that both she and Rasputin are German spies and, as she *is* a German, it is why – one way or another – both of them have to go. Unless they do so, and soon, there's going to be a full-scale revolution and, when Nicky is brought down by it, we will be brought down with him.'

Miechen's reaction was swift and blunt. 'Then the only answer is Nicky's abdication.'

Ella said cautiously, 'Kyril and Ducky aren't with us, Miechen, and as Kyril is third in line to the throne, he needs to be with us if abdication is to be under discussion.'

'Kyril isn't with us because Nicky posted my son as far away from Petrograd as possible and he's serving with the Northern Fleet in Murmansk.' Miechen's voice was clipped and tight.

'And Ducky is ambulance-driving at the Front.' Felix, who rarely admired anyone other than himself, was obviously deeply impressed. 'She has formed her own ambulance unit. Every driver is a woman. I've suggested they descend on the battle-fields bare-breasted, like the women warriors of Greek mythology. It would give severely injured men a reason to live, don't you think?'

With difficulty, Nicky's brother Misha put from his mind the arousing picture Felix had conjured up. 'Alexei is still a child, Miechen. If Nicky abdicated, who would act as regent?'

'As Dowager Empress, Minny would. Or she and Paul could act as co-regents.'

There was silence, but it was silence because no one had any objections to what Miechen had said – or wouldn't have, if it could be achieved.

Paul said grimly, 'Such a prospect could only happen if Rasputin was no longer on the scene. With Rasputin pulling Alicky and Nicky's strings, Nicky is unlikely to abdicate, no matter what pressure we, as a family, bring to bear on him.'

'Then the answer is obvious, and Rasputin must no longer be on the scene.' Languidly Felix rose to his feet. 'No doubt, if you all put your heads together, you will come up with a solution, but Dmitri and I can't stay to help. We have an assignation at the House of Fabergé. Dmitri is going to help me choose Irina's Christmas gift.'

'Am I?' Dmitri asked as they left the palace in a horse-drawn sleigh.

'No, of course not. Prince Felix Yusupov doesn't go to the House of Fabergé. Monsieur Fabergé comes to Prince Felix Yusupov. We are now heading to my palace on the Moika in order that, over champagne, we can plot how we can make the family happy by disposing of Alicky's mad monk. Poison, I think. Poison would do away with the sight of blood – and blood is so messy. Even a glimpse of it makes me feel faint.'

A week later Alicky's daughter, Olga, said to her mother, 'I think there's a member of the family who is trying to build bridges with Grishka, Mama. Felix Yusupov has invited him to a late-night supper at the Moika Palace tonight, in order for him to meet Irina.'

'How extraordinary!' Felix wasn't one of Alicky's favourite people. He was too outrageous and bohemian, but his marriage to Nicky's niece had made him family, and if he was extending the hand of friendship to Grishka, then she was willing to begin thinking differently about him. 'Although I don't think the invitation can have been for tonight,' she added, 'I happen to know that Irina is in the Crimea.'

'Then I must have heard wrongly. It was Dmitri who told me. He's on leave from his Cossack regiment. Do you know he's been awarded the Cross of St George for gallantry in action? Uncle Paul must be very proud of him.'

The next day, when Alicky made her daily telephone call to Rasputin, she was told that the previous evening he had been Prince Yusupov's supper guest and hadn't been seen since he had left for the Moika Palace in one of the Prince's chauffeur-driven Daimlers.

With Nicky at the Stavka, Alicky did what she had long been doing. She acted in his stead, telephoning the Chief of Police and demanding that he make a full and instant investigation.

His report, the next day, wasn't reassuring.

'Pistol shots were heard coming from the Moika Palace the night Rasputin was there,' he said, privately hoping that at least one of the shots had found its mark and that the biggest troublemaker in Russia was now as dead as a door-nail, 'and there are blood stains leading out of the palace and across the courtyard. According to Prince Yusupov, it was a small party, the only other guests being Grand Duke Dmitri, an army officer named Sukhotin and Purishkevich, a member of the Duma. Prince Yusupov says there was a lot of heavy drinking and the party got a little out of hand, when Sukhotin shot a dog that was making a nuisance of itself. He showed me the body of the dog, which was in a corner of the courtyard, awaiting removal. Prince Yusupov says that the last he saw of Rasputin, he was weaving drunkenly in the direction of

Gorokhovaya Street, swigging from the neck of a bottle of brandy and bawling lewd songs.'

Even though she was exceedingly fond of Dmitri, and even though Felix was now part of her extended family, Alicky gave orders that both of them were immediately to be placed under house arrest.

Then she fired off a telegram to Nicky updating him on the situation.

After that there was nothing she could do but wait, and she did so with a rising fear, as her four bewildered and distressed daughters huddled around her.

Three days after he was last seen, Rasputin's frozen body was found in the ice below a bridge in the northern part of the city. With its discovery, Felix coolly admitted that he and Dmitri were responsible for, as he said, 'having saved the dynasty'. That Felix was capable of such an action was no great surprise, but Dmitri having been a party to it was something none of the family could quite believe.

Paul was as glad as anyone that Rasputin was dead, but his son having taken part in the murder plot horrified him.

'And Nicky is punishing him for the crime by sending him to Qazvin on the Persian front! Where the hell is that?' he said despairingly to Miechen. 'And the dire way this war is progressing under Nicky's leadership, what is the likelihood of my ever seeing him again?' To Miechen's distress, he covered his face with his hands, tears streaming through his fingers.

'And I,' Felix said unconcernedly to Misha, 'am to be banished eight hundred miles distant to my estate in Kursk. All in all, it's not too severe a sentence for having freed an empire from the rule of an insane *moujik*.'

'Is it true that, until the very end, you couldn't kill Rasputin, no matter what you did to him?'

Felix shuddered. 'You have no idea, Misha, *mon ami*. Dmitri, Sukhotin and Purishkevich were in another room, ready to come and dispose of him when poisoned cakes had done their business. I was alone with him – Rasputin thought we were waiting for Irina to join us. He ate enough cyanide-filled cakes, washed down with poisoned wine, to fell a regiment and the only effect they had was that he asked me if I would sing for him! In desperation, I did the only think I could think of doing. I made an excuse to leave the room, snatched Dmitri's army revolver from him, sprinted back and shot Rasputin. He fell, foaming at the mouth, but still the Satan didn't die. I have never been more terrified in all my life and then . . . Oh God, Misha – he came after me like a wild animal on his hands and knees!'

Felix broke off and, with a shaking hand, lit a cigarette.

'Having heard the gunshot, the others rushed into the room; and, after the cyanide-filled cakes, the poisoned wine and being shot, the Fiend got to his feet and began running out of the palace. It was incredible! Unbelievable! We chased him across the courtyard, shooting as we ran, until finally he fell into the snow, and even then . . . even then as we bound him with rope and rolled him up in a rug, *an eyelid twitched.*'

There was nothing faked about the horror Felix was remembering.

'Then we hoisted him into the boot of a car, drove him to the north of the city, dug a hole in the ice beneath the Krestovsky Bridge and dropped him through it. We figured that, with all the ice and snow, he wouldn't surface for months, but in the dark we didn't notice that in between dragging him from the car and dropping him into the water one of his boots had fallen off. If it hadn't been for that being recognized, Rasputin would still be at the bottom of the Malaya Nevka River.'

* * *

In the days that followed, Alicky didn't leave her mauve boudoir. She was too overcome with grief at the murder of her beloved friend, and with terror at the thought of what would happen the next time Alexei had an uncontrollable bleed. It was Nicky who dealt with the family – or who tried to deal with them, for although no one made too much hue and cry when Felix departed for Kursk, they were united in their indignation over Dmitri being sent to the Persian front.

'It's a death sentence!' his father said, no longer the suave and sophisticated Paul they were all familiar with, but a man heartbroken and despairing. 'How can Nicky do this to him?'

Even Nicky's mother begged him to rescind the Army order sending Dmitri to Persia. 'The climate alone will be enough to kill him,' Minny said passionately. 'And you must be aware of how detrimental to you the monk was. All the fifteen months you have been at the Stavka, it has been Rasputin who has been ruling Russia through Alicky – not Alicky who has been ruling it. When Nikolai tells you that Rasputin's death has saved the monarchy, he is telling you the truth. Whatever Dmitri did, he did out of love for you. You cannot send him to what is sure to be his death.'

Nicky had been immovable.

Ella, her face as white as the wimple that covered her head and bound her chin and neck, pleaded with him as well, but to just as little effect.

Nicky merely said time and again, 'A murder is always a murder. There has to be punishment.'

A week later Alicky left her boudoir and the palace in order to bury her beloved friend in a quiet corner of the Alexandra Park.

Dressed in boots and an ankle-length black fur, looking years older than her forty-four years and carrying seven hothouse roses, she had become wraith-thin. The burning certainty she had lived with – the certainty that, because of Grishka, haemophilia wouldn't kill Alexei and that he would survive to inherit the throne of the Russian Empire and rule it as an autocrat, as Russia had always been ruled – had been savagely and cruelly annihilated. From now on, fear and tension would again be her constant companions, for how, without Grishka, could it be any different?

As she walked through deep snow with Nicky and Alexei and the girls towards the freshly dug grave, more snow was falling. Ever since she had first come to Russia it had always been the same. At all the major moments in her life there, it had been winter. It had been winter and Russia had been covered in snow when Nicky's father had been dying, and when Nicky had urgently telegrammed to Hesse-Darmstadt that he needed her by his side.

And when Nicky's father had died and Nicky had become Tsar, and when it was imperative that they marry as soon as possible, it had still been the middle of an Arctic winter. Snow had been falling as she had entered the chapel of the aptly named Winter Palace; and it had been falling when, as her darling's wife, she had left it to shouts from vast crowds that she was their Winter Bride.

And now it was winter again and this time there was no springtime of hope awaiting her. Before Grishka's coffin had been closed she had written him a letter:

My dear Martyr, give me thy blessing that it may follow me always on the sad and dreary path I have yet to follow here below. And remember us from on high in your holy prayers.

And when she had sealed the envelope with a kiss, she laid it on his mutilated breast.

As she had reached the graveside, Anastasia slid her hand in hers. 'What mattered, Mama,' she whispered in an effort to bring comfort to her mother, 'is that we were lucky enough to have had him in our lives for a little while, and that he loved us and we loved him.'

The coffin was lowered into the grave. A lone priest conducted the Requiem Mass and, when it was at an end, she and Nicky each threw a handful of earth onto the coffin.

'Here, my darlings.' Beneath her thick veil, Alicky's tears flowed freely as she handed a rose to Nicky and Alexei, and then to Olga, Tatiana, Marie and Anastasia. 'May we always remember him, and may he never be far from us.'

Stepping up to the edge of the grave, she kissed the rose she was holding and then gently dropped it on the coffin. Solemnly and in turn, Nicky, Alexei and the girls each did the same.

It was over. Their goodbyes had been said, but as Alicky walked unsteadily away from the graveside, her heart told her that it was not the end – only the beginning of the end. For without Rasputin the future was a yawning black abyss; an abyss that would need every last drop of her iron determination and courage, if she was not only to face it, but survive it.

Chapter Forty

MARCH 1917, ALEXANDER PALACE, TSARSKOE SELO

'Alexei has measles,' Alicky said on the telephone to Nicky, who was at the Stavka. 'Botkin says it will be three or four weeks before he begins to get over it. Olga woke up with a rash on her head and a sore throat this morning and, as measles are so infectious, I think Tatiana, Marie and Anastasia will also soon be showing symptoms.'

Nicky had been lovingly sympathetic, but nasty as measles were, with his mind focused on the war effort, he could see no reason for returning to Tsarskoe Selo. Alicky was a trained nurse, and Botkin had always shown himself calmly efficient when it came to dealing with the children and their illnesses.

The first intimation at Tsarskoe Selo of more-than-usual unrest in Petrograd was when a senior member of the palace staff, who had been given a day's leave to attend his mother's funeral in Petrograd, failed to report for duty.

More snippets of information came in during the morning. Women had taken to the streets, protesting at the lack of bread. Men had walked out of several factories. Crowds were surging into the city, carrying Bolshevik red flags and banners. Trains had stopped running.

'Hooligans,' Alicky said dismissively when she was told.

Alexei's temperature had soared to one hundred and four degrees, and she had far more on her mind than worrying about yet another wave of unrest in Petrograd – unrest the Cossacks of the Petrograd Garrison would soon put an end to.

It was a telephone call from Ducky that first alerted her to the fact that the unrest was a little more serious than usual. 'Are you and the children still quite safe, Alicky?' she had asked, her voice tense and deeply concerned.

'Safe?' Ever since Ducky's divorce from Ernie, she and Ducky had never been close, and they certainly weren't in the habit of making telephone calls to each other. 'Of course I'm safe. Why wouldn't I be?'

There was a stunned silence from the other end of the line, and then Ducky said, 'Because I'm in Petrograd and I don't feel at all safe. There is uproar on the streets. Government buildings are being set on fire. A red flag is flying above the Peter and Paul Fortress. The sooner Nicky gets here and restores order, the better. What time do you think he will be arriving?'

'He won't be arriving. He can't just leave army headquarters because of a disturbance in the streets – it's nearly five hundred miles away. Are those gunshots I can hear in the background? Is a wedding being celebrated?'

Ducky said a word so rude that Alicky didn't even know what it meant.

'Ring Nicky, while you still have telephone contact with him,' Ducky said, when she could trust herself to speak. 'He *has* to return to Petrograd. Tell him that if he doesn't do so as fast as is humanly possible, there won't be a Petrograd for him to return to!'

Over the telephone came the sound of an almighty crash and then the line went dead.

Alicky frowned. Ducky was quite obviously drunk, and she

could only suppose that the crash she had heard was her falling to the floor in a drunken stupor.

Nevertheless, she telephoned Nicky right away. 'Sorry to be disturbing you, when you must be so busy, my darling. Ducky has telephoned to say there is civil unrest again in Petrograd and she wants to make sure you are aware of it.'

'I am aware of it, sweetheart. Members of the Duma cabled me earlier this morning with an urgent request that I return at once. They are, of course, a bunch of old women, and I have dealt with the situation by telegraphing the military governor of Petrograd and insisting that he bring order to the streets immediately, and that calm must be restored by tomorrow at the very latest.'

Alicky loved it when Nicky sounded every inch an autocrat. 'I wish,' she said, her voice thickening, 'that we were in bed together, my love.'

'It is all I ever think about. Our being together. Making love. Being happy.'

By the time she came off the phone she'd forgotten all about Ducky's near-manic telephone call.

The next morning it was obvious that Anastasia, too, had measles. All that day no news of what was happening in Petrograd reached Tsarskoe Selo. Helped by Dr Botkin and her two ladies-in-waiting, Alicky nursed her sick children around the clock until she was near to collapsing from exhaustion.

'You must rest, Your Imperial Majesty,' Botkin said to her time and again. 'You cannot keep pushing yourself as you are doing.'

She had taken no notice of him. Alexei's temperature was now beginning to drop, but Olga's and Anastasia's had soared.

Only when she was told that the telephone line to the Stavka was down did she begin to feel uneasy.

'Mama! Mama!' she heard Tatiana shouting, 'I've got red spots, too, and my ears are hurting.'

Two days passed. Alexei was over the worst, but was wan and pale. Olga was now delirious with fever, Anastasia was constantly slipping in and out of consciousness and Tatiana had developed abscesses in her ears.

The only member of the family to make physical contact – other than Ducky – was Nicky's brother, Misha. He arrived by car, striding into the palace in great agitation, saying, 'You and the children must leave, Alicky! The city is in the complete control of the revolutionaries. It's a miracle they aren't yet at Tsarskoe Selo.'

Alicky stared at him as if he was mad. It was incredible to her that Misha would show such panic in the face of danger, and although he was obviously about to head south until the unrest was over, she most certainly was not going to do so.

'I can't leave. The children have measles and are in no condition to travel anywhere. Although I now have no communication with Nicky, as all the lines are down, I know he will be on his way here and, when that happens, order will be restored.'

'Nothing on God's earth is going to restore order in Petersburg, or in the rest of Russia, while Nicky remains Emperor. It's over, Alicky. And if you won't take my word for it – and if you won't leave for the south and safety, while there is still a chance of you doing so – then you must pray your palace guard are still loyal.'

'Of course they are still loyal! Why on earth wouldn't they be?'

'Because the troops in Petersburg aren't. One last time, Alicky. Join my mother in Livadia, or join Miechen in Kiev.'

'No,' she said unhesitatingly. 'Nicky will be here soon, and I must be here for him when he arrives.'

Accepting defeat, knowing that he had done his best, which

hadn't been good enough, Misha hugged her, said his goodbyes and left.

They had been talking in one of the marble-pillared, magnificently mirrored rooms of the palace, rooms that Alicky never normally ventured into, and suddenly she was aware of how quiet everything was. Where were the footmen who would normally be standing to attention and lining the walls of the room? Why, in a palace that had a staff of hundreds, was there no sound of movement?

'The vast majority of the staff have either not shown up for work or have run away,' Count Benckendorff, the Grand Marshal of the Court, said, when she made enquiries. 'They are frightened the palace is about to be attacked.'

'The palace will *not* be attacked! It is far too protected by loyal troops.'

She made a mental count of them. There were two squadrons of Cossacks of the Emperor's Escort, a hand-picked regiment of the Imperial Guard and a battalion of the marine regiment whose sailors manned the imperial yacht. More than enough to deal with a mob, however large.

On impulse, accompanied only by Marie, she went outside to thank the troops for their staunch loyalty.

It was dusk and the men were in battle order. Slowly, with a fur coat draped around her shoulders, she walked along the lines, stopping every now and then, telling them their Tsar would soon be with them. She made it clear to them that the lives of her children were in their hands and she had complete trust in them.

In the morning she woke to the news that Nicky had left the Stavka and was on his way back to Petrograd.

'Thank God!' If she had been on her own when the news was given her, she would have wept with relief.

'And because of revolutionary activity on the track,' Count Benckendorff added, keeping the anxiety he felt from his voice, 'the imperial train has had to make a diversion to Pskov.'

'Pskov? Where is Pskov?'

'It is south and west of Petrograd. A distance of one hundred and sixty miles.'

A day later the palace water and electricity supplies were cut off, and the troops she'd had so much faith in deserted her.

It was a blow of disloyalty so deep Alicky could scarcely comprehend it. 'All of them?' she gasped. 'Even the sailors who so often served as crew aboard the *Standart*?'

'All of them,' Benckendorff said bleakly.

Alicky held onto the back of a chair to steady herself. 'Are you telling me that I and my children are now utterly defence-less, should the palace be attacked?'

'Yes, Your Imperial Majesty.' There were now white streaks in his hair, where days before there had been none. 'As for the household staff, your two closest ladies-in waiting are still here, as are thirty of the footmen, approximately the same number of valets, a dozen chambermaids, a few cooks and a handful of kitchen staff. The girls' tutor, Mr Gilliard, is still here, as are Dr Botkin and Dr Derevenko.'

They were interrupted by the arrival of Nicky's uncle, Paul.

Dismissing Count Benckendorff, she ran towards him, saying urgently, 'Have you news of Nicky? The last we heard, his train had been diverted to Pskov.'

'Yes, I have news.' His face was grey with fatigue.

'Is he still at Pskov? Have you spoken to him on the phone? I haven't been able to – all our lines are down. Please tell me he is all right and that he will be home soon. The children are so ill and . . .'

'He's all right, Alicky. And he will be home soon.' And then, breaking the dreadful news as gently as he could, he said, 'But when he comes home, it will not be as Tsar.'

She stared at him, not understanding. Not even beginning to understand.

'He's abdicated, Alicky. Both for himself and for Alexei.'

'Abdicated? *Abdicated?*' She tottered backwards and he thought she was about to fall. As he reached out to steady her, she pushed him violently away. 'How can Nicky abdicate?' There was hysteria in her voice. 'He is God's anointed!'

She was clutching at her heart and he was terrified she was about to have a heart attack.

'He had no choice. Every regiment and battalion in the Army has joined the revolution.'

'All of them? *All?* Even the Cossack Escort and the *Garde Equipage?*'

'All of them. The Navy has mutinied. Not even the Duma is loyal to him any more.'

'Oh, my poor darling!' There was deep passion in her voice, and he knew she was referring not to him, but to Nicky. 'To have had to undergo all this by himself! To have had to make such a decision with no one there to guide or to support him. It doesn't bear thinking about.'

Her legs gave way and she half-fell into the nearest chair. 'How could Nicky abdicate on Alexei's behalf? To be Emperor of Russia is Alexei's birthright! That Misha is now Tsar is unbelievable.'

'He isn't Tsar, Alicky. Misha abdicated within the hour. And Kyril hasn't become Tsar. Kyril,' he added, 'has thrown in his lot with the revolutionaries, even to the extent of flying a red flag on his car.'

She stared at him, struggling to believe that a close member of the family could have behaved in such a way. Dazed, her head spinning, she said, 'Then in the name of God, who is now ruling Russia?'

'I've no idea, and I'm not staying around to find out. I've lived in France before, and I intend living in France again. For the sake of Alexei and the girls, will you now do what I know Misha has already asked you to do? Will you leave Petrograd and join either Minny in Livadia or Miechen in Kiev, before what is being called "the Soviet" puts you and the children under house arrest?'

Alicky shook her head and, not for the first time, he was aware of her formidable inner strength. 'No, Paul. I'm going nowhere until my poor, darling Nicky arrives. And then, when the children are fit enough to travel, we will leave for wherever it is Nicky wants to go.'

'If you can by then,' Paul said tautly. 'If you are still able to.'

Later that night a fleet of army vehicles swept up to the palace.

Minutes later, an ashen Count Benckendorff informed Alicky that a general by the name of Kornilov wished to speak to her.

Alicky clasped her hands together tightly. It was eleven o'clock at night – the kind of time when arrests were made.

'I'll speak to him in the Audience Room,' she said, knowing that she had to fight down her fear; that she couldn't allow it to show.

Minutes later she was facing Kornilov, still dressed in her Red Cross nurse's uniform.

The first thing she noticed was that he was very young to be a general. The second was that his Imperial Army badge had been replaced by a badge showing a red star with a crossed hammer and sickle in the centre of it.

For the first time in her life, a minion did not respectfully address her by her proper title.

'Alexandra Feodorovna Romanov,' he said, without preliminaries. 'I am here to place you under house arrest. Your husband is also under arrest and will be returning to Tsarskoe

Selo tomorrow. I am also here to tell you that as soon as your children's health permits, the Provisional Government's intention is for you and your family to be escorted to Murmansk, from where a British cruiser will take you to England.'

Relief flooded through her so intensely that she thought she was going to faint. She wasn't going to be taken away and incarcerated in the prison of the Peter and Paul Fortress, whose very walls were steeped with the blood of those who had been tortured and had died there. Nicky would be with her sometime tomorrow, and she now knew what their future as a family was to be. England was a land that was as much a part of her childhood as Hesse-Darmstadt had been. A land over which Georgie and Kindred Spirit May were constitutional rulers. A land of green fields and bluebell woods, calm common sense and sweet reason. One world had come to an end, but another world was waiting.

In the seconds before the general left the room, and to his great amazement and discomfiture, she took both his hands in hers and thanked him.

'What was the German bitch like?' was the first question his aides asked, when he walked out to his car.

'She was dignified,' he said, trying not to show how much she had impressed him. 'Unafraid and very dignified.'

Despite the severe restrictions they had to live under – being unable to send or receive mail or make telephone calls, and forbidden to walk anywhere other than a restricted area of the palace park – after Nicky arrived, life settled into a routine that was bearable only because of Alicky's determination that they would all find it so.

In the mornings Pierre Gilliard gave the girls their French lessons, just as he had always done. Nicky gave history and geography lessons to Alexei, and Alicky gave him English lessons and undertook his religious instruction. In the afternoon they all took what exercise they could, and the girls and Alexei followed their parents' example by behaving as if there were no guards leering at them, constantly making uncouth comments.

'Close your eyes and ears to them,' she said, time and again. 'Soon they will be there no longer. Soon we will be in England.'

Nicky and Pierre Gilliard spent their exercise time in clearing snow and chopping down trees, but as the weather warmed, the entire family took to digging a mammoth kitchen garden and, under the mocking eyes of the guards, planting vegetables.

In the evenings they entertained themselves in the modest ways they had always done. In preparation for making England their home, Nicky read English novels to them: Hardy's *Tess of the d'Urbervilles*, Charlotte Brontë's *Jane Eyre*, Arthur Conan Doyle's *The Hound of the Baskervilles*. They did jigsaws and played Halma and dominoes. Whatever they did, wherever they went, the guards were present, always surly, always foul-mouthed, always listening in on their private conversations.

Of all of them, Alexei found it hardest to bear the constant humiliations, especially the humiliations his father had to endure.

'How can Papa bear it?' he said between sobs, as he knelt with his head in Alicky's lap. 'He was the Tsar and now he is treated as if he were a nobody; as if he were a peasant.'

'He bears it because he has no option,' she said, her heart hurting for him. 'He bears it in order that we keep the small freedoms we have been allowed. He bears it because at least we have a future to look forward to. In England we will be able to live as we want. Do you know that Papa has always dreamed of having no reports to read and no ministers to see, and he has always had a secret desire to be a farmer? I think

474

Papa would be a very good farmer. Perhaps in England we will have a farm near the sea; a farm in Norfolk, close to Sandringham.'

A new visitor began calling on them: Alexander Kerensky, the Minister of Justice in the Provisional Government that had been established on Nicky's abdication. Oddly enough, Nicky quite liked him.

'Your relatives abroad are taking a keen interest in your welfare,' Kerensky said to him on one of his visits. 'The English Queen especially asks that your wife is aware that all her thoughts are with her.'

The knowledge that May was thinking of her, and doing her best to make some kind of contact, was balm to Alicky's increasingly troubled soul.

But the weeks turned into months, and still they weren't told to prepare to leave for England. Her general health deteriorated, her sciatica becoming so acute that she could no longer walk more than a few steps unaided and had to use a wheelchair, when accompanying Nicky and the girls and Alexei as they took their outside exercise.

It was summer when Kerensky, now head of the Provisional Government, had a long, difficult conversation with Nicky.

'England is no longer possible,' he said, constantly amazed at Nicky's ability to take appalling news unflinchingly. 'The fear of a left-wing revolution in Britain is such that the British Prime Minister has withdrawn his offer of sanctuary. It is his government's belief that if sanctuary were to be given to a family who have ruled so autocratically and despotically, the very large number of British people in sympathy with revolutionary Russia would rise in protest and topple the monarchy, just as has happened here.'

Nicky, who had never understood how limited George's powers as a constitutional king and an emperor were, gaped at him.

'But if not England, where?' he asked, struggling to get his thoughts in order. 'We can't be kept under house arrest forever! My wife and daughters have no privacy. The soldiers wander in and out of our rooms as they like. Perhaps Denmark? The King is my cousin.'

Kerensky didn't have the heart to tell him that the Danish government had been approached and that their reaction had been identical to the British one.

'I thought the Crimea,' Kerensky said, 'but wherever your destination, you will be leaving Tsarskoe Selo within days, for I can't guarantee your safety here any longer. The Bolsheviks are now headed by a returned exile, Lenin, and there are rumours that he is plotting to overthrow the Provisional Government. If he does, it will be the end of me, as well as the end of you and your family. Begin packing, Nicholas. You will soon be leaving.'

'The Crimea!' It was the place they had always been happiest in, and Alicky could hardly believe that such good news was true. 'And from there, when the war is over, we can quite easily be taken by boat to England.'

He didn't tell her that England no longer wanted them. He merely said, 'You and the girls must begin packing – and not only clothes. If something has great sentimental value to you, then see that it goes into one of the chests or boxes.'

It was when she was packing up mementos of Grishka that she came upon an envelope addressed to Nicky in the monk's handwriting. Anything written by Grishka was to be treasured, for he had rarely written anything. As a peasant, writing had been something that he was uncomfortable with. The envelope wasn't sealed and she slid the letter out, eager to read its contents.

In heavy black ink, it was dated December, shortly before his murder, and at first Alicky thought it was a will:

I write and leave behind me this letter at St Petersburg. I feel that I shall leave life before 1 January. I wish to make known to the Russian people, to Papa, to the Russian Mother, to the Children, to the land of Russia what they must understand. If I am killed by common assassins, and especially by my brothers the Russian peasants, you, Tsar of Russia, have nothing to fear and your children will reign for hundreds of years.

But if I am murdered by nobles, and if they shed my blood, their hands will remain soiled with my blood. For twenty-five years they will not wash my blood from their hands. They will leave Russia. Brothers will kill brothers and hate each other, and for twenty-five years there will be no nobles in the country. Tsar of the land of Russia, if you hear the sound of the bell that tells you Grigory has been killed, know this: if it was your relations who wrought my death, then no one in your family – none of your children or relations – will remain alive for more than two years. They will be killed by the Russian people. I shall be killed. I am no longer among the living. Pray. Be strong and think of your blessed family,

 Grigory

The blood thundered in Alicky's ears. The ground felt as if it was shelving away beneath her feet. The world was spinning and she couldn't breathe. Had Nicky ever received this letter? Common sense told her that he had to have done. The envelope had been opened. It had been in the same small box as several icons that Grishka had blessed. And Nicky hadn't shown it to her. How could he have shown it to her? Grishka never spoke a word that wasn't true. *If it was your relations who wrought my death, then no one in your family – none of your*

children or relations – will remain alive for more than two years.
They will be killed by the Russian people. The words leapt from
the page as if written in fire.

She looked again at the date of the letter. It had been
written in December. She read his second opening sentence.
I feel that I shall leave life before 1 January. His murder had
taken place on 30 December. It was a prophecy that had
been fulfilled to the letter – and she had not a shadow of a
doubt that his other prophecy would be just as accurately
fulfilled.

She slid down against the nearest wall and, trembling uncon-
trollably, hugged her knees to her chest. Nicky's reaction would
have been to assume that Grishka had been drunk when he
had written his letter to him, but then Nicky had never believed
in Grishka as fervently as she had always believed in him. And
he hadn't shared the letter with her because, although he would
have discounted it, he would have known the very different
effect it would have on her.

She could feel that effect flooding through her like iced
water from top to toe. All joy at the thought of the Crimea
vanished. Wherever they went, she, Nicky and the children
wouldn't be safe. Because Grishka had died at the hands of
their family, there would be a terrible price to pay.

She never knew how long she sat huddled on the floor,
coming to terms with the stark prophecy of Grishka's letter,
but when she finally rose to her feet, Alicky knew how she was
going to handle the horrific knowledge she now had.

She wasn't going to let Nicky know that she had read the
letter, and she certainly wasn't going to burden her beloved
children with the letter's contents. Instead she was going to
ensure that, under whatever conditions awaited them, their
family life was going to remain as untroubled as she could
possibly make it. And she was always going to remember that

she was an empress. From now on, no matter the circumstances, no one was ever going to see her cry.

As they packed to leave, the children chattered happily about how different life would be for them in the Crimea.

'Even if we are still held under horrid house arrest, the sun will be shining and however small a section of Livadia Palace's gardens we are allowed in, we can put up a net and play tennis,' Anastasia said as she squeezed a rag doll into one of the trunks they were packing.

'And we won't be under house arrest in the Crimea,' Nicky said reassuringly. 'Prime Minister Kerensky is sending us there because it is safe. There is no revolution in the Crimea.'

'And lots of our relatives are there.' Marie took another armful of clothes out of one of the cupboards. 'Granny Minny, Aunt Miechen, Great-Uncle Nikolai and lots and lots of other Romanov aunts and uncles and cousins.'

The mood was almost holiday-like as they selected favourite pictures and ornaments and keepsakes to take with them.

Alicky coped by not taking part in the general packing. Instead she oversaw the stowing of Romanov jewellery into large portable jewel chests. The jewellery was the only kind of finance they were now left with and, whatever else was going to be left behind to be looted, she was determined it wasn't going to be her family's future financial security.

The day before they were due to leave, Kerensky sent a message that they would not be going to the Crimea, as the railway line to the south was in the hands of the Bolshevik revolutionaries. Instead they would be travelling east.

'And he said that we should pack warm clothes and furs,' Nicky told the devastated children. 'And he also said we should expect a journey of at least five days.'

'Five days?' Olga did the maths. 'The only place five days' train travel east is Siberia.'

At Marie's gasp of horror, Alicky said swiftly, 'Grishka was born in Siberia, in a village called Pokrovskoe. Perhaps we will be able to see it from the train.'

'And he once lived in Tobolsk, in Siberia,' Tatiana said. 'I know, because he told me that although Tobolsk is only a small town, it seemed a vast city to a village boy like him.'

'Then if it is a town, perhaps the train line will run through it.'

The difficult moment was over. The packing continued.

They were to begin their journey in darkness, at one o'clock in the morning. Scores of steamer trunks, large chests and wooden boxes were piled in the lapis- and malachite-decorated entrance hall and the rooms leading off of it. Kerensky, who was overseeing their departure, had asked that they gather in the entrance hall with their luggage.

The hours ticked by. Two o'clock. Three o'clock. Curled up in whatever comfortable chairs they could find, the girls dozed. Alexei struggled to keep awake, helped by his little dog, which thought it only reasonable that the two of them keep going for walks through the surrounding rooms.

Nicky paced the marbled floor, smoking cigarette after cigarette.

Kerensky was repeatedly on the telephone, furiously demanding to know what the hold-up was; demanding to know when the cars that should have been there hours ago, to ferry them to the waiting train, were finally going to arrive.

Dressed in a wine-red travelling suit and with a matching hat tilted so that it shadowed her eyes, Alicky was seated on a chair that had once belonged to Marie Antoinette, her kid-gloved hands clasped tightly in her lap.

Siberia. How ironic that the only place deemed safe for them was the place Grishka had come from.

Finally there came the sound of cars and trucks approaching the palace.

Kerensky said tautly, 'The family will leave first. The household staff accompanying them will leave second, and only then will soldiers begin loading the luggage into the trucks.'

The girls stirred and rose wearily to their feet.

Alexei picked his little dog up in his arms.

Nicky stubbed out his cigarette and held out his hand to help Alicky rise from her chair. 'You will be able to sleep, my darling, when we are aboard the train,' he said comfortingly.

'Yes.'

How she envied Nicky his calm and untroubled thoughts. He was a fatalist. It was how he had been able to cope with his enforced abdication; the humiliations of the last four months; this leaving in the night, for a journey of thousands of miles to heaven only knew where. For Nicky, whatever would be would be. Everything was in God's hands, and railing against fate was pointless.

He tucked her gloved hand into the crook of his arm. 'I love you with all my heart, body and soul,' he whispered, sensing her tension and fear. 'Always and forever.'

'For eternity?' It was what they always said to each other.

'For eternity.'

For the first time since she had read Grishka's letter, a feeling of peace flooded through Alicky. Whatever happened, they would always be together, of that she was absolutely certain. And with renewed courage and a heart full of the most passionate, burning love, she walked with Nicky into the all-enveloping, waiting darkness.

Chapter Forty-One

OCTOBER 1918, LONDON

May was about to leave Buckingham Palace for another long day of hospital visits to wounded and maimed soldiers, when George hurried breathlessly into her sitting room. 'The latest news from the Front is that the Germans are falling back! At last we have them on the run, May.'

May sucked in her breath. Ever since August there had been glimmers of hope that the Allies were gaining the upper hand. Fifteen months ago America had entered the war and only three weeks ago had inflicted a heavy defeat on German troops at Saint-Mihiel in northern France. This, though, was the first time George had sounded so optimistic of overall victory being within sight.

With a trembling hand he lit a cigarette. 'And the rumour from Germany is that Willy's Chancellor, Max of Baden, has formed a liberal government that just might be interested in an armistice. Wasn't he an old suitor of yours?'

'There was a time when Mama hoped he was, but it wasn't a hope I ever shared.'

'Still, he sounds a good man. Louis says he is.'

Louis of Battenberg, Vicky's husband and now Louis Mountbatten, since George – having got cold feet about his surname of Saxe-Coburg-Gotha – had changed it to Windsor and had anglicized all other German surnames in the family at the same time, had once been a close friend of Max's.

'I believe he is. Mama wouldn't have considered him a suitable husband for me if he hadn't been.'

Oblivious to the fact that May was wearing a light tweed walking dress, one of her distinctive toque hats and had been in the process of putting on a pair of kid gloves, he sat down, wincing with pain as he did so.

Three years ago, when making one of his self-imposed visits to the Western Front to bolster the spirits of the troops, the horse he was riding had been spooked by the sound of the men cheering and had reared up and fallen on him. The injuries he had received – one of which was a badly fractured pelvis – had meant that he had never fully recovered, and he still regularly walked with a stick. Combined with the crushing burden and griefs of the war, it had ensured there was nothing whatsoever left of the rosy-cheeked, joke-loving Georgie of those long-ago days when Eddy had still been alive.

He was fifty-three, but he looked seventy-three. His always-trim Van Dyke beard was almost white. There were bags beneath his eyes, his face was deeply lined and even before the news that had come from Russia in late July, his eyes had held nothing but sadness for the hundreds of thousands of young men cut down in their prime on foreign soil.

After July, stupefying grief had been yoked with crippling guilt – emotions that May knew he would carry with him for the rest of his life.

Suddenly aware that she had been about to leave the palace, he said, 'I didn't mean to keep you, but I knew you would want good news from the Front. There is also a family letter for you from Irène, via Sweden. The Prime Minister is waiting to have a word with me, so you will have to update me on its contents later.'

When he had left the room, May opened the envelope he had given to her. George's first cousin, Daisy Connaught, was married to the Crown Prince of Sweden and, ever since the beginning of the war, Daisy had acted as an intermediary between family in England and Germany. Irène had written in hasty-looking handwriting:

> *Dearest May,*
>
> *Things are moving at a great pace here. It is Heinrich's opinion that the war is all but over – and that Germany will capitulate. Willy is still at military headquarters, but not in any kind of command. If the truth be told, Our Great Warlord has never been in command. He has only ever been a play-acting, sword-waving figurehead, and the word is that now reality has at last intruded he has had a complete nervous collapse. Revolution is on the verge of breaking out here, as it did in Russia, and Heinrich believes things can only end in Willy's abdication. What will then happen to us (Heinrich and the children and me) when that occurs, I haven't the faintest idea. And if Willy abdicates, where will he and Dona go? Ironically, the only country Willy has ever truly wanted to live in is England. If God is good, Heinrich and I will find ourselves at Hemmelmark, our estate in northern Germany. This is just to let you know how volatile things now are here, and for you not to worry too much if you don't hear from me for a little while.*
>
> *Much love to Georgie, Irène*

With Irène's letter in her hand, May looked unseeingly out of the window. Everything Irène had written indicated that George was right in his assumption that the war would soon be over. A world at peace again would be the greatest mercy imaginable, and the rejoicing and celebrating would no doubt go on for months, but although Georgie's thankfulness would be bone-deep, it would not bring him peace of mind. Nothing was going to be able to do that ever again.

Exerting all her mental strength, she forced herself to carry on with her day. When George had walked in on her, she had been on the point of leaving the palace to visit critically injured soldiers in Great Ormond Street Hospital, where their daughter, Mary, was doing a nursing course. No matter what the private nightmares, life had to go on and, picking up her gloves, May walked briskly downstairs to the courtyard and her waiting car.

Over the last four years barely a day had gone by when she hadn't spent the greater part of it in hospital or visiting convalescent centres or, with George, visiting a shipyard or a munitions factory, letting people know how at one with them they were. She had even accompanied George on one of his stressful visits to the Western Front, a visit of such unimaginable nightmare that only her lifelong habit of rigid self-discipline had helped her survive it.

The strain of the war showed in May's face. It was very seldom now that any of her natural merriment showed in her eyes. At fifty-one her distinctive hairstyle was still the same as it had always been, although her dark-gold hair was now flecked with white and, because George disliked change of any kind, her way of dressing had barely changed over the years. She still wore off-the-face toques that didn't interfere with her poodle fringe, and she still favoured several-stranded chokers of pearls and, at the same time, invariably wore long, waist-length ropes of pearls. Her still-slender figure was always stiffly corseted and she had lost none of her ability to move gracefully.

The Prime Minister, David Lloyd George – no lover of royalty – had been heard to say admiringly that never had any queen been as effortlessly stately as May Teck.

The memory of the horrors she had seen on the Western Front were not ones that she wanted at the forefront of her mind when trying to bring a little cheer to badly injured men and she blocked it from her. She must think of the day ahead. A day when Marie-Louise would be acting as her lady-in-waiting.

Since her divorce from Aribert, Marie-Louise had never remarried, but had always kept herself busy. At one time she had been the owner of a smart little hat shop in Knightsbridge, something that shocked the majority of her family just as deeply as her divorce had done.

May hadn't been shocked. She had thought it very enterprising.

'There was a time, before my engagement to dear Eddy, when I thought of doing something similar,' she had said, 'although not in London, but in Florence.'

On the outbreak of war, Marie-Louise had turned a Girls' Club that she had established and run in Bermondsey into a hospital of one hundred beds and, under the direction of the government, she was its hands-on administrator.

As they sat together in the back of the royal Daimler, Marie-Louise said, 'When my father died a few months ago, Willy sent me a very kind letter of condolence via Daisy. Not a word about the war, of course; just family matters. Adalbert and his wife have had another daughter. Is Adalbert Willy's second son?'

'Third.' May was never at a loss when it came to fathoming family relationships.

'And Sissy and Ernst have had a daughter, Frederica.'

May felt a pain in the region of her heart. Was it only five years ago that they had been at Sissy's and Ernst's wedding in Potsdam? All the royal houses of Britain, Germany, Austria and Russia, united in celebrating a happy family event? How could the unspeakable monstrosity of what had happened since then have occurred?

'Willy asked to be remembered to you,' Marie-Louise said as the Daimler drew to a halt outside the front entrance of the hospital. 'He wrote that you were a kindred spirit. I thought it a very droll expression, but then there were always times when Willy's English was droll. I remember him once saying he had a very gentle chair, when he meant to say he had a very comfortable chair.'

Later, when they were once again in the Daimler, Marie-Louise said hesitantly, 'I hope you aren't thinking me as unfeeling for not having spoken of . . . of July . . . but I thought you wouldn't want to be reminded. It was all so terribly, terribly ghastly . . .' Her voice tailed off in awkward embarrassment.

'No.' May kept her eyes focused straight ahead on the traffic. They were nose-to-tail with an ambulance. A boy who was mercifully too young for army service cycled past them, his pannier piled high with fresh bread. 'No,' she said again. 'You were quite right, Marie-Louise. Like the Battle of the Marne and Gallipoli, and Verdun and the Somme and endless other blood-soaked battlefields, there aren't enough words in the English language for it, and so it is best not spoken of.'

Not spoken of, but never for a moment forgotten.

When Marie-Louise had been dropped off at the small Knightsbridge flat she lived in, in glorious independence, May massaged her aching temples. The nightmare best not spoken of had started after Nicky's abdication eighteen months ago, when Russia's Provisional Government had asked the British government if the former Tsar and his family could be given refuge in England.

'Of course I have agreed,' George had said to her at the time. 'How could I not? Nicky is my *doppelgänger*. We are so alike physically that whenever we are together at any family event, we are constantly mistaken for each other. And besides, I like Nicky. He's a grand chap. Always so sweet-natured and amiable.'

The Daimler rolled into Buckingham Palace's inner court-yard. Without betraying a flicker of her mental agony, May stepped from the car and thanked the driver, her thoughts going relentlessly over the terrible, fateful days in March.

A meeting between the Prime Minister, George's private secretary and the Permanent Under-Secretary at the Foreign Office had taken place in Downing Street. Agreement had been swiftly reached and a message sent to the Russian government, stating that Britain was prepared to offer asylum to the former Tsar and his wife and children.

It had all seemed so straightforward. It had even occurred to May that once the family was domiciled in Britain, her eldest son might stop philandering with married women and become engaged to Olga or Tatiana, something she knew would delight Alicky just as much as it would her.

But there had been a delay from the Russian end in putting what had been agreed into practice, and during those delays a huge swathe of the British public, sympathetic to the Bolshevik cause, had made their feelings known. The revolution in Russia had sparked a countrywide revolutionary movement in Germany, as Irène had indicated in her recent letter, and the same kind of political unrest was happening in Britain. All over the country there were worker-led strikes, and trade-union leaders were loud in their support of Comrades Lenin and Trotsky. Buckingham Palace was deluged with letters from outraged members of the public, all expressing the belief that a dynasty that had ruled as autocratically and despotically as the Romanov dynasty had deserved all that it got and was most definitely not wanted on British soil. In Parliament, Labour and Liberal MPs vehemently expressed the same opinion. Labour clubs from Land's End to John O'Groats let it be known that the Tsar and his family were most definitely not welcome.

George had been appalled. 'I thought my decision was simply a family decision,' he had said to May, ashen-faced and bewildered. 'And look at the outcry it's aroused. In today's *Times* a letter to the editor has suggested that all the ancient trappings of throne and sceptre should be done away with! By which I take it he means *I* should be done away with.'

In the end George had decided that he could not risk inflaming revolutionary passions in Britain by giving Nicky and his family asylum. The risk of it triggering a wholescale revolution in Britain that would sweep him from his throne was too great for him to be able to do so. He had changed his mind and, without telling her, had withdrawn the offer of asylum.

'It isn't as if Britain is the only place Nicky can resettle,' he had said when the regret-telegram had been sent. 'There are other countries Nicky and Alicky have links to. Denmark, for instance. Or Sweden. Or even Maudie and Haakon's Norway. Later, when the war is over and the dust has settled, that will be the time for them to come to England – assuming, of course, they still want to do so.'

As she stepped inside the palace, May was greeted by a euphoric George.

'Great news, May! Wonderful news!' He nearly knocked her off her feet. 'The German Navy has mutinied. The sailors are demanding political reform and Willy's abdication. Your old boyfriend Max of Baden is talking of an armistice.'

May's knees gave way in relief and she sank down onto the nearest chair. An armistice. A truce. An end to the hostilities while a peace was negotiated. Never had any news been so welcome. 'Oh, thank God,' she said weakly, from the bottom of her heart. 'Thank God!'

* * *

Willy wasn't thanking God. He was struggling with all his might to understand the disaster happening all around him.

'The war,' Prince Max of Baden, his newly appointed Chancellor, said to him grimly over the telephone on 8 November, 'is not as good as lost. It *has* been lost – and if civil war in Germany is to be avoided, there is no other alternative but for you to abdicate.'

Max was in Berlin. Willy was at Military Headquarters, hundreds of miles away at Spa.

'Abdicate?' Willy roared, hardly able to believe his ears. 'I'm not a lily-livered ninny like Nicky Romanov! I'm a successor of Frederick the Great, and a successor to Frederick the Great does not abdicate.' And, with great fury, he slammed the receiver back on its rest.

He swung round to view himself in the nearest mirror. He was fifty-nine and, unlike a lot of the men his age, was still a fine figure of a man. His figure had thickened over the years, but he didn't have a paunch. His strong-boned facial features had held up well. His jawline was still arrogantly firm; his nose, unmarked by red veins, was just as jutting as ever; the cleft in his chin still gave him a look of great panache.

Rather than abdicate, he would go to the Front and lead his army himself. In his mind's eye he could see himself doing it. He could see himself, like a legendary hero in a romantic saga, dying a glorious death at the head of his troops.

Unfortunately, no one else could. With capitulation staring them in the face, all his generals were unanimous that the war was lost; and they, like Max, insisted that his abdication was the only thing that could save Germany from disintegration.

'Then I shall abdicate as German Emperor but remain King of Prussia,' he announced grandly, when faced with the inevitable, only to discover, with overwhelming disbelief, that no one was listening to him any longer.

Two days later, without even having had another conversation with Willy, Max announced his abdication, and the abdication of his eldest son and heir.

'Impossible!' Willy bellowed when the news was brought to him. 'Preposterous! No one can abdicate a throne except the person sitting on it.'

'But they have,' he was told bluntly by his generals. 'Germany is now a republic, you are no longer Kaiser – and you cannot,' they added, even more bluntly, 'remain in Germany, not unless you want to meet the same fate as the Tsar did. You must go into exile.'

Exile. His first thought was England, but having waged war against it for four years, even he realized that England was an impossibility. One of his generals suggested Holland.

'Queen Wilhelmina is a cousin of yours, isn't she?' the general in question said. 'I'm sure she will grant you asylum.'

Within hours, news came back from The Hague that Willy would be welcome in Holland as a guest of a Count Bentinck at the count's castle at Amerongen. He was to leave for Holland immediately. Dona, and other members of his family who wished, would follow afterwards.

On the imperial train and in a private carriage in which, ironically, hung a photograph of his grandmother taken at Osborne House, Willy left Germany behind for good. He was no longer the Kaiser. He was no longer Germany's All-Highest. And all he felt was the most incredible, overwhelming relief. Never again would he have to pretend to be someone he wasn't, in order to fulfil his position as an emperor. Never again would he have to play-act. From now on he could simply be himself. An entire new world of freedom was opening up before him. And he knew how he was going to celebrate it.

Looking out at the flat fields of Holland, he rang the bell

that summoned his aide-de-camp. 'I would like,' he said to him in great good humour, 'a cup of very good, extra-strong English tea.'

In England things were moving with such speed it was hard for May to keep up. From Germany had come news of Willy's abdication and exile in Holland.

'And at any moment we will be receiving news that the armistice has been signed,' George said to her. 'When news of it is given, the British people are going to descend on the palace in cheering hordes. We are going to have to make appearance after appearance on the balcony.'

'Yes, George.' She knew what it was that he was really telling her. He was telling her it was imperative there were no dark thoughts on their minds when, from Buckingham Palace's balcony, they faced the jubilant crowds. He was telling her that, for a short while at least, they must somehow shut out the memories of July.

When he had hurried away to meet Prime Minister David Lloyd George, she walked into her private sitting room. It wasn't much different from how Queen Victoria's sitting room had been. If it was one thing her Aunt Queen's descendants had in common, it was the need to surround themselves with family photographs and memorabilia.

Central on her desk was a photograph of Nicky and Alicky and all five of their children. It was a carefree, happy photograph that had been taken at Cowes when they had last visited England.

Slowly she took off her hat and removed her gloves, thinking back to July. Remembering.

The news had come totally out of the blue. They had known, of course, that ever since Nicky's abdication eighteen months earlier, he and Alicky and the children had been living under house arrest. They had received news via the British Ambassador in Petrograd when the family had been moved – for what had been described as their own safety – to Tobolsk, in Siberia. Later they had received the information that they had been moved again, this time to Ekaterinburg, a town three hundred miles to the west.

She and George had been at Windsor, enjoying a Sunday lunch with Marie-Louise and her parents, when George had been called away from the table to take an urgent telephone call.

When he re-entered the room, the man she had always known had vanished forever. In his place was a man suffering mental agony; a man who had aged two decades.

'Nicky,' he had said dazedly. 'Those damned bloody Bolsheviks have murdered Nicky.'

There had been no news of Alicky and the children. Even after the atrocity of Nicky's murder, it hadn't occurred to anyone to wonder if they, too, had suffered a similar fate. That such a thing might have happened to them had been beyond imagination.

Twenty-four hours later they had been faced with the ultimate horror.

'How,' George had said to her, struggling for speech, 'was I to know that because I had refused them asylum, they would be killed in such a ghastly manner? Who could possibly believe that such a thing could happen?'

Hunched and ashen in the seventh circle of hell, he had locked himself into his stamp room, tears streaming down his face.

May looked at the photograph now. Nicky had his arm around Alicky's shoulders. Alicky was staring straight at the camera, not smiling, but then Alicky never smiled in photographs. Her eyes, though, were smiling. She had been happy that day; happy to be back in England where she had spent so much time as a young girl; happy with her family around her. Olga, Tatiana, Marie and Anastasia were all wearing straw boaters decorated with wild flowers. Alexei's arms were around the neck of his little pet dog. How, when that photograph had been taken, could anyone possibly have imagined the horror lying in wait for them?

With an unsteady hand she poured herself a stiff brandy.

Details of what had happened had reached them a week later, when White Russian forces loyal to Nicky had taken Ekaterinburg and one of the executioners had been captured and interrogated. According to his statement, on the night of 16 July the family had been told that, as White Russian forces were advancing on Ekaterinburg, they were to be moved to yet another destination and were to go into one of the basement rooms to await the arrival of their transport.

This, together with three members of their household, they had done. There had been no chairs in the room and, at Nicky's request, two chairs had been brought in, one for Alicky and one for Alexei, who was recovering from a bleed in his knee and couldn't stand. Then, under the orders of Yakov Yurovsky, the man in charge of the family's captivity, eleven men had entered the room armed with revolvers. Yurovsky had told Nicky that he and his family were about to be shot. Nicky had said a bewildered, 'What? What?' and then the executioner had shot him between the eyes. Then the men had opened fire on Alicky, Alexei, Olga, Tatiana, Marie, Anastasia and the three members of the household. The room was small, the shooting chaotic, the smoke thick, and the men resorted to bayonets. The jewels sewn into the girls' clothing acted as armour, and as they screamed and ran, they were bayoneted time and again. The floor became slippery with blood and what should have taken five minutes had taken twenty.

The account was so graphic May knew she would never forget a word of it; that the words – and the unspeakable images they conjured up – would be her private nightmare for as long as she lived.

On the day she, George and other members of their family attended a memorial service for Nicky, Alicky and their children, news arrived that Ella, too, had been murdered by the Bolsheviks.

'They threw her down a mine shaft,' George said, his voice cracking and breaking, tears rolling down a face that the war had lined with deep grooves. 'She was still alive, May, and the fiends threw her down a mine shaft and left her to die. The local peasants say that for days they could hear her singing hymns and that her singing grew fainter and fainter and then – nothing.'

It was a long time before May could trust herself to speak and, when she did, she said unsteadily, 'Do you think Willy knows? Ella was the only woman he ever truly loved and I don't believe he ever stopped loving her. He offered her sanctuary many times, but she always said that her heart belonged to Russia and that she would never leave it. Her death – and for her to have died in such a cruel, hideous manner – is going to break his heart.'

On 11 November 1918, in a stationary railway carriage in the forest of Compiègne, an armistice was ratified by six signatories. The news was formally announced in London a little before eleven o'clock, and immediately great crowds began descending on Buckingham Palace from every direction, choking every inch of The Mall, from the palace gates all the way back to Trafalgar Square and the Strand.

Inside the palace, George had dressed in his admiral's uniform. 'Has Mary arrived?' he asked May anxiously. 'I so want Mary to share in this moment with us, even though the boys can't.'

'Mary is here, and so is Uncle Arthur.'

Uncle Arthur was Daisy Connaught's father.

She, too, would have liked the boys to have been able to step out onto the red and gold-draped balcony with them, but in the end the Armistice had been so sudden that none of them had been able to reach London in time. David was with his regiment. Bertie, who had transferred from the Royal Navy to the Royal Air Force, was completing pilot training at St Leonards-on-Sea. George was at naval college, Henry was at Eton and their disabled youngest son, John, was with his nurse at Sandringham.

From beyond the open windows came the deafening roar: '*We want the King! We want the King! We want the King!*'

'What a day,' George's Uncle Arthur said emotionally, dabbing at his eyes with a huge purple handkerchief. 'There's never been one like it in history! Never!'

Shouts of '*We want Queen Mary!*' had now joined the shouts of '*We want the King!*'

'I think it's time, darling,' George said.

'Yes.' She was bare-headed and had slipped a fur coat around her shoulders. 'I'm ready, George.'

With Arthur and their daughter behind them, they stepped out onto the balcony and, amidst a sea of waving Union Jacks and streamers, the world erupted into a maelstrom of deafening cheers and whistles and the singing of the national anthem.

They had survived, and so – no longer Saxe-Coburg-Gotha, but Windsor – had their dynasty.

'I think,' George said, under cover of the tumult and for the first time in their long married life, 'that I love you with all my heart, May Teck.'

'Yes, George.' Her face was radiant. 'I know.'

Acknowledgements

Huge thanks are due to my life-enhancing publisher, Wayne Brookes, and to my editor, Alex Saunders. Without Alex's constant support *The Summer Queen* might never have been finished and certainly wouldn't have been as much fun to write. Thanks are also due to copy editor Mandy Greenfield, desk editor Sam Sharman, my eagle-eyed proofreader, Marian Reid, and to my agent at Curtis Brown, Sheila Crowley, and her assistant, Abbie Greaves.

Select Bibliography

Theo Aronson, *Crowns in Conflict* (John Murray, 1986)

E. F. Benson, *The Kaiser and English Relations* (Longmans, 1936)

Gordon Brook-Shepherd, *Royal Sunset* (Weidenfeld & Nicolson, 1987)

Deborah Cadbury, *Queen Victoria's Matchmaking* (Bloomsbury, 2018)

Miranda Carter, *The Three Emperors* (Penguin Books, 2009)

Christopher Clark, *Kaiser Wilhelm ll: A Life in Power* (Penguin Books, 2009)

Virginia Cowles, *The Last Tsar & Tsarina* (Weidenfeld & Nicolson, 1977)

Christina Croft, *Queen Victoria's Granddaughters* (Hilliard & Croft, 2013)

Anne Edwards, *Matriarch: Queen Mary and the House of Windsor* (Hodder & Stoughton, 1984)

Carolly Erickson, *Alexandra: The Last Tsarina* (Robinson, 2003)

Greg King, *The Last Empress* (Aurum Press, 1994)

Elizabeth Longford, *Victoria R. I.* (Weidenfeld & Nicolson, 1964)

Diana Mandache, *Dearest Missy* (Rosvall Royal Books, 2011)

Robert K. Massie, *Nicholas and Alexandra* (Phoenix, 2000)

Simon Sebag Montefiore, *The Romanovs* (Weidenfeld &

Nicolson, 2016)

Harold Nicolson, *King George V: His Life and Reign* (Constable, 1952)

Hannah Pakula, *The Last Romantic* (Simon & Schuster, 1984)

James Pope-Hennessy, *Queen Mary* (George Allen & Unwin, 1959)

Prince Michael of Greece, *Eddy & Hélène* (Rosvall Royal Books, 2013)

Helen Rappaport, *Four Sisters* (Macmillan, 2014)

John C. G. Röhl, *Kaiser Wilhelm ll* (Cambridge University Press, 2014)

Kenneth Rose, *King George V* (Weidenfeld & Nicolson, 1983)

John Van der Kiste, *The Last German Empress* (A & F Publications, 2015)

Justin C. Vovk, *Imperial Requiem* (iUniverse, 2012)

A. N. Wilson, *Victoria, A Life* (Atlantic Books, 2014)